The Gia

BY JAMIE EDMUNDSON

THE WEAPON TAKERS SAGA
TORIC'S DAGGER
BOLIVAR'S SWORD
THE JALAKH BOW
THE GIANTS' SPEAR

BOOK FOUR OF
THE WEAPON TAKERS SAGA

THE
GIANTS'
SPEAR

JAMIE
EDMUNDSON

Rarn
Publishing

The Giants' Spear
Book Four of The Weapon Takers Saga
Copyright © 2019 by Jamie Edmundson. All rights reserved.
First Edition: 2019

ISBN 978-1-912221-05-9

Author newsletter
http://subscribe.jamieedmundson.com

Cover: Streetlight Graphics

For Julie

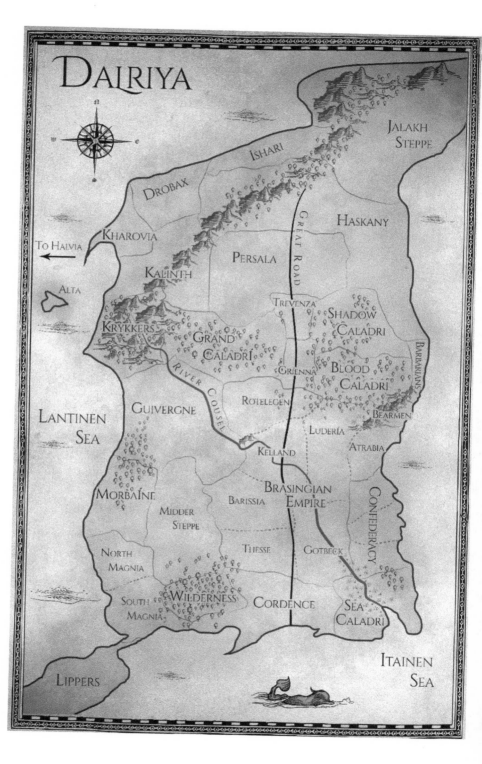

Dramatis Personae

South Magnians

Soren, a wizard

Belwynn, Soren's sister

Herin, a mercenary

Clarin, Herin's brother

Farred, a nobleman of Middian descent

Gyrmund, Farred's friend

Edgar, Prince of South Magnia

Brictwin, Edgar's bodyguard

Morlin, Elfled's bodyguard

Wilchard, Edgar's chief steward

Wulfgar, high-priest of Toric

Otha of Rystham, magnate, Wulfgar's brother

Aescmar, a magnate

Ulf, a smith

North Magnians

Elana, a priestess of Madria

Cerdda, Prince of North Magnia

Mette, Cerdda's mother

Elfled, Cerdda's sister

Irmgard, Cerdda's wife

Middians

Brock, a tribal chief

Frayne, a tribal chief

Kellish

Moneva, a mercenary

Baldwin, Duke of Kelland, Emperor of Brasingia
Hannelore, Empress of Brasingia
Katrina, their oldest daughter
Liesel, their second child
Leopold, their son
Walter, Baldwin's younger brother, Marshal of the Empire
Rainer, Baldwin's chamberlain
Decker, Archbishop of Kelland
Gustav the Hawk, Archmage of the Empire
Inge, Gustav's apprentice
Lord Kass, a nobleman

Rotelegen

Jeremias, Duke of Rotelegen
Adalheid, Dowager Duchess of Rotelegen, his mother
Rudy, an escaped prisoner from Samir Durg
Jurgen, his cousin

Other Brasingians

Arne, Duke of Luderia
Tobias, his son
Godfrey, Archbishop of Gotbeck
Coen, Duke of Thesse
Emmett, a nobleman of Thesse
Gavan, Prince of Atrabia
Gervase Salvinus, a mercenary leader

Guivergnais

Nicolas, King of Guivergne
Bastien, Duke of Morbaine
Russell, Bastien's man

Kalinthians

Theron, Count of Erisina, Knight of Kalinth

Evander, Knight of Kalinth

Sebastian, Count of Melion, former Grand Master of the Knights of Kalinth

Alpin, Sebastian's squire

Tycho, Knight of Kalinth, Theron's friend

Philon, Knight of Kalinth

Leontios, Knight of Kalinth

Coronos, Knight of Kalinth

Jonas, King of Kalinth

Irina, Queen of Kalinth

Straton, eldest son of Jonas

Dorian, second son of Jonas

Diodorus, Count of Korenandi

Lyssa, a girl from Korkis

Haskans

Shira, Queen of Haskany, member of the Council of Seven

Koren, Shira's uncle

Rimmon, a mage

Etan, Isharite general

Persaleians

Pentas, a wizard

Cyprian, an escaped prisoner from Samir Durg

Zared, an escaped prisoner from Samir Durg

Mark, deposed King of Persala

Duilio, soldier

Ennius, flamen of Ludovis

Linus, Isharite general

Vismarians

Sevald, a Vismarian leader

Gunnhild, a Vismarian

Nemyr, a West Vismarian

Dalla, his daughter

Ketil, his older son

Jesper, his younger son

Krykkers

Kaved, a mercenary
Rabigar, an exile

Maragin, chieftain of the Grendal clan
Jodivig, chieftain of the Dramsen
Stenk, a young warrior
Wracken, chieftain of the Binideq

Caladri

Dorjan, King of the Shadow Caladri
Lorant, King of the Blood Caladri
Hajna, Queen of the Blood Caladri
Ignac, a wizard of the Grand Caladri

Isharites

Siavash, Lord of Ishari
Arioc, former King of Haskany
Harith, servant of Diis
Peroz, servant of Diis
Mehrab, a wizard
Roshanak, a wizard

Orias

Oisin, King of the Orias
Cillian, Oisin's brother
Niamh, Oisin's wife

Other

Kull, a Drobax
Tana, Queen of the Asrai
Gansukh, Khan of the Jalakh Horde

Recap: Toric's Dagger, Book 1

Toric's Dagger, a holy relic, is apparently stolen by Gervase Salvinus and his group of mercenaries from its resting place in Magnia. Prince Edgar asks his cousins, Soren and Belwynn, to lead a team tasked with its retrieval. The twins are joined by their friends, warriors Herin and Clarin; Krykker bladesmith Rabigar; mercenaries Moneva and Kaved; priests Elana and Dirk; and the ranger, Gyrmund. They follow the trail into the Wilderness, where they are attacked by the vossi. Surrounded and close to defeat, Soren casts an illusion that makes the vossi's god appear. They turn and run, but Soren has overextended himself and lost his ability to use magic.

They continue to follow Salvinus to Coldeberg, in the Brasingian Empire. On the road to Coldeberg they are attacked by a powerful Isharite wizard, Nexodore, and saved from him by Pentas, a red-eyed wizard. In Coldeberg, they learn that Emeric, the Duke of Barissia, has declared himself king. Many of the group are captured by Salvinus, and taken to Emeric's castle. Belwynn, Soren, Clarin and Dirk must rescue the others from the castle prison. Dirk reveals that he stole Toric's Dagger from the temple and has had the relic all along. In the castle dungeon, Rabigar is tortured and loses his eye. He is rescued by Moneva. In the duke's private rooms, it is revealed that Kaved betrayed them to Emeric. They escape the castle, chased by Salvinus. Walter, Marshal of the Empire, saves them from Salvinus and takes them to the capital of the Empire, Essenberg.

After a meeting with Emperor Baldwin and his Archmage, Gustav, Soren decides to take Toric's Dagger to the lands of the Blood Caladri, and his friends are persuaded to go with him. Here, they learn that Toric's Dagger is one of seven weapons made by Elana's goddess, Madria, that can be used to defend Dalriya from the Isharites. Elana is attacked by Nexodore, who is killed by Dirk, wielding Toric's Dagger.

Farred leads an army of Magnians north, to help the Brasingian Empire against the imminent Isharite invasion.

Looking for more information about the weapons, as well as a way to restore his powers, Soren leads the group to the lands of the Grand Caladri. When they reach the capital, Edeleny, they find it under attack by the Isharites. Amidst a magical battle, Soren finds a way to restore his lost powers. Belwynn, Elana, Dirk and Rabigar retrieve a second weapon, Onella's Staff. They are then transported to safety by Pentas. The rest of their friends are captured in the invasion by Arioc, King of Haskany.

Recap: Bolivar's Sword, Book 2

Belwynn and her friends find themselves in Kalinth. Rescued by a Knight of Kalinth, Theron, and taken in by his uncle, Sebastian, they find themselves involved in a conflict between the Knights and the crown. Taking on the mantle of Grand Master, Sebastian takes the capital of Kalinth, Heractus, and seizes control of the government.

Brasingia is invaded by a huge Isharite army led by Queen Shira of Haskany, containing hundreds of thousands of Drobax. Farred works with Prince Ashere of North Magnia to frustrate the invasion. Ashere is mortally wounded and Farred's Magnians take refuge with the army of Emperor Baldwin in his mighty fortress, Burkhard Castle.

Moneva and the rest of her captured friends are taken to Samir Durg, capital of Ishari. Moneva is taken to the rooms of King Arioc. Herin, Clarin and Gyrmund are sent to work in the mines and Soren is delivered to the Order of Diis. Submitting to Arioc, Moneva is given some freedom by him, and meets with Pentas, who tells her where her friends are being held.

Rabigar leaves Kalinth to return to the lands from which he is exiled. Despite his past crimes, he persuades the Krykkers to make a stand against the Isharites. The Krykkers lead an army to Kalinth, bringing with them the third of Madria's weapons, Bolivar's Sword. The combined Krykker-Kalinthian army invades Haskany, causing panic in Samir Durg.

Prince Edgar personally leads a Magnian army the Empire. Allying with Duke Coen of Thesse, he defeats the army of Duke Emeric. After a failed attempt to assassinate Edgar, Emeric is besieged inside Coldeberg. Gervase Salvinus betrays his master and brings Coen the head of Emeric, ending the siege and the Barissian rebellion.

Moneva successfully frees Herin, Clarin and Gyrmund from the mines. With a small force of escaped prisoners, Herin and Clarin cause havoc in the fortress of Samir Durg. Moneva and Gyrmund locate Soren and free him. Soren insists that he is taken to the throne room of Samir Durg. Here they find that Pentas has taken Belwynn to the throne room, too. Their attempt to kill Erkindrix, the Lord of Ishari, looks like it will fail, until King Arioc betrays his master. Moneva kills Erkindrix with Toric's Dagger.

The death of Erkindrix sees the recall of the great Isharite army, saving Burkhard Castle and Brasingia. It also saves Clarin and his force of escaped prisoners. Herin, however, is missing.

Recap: The Jalakh Bow, Book 3

The death of Erkindrix leads to a civil war in Ishari, giving time for the search for the remaining weapons of Madria to continue. Soren, Moneva and Gyrmund travel to the lands of the Jalakh tribes, looking for the Jalakh Bow.

Belwynn remains in Kalinth. Clarin, escaping from Samir Durg by foot, finds her here and agrees to fight for Kalinth, though he becomes jealous of her relationship with Theron. Threatened by civil war, Theron and Sebastian defeat their enemies, led by Prince Straton, who is confined to his rooms in the castle.

Farred travels to the lands of the Sea Caladri. He persuades them to send a fleet into the Lantinen Sea to challenge the dominance of the Kharovians. This allows Rabigar to cross to Halvia, where he finds clues to the whereabouts of the Giants' Spear.

The civil war in Ishari ends with the Battle of Simalek. The forces loyal to Siavash surprise those of his enemies. Queen Shira is slain and Arioc and Pentas are both forced to escape. Diis uses Siavash to bring forth two new weapons: Siavash's shadow is separated from him; and a dragon is brought into Dalriya. The dragon supports an army of Drobax to retake the lands of the Grand Caladri, and to invade the lands of the Krykkers. Unable to stop the dragon, Maragin leads her rock walkers underground, while Rabigar returns to Halvia. During the crossing, the Sea Caladri fleet is destroyed by the dragon. Rabigar takes an army across the Drang, but it is ambushed by Drobax.

Siavash uses his shadow to infiltrate Heractus, killing both Sebastian and Elana. Before she dies, Elana passes on her connection with Madria to Belwynn. Siavash's shadow, taking on the form of Prince Dorian, unites Theron's enemies against him, raising an army loyal to Prince Straton. Belwynn uses her powers of telepathy to raise a loyal force for Theron and they march south.

Clarin goes to Persala to search for the Shield of Persala. It is revealed that his friend, Zared, is the heir to the Persaleian throne. Zared uses his contacts to get them into Baserno, where Clarin gets his hands on the Shield. However, their force is surrounded by an Isharite unit led by Herin, now working for Siavash. Herin defeats Clarin in a sword-fight to the death and takes the Shield for Ishari.

In exchange for helping Gansukh to become khan of the Jalakhs, Soren, Moneva and Gyrmund claim the Jalakh Bow. Pentas transports them back to Kalinth just in time for them to help in the battle. Pentas is killed, but the shadow is destroyed when Belwynn strikes it with Toric's Dagger.

'The king with his guard and Merry at his side passed down from the gate of the Burg to where the Riders were assembling on the green. Many were already mounted. It would be a great company; for the king was leaving only a small garrison in the Burg, and all who could be spared were riding to the weapontake at Edoras.'

JRR Tolkien, *The Return of the King*

Prologue

S IAVASH SAT ON THE THRONE where Erkindrix once sat. His arms rested on the carved red crystal. It was his now, and he had got more than used to that idea. Golden light shone down from the dome high up in the vaulted ceiling, bathing him in warm colours. He would have felt like a god, if he didn't already have one living inside him.

Diis was with him: an oppressive presence, impatient for the victory over Madria that still eluded them.

His mind repeated the moment when that bitch, Soren's sister, had struck the corpse of Prince Dorian with the dagger. There had been a blinding flash, a bang, and Siavash's shadow was shattered, evaporating away into nothingness. It was lost to him forever—and lost cheaply, because he had not even succeeded in defeating the Kalinthians.

The doors opened and the Magnian, Herin, strode in, walking towards the throne in a self-assured way. Siavash could feel Diis focus his malevolence on the human, and Siavash could see the human's spirit quail, though he maintained an admirable show of bravado.

'I am honoured to present you with these gifts, Lord Siavash,' he said, bending down on one knee in front of him. From a sack he pulled a decapitated head.

'King Mark evaded us long enough, but he has met his end now,' Herin said, holding the face towards Siavash so that he could see the former King of Persala's features. Siavash had never met the man, but his informants had already confirmed that this was indeed the head of the king-in-exile.

'My force also successfully recovered the Shield of Persala, as you ordered,' said Herin.

Dropping the head unceremoniously to the floor, he now held up the shield, the leather exterior decorated in the gaudy colours of the Persaleians.

Siavash felt Diis stir, a mix of hatred for the object brought before him, and elation—that at last one of the weapons of Madria was in their hands.

'You have served us well,' Siavash admitted, 'and will be rewarded. I need generals with the ability to carry out orders. You will be given your own host to command.'

Herin lowered his head, acknowledging the scale of the reward. 'I am honoured,' he said, raising his eyes to look at Siavash once more. 'What orders will this host have?'

'Same as the three others. All four hosts will leave for Kalinth immediately.'

'Four?' Herin asked. 'All for Kalinth?'

'The Kalinthians must be crushed!' Siavash shouted at him, letting loose the anger and loathing he had carried since his defeat. 'Everywhere in Dalriya, and even in distant Halvia, our enemies are subdued or on the verge of defeat. And yet that pathetic kingdom still holds out. Almighty Diis demands its destruction!'

A shadow passed over Herin's face, but he bent his head in obeisance yet again.

'Leave your gifts here and go,' said Siavash, tired of the man's presence.

He waited for the Magnian to exit the doors at the end of the throne room before calling out to the shadows behind him, where he had his private rooms.

'Well?' he shouted irritably. 'Come, then.'

Out came Peroz, servant of Diis. Siavash had reformed the Isharite military, so that every unit had at least one servant attached to it, reporting back directly to him. It imposed discipline and loyalty, reducing the chances of another such as Pentas from betraying them.

Siavash allowed himself a smile at the thought of the red-eyed wizard. He recalled the sensation as the spear, wielded by his shadow in the body of Dorian, penetrated deeply into his enemy. It hadn't quite all been for nothing in Kalinth, he reminded himself.

'What of him?' Siavash asked Peroz.

'He can't be trusted, my lord.'

'I don't trust him. That's why you have this task. But he's able.'

'He fought and killed his brother for the Shield. But then he let the rest of our enemies leave, no doubt to return to Kalinth.'

'There's something I've learned of humans,' Siavash explained to his servant. 'Despite all the evidence of what Diis will do to this world, they still think they will be saved. If they show loyalty, or are useful in some way, they think we will spare them; their family; their friends. It is the way their minds work. This Herin will do as he is ordered because he thinks it will save him.'

Siavash studied Peroz, looking to see whether the lesson had been taken.

'And if he doesn't,' Siavash added, 'you know what to do.'

I

A SALMON SUPPER

WAIT A MINUTE,' Belwynn said to Moneva. 'You're going too fast for me.'

She scratched the quill on the paper, recording the items that her friend seemed able to recite from memory.

'Shoes and clothing,' said Moneva patiently, wandering around Belwynn's room in the castle as she spoke. 'Saddles, stirrups, bridles, and whatever other horse tack the Knights require. Oil and timber. Nails, rivets, hammers—'

'How do you know all this?' Belwynn asked her.

Moneva had walked over to the window, and was peering down into the courtyard. She turned to give Belwynn one of her enigmatic smiles. 'I've been in the business of supplying armies before.'

'Hmm. Is that it?'

'Isn't that enough for now?' Moneva replied, her attention drawn back to the castle courtyard, from where Belwynn could hear dogs barking.

'Yes, I would say so.'

Belwynn would take the list to her service at the Church of Madria, and ask her congregation to supply as much as they could. With Theron and most of the knights out in the Kalinthian countryside, gathering as much in the way of supplies as they could, she had the task of managing the war effort here in Heractus. For no-one was in any doubt, that Siavash of Ishari would be sending his armies to punish the Kalinthians for their resistance.

Belwynn's thoughts, which now always found their way to armies and war, were diverted back to her friend, whose attention remained fixed on the goings-on outside.

'What *is* so interesting down there?' she demanded.

'Didn't you say that Clarin made friends with two Dog-men?' Moneva asked.

Belwynn narrowed her eyes. 'They're down there now, aren't they?'

Moneva nodded.

'Come on,' said Belwynn.

Belwynn and Moneva descended the steep circular tower steps, before exiting into the castle courtyard.

It was busy with bodies, standing around a horse and travois. Belwynn recognised some of the faces, even if she hadn't learned the names, of men who had escaped from Samir Durg with Clarin, and gone with him into occupied Persala to fetch the Persaleian Shield. But no-one was holding aloft a shield. Instead, they were looking at what was on the travois.

They were looking at Clarin.

He was unconscious, wrapped up in a pile of blankets, but she could see his face, and it was a strange, grey colour.

'What happened to him?' Belwynn asked, alarmed.

She looked from the two Dog-men, whose heads swivelled about them uncomfortably, to the two men she recognised as Clarin's friends. One of them was sitting on the floor, with a wan, exhausted look to his face. The second answered her.

'My lady, I am Rudy of Rotelegen. Clarin fought with his brother. At first we thought he was dead—'

'Wait,' Moneva interrupted him. 'With his brother?'

'Yes. Herin. He found us outside Baserno. He led a unit of Isharites and Drobax.'

Belwynn shared a look with Moneva. The information was hard to process, impossible to understand. Not that Herin was alive, which would ordinarily have been something to celebrate. But that he now led the forces of the enemy and had fought with Clarin? Belwynn shook her head. Questions about Herin would have to wait. They had to focus on Clarin.

'You said you thought him dead?'

'Aye. We were talking about burying him, before Jurgen detected a faint breath. But he hasn't woken up since. Can he be healed?'

Eyes turned to Belwynn, as they always did now when there was an illness. She was Elana's successor, the Voice of Madria some now called her. But where Elana had been gifted with healing powers by the goddess, Belwynn had none. Instead, she could talk to her congregation telepathically. Her gift had its uses, but in situations like this, when people looked to her as they had once looked to Elana, she felt useless. She felt like a fraud.

5

But she had worked with Elana as her disciple, and had learned enough of medicine to know how to treat the injured, even if she couldn't call on Madria for aid.

Soren, she said, using her oldest and strongest telepathic link to speak with her brother. *Clarin is here. He's unconscious. Can you come down to the chapel?*

Clarin? Repeated Soren, his mind sounding befuddled. No doubt she had interrupted him while deep in a book. *I'm coming now. I'm in the library, I'll be there shortly.*

Belwynn looked around. The courtyard had continued to fill, as more residents of the castle had come to find out what was happening.

Lyssa, her young charge, was one of them. Belwynn was sure the girl should have been in a lesson at church, but that conversation was another thing that would have to wait.

'Lyssa,' she called out, and the girl came over, a slightly guilty look on her face.

'Can you go to the kitchen for me, tell the cook what has happened. We'll need hot water, honey, towels, anything else she can think of.'

'Yes, Belwynn,' said the girl, before running off.

'He needs to be carried to the chapel,' Belwynn announced, gesturing at Clarin. Carrying the big man up the winding stairs was not practical, and they needed somewhere where he could rest undisturbed for as long as necessary. 'He's not light, either,' she added, encouraging a few more men to volunteer.

'I'll see to his friends and join you shortly,' said Moneva.

Moneva led the two young men and the Dog-men away.

Half a dozen men had managed to lift Clarin, made easier because his limbs had been wrapped in blankets. Belwynn walked ahead, clearing people out of the way as she led them to the castle chapel.

Once there, she cleared the table of its ornaments, and Clarin was laid down upon it. She got the men to shift his body to one side then the other, while she unwrapped the blankets from around him. It was time to check his injuries.

She had done this many times now, in the aftermath of battles when the wounded had come thick and fast, their bodies butchered so badly that it had seemed inconceivable that they still lived. It meant that even though it was Clarin she was dealing with, she could concentrate on what she needed to do.

In fact, the more she looked, the odder she found it. Clarin had clearly been in a fight, and she had found injuries: aside from bruising, a wound under his arm, and gashes on his ankle and thigh. They were deep cuts, that looked like they had been inflicted by one of the crystal swords that the Isharites wielded. But they were hardly severe, and certainly didn't explain why he had been unconscious since the fight.

Moneva arrived with the cook, two kitchen maids, and Rudy. Between them they carried an array of items that might be used for medicine. Belwynn saw that the cook had brought a sharp knife and a bone saw, and gave a silent prayer to Madria that they wouldn't be needed.

'Well?' asked Moneva, gently lifting Clarin's head and placing a folded towel underneath.

'Take a look, will you. I can't see anything, save for three cuts where Herin's blade must have pierced him.'

Belwynn turned to Rudy. 'Is there anything else you can tell us? Did he take a blow to the head, for example?'

'Not a full strike, I'm sure of it. Herin gave him a kick at the end, but more of a push than a real blow. He was already on his knees by then.'

A clacking sound on the floor signalled Soren's arrival. He made his way into view, leaning heavily on Onella's Staff as he walked.

Belwynn worried for him. He had never fully recovered from his ordeal in Samir Durg, despite Elana's ministrations. On his journey to the Jalakh Steppe with Gyrmund and Moneva he had fallen ill. He had expended much magic there, as well as at the battle of the Pineos when he had returned to Kalinth with Pentas. Now, with Elana gone, his recovery was slow.

'I don't see anything else,' said Moneva, having checked Clarin for herself. She bit her lip as she thought. 'Poison is possible.'

'Poison?' asked Soren, hobbling over to examine the patient. He peered at Clarin's wounds, his ability to see clearly only possible because of the power of the staff he gripped, strengthening his eyesight as well as his body.

He sniffed at the wounds.

'I don't smell anything unusual. The wounds need a proper clean, but there's no serious infection that I can see,' he added doubtfully.

'It could be nightwort,' Moneva said.

Belwynn had never heard of it. Soren raised an eyebrow.

'Go on?' he asked.

'It's taken in small quantities, dried and added to a mixture, to aid sleep. In medium quantities to induce sleep. I've heard that taken untreated it can result in a prolonged sleep. But it's dangerous. Too much and the victim never wakes up.'

'I take it you've used this yourself?' said Belwynn archly.

'No,' said Moneva, sounding somewhat defensive. 'If you think about it, you would only use it for very specific purposes. If you want someone dead, for example, you would use something else entirely. But if Herin wanted it to look like he had killed Clarin, while giving him a chance to live, it was perhaps his best option.'

'What do you think?' Belwynn asked Rudy.

The man was clearly thinking the suggestion over. 'It looked like a real fight to me, like they were both trying to kill each other. But Clarin did go over easily. Maybe Herin's blade *was* poisoned. And he *was* the one who suggested the fight.'

Soren nodded, as if he had been convinced. 'If it is nightwort, how is it treated?'

'There is no treatment that I know of,' Moneva said. 'Just take care of him and let it run its course.'

No treatment needed. That eased Belwynn's immediate anxiety. As she relaxed a little, a thought occurred.

'Rudy,' she began. 'The Shield of Persala. Did you find it?'

The man nodded, a worried look on his face. 'We travelled to Baserno. Clarin got it. But Herin found us. He has it now. That's bad, isn't it?'

Belwynn looked from Soren to Moneva. They had the same, tired look on their faces. They had worked so hard to acquire the weapons of Madria. Soren and Moneva had gone with Gyrmund to the steppe lands of the Jalakh tribes, where they had persuaded the Jalakhs to part with their bow. As well as the staff that Soren now carried, Moneva had Toric's Dagger in her belt, and somewhere, perhaps still in his homeland, their friend Rabigar the Krykker had Bolivar's Sword. They had four of the seven weapons they had been searching for. But if Herin had now handed the Shield of Persala to the Isharites, it seemed that it had all been for nothing.

'It's not good,' said Soren finally. 'But we'll just have to take one step at a time. Get Clarin better first. Then we decide which weapon to go after next. In Coldeberg, Rabigar spoke of contacting the Krykkers in Halvia, to find out the location of the spear. It was once owned by the Giants, a people that Szabolcs called the Orias. We must hope that Rabigar has met with success.'

***

IT HAD been ten days since the Drobax had ambushed the mixed army of Krykkers and Vismarians who had crossed the Drang into enemy territory. Teleported away from the fighting, Rabigar was now one of only four people left to continue the search for the Giants' Spear. Relying on Gunnhild, the large Vismarian who knew the lands of the far north, to lead the way, they had so far avoided any further conflict with the creatures. Ignac, the Caladri medium, had come with them, his strange, bird-like walking gait keeping pace with the long legs of Gunnhild. Rounding out the group was young Stenk. It had been an instinctive decision on Rabigar's part to bring the Krykker with them, motivated by a desire to save him from danger. Time would tell whether it was the right one.

For the first few days Rabigar constantly thought of the men they had left behind. They would have to make a retreat all the way back to the Drang, while being harried by the Drobax. The monsters were now led by the taller, new breed of Drobax, who could talk, think, and plan. Rabigar had left them to it, taking Bolivar's Sword with him, when they had been in desperate need of his help. He had done it so that he could continue the search for the Giants' Spear. At times he wondered whether it had been the right thing to do. But as the days passed, Rabigar thought of it less. It was done now.

There are no second chances, he reminded himself. *You must learn to live with your mistakes, and if this was another, you've made worse.*

The farther they walked, Gunnhild taking them in a north-westerly direction, the colder it got. When the wind came from the direction they walked in, it harried them, bitingly cold. When it rained the water was cold, so close to snow it might as well have been. At night they were careful to avoid any kind of fire that might be seen, so that Rabigar never warmed up. His feet felt permanently frozen, and as he lay on the cold ground, his teeth would chatter, and he would admit, even if just to himself, that he was too old to punish his body like this.

In such a way ten days passed, each one more difficult than the last, even if they all knew that it would be so much worse should the Drobax find them.

Finally, faint at first, but getting louder as each hour passed, they heard the Nasvarl. This was the river that Gunnhild said flowed west. It was the route they would take to search for the Giants, at the edge of the world.

'Travelling west on foot is suicide,' she told them that night. They sat around the fire, consuming the last of their rations. Gunnhild was confident that no Drobax would be in the vicinity. Apparently, they were miles from any settlements, and they hadn't seen any signs of the creatures for days. Rabigar was grateful for the warmth. 'The ice fields are treacherous. Those who have explored west and returned to tell the tale did so by boat.'

'Did they find the Giants?' Stenk asked.

'Some said so. But the better the story round the fire at night, the better the food and drink the storyteller gets. Tales of giants abound, friend Stenk, but hard facts are much thinner on the ground. If they still live out in the wilds of Halvia, it is many leagues from here.'

Gunnhild giggled to herself.

'What is so funny?' asked Rabigar.

'Sorry,' she said. 'I just broke wind down below.'

Stenk, positioned next to the Vismarian, suddenly put his hands to his mouth and nose.

Gunnhild pointed at him, bursting out into guffaws of laughter.

'It's travelled on already!' she said, clearly delighted.

Ignac stared at her, a look of horror on his face.

Rabigar sighed inwardly. This was going to be a very long journey.

The next morning, Gunnhild led them to the south bank of the Nasvarl. It gurgled and frothed busily, still full of melted ice from the northern reaches of the continent. The water was crystal clear, the rocky bed of the river visible beneath. When Rabigar scooped up a handful it was cold and fresh. Now all they needed was some food to break their fast.

He spotted a salmon breaking the water in the river and pointed it out to the Vismarian.

'Not here,' she said.

Gunnhild looked about her, gathering her bearings, before continuing downriver. The morning was still young when they came upon a small collection of wooden buildings, that made up a fishing lodge. Gunnhild led them into the main building. It was deserted, but had been untouched by

Drobax, with fuel in the fireplace and pallets for sleeping. They shrugged off their packs, before heading back out to explore further.

Gunnhild opened the doors of a low hut and grunted with pleasure. Leaning in, she heaved back on an object, pulling a long canoe onto the riverbank. Rabigar peered in and spotted a second boat. He and Stenk grabbed a side each. It slid pleasantly on the rocks, and they deposited it next to the first.

The canoes were of similar length. Each was long enough to carry all four of them, but with their packs and weapons, two to a canoe would be more comfortable. Rabigar ran a hand along the length of his canoe, admiring its construction. It had been dug out from a single tree and was strong looking. That said, it looked like it had not been used recently.

'They'll need a bit of work on them,' he said to Gunnhild.

'We have two jobs here,' she said. 'The canoes need sanding and oiling. Out in the river there is a salmon trap. We need at least one person to catch the fish, and one to cure them.'

'Let me deal with the canoes by myself,' said Rabigar, who had little experience of fishing. 'I will enjoy getting them ready.'

'Alright, if you can manage it yourself, that will allow the three of us to catch enough fish to feed us comfortably for a week at least. Scrape the surface, and check—'

'Please,' interrupted Rabigar, holding up a hand. 'Just get me what tools you have and leave me to it.'

Gunnhild could be irritating, but she didn't offend easily, and she happily fetched what the lodge had, before heading off with Stenk and Ignac to teach them fishing.

Rabigar knelt by the first canoe. He soon had a little grin on his face, the first in a long time. He had got used to working with his hands every day as a bladesmith, and while this wasn't metal, the wood was beautiful to work with.

He pressed an ear to it. Every tree has a heart and objects such as this canoe, built from a whole tree, kept the heart intact. After he had scraped away the outer layer of the canoe he had got closer to the heart of the tree, and he could hear its faint beat had become stronger.

Rabigar worked on the first canoe, then the second, then the paddles. His mind wandered to his friends in Dalriya. Beautiful young Belwynn, who had found a place for herself in Heractus as a disciple to Elana. Her brother, Soren, who had been keen to search out the Jalakh Bow. Rabigar hoped he had met with success. In Magnia, his apprentice, Ulf, would be running Rabigar's smithy, and his wife Bareva would have given him a child by now. He wished them well, too. Herin, the man who had persuaded him to leave his forge in the first place and get involved in all this nonsense. Last Rabigar had heard, he and his brother Clarin had made it out of the slave pits of Samir Durg, but no-one knew whether they had escaped the fortress itself. He hoped they had.

Finally, in his Krykker homeland, a place from which he had been banished for so long, Rabigar thought of Maragin, the woman he had loved all these years, the woman whose father he had killed in a drunken fight. She was now buried beneath the rubble of the Krykker mountains, leading her rock-walkers against the Drobax who had invaded every part of their homeland except for those that lay underground. He hoped that he would get to see her again.

When he was done his body creaked and ached from kneeling all day, and he walked over to see how the others were getting on.

Gunnhild sat by the river. Her hands worked furiously, gutting the fish that Stenk left for her, throwing the unwanted bits back into the river, before covering the pieces in a salty dry cure and laying them out on the rocks behind her. Rabigar was amazed to see how much they had caught, close to a hundred salmon had been processed and now lay glistening on the rocks.

'You've done well,' he said.

'The salmon are running, and there's been no-one else around to catch them, save for the bears. We're going to keep at it a while longer: they're active in twilight. If you're done, maybe you could get a fire going in the lodge and we can cook ourselves a nice supper. We've earned it after today's work.'

They took their supper out by the river: two Krykkers, a Caladri and a Vismarian woman. A clear sky allowed them a perfect view of the stars. Whatever perils lay ahead, Rabigar was wise enough to appreciate moments like this.

II

THE DUKE'S CRAG

EDGAR LISTENED POLITELY to Lord Kass as he made his pleas for assistance. A Drobax army was on its way to the Empire, sent to finish the job that had been interrupted last summer. Edgar's friend Farred, who he had last seen a month ago, was now in Brasingia, and had written a note detailing the invasion of the Krykker lands. It included a description of a flying dragon that had destroyed the Krykker army. Kass's handlebar moustache wriggled particularly violently when he talked about the dragon, as if it were trying to detach itself and hide from the great beast.

In fact, Edgar knew all about the dragon. The remnants of the Sea Caladri fleet had stopped in Magnian harbours on their way south only two weeks ago, with stories of how a green dragon had destroyed all but a few of their ships. Since then the Kharovians had been sighted as far south as the Magnian coast, now in complete control of the Lantinen Sea.

'How has the Emperor disposed of his forces?' he asked Baldwin's man, glancing across at the other two people present for the meeting.

Wilchard was listening intently to the reply. Edgar's friend since childhood, he trusted the man completely, and also relied on his mastery of the facts. The prince's new wife, Elfled, had insisted that she should also be present. He watched as she passed a hand over her abdomen. Realising he had stopped listening to Kass, he refocused.

Kass was explaining that six of the seven duchies of Brasingia had sent their armies to Burkhard Castle.

There were only four duchies there last year, Edgar said to himself. He had led a Magnian army into the south of the Empire, joining up with the Thessians to defeat Emeric, the Duke of Barissia who had made himself a king. *Surely, the armies of six duchies can hold off the Isharites*, a part of Edgar demanded. Another part of him knew full well that they couldn't.

'So you see,' Kass said, 'the rest of the Empire has been stripped of fighting men. If you could manage to bring a force to Essenberg, the capital would be reinforced. Empress Hannelore, the prince and princesses would be properly protected. Emperor Baldwin would be eternally grateful. And if the worst should happen, and Burkhard does fall, some resistance could continue.'

The Brasingians were only asking him to take an army to Essenberg, not to fight. But Edgar knew well enough that once he was in the Empire, the chances of getting sucked into the conflict would be high.

'I thank you, Lord Kass. I must discuss what you say with my wife and chief steward.'

'Your Highnesses,' said Lord Kass, bowing, before taking his leave.

Edgar sighed. After last year, he had vowed he would not lead the Magnians into another war on foreign soil again. Even if the intervening months had dulled the sharpness of it, the battle of Lindhafen remained imprinted on the prince's mind. The deaths of his subjects, the disability and disfigurement of others, fighting for reasons many of them didn't fully comprehend, had been hard to take. Even worse than that had been the night time assassination attempt on his life, when the agents of Emeric had nearly succeeded in killing him. He had lost his chancellor, the wizard Ealdnoth, and Leofwin his bodyguard that night. He wasn't ready to lose anyone else.

'I'm not taking an army to the Empire again,' he declared. 'It's harder to say it to Kass's face, but there it is. Maybe we can offer him supplies.'

Wilchard nodded.

Elfled shook her head.

'How can Magnia not help when the Isharites are close to destroying every civilisation in Dalriya?'

'It's not that simple, Elfled. If the Isharites come to Magnia, our people will defend our lands. But they won't go abroad to fight for others again. We shed enough blood in Brasingia last year. Too much.'

'If the armies of Ishari reach Magnia it is already too late, Edgar. You know that.'

'Our people don't.'

'Then you must explain it to them, Edgar. They will follow you. Especially after what you did last year.'

'What do you say, Wilchard?' he asked his friend, hoping for some support.

Wilchard looked uncomfortable, caught between a difference of opinion between his prince and princess.

'Maybe we can give them some other kind of support?' he offered.

'Yes,' Edgar agreed.

'No,' said Elfled. 'I know people have suffered. But we have to look to the future. To the world we want to create. That our child can inherit.'

Elfled put a hand to her belly again. Her menses hadn't come this month and she was convinced that she was pregnant. It had happened so quickly that Edgar, while happy, hadn't really been ready for it.

Wilchard stared at the floor, not knowing where else to look. Edgar was on his own.

'Look Elfled, even if the South Magnians were willing to follow me, last year I had the North Magnians and Middians with me as well. I just don't think it's possible.'

'You and Wilchard can work on the Middians,' she answered. 'I will persuade Cerdda to act.'

Edgar shook his head, though he couldn't help smiling at her. He was in no doubt that she would.

***

IN THE Emperor's Keep, in Burkhard Castle, Baldwin waited for his councillors to arrive. His own flag of Kelland, the Eagle, flew from the turrets, and he had brought the largest force of all. But his men shared the Emperor's Crag now. The Mace of Gotbeck, and the Spoked Wheel and Crossed Corn of Thesse, flew alongside the Eagle. Their rulers had the shortest distance to answer his summons and they arrived together. Godfrey, Archbishop of Gotbeck, had been here last year, and entered with his usual confidence. Duke Coen of Thesse had not been here, but he had put an end to the rebellion of Emeric of Barissia, and Baldwin had to admit, the man had played his hand well. He had a keenness about him, an energy, and Baldwin had decided that Coen and his men would make a good addition to the army.

From the Duke's Crag came the final three dukes. Most important to him was his brother Walter, the new Duke of Barissia. Walter had prepared the fortress for the siege, and he knew what he was doing, for like Baldwin, he had endured it last year. Walter flew the Boar of Barissia, his predecessor's symbol. Baldwin would have preferred it if his brother had chosen a new design, but it was his choice. The Red Rooster of Rotelegen and the Tree of Luderia could be seen next to the Boar on the Duke's Keep. With Walter was Jeremias, the young Duke of Rotelegen. The boy had proven to be stout-hearted, though it

15

was hard not to wish his father were here in his stead. Finally, Baldwin's brother-in-law, Tobias. Tobias had been sent in place of his father, Duke Arne. Baldwin wasn't surprised at Arne's absence. It was a hard thing for every man to return to this place. And Arne had never been a soldier.

Just as they were seated and about to begin, Gustav, Archmage of the Empire, appeared and took a seat. It was never clear where Gustav had arrived from, and most men preferred not to ask. Some of Baldwin's dukes still gave that look of distaste whenever the mage entered the room. But such an attitude made them look foolish, for none were able to cast doubt on his value.

'Whether you are here for the first time,' Baldwin began, 'or have returned, you are welcome, and the Empire gives you thanks.'

Baldwin's dukes returned his words with murmurs. It looked like Godfrey was readying himself for a speech, and so Baldwin quickly pressed on. 'In case there are doubts amongst anyone on strategy, we are here to hold up the enemy for as long as is possible. Each extra day means a day when the Drobax are here and not in the homes of the Brasingian people. I need you and your men to be ready to die for the Empire. Tell me now if you are not.'

Of course, none would say such a thing. The dukes of Brasingia looked at one another and at their emperor. Baldwin was surprised that it was Jeremias who cleared his throat.

'The men of Rotelegen have already lost their homes. We are ready to die here.'

Baldwin nodded. 'It is my deepest regret, but Rotelegen is now a wasteland. The same will be visited upon the other parts of the Empire once we are done here. Gustav, the latest from the north?'

'The Drobax are being marched here at speed. At their current rate, they will be here within a day or two.'

'And the dragon?'

'Still with them.'

'But the brave men of six duchies will meet them here,' Baldwin declared. 'To their eternal shame and dishonour, the Atrabians are the only ones absent.'

There was a mixture of reactions to that statement, as Baldwin knew there would be. The matter of the Atrabians was one of the few areas where he and Walter disagreed. He knew them to be treacherous swine, and for some reason, Walter continued to make excuses for them.

'Do you think me wrong, Duke Walter?' he asked him. 'Do you expect Prince Gavan to make it here before the Drobax?'

'Prince Gavan will stay in Atrabia, no-one would put money on anything else,' Walter replied. 'Our father forced the Atrabians to bend the knee to the Empire, but he didn't make a single one of them loyal to it.'

'The execution of that false prince might persuade them of their loyalty,' Godfrey suggested.

Baldwin noted how his brother-in-law's eyes widened at the remark. The Luderians loved the Atrabians nearly as much as Walter did. Bah. This was foolery on his own part, he knew. His dukes were divided on the subject and they were in no position to punish the Atrabians, even if they were to agree on it. But sometimes, his anger came out regardless. The Brasingians would soon shed their lifeblood on this rock, while the rest of Dalriya would look on and wait to see the outcome.

***

IF FARRED hadn't seen it once before, he might not have believed his eyes. From his position on the bridge of Burkhard Castle, he could see the Drobax army arrive, and they came as a swarm; as a plague. Burkhard Castle, made up of two giant karst rocks, was surrounded by a flat plain, and the Drobax army filled it. They looked like hundreds of thousands of tiny black specks, circling the castle like the sea coming in around the rocks on a beach.

There were, perhaps, no more of them than had come last summer. But this time their progress had been quicker. Farred had led a force of South Magnians last year, and together with Prince Ashere's North Magnians and Brock's Middians, they had harried and troubled the Isharite advance enough to allow the Brasingians to prepare the defences at Burkhard. This time, the Brasingians had sent one force of skirmishers against the advancing horde, and the dragon had destroyed it in a matter of minutes. No more soldiers were sent after that, and the people of Rotelegen had fled south, looking for refuge in the Empire's capital, Essenberg.

That was the problem they now faced. Last year they had held out for two weeks against the Drobax, before the enemy recalled them after Gyrmund and his friends had killed Erkindrix. This time, the Isharites had sent the dragon as well as the vast Drobax army, and there simply didn't seem to be a solution.

A bridge linked the Emperor's Keep on one rock with the Duke's Keep on the other. It was the latter where Farred now lived, having attached himself to the force of Walter, Duke of Barissia. Walter was the man tasked with organising the defences. He had added ballistae to the towers of each keep, to counter the threat from the dragon. Farred looked up and saw one poking over the edge of the battlements, a giant arrow already loaded onto the machine. Next to it fluttered the Boar of Barissia. Walter had decided to retain the symbol for his new duchy, entrusted to him after Emeric's defeat and death. The other two flags were the Red Rooster of Rotelegen and the Tree of Luderia. Arne of Luderia, who had endured the siege of Burkhard last year, had sent his son Tobias in his place.

Farred didn't blame Arne for not coming a second time. Indeed, he wondered to himself how he had wound up here a second time. Farred had come to the Empire to warn them of the dragon, that had helped the Isharites to conquer the lands of the Krykkers. Now he was firmly ensconced in this hell again. No doubt he deserved it. Edgar had offered him lands and titles in Magnia, and Farred had walked away.

Still. He was free of the responsibility of last year. He had become the leader of the Southern army after Ashere had died, infected with Isharite poison. Now he had no men to lead. He would just be called on to fight the enemy.

Footsteps behind him made Farred turn around. It was Inge, the witch. He had first known her as the apprentice to Archmage Gustav, but more recently it was in her position as Baldwin's mistress that he had encountered her. She smiled slyly at him, that fake smile, as if she was in on some great joke that he wasn't.

'Enjoying the view?' she asked him, indicating the Drobax moving down below them.

'No,' he replied curtly. 'But it's one I've seen before. You are not with the council?'

'No, I have no position in the Empire that would demand an invitation. Still, the Emperor is free to ask me for advice, any time of day or night.'

He was used to this now, the not so subtle hints that she was bedding Baldwin. He wondered what pleasure she still took from it, since the affair now seemed to be common knowledge.

'Well, he is blessed with advisers,' Farred said, just for something to say.

Inge let out a tinkle of laughter. 'Oh Lord Farred, you don't like me very much, do you?'

Farred shrugged. Perhaps Inge was under the impression that she was tormenting him with these conversations. The truth was, he really didn't care.

'Not at all. I don't know you.'

'Well, maybe we should get to know each other better. Maybe I should sprinkle a love spell on you, to make you like me a bit better?'

Farred looked at her coldly, not even bothering to reply to her any more.

'Maybe not,' she said. 'I don't think I'm your type.'

This wasn't the first time Inge had dropped that hint, either. Farred and Ashere had had a brief relationship before the prince had died. It seemed that Inge had worked that out, perhaps when she was treating Ashere's infected wound.

'There's a million Drobax, a dragon, and Toric knows what else out there, waiting to kill us all. I would be very surprised if anyone here really cares what my type is.'

She smiled at that. 'Well, I think I'll give up trying to lighten the mood, it's not working. You still don't like me, Farred, but you're one of my favourites. When you're fighting, I will look out for you, protect you as much as I can.'

With that, she walked off in the direction of the Emperor's Keep. What had that last comment meant? Farred didn't know if it was a flippant nonsense or a cryptic threat. Surely things are bad enough, he thought, without adding witch's curses to the mix.

IT WAS only right, of course, that the Barissians should be the first to defend the path up the Duke's Crag. Last year they had been fighting on the enemy's side, and now they had a debt to pay. But that meant that Farred would be fighting with them.

Waiting outside the keep, Walter's soldiers readied themselves, checking the straps on each other's armour and shields one last time; testing the tips and edges of weapons, just for something to do. Farred stood with the core of Walter's troops, men who had served him for years as Marshal of the Empire. They would stand with him at the front. The Barissians, his new subjects, whose loyalty and bravery were not yet tested, would fill in behind them.

Across the bridge, Farred could make out Baldwin's Kellish soldiers, deployed to defend the Emperor's Crag. But the biggest threat was here, and everyone knew it.

Then Walter was there, striding towards them energetically, and Farred could feel the mood lift. Experienced, professional, the soldiers trusted him. Farred had learned that while Baldwin was respected as Emperor, his position made him a more distant figure. Walter had campaigned with these men, and they fought with him as a brother in arms, not for his titles.

'For Baldwin and Brasingia!' he shouted, raising his sword. A gruff cheer went up, before he began marching them towards the path that wound its way around the steep crag. Indeed, the Duke's Crag was much the steeper of the two giant outcrops, but the path that had been carved into it was the only route up to the top, making it the obvious point to attack.

It was said that the Krykkers had a hand in building the fortress for Duke Burkhard all those years ago. Whoever it was, they had made it a death trap. Walter led them through the walled section at the top of the path, where attackers were presented with three options. The two to their right were fake, leading nowhere, except perhaps to a bloody greeting by the defenders.

They descended now, the path steep, and interrupted at regular intervals by wooden gates and ledges that had been added by Walter himself. These had worked well last year, impeding the progress of the Drobax and giving defenders an extra height advantage. As they went, Walter stationed small groups of Barissians at each one, ready to defend the position or open the gates as required. Farther down, a massive boulder was positioned just off the path, kept in place by a wooden buttress. A wicked part of Farred wanted the Drobax to get this far, so that he could see what happened when it was released.

Finally, Walter called a halt to their progress just before the path levelled out. This was where they would make their stand. Walter looked about him. 'Farred!' he said. 'Come, fight by my side.'

Honoured, Farred moved into position next to the duke. Ahead of them, the front row held spears, but otherwise short weapons were the order of the day in this tight space. Both Walter and Farred carried short swords. It was the weapon that Farred had always been more comfortable with. But most other men held blunt weapons, hammers and clubs, and in all honesty, Farred thought they looked the better choice.

In the distance, the Drobax could be seen, edging forwards as they readied themselves to advance. But it wasn't just the Drobax that occupied Farred's mind. He looked up at the sky, searching for a giant lizard with wings. All he saw was the sun overhead, blindingly bright.

They waited in the sun, and the smell of his neighbour's sweat filled Farred's nostrils. The smells would be worse before the day was done.

Then the drums started, the heavy thuds telling the Drobax that the order to attack had been given. Farred could see them shuffling forwards, great lines of the monsters advancing towards the Barissians who stood only half a dozen wide. The Drobax funnelled towards the path, barging into each other in the surge.

Farred heard voices. Initially, he looked about him, wondering where they were coming from.

'Out there,' Walter said into his ear. The duke pointed out in front, towards the Drobax.

Farred frowned at the idea, but he listened. Some of the Drobax were giving orders.

'Advance!'

'Steady!'

'Wait!'

As he looked closer, he could see which Drobax spoke; saw their lips move. Scattered in amongst the rest, they were taller than the others. Drobax that could speak? What devilry was this?

But there was no more time to think about it, because the Drobax were onto them. The front row prodded forward with spears, but the surge was too strong to hold off. Drobax plunged into the cold metal of the spear tips, but more followed, pulling spears out of hands, climbing on the fallen and hurling themselves into the defenders.

Farred worked with his sword, thrusting the blade into faces, necks, chests. His hand and forearm came back bloody, his grip on his sword hilt slippery. There was no other choice but to retreat from the force of the attack. But it was difficult, because the men behind them had to give them room. Walter slipped, and Farred caught his arm, keeping him upright.

Next, Farred felt hands on his shoulders and he allowed himself to be guided backwards, through one of the wooden gates. Barissian soldiers shoved the gate closed and bolted it, giving them a chance to breathe. Above them, more soldiers stood on the ledge, hurling missiles down at the Drobax who approached the gate.

'Alexia preserve us!' came the shout, and instinctively, Farred looked up.

A great shadow passed over them. The dragon had come, sweeping over the siege.

But at least Farred had given the Brasingians warning, and they met it with a volley of arrows. Archers manned the towers and walls of the Duke's Keep, firing high into the sky at the beast. The large ballista bolts followed, tearing through the sky at velocity.

Like everyone else, Farred stared at the dragon. Green in a blue sky, it was all neck and tail and wings. A sick feeling of dread rolled from it onto the soldiers below. They were helplessly exposed. Farred saw some of the arrows hit the target, but the creature seemed unaffected. When the bolts came some were diverted away, the Isharite wizards down below protecting their greatest weapon. Others the dragon itself avoided, displaying its agility. It used its wings to stop, then move its bulk to the side, dodging the larger missiles that might have pierced its scaly skin. Then it roared its fury at them. Farred felt a guilty sense of relief when the dragon furled its wings and dived, not towards his position, but at the archers on the keep.

A noise competed for his attention. Slowly, as if spellbound, Farred wrenched his fearful gaze away from the dragon and onto the gate in front of him. A multitude of grey hands had reached around the sides of it and were pulling at the wood. The gate was ripped apart in front of his eyes.

He went to shout and found he was voiceless, his jaws still clamped tight from fear. The Drobax advanced, crude weapons held at the ready. Farred felt hot piss on his legs.

'Kill them!' ordered one of the Drobax.

For some reason hearing those words released Farred.

'Drobax ahead!' he bellowed, and the Barissians around him shouted too, many just making mad, animal noises.

The Barissians and the Drobax moved on each other, both sides hungry for bloodshed. Farred hacked and thrust with his sword, until his shoulder ached so much it felt like he couldn't raise his arm any more.

A Drobax leapt at him. With the space so constricted, Farred couldn't move out of the way, having to rely instead on stabbing the creature as it came at him. But it grabbed his arm, moving his weapon aside, and Farred collapsed, with the Drobax landing on top of him. He fell heavily onto his back, the wind knocked from him. He could smell the foul breath of the creature as it pinned him to the ground, before raising its arm, a sharp looking rock in its hand ready to dash his brains out. But the blow didn't come, instead it remained in position, as if frozen. Fumbling with his right hand, Farred found the hilt of his sword and stabbed into the throat of the Drobax. Now it fell, and then Farred felt hands grabbing under his arms, getting him back on his feet.

The battle resumed. The defenders had the height and consequently the better of the fighting, but the Drobax were relentless, an endless supply of reinforcements ready to take the place of the fallen. Walter's men were gradually driven back up the path to the next gate, which was locked in place.

'Come' said Walter breathlessly to the men around him. 'We've fought enough for one day. Time to let others take our place. There is no benefit in getting ourselves killed.'

Walter led the group back up the path, leaving the Barissians to take the front. Farred didn't think he had the strength to climb all the way back to the top. Collapsing on the path wasn't much of an option either, though, so he kept moving, one step at a time.

He summoned the energy to turn and look into the sky for the dragon, but he saw nothing, neither the monster nor arrows from the defenders.

When they reached the top of the crag Farred heard gasps. Walter and his men were gesturing to the keep. The top of it was smoking.

Tobias of Luderia had come to meet them.

'We drove it off in the end,' he told them. 'Not before it scorched the roof. The ballistae are burned to a crisp, I am afraid.'

'The archers?' Walter asked wearily.

'We lost some of them. Some of the boys had to hurl themselves from the roof to avoid the flames from the beast. The heat up there was extraordinary. We kept shooting and shooting, Walter. We don't have many arrows left now.'

'Did it seem injured?' Walter asked.

'Hard to tell. The arrows don't seem to bother it too much. Most bounced off it, but some stuck. Perhaps if we aim for the eyes, the wings, they might work. It was worried by the ballista bolts, but it avoided all of them.'

'What happened at the end?'

'Once it destroyed the ballistae it flew off. It was beginning to resemble a pin cushion by then,' the duke said, allowing himself a grim smile.

Walter nodded. 'Well done, Tobias. Tell your men too, from me, the archers of Luderia have done well. From what you say, the monster could be back tomorrow. We still have the ballistae on the Emperor's Keep. It might be worth transferring them over here.'

The drums of the enemy took up, banging out a new rhythm. To a man, they all looked down to see what new menace would appear. But the drums were beating out a retreat. The Drobax began to move back down the path, a bloody trail of destruction left in their wake. Across the bridge, the Drobax who had been toiling up the sides of the Emperor's Crag did the same.

'What does that mean?' Tobias asked.

Walter shrugged.

Farred thought he knew. 'They'll wait until the dragon is ready to attack again. Perhaps not until tomorrow. I think the creature uses a lot of energy to keep itself in the air, not to mention the fire-breath. When it attacked the Krykkers, it did so in short bursts.'

'Whenever they come, we need to be ready,' said Walter. 'I will speak with Gustav. Whether we like it or not, we will need his magic to help us next time.'

III

THE QUEEN OF KALINTH

I T WAS A RELIEF TO SEE the Knights of Kalinth return to Heractus. Belwynn and Lyssa watched them from the battlements of the castle as they rode past to the city gates, the Kalinthian flag of the Winged Horse carried ahead to alert the city guard.

Lyssa enjoyed pointing out the people she knew: there was Theron, riding next to his friend Tycho, for whom she had a soft spot. Not far behind was Evander, Theron's former squire. He was not much older than Lyssa really, but they had made him a knight because they needed as many warriors as they could get. There was Gyrmund, who had accompanied the Knights on their travels. Lyssa giggled.

'Why does he look so different?' she asked.

Belwynn wasn't quite sure what the girl meant. He wore the comfortable leathers he always travelled in, rather than the armour the knights wore. He also had the dark skin and long hair of the Middians, which set him apart from the fairer skinned Kalinthians around him.

'What do you mean, Lyssa?'

'Why isn't he dressed like a knight?'

'Well, he's not a knight, is he?'

'Why not? Won't they let him join?'

'No, Gyrmund doesn't want to be a knight. He's not from Kalinth, remember? He's from Magnia, like me.'

'But you're the Lady of the Knights, now. So why doesn't Gyrmund become a knight?'

'Hmm,' Belwynn said, thinking. 'Good point. I guess—'

'Look, there's Coronos,' said Lyssa, evidently ready to move on from that topic of conversation.

Belwynn studied the force. Theron had spent the last week recruiting and gathering supplies. But his numbers didn't seem so much larger than when he had set out, and the supply wagons that trundled past were far from full. It suggested that the expedition hadn't gone as well as they had hoped.

'Come on, Lyssa,' she said. 'Let's go down to the yard to greet them.'

The courtyard was a confusion of bodies as squires rushed over to take horses away to the stables. Belwynn saw Moneva standing to one side, waiting to see Gyrmund. They shared a smile. It pleased Belwynn no end to see her friends happy again.

Next, she spied Theron. He had dismounted and was looking around the courtyard, his face grim. When he met eyes with Belwynn his face relaxed and he smiled. At least that was something.

He walked over to see them.

'Has the city been running smoothly under your command?' he asked Lyssa with a straight face.

'Yes, it's been fine, but they still made me go to lessons, so I couldn't really be in charge all the time,' the girl answered, sounding almost apologetic.

'Well, I know you will have done a good job.'

'Look Lyssa, there's Evander,' Belwynn said.

The young man waved at them and Lyssa went over to speak with him.

'Well?'

'Not so good,' Theron said. 'There is more suspicion out there than I imagined. From the nobility and ordinary folk alike. The deaths of Straton and Dorian are part of the problem for us. As are all the years they have suffered from Drobax and Kharovian incursions and had no support. Then we suddenly show up asking for soldiers.' He shrugged. 'Anyway, I'll talk to you properly soon. But I've been daydreaming of having a bath for the last few days.'

Belwynn wafted a hand over her nose. 'Good idea. I will come to your room later.'

'Yes please.'

Belwynn made her way over to Moneva and Gyrmund.

'Clarin's here?' he asked, looking excited.

'Shall we all go and see him?' Belwynn suggested.

Clarin was still staying in the castle chapel for now, having only woken from his prolonged slumber yesterday. They had set up a bed for him, but it wasn't the most private or convenient of spaces and Belwynn would find him a room when he was ready to move.

They found him dozing, but he soon got up when he saw he had visitors. Gyrmund and Clarin wrapped their arms around each other and stayed that way for a while. It was the first time they had seen each other since Samir Durg. They had gone through a lot there, and sometimes Belwynn could forget that.

'You saw Herin, then?' Gyrmund asked as he extricated himself.

Clarin nodded. 'A bittersweet meeting. He is alive and well, even if he now serves Siavash of Ishari. We fought. He won and took the Persaleian Shield from me. The Isharites must have it now. He cheated,' the big man added with a frown, as if that was the worst part of it. 'Used poison that made me sleep. That's what Moneva thinks anyway. But I'm alive, and the rest were spared, too. So—' he gave a little shrug, suddenly looking tired again. 'I don't really know what to think.'

'Well you rest up,' said Gyrmund. 'We're going to need you.'

'How's that?'

'Kalinth still doesn't have much of an infantry force. And I don't think it will be long before the Isharites send their armies here.'

'Hmm,' said Clarin, pondering that. 'Fighting to be done, eh? Well, I might be getting some of my appetite back. That's a good sign, isn't it?'

'Anything we can get you?' Belwynn asked.

'Eggs and toast would be nice,' he suggested. 'Maybe with a bit of ham or bacon. Don't know if the kitchens here could spare some milk to wash it down with?'

Belwynn shared a look with Moneva, trying not to smile.

'Do you know, Clarin,' said Moneva, 'I think you might make a full recovery after all.'

'I hope so,' said the big man, settling back down onto the bed and closing his eyes. 'Make sure to wake me when the food arrives, won't you?'

'So the shield is lost to us,' said Theron, after Belwynn had fully explained what Clarin had told her. 'Is it necessary to have all seven weapons?'

They sat on his bed in his private rooms. It was nice to spend some time alone together. Belwynn couldn't recall the last time they had got the chance.

'No one really knows for sure,' she answered him. 'But I think that's the idea.'

'Could we get it back? Will it be in Samir Durg?'

'I don't know.'

'Can't you—you know. Ask Madria?'

Belwynn smiled. Theron wasn't the only one who had trouble understanding the boundaries of her powers.

'So, from being able to talk to people telepathically, it's now become identifying the locations of objects,' she said, not refraining from letting a bit of sarcasm enter her voice.

'You could try,' he said, smiling.

'Alright, Theron. I'll try. We'll have to see what Soren thinks. There are still two other weapons that haven't been found.'

Theron nodded, but she saw his eyes glazing over somewhat. She understood. It wasn't that he didn't believe the weapons were important. That had been proven for all to see when they had defeated the army led by Siavash's shadow. Belwynn herself had wielded Toric's Dagger to destroy the creature. It was that his head was filled with problems of recruitment and supply. And they were vital too. Kalinth's stubborn resistance to the Isharites had given them the time to search for the other weapons.

'You will head south next?' she asked, changing the subject to one more relevant to his priorities. 'At least the people there have now witnessed the threat from the Drobax.'

It was from the south that the Drobax had invaded Kalinthian territory. From the Krykker lands. Whenever she thought of it, a cold feeling clamped at her insides. What had become of Rabigar and their Krykker allies?

A shadow passed over Theron's face. 'Yes, in due time. There are things to be done here in Heractus first.'

'What things?'

Theron hesitated. He looked torn over what to say to her. Belwynn didn't like the idea that he might be keeping things from her.

'Well?' she insisted, her voice becoming sharp.

'I've decided to resign as Grand Master of the Knights.'

'What?' Belwynn let out, caught completely by surprise.

'I could do with someone else taking on that responsibility. And I have come to realise, I am not universally popular. I occupied Heractus and imprisoned the royal family. I executed Count Ampelios, I killed the princes, Straton and Dorian. That's how people see it, at any rate. It didn't matter before, because Sebastian was Grand Master. It kept him free of any blame. But I'm the leader of the Knights, and my name is tainted. If I resign, the taint is removed from the Knights. They will once more be seen as nothing but the defenders of our country. That is all I have ever tried to do—'

He stopped, finding it hard to continue, and Belwynn reached over to hold his hand. She knew it was an issue. That was why she had agreed to play the role of the Lady of the Knights, and accepted her new one, the Voice of Madria. So that she could support what Theron was doing.

'Who, then?' she asked softly. 'Tycho?'

Theron shook his head. 'He is too close to me. I have discussed it with him the last few days. We are both agreed on Leontios.'

'Leontios!'

When she first met Leontios he was an untried young knight, one of the group who had asked Belwynn to bless their swords on the journey from the High Tower to Heractus. But she could see why Theron and Tycho had picked him. He had taken on much responsibility since then, and he was the leader of that younger generation of knights, who had come into their own in the last year. Good natured, popular and resourceful. He would have been a perfect candidate in ten years' time. But, just like Evander becoming a knight too early, the men of Kalinth were having to fill vacancies before their time.

'Well, not a bad choice,' she conceded. 'And there's one other benefit.'

'What's that?'

'If you're not the Grand Master any longer, your vow of chastity is conveniently removed.'

'That,' Theron replied, leaning in to her, 'was reason number one.'

Belwynn woke from a dream. When she tried to recall it, it evaded her grasp, like smoke from a fire. The feeling left her unsettled.

She realised that she was in Theron's bed and she reached over to him for comfort.

He wasn't there.

Belwynn sat up, looking around his room. It was chilly—pitch black—and the fear of the dark that night brings clutched at her. Theron wasn't in his room.

Theron? she demanded, using her telepathy to call out to him.

There was a pause before he answered.

Belwynn? What is it?

Where are you?

Nowhere. I mean, it's nothing. Go back to sleep.

His tone and his words raised Belwynn's suspicions further. Go to sleep? I can hardly get back to sleep now, she said to herself.

Her mind made up, she left the warm blankets and put her cold clothes on, then left Theron's room.

She walked along the corridor and down the steps to the ground floor. Maybe, a few months ago, Belwynn would have just settled back to sleep. But Siavash's shadow had changed all that. It had taken control of Remi, Sebastian, and Prince Dorian. It had used their bodies to kill. It had killed Elana, and she had failed to stop it. Something didn't feel right tonight, and she wasn't going to bury her head in her pillow and do nothing.

Belwynn made her way into the Great Hall of the castle. It was full of slumbering men, mostly recruits that Theron had gathered from the northern estates of Kalinth. She tiptoed through the room, trying carefully not to wake anyone.

She found herself approaching the royal suite of apartments. Two knights stood guard by the door that allowed access to the rooms, talking quietly together, no doubt to help them stay awake through the night hours. Belwynn suddenly felt foolish, wandering around the castle like this. What was she going to do, approach the two men to tell them she had woken from a funny dream? She turned, ready to go back to her own room.

Then she heard a scream from the royal suite.

She ran forward to the two knights, recognising both men.

'Did you not hear that?'

They both wore awkward expressions. One of them was Coronos, one of Lyssa's favourites. 'Yes, my lady. It's just that Lords Theron and Tycho told us to stay here.' He looked at her, going a bit red. 'Not to let anyone past.'

'Well I don't think I'm just *anyone*, do you?' she demanded coldly.

'No,' Coronos said quickly, his resistance broken, and he stepped aside to let her past.

Belwynn opened the door and went through. Here was an open plan area, off which doors to private rooms were located. In the middle of the area she saw Tycho struggling with someone. At first, she thought he was being attacked, but then she saw that he was restraining Queen Irina.

'Get your filthy hands off me,' the queen shouted.

'I can't do that, Your Majesty,' he said, holding her by the wrists. 'Please, come with me,' he added, making an effort to guide her away towards Belwynn.

They didn't see Belwynn approach until she was on them.

'Belwynn!' Tycho said in surprise, a guilty expression crossing his face.

'What's going on here?' Belwynn demanded.

'Come to gloat?' Irina said to her, voice raw with emotion. 'The Lady of the Knights,' she said, full of sarcasm. 'You've killed my boys. Now it's to be my husband's turn.'

Irina spat at her from close range, her spittle landing on Belwynn's face. Belwynn wiped it away. Confusion and anger began to boil within her.

'Where is Theron?' she demanded of Tycho.

His eyes flickered towards one of the doors and she walked towards it.

'Don't go in there,' he warned weakly.

Ignoring him, Belwynn shoved the door open. It was the royal bedroom. Inside she saw Theron kneeling on the floor. He was cradling the head of King Jonas, who lay on the floor in a pool of blood.

'I let him pray first,' said Theron quietly, turning to her. 'He was at peace with it.'

'Why?' Belwynn asked. She stared at the scene, her brain refusing to process what she was seeing. Is this what she had dreamt?

'It had to be done, Belwynn,' Theron said, his voice still quiet, no emotion in it. 'We should have done it before. It would have saved a lot of lives. The people were never going to accept the situation. Never. Me giving out orders, while their king was locked away here. The Knights *defend* Kalinth. They don't rule it.'

Understanding slowly dawned on Belwynn. 'That's why you are resigning as Grand Master. You are going to make yourself king.'

Theron smiled at her. 'Yes. And you will be my queen.'

Belwynn shot a hand to her mouth as bile rose up her throat. She felt like she was going to vomit. She turned away from Theron as hot tears came to her eyes.

'Belwynn,' he called after her as she left the room.

Belwynn stumbled back into the area beyond. She was grateful that Tycho had succeeded in manhandling the queen away somewhere. She ran through, past the two knights standing guard outside, not looking at them, not speaking.

Soren! she said to her brother telepathically, not knowing who else to turn to, where else to go. She assumed he would be asleep, but he answered immediately.

Belwynn? What is it?

Where are you? she asked.

In the library.

What are you doing there? she demanded, changing course for the library.

Soren was somehow able to communicate a heavy sigh telepathically.

What do you think I'm doing here?

She ascended the tower stairs and ran for the room. Inside she found her twin sat at a desk, surrounded by candles. A pile of books lay to one side, and one was open in front of him. One hand clutched Onella's Staff. It gave him the ability to see clearly even in this dingy light. Without it, he wouldn't have been able to read a word.

'What are you doing up at this hour?' she said, the need to reprimand her brother temporarily outweighing the need to tell him about what she had just witnessed.

'Reading.'

'How is that going to help us? You should be resting. We need you to be fit and well for what is to come.'

'What is to come will soon be here. This may be the last chance I ever get to read. Anyway, what is it, Belwynn?'

'I've just come straight from the royal suite. Something drew me down there. When I got there, I found Theron. He has killed King Jonas.'

'Hmm,' Soren said, sounding interested but not as shocked as Belwynn expected. 'Why?'

'He is going to take the throne.'

'Well, it may not work out so bad. Theron will be a powerful king. Better able to muster the forces of Kalinth.'

'But it's *wrong*, Soren. Can't you see that?'

She was shivering, the shock of what she had just witnessed beginning to affect her body.

Soren looked her up and down. He stood up, leaning on Onella's Staff. He grabbed a chair from a nearby table and dragged it over next to his. 'Come, Belwynn, sit down.'

She did as he said, and he took off his cloak and put it around her.

'When we were in Tosongat,' Soren began, 'amongst the Jalakhs, we needed Gansukh to win the Great Contest and thereby become khan. Only then would we get the Jalakh Bow. He had to win a fight each day to win the Contest. But he became injured, and had to fight fresh fighters the following days—the best the other tribes had. He wasn't going to win. Our chances of getting the Bow were fading. I used magic against his challengers. Moneva killed fighters from the other tribes before they could even challenge him. We killed in cold blood so that we could bring the Bow back. It didn't feel right when we did it. But it was what we had to do. Better than failing, because the consequences of failure would be more terrible. Theron has done something similar. He has killed his king. No doubt he feels wretched about it. But if he did it for the good of his people, then—'

Soren ended his speech with a shrug.

Belwynn nodded. 'I understand that. We've all had to do hard things. But I am complicit in it. As Madria's priestess, as the Lady of the Knights, I support Theron. And he did this behind my back, without talking to me about it.'

'I know you have made a place for yourself here, Belwynn. I am happy for you. But in the big picture, either we defeat Siavash, destroy Diis once and for all—or we don't, and they destroy Dalriya as we know it. What happens to one man, even though he may be a king, must be set in that bigger picture.'

Belwynn felt dizzy. This conversation with her brother, in a library in Kalinth in the middle of the night, felt surreal. She wasn't sure what she thought any more—what she believed in. What was important. She struggled to gather her thoughts.

'You don't care much what happens to Kalinth, Soren, but I do. It is my home now. And Theron was special to me. I loved him. When I went downstairs he told me he would make me his queen.'

Soren's eyebrows raised at that, but he didn't interrupt her.

'But I can't get that image out of my head now. I don't think I can look at him, speak to him ever again. Why didn't he tell me?'

'I expect he wanted to spare you. What would you have preferred? Joint regicide, each of you sticking a knife in? He didn't want you to have that image in your head, but you decided you had to find out. I can't tell you what your feelings for Theron are, Belwynn. You will have to work that out for yourself. Give yourself time. All I can say is, for the good of the world, we need to focus on our task. We need to get the weapons. We need to kill a god. If we are still here after all that, then we can decide who we love. Decide whether we want to be a queen, or a priestess. Or a sister.'

'I'll always be a sister, you idiot.'

Soren smiled at that. 'And what of Madria?'

'What of Her?'

'Is that a choice, too? Will She leave you if you ask Her to?'

That was a question that had never crossed Belwynn's mind. Why hadn't it? She reached out for the goddess, wondering if she was listening to the conversation. But she wasn't there to connect with.

Soren looked at her, concern visible in his expression.

IV

A WATERY GRAVE

RABIGAR DIPPED HIS PADDLE into the waters of the Nasvarl. The canoe didn't immediately sink, which was something.

Ahead of him sat Stenk, and in between them their armour, weapons, blankets and other supplies: mostly the fish they had taken yesterday. Gunnhild had given them a rudimentary lesson in paddling but insisted that they would only learn by doing it. She and Ignac were in the second canoe, already some distance ahead.

'Rocks ahead!' shouted Stenk.

Stenk was in the front because his eyesight was better, although Rabigar wasn't convinced about the boy's brains.

'Which way?' Rabigar shouted back.

'What do you mean?' Stenk shouted back, a note of panic in his voice.

Rabigar felt the shudder as the canoe banged into the rocks.

'Stenk!' he shouted. 'When you see an obstacle, you're going to have to decide whether we're going left or right, and tell me. Just shouting "rocks ahead" isn't very helpful.'

'Righto, Rabigar,' replied Stenk as he prodded with his paddle at the rocks, pushing the front end of the canoe away from the hazard. He chuckled. 'I've always been a bit uncertain between my lefts and rights.'

Rabigar sighed inwardly. This was going to be a very, very long journey.

Once they got the hang of it, Rabigar and Stenk began to make good time in their canoe. Although they were travelling with the flow of the river, they still had to paddle hard to maintain a good speed. They soon learned where the fastest parts of the river were and by mid-morning they were keeping the same pace as Gunnhild and Ignac. Rabigar's shoulders began to ache, but it was a good ache, and he didn't mind it at all.

It was hungry work, but the canoe was full of their salted salmon and it kept them going until midday, when everyone agreed they should pull in to the riverbank for a rest. Stenk managed to steer them onto a gravelly flat spot and they climbed out, before dragging the canoe up a bit farther. They didn't want to see it go floating off down the river or their weapons tipped into the water.

Rabigar was grateful for the chance to stretch his legs and back out. He wandered up to the top of the bank. A stark world of whiteness lay before him, interrupted only occasionally by black rock. Gunnhild approached him, having beached her own canoe a little further downstream.

'It's impossible to know which ice is safe to stand on,' she commented, looking out with him. 'Especially this time of year, when the sun is strong enough to melt it in places. It would be slow going walking on foot. We'd need ropes round our waists, so we could pull each other out. No,' she said, as if Rabigar had suggested leaving the canoes behind and travelling the rest of the way on foot, 'this river is the only safe way to go west.'

'If the Nasvarl empties into the sea off the west coast,' Rabigar said, 'how will we know when to stop? Where exactly should we look for the Giants?'

'We'll keep going until we see a sign.'

'What sign?'

'I don't know, Krykker. A sign left by the Giants, I suppose.'

'What do the stories say?'

Gunnhild spat. 'The stories say all kinds of things. We can't rely on *them*.'

'And what if there are no signs?'

'Then they can't be found.' The Vismarian pointed out to the ice fields. 'You think you can wander around out there until you bump into a Giant? Impossible. You would spend the rest of your life looking and get nowhere. Except your life wouldn't be a long one, what with the white wyrms.'

'White wyrms?' Rabigar found himself asking, despite being quite sure he didn't want to know about them.

'Giant white lizards. If they don't see you crossing the ice, out in the open with nowhere to hide, they'll smell you. We can't trust to blind luck out here. We're looking for a sign. Pray to your gods if you think that will help.'

Mention of gods made Rabigar think of Belwynn. She had become a disciple of Madria—a replacement for Dirk, who had succumbed to his injuries. He wondered what would come of that decision.

'Gods aren't interested in what we want,' he said. 'They're only happy when we're dancing to their tune.'

They paddled for the rest of the day until the light started to give out, then found a spot by the bank to make camp. It didn't feel right to Rabigar sleeping so close to the river, and he woke with a start more than once, fearing he had rolled into the water in his sleep.

The next day was more of the same, and the next. The novelty of paddling a canoe started to wear thin. The scenery became tedious and the taste of salmon monotonous. More of the fish swam past them constantly, on their way to their spawning grounds, where, according to Gunnhild, they would die. It seemed a rather pointless journey to make, yet they all did it, swimming upriver in their thousands. Rabigar was beginning to think that their own journey might end up being even more pointless.

A rushing sound ahead gradually got louder, and Gunnhild and Ignac pulled in next to them for a discussion.

'That sounds like a pretty big waterfall coming up,' said Gunnhild, having to speak loudly to be heard.

'Sounds like it,' Rabigar agreed.

'Normally, we'd have to leave the river and carry the canoes down to the next stretch.'

Rabigar didn't like the sound of that. They weren't easy to carry, and the route might be treacherous.

'But Ignac has an idea.'

'When we approach the fall, I can teleport us to the next stretch of water. It should be possible for me to gauge the correct place to move us to, give or take. But there's a risk that I get it wrong.'

Rabigar's instincts were against the use of magic. But Soren's interventions had helped them more than once in the past. And why bring the Caladri medium with them, if they weren't going to use his powers?

'Alright,' he agreed. 'It sounds like it could save us a lot of time.'

They paddled further, staying close, until they could see the drop ahead. Here the water travelled faster, and the rush of the waterfall had become a roar.

Ignac reached out and Rabigar held his hand, keeping the two canoes together. Gunnhild and Stenk kept them facing the waterfall. They approached. They would go over in mere seconds. Rabigar looked over to Ignac. What was he waiting for?

The Caladri peered ahead, concentrating, then closed his eyes. That shifting feeling in the stomach hit Rabigar. The waterfall disappeared. He could feel his canoe falling through the air, but only for a moment, before it hit the river with a splash. Rabigar looked around. Gunnhild and Ignac were next to them. Behind them the waterfall loomed tall, cascading into a pool.

Stenk let out a relieved whoop. 'You did it, Ignac!' he hollered enthusiastically.

Ignac gave the lad a smile. 'I dropped us slightly too high, but not a bad result.'

Rabigar looked over at Gunnhild. It was unlike her to not add a comment. She was staring ahead to a bend in the river. When Rabigar looked he got a shock and put a hand to his heart, nearly dropping his paddle in the process.

A giant stood there. It was huge and stood looking across the river as if it owned it.

'Gunnhild?' he murmured, not sure what they should do.

'It's a statue,' she said.

'Huh?' Rabigar peered at it. It wasn't moving, that was true, but he couldn't see it clearly enough to fully satisfy himself.

'Come,' said Gunnhild. She and Ignac began to paddle towards the river bend, and Rabigar and Stenk followed them.

Gunnhild was right. As Rabigar neared, he could see that it held the same dynamic pose, as if it were looking at the waterfall. The giant's legs were squat and powerful looking, its torso long and muscular. The statue was a pale green colour, and Rabigar knew that it must be made from bronze or some similar metal.

They ran their canoes ashore and walked over to the statue of the giant. Rabigar ran a hand over the metal admiringly. He looked up.

'Must be twelve feet tall. Do you think it's meant to be life size?'

'I would think so,' said Gunnhild.

'Is this the sign we were looking for?' he asked the Vismarian.

'Yes,' she said, sounding certain.

Gunnhild pointed to the west. They could see a mountain range on the horizon. Between the statue and the mountains lay ice, interrupted every now and again by black rock, some of it protruding quite high from the ground.

'We must go on foot from here,' she said. 'Stow the canoes nearby for our return.'

Rabigar looked about. The Nasvarl flowed away in a more northerly direction than the mountain range. It wouldn't be an easy journey getting to those mountains on foot.

'Are you sure?' he asked her.

'Yes,' she replied.

Rabigar looked at Ignac, who gave a slight shrug, as if to say what choice did they have but to trust her. They had none.

'Alright,' Rabigar agreed.

They spent some time preparing for the walk. Armour now had to be worn, and supplies carried. Rabigar was already missing the comfort of the canoes, which had carried everything for them.

Gunnhild insisted that they be roped together.

'If you fall in,' she explained, 'the water can pull you away under the ice in seconds. That's it. Gone. At least this way we have a chance to pull each other out. Now, I'm the heaviest. If I go in I could take you all with me. I go last. Ignac is the lightest, so he goes first. All we're doing is travelling from one outcrop of rock to the next, until we get to the mountains.'

They set off, gingerly walking across the icy surface. In some places the surface had melted and was slushy underfoot. In other parts it was still frozen solid, and the ice was slippery. Ignac walked barefoot, his birdlike feet seemingly able to find purchase on the hardest ice. Rabigar, second in line, did not find it so easy. More than once a foot went from under him and he found himself tottering, or going down on his knees or arse. If it wasn't him it was Stenk. Gunnhild carried her hammer, one side of which had a sharp spike, ready to be smashed into the ground should the need arise.

It was Rabigar who fell in. His eyes on Ignac in front of him, he wasn't looking at the ground with enough care. As he put his weight on his front foot it kept going, down into the icy water, and he couldn't stop himself from falling over. As he landed, the ice all around him gave way. Worse, the rope he wore only went taut for a second before it loosened again. Ahead he could see Ignac had lost his footing, pulled backwards towards the hole Rabigar had made.

The Caladri fell towards him. Rabigar made to reach an arm out of the water to stop Ignac from falling in, but his arm wouldn't do as it was told. Instead, starting to panic now, he submerged under the icy water.

As he struggled, Rabigar felt Ignac's body knock into him, and he swallowed water. Choking, he saw the hole, lighter than the solid ice around it, was receding as he drifted away.

Then, somehow, he was moving back towards the hole. His head was raised above the water and he spluttered and coughed, desperately trying to breathe in air.

'Steady,' came a voice, maybe talking to him. He felt himself move now, dragged up then along, his chin coming down hard on solid ice. He was left there for what felt like an age, legs still in the icy water, face pressed against the ice, sucking in whatever oxygen he could, though it was never enough. Then he was moving again, this time dragged completely out of the water, turned over, faces peering at him. He heard the sound of talking, but not the words.

'Get up!'

Gunnhild shouted in his ear, and this time he heard it. Rabigar worked with her now, getting to his feet. He was shivering violently. She put an arm around his shoulders and led him, like a child, away from the hole.

Rabigar was sopping wet and the cold air on his skin was excruciating. He had never been so cold. His lungs burned, his heart was racing, and he felt dizzy. It was all he could do to put one foot in front of the other. Without Gunnhild supporting him he would have collapsed to the ground, and the others would have had no choice but to leave him there. He wanted to ask her how much farther she intended on making him walk, but his teeth were chattering so much he couldn't get any words out.

They made it to a rocky outcrop, that rose gently enough for Gunnhild to lower him onto.

'I have to get these clothes off you,' she said, tugging at his top. Rabigar did his best to raise his arms so that she could pull it over his head. She pulled at his trousers.

'Get off!' he demanded, finding his voice at last.

But his hands were so numb with cold that there was no way he was going to be able to grip his trousers himself.

'Don't be so bloody stupid,' Gunnhild snarled, pulling at his trousers until they came loose. She rubbed at him with one of the blankets before putting it over him. Next thing, Ignac was deposited next to him. The Caladri looked half drowned and was making a horrible rattling sound when he breathed.

Gunnhild and Stenk covered them both in whatever blankets and spare clothes they could find.

'Lie down with them,' Gunnhild ordered Stenk. 'They need your body heat.'

Stenk lay down on top of them, putting his arms around them.

'Get off me,' Rabigar demanded, his words slurring. He was naked under the blanket and the last thing he wanted was a three-way cuddle with two men.

Stenk lifted himself up.

'Rabigar doesn't want me to,' he called out to Gunnhild.

'If you don't lie down there right now, I'm going to break your limbs and dump your bleeding body on top of them.'

Rabigar had rarely heard a voice sound so angry and he wasn't surprised when Stenk lay straight back down.

'What are *you* doing?' Stenk shouted out.

'I'm going to try to make a fire,' Gunnhild's voice drifted back. 'It's going—oh no.'

The last two words were quieter, but something about the way in which they were said made Rabigar take notice. He struggled to a sitting position. Stenk, too, got up to see what the problem was.

'Quiet,' Gunnhild hissed. She turned around to see the two Krykkers looking at her, and pointed out to the ice. 'White wyrm.'

A feeling of dread passed through Rabigar. He looked out to where Gunnhild pointed but saw nothing.

'Do you see it?' he asked Stenk.

The Krykker shook his head, nervously getting to his feet.

'Stenk. Fetch me Bolivar's Sword, will you?'

The young Krykker ran over to where Rabigar's clothes had been spread out on the rock and picked up the weapon. Rabigar made himself stand, and reached out for the sword when Stenk returned with it. *Bolivar, Madria—whoever; give me strength*, he asked, and forced his hand open enough to grip the hilt.

The sword poured heat into him, steaming away the cold that had settled in his bones, the fogginess that had clouded his mind.

He marched forwards to stand with Gunnhild, and he saw the beast. It was so large that it took him a while to understand what he was seeing. Four legs, with what looked like a thick body, though it seemed to be covered in a white

41

fur that perhaps made it look bigger than it really was. A long bony head, ending in spikes where it met the sinewy neck, was raised in the air, as if it smelt them on the wind. It padded towards them, in no rush.

'What do you know of them?' he asked Gunnhild.

'They live alone, ruling their own territory which stretches out for miles. There will only be one of them. It heard us or smelt us; or both. It will come for us now. We would make a fine meal in these parts.'

'I'm not sure we can kill that,' said Rabigar, desperately trying to think through their options as the creature neared them.

'Nor am I,' Gunnhild agreed, eyes fixed on the wyrm. She unbuckled her great hammer from her belt. 'Maybe I can keep it occupied for a while.'

Rabigar turned around and returned to the rock. He grabbed Ignac's hand and placed Bolivar's Sword into it.

'Ignac,' he said, hoping the weapon would have a similar affect on the Caladri as it did on him. 'We're in trouble. Can you teleport us away?'

Ignac looked at him, some colour returning to his features.

'Get me up.'

'Come, Stenk.'

They lifted the Caladri to his feet. Rabigar pointed out the wyrm that was approaching them. Its head was down now, and it was coming more quickly, perhaps content after having determined what kind of prey it had found.

Ignac studied the mountain range they were aiming for. 'I perhaps have the strength to move all four of us two miles in that direction. Then I will be spent. I can't guarantee that we will finish anywhere safe, either. Meanwhile, the creature will be able to track us down from two miles away.'

'If there were three of us rather than four?'

'It wouldn't make much difference, Rabigar. Maybe I could carry us a little farther—'

'I'm sorry,' Rabigar said. 'This is my fault.'

'We certainly don't have time for that nonsense,' said the Caladri medium.

From somewhere, Rabigar found a smile.

'Then we fight?'

'I think so.'

They waited on the rock for the white wyrm to approach. Gunnhild stood on the highest part of the outcrop, her hammer held in both hands, her face grim.

Rabigar had Bolivar's Sword and Stenk gripped a short spear. He stood bravely and Rabigar was proud of him. Behind them was Ignac. He had no weapon. Perhaps he would find the strength to help them with his magic.

The wyrm approached. A rancid smell came with it, and Rabigar gagged when it carried to him on the wind. It reached as high as the rock and it stopped in front of Gunnhild, opening its mouth to shriek a challenge at her, revealing rows of sharp teeth and a long red tongue.

Suddenly it moved, faster than Rabigar could have imagined. It launched itself at Gunnhild, rising onto its hind legs and swiping at her with a clawed front leg. The rock on which she stood exploded into pieces and she was gone from sight.

Rabigar and Stenk moved together, no option left now but to attack. Stenk ran ahead to where the wyrm's tail flicked, trying to approach the beast from behind. Rabigar took the direct route, hoping that a strike from Bolivar's Sword might inflict enough damage.

The wyrm sensed their approach, backing away from them. At the least, they had driven it away from Gunnhild.

Stenk thrust his spear at it. With a screech, the wyrm whipped its tail and caught the young Krykker, who flew into the air before landing with a crunch. Rabigar stared, fearful that the weight of Stenk's landing would crack the ice, but the ground held. Stenk didn't move.

Rabigar ran at the wyrm and from the corner of his one eye he saw Gunnhild on her feet doing the same. The creature came for Rabigar, the claws of its front foot reaching for him. Rabigar swung, connecting with the wyrm, and was rewarded when the weapon sliced clean through, sending a claw spinning to the ground.

In a roar of anger, it leapt at him, its bloody foot coming to crush him into the ground. Rabigar skipped and slid away to the side, but only into the path of the wyrm's cruel maw. It clamped above and below his right knee, Rabigar feeling those sharp teeth cutting through flesh and tendons as its powerful jaw clenched shut. He shouted out in pain, then fear, as he found himself rising into the air, the powerful neck of the wyrm strong enough to pick him up.

Rabigar flailed out with the sword. Maybe he connected, maybe Gunnhild did, because the wyrm opened its mouth and let him drop to the ice. He clattered back down to earth, losing his grip on his weapon as he did.

Pushing himself up with his elbows, he saw Ignac run past him. With no weapon, the Caladri ran straight for the wyrm, past its clawed feet, past its snapping mouth. Rabigar stared aghast as time stood still.

Then the wyrm disappeared.

It seemed to flow, somehow, into the ice beneath it.

'Where is Ignac?' Gunnhild shouted at him, the Vismarian still on her feet, still clutching her hammer.

Rabigar reached over for Bolivar's Sword. Using its strength to help him, he got the foot of his good leg onto the ice, then pushed himself up, crying out in pain as he did so. He went woozy, as if he might faint, but pushed the feeling away.

Rabigar understood what Ignac had done. He looked under the ice.

'There!' he called out to Gunnhild, gesturing.

Beneath the ice, the pale, monstrous form of the wyrm could be seen.

Then one clawed foot erupted up through the ice, before finding purchase on the ground. The second foot came next, still bloody, but powerful nonetheless. Its head banged against its icy prison, trying to break through.

Gunnhild threw herself at the feet, smashing down with her hammer to send the creature back down into the icy depths.

Rabigar dragged himself towards the lizard, his injured leg threatening to give way if he put the slightest weight on it. As its head pressed against the ice a second time, Bolivar's Sword came down, breaking through ice and bone, burying into the brain of the wyrm.

It stopped moving. Its feet retreated into the water, its head began to sink, and Bolivar's Sword slid free.

The threat gone, Rabigar collapsed to the ground.

'What of Ignac?' Gunnhild asked.

'If he lives, and has the strength, he will teleport himself back.'

They sat by the hole where the wyrm had tried to escape its watery grave. They waited, but Ignac never came.

V

THE HAWK AND THE DRAGON

IT WAS THE TURN OF THE Luderians to defend the path up the Duke's Crag. That didn't mean Farred was spared. He stood atop the Duke's Keep, which had been scorched black by the dragon yesterday. With him were Walter, along with the best archers the marshal had, and men deployed to use the two ballistae that had been brought up. Finally, Gustav, Archmage of the Empire, was there as well. All of them ready to defend against the dragon should it reappear.

The pounding of the drums began, signalling that the Drobax were marching to the path once more. Farred strung his bow. He pulled it back, testing the resistance. He was a decent shot with a bow. He would have liked Gyrmund to be with them though. If anyone could make a shot into a dragon's eye, it would be him.

Farred stood in a line with three other men. They shared a pail of arrows. There weren't many in there, Walter making it clear that each shot had to count. The Luderians had released a vast quantity into the sky yesterday. Understandable, given a great green fire-breathing dragon had been flying towards them.

As he thought of the beast, so it appeared in the sky, coming from the direction of the Isharite army. It headed for the keep at an alarmingly fast pace, getting larger with each flap of its great wings as it neared them. It was heading straight for their position on the keep's battlements, presumably having learned that this was where the threat would come from.

'Wait until it nears!' Walter shouted out, dissuading his archers from loosing missiles prematurely.

The dragon was high above them in the sky, the sun behind it, making it harder to see. Then, with a roar, it dived at their position.

Walter hardly needed to shout 'Now!' as men moaned and murmured. The fire hadn't come yet but the fear had, rolling off the monster onto the keep, so palpable that Farred felt he could reach out and touch it. Instead, he drew and fired at the approaching monster. The ballistae made a cracking sound as they released their bolts.

An invisible, yet powerful, protective shield enveloped the dragon, sending even the most well aimed missiles astray. And then the dragon was above them. It emptied fire onto them. Farred felt the heat. He was sure he would have been cooked there and then, but Gustav created a shield of his own, straining to resist the deadly blast, before the dragon flew past, just a few feet above, a roar of frustration deafening them as it did.

Gustav turned and aimed a bolt of magic at the dragon. Farred watched it arc through the sky, before it dissipated as it got near. The Isharites, located somewhere on the plain below, still protected their most valuable weapon.

The men on the battlements didn't let the dragon out of their sight as it swung around in a slow, wide arc, lazily circling back to the crag. Instead of returning to the high battlements of the keep, it made for the beginning of the path up the crag.

Farred ran to the far side of the keep, from where he could see what the dragon would do. Many others joined him, Walter finding a space next to him and peering down with a grim face.

The Drobax had already made some progress up the path, pushing the Luderians back. The dragon let loose where the fighting raged, killing Drobax and Luderians alike, before continuing the circular journey up and around the crag. As it flew higher and higher, the wooden gates and ledges were torched, and the Luderian defenders turned into black ash.

'We must stop it!' Walter shouted, frantic.

They fired down upon the creature, having to ignore the chance that their arrows might strike Luderian defenders instead. The ballistae were readied, each firing a bolt when the dragon came around, still following the path. But arrows and bolts were repulsed.

Gustav tried now, covering the defenders with a magic shield. For a precious few seconds it worked, and for each second it lasted scores were saved. But the Isharite wizards, lurking somewhere down below, were many, and Gustav just one. Gustav fell to the floor from the unequal fight, his shield shattered, and the dragon completed its deadly work.

Farred fired again. This time he was sure his arrow hit, and his wasn't the only one. The dragon flew away now, roaring again, perhaps this time in triumph. The Luderian army was destroyed. The path up the crag smouldered, but large sections looked empty, the heat so intense that the soldiers had been incinerated.

Walter grabbed Farred's arm. Farred turned to look where the duke pointed. At the bottom of the crag, the Drobax surged onto the path unopposed. It wouldn't be long until they reached the top.

'The boulder!' Walter hissed and made for the stairwell.

Without time to think, Farred followed him, descending the narrow stairs as fast as he could, hands on the walls to prevent himself from falling and breaking his neck at the bottom.

Farred exited the stairwell into the keep's courtyard. Walter was running for the gates, not stopping to see whether Farred followed. Out of the gates, they ran for the top of the path.

Heat and fumes still came off the path, but into it Walter ran, and Farred ran after. The stench was bad. Worse was the heat from the floor. Farred could feel his feet blistering through his boots. He would have stopped to go back if Walter hadn't kept going. Then they had gone so far that turning back seemed pointless.

The Drobax would keep coming. And if they reached the top...

Farred caught up with Walter. The duke had stopped as he came upon the Luderians who Gustav had saved, making their way back up the path. Walter tried talking to them, saying he needed to release the boulder. But these men were wild eyed survivors of a massacre, and didn't listen to this duke raving about going back down for a boulder. So instead Walter grabbed an axe from one of them, and Farred did the same. They shouldered their way through the Luderians, desperate to reach the boulder before the Drobax.

The path wasn't quite so hot now and once free of the Luderians they ran until they reached the boulder. A wooden buttress held it in place and Farred and Walter smashed into it with their axes, until it splintered and gave way.

The boulder didn't move. Farred heard the Drobax approaching them.

'Push it!' said Walter, and they both heaved, but of course it didn't budge. Two men couldn't move this thing.

They looked at one another. They didn't have the energy to run back up the crag now. The Drobax would catch them soon.

They pushed again, the futility of it driving Farred to tears. Then a third force joined them, and they felt it move.

'Gustav?' Walter gasped.

'Or Inge,' said Farred.

Somehow, he knew it was the witch.

They pushed, using all of their strength, and now it rolled, gaining enough momentum to push it onto the path. The slope now began to pull it down. It was slow, though, and Farred and Walter continued to push at it, trying to give it enough speed so that it became what it was meant to be, an unstoppable tool of death.

It rolled down and it gained speed, the tilt of the steep path encouraging it to get even faster, the pummelling noise of rock on rock echoing outwards. They watched until it disappeared around the corner. Farred was sure it would roll off the edge, but the path was so circular and smooth that it kept going, hugging the inside of the crag.

Then they heard the first screams as the boulder met the Drobax, and the screams didn't stop, they just got louder, as the boulder continued its path, crushing anything that got in its way. Farred dared to peer over the edge below. He saw the path beneath packed full of Drobax, then saw them wiped away as the boulder came careening into view.

Walter gave Farred an embrace, virtually collapsing into him with exhaustion.

'Praise Gerhold,' said the duke, gasping for breath. 'I think we just saved the crag.'

Tobias, the heir to the duchy of Luderia, and well over half of his men, had died yesterday. It didn't really matter that Farred and Walter had killed the same number of Drobax with the boulder, because their numbers were endless. More would always come.

They came now. Today it was Godfrey and the men of Gotbeck who stood in their way, the Mace of the duchy held aloft in defiance at the place where the Tree of Luderia had been turned to ashes.

Farred had once had cause to dislike the Archbishop of Gotbeck, with his authoritarian brand of religion. But his sense of righteousness had not only led him to stand in the spot where young Tobias had been obliterated by dragon fire the day before, but had led his soldiers to stand with him. It was just as well, because Farred had his doubts that any other units would have willingly exchanged places with the Gotbeckers.

Farred found himself on the battlements of the Duke's Keep once more. They had fewer arrows than they did yesterday, when they had failed to stop the dragon. In Gustav's place stood his apprentice, Inge. The men around Farred cast her nervous glances. Did she have the power to defend them from dragon fire as the archmage had done?

The Drobax marched to the sound of the drums, and in the sky a speck in the distance became a green dragon, come to kill them. Bows were strung, ballistae readied. Prayers to the various gods of Brasingia were muttered.

As the dragon neared, it flapped its huge wings, gaining height in preparation for one if its deadly dives. But as it did so, the dragon found itself under attack. A hawk, tiny compared to its adversary, swooped in, sharp claws reaching for the dragon's face.

Farred and Inge shared a look. Neither had liked Gustav's decision to fight the dragon by himself. But nor could they come up with an alternative strategy that would prevent another massacre.

The dragon roared in anger, trying to swat the bird away with its own claws, but its movements were slow compared to the hawk, which had already twisted away and powered itself out of range.

As the hawk banked around, the dragon hung in mid-air, following its progress. The element of surprise had gone now, and the dragon was waiting for Gustav to make a move. As the hawk flew closer, the dragon let out a long fiery blast, forcing the wizard to quickly change direction, unable to get close.

Like everyone else, Farred stood transfixed watching the cat and mouse game, until he realised that they might help.

'Shoot the dragon!' he shouted, grabbing an arrow himself. 'We can distract it!'

The archers and the ballistae fired, forcing the dragon to evade the missiles, and the Isharite wizards, stationed somewhere down on the plain, to focus on this new threat.

Gustav took advantage, soaring around behind the great monster, so that it lost sight of his position. Then he attacked, this time going for one of the wings, tearing with its beak and talons.

Another roar from the dragon, but this time one of alarm. As it flapped its wings in an attempt to shake off the hawk, it lurched, then began to spin uncontrollably, the damaged wing no longer working with the same power as the intact one. Spiralling downwards, it vented a blast of fire up towards the hawk, enveloping it in flames.

While the dragon was able to manage its descent, floating down to the ground, the hawk dropped out of the sky like a dead weight. As it fell, the bird turned back into the man, and the people about the keep gasped or cried out at the sight.

Gustav came hurtling down to the crag; no sign of movement coming from his body. He would either hit the walls or the rocks beneath them. Farred wanted to turn away, but something made him watch.

Then a force reached out to the wizard, swirling about his figure, and cushioning his fall.

Farred turned to Inge, her face straining with the magic she deployed. She pulled her arms into her body, and the archmage drifted towards her. Inge deposited him safely onto the roof of the keep, before doubling over in pain.

Farred rushed over, placing a hand to Gustav's neck, searching for a pulse. His skin was red raw in places, but he lived.

'We need to get him inside!' Farred shouted at the crowd that had assembled. Though he wondered how they would get Gustav down the twisting stairs without damaging his scorched body further.

'Wait,' said Inge, standing upright once more. 'I will do it. I will take him to his room in the Emperor's Keep. Please fetch water there, as much as you can.'

The witch turned her arms over, palms facing up, and lifted Gustav up into the air. She began to walk towards the stairwell, the mage's body suspended in the air before her.

The Brasingians on the roof of the keep looked on, expressions of distaste and revulsion on their faces. But Farred knew that the crag would have been overrun if not for the work of the two wizards.

'You heard her! There's water to fetch,' he snarled, making his way to the opposite stairwell.

Rising from the path below him came the sounds of the Gotbeckers, fighting and dying. A horde of Drobax came at them—but no dragon. And here on Burkhard Castle, that counted as good news.

VI

UNDER ROCK

IT HAD BEEN A SOMBRE FEW DAYS, and Soren's heart ached for his sister.

First, the funeral of King Jonas. No lying in state; no invites sent out to the great and good of the nation. Theron wanted it over with. Belwynn had the duty of leading the ceremonies in the Church of Madria. Soren knew the hypocrisy of it twisted at her insides like a knife. She had always been the sensitive one. But she made herself play the part, delivering the eulogy even as the widow of the king was taken from Heractus and deposited in a holy house somewhere remote, where she couldn't be a nuisance.

The very next day saw the coronation of Theron as King of Kalinth. Again, it was a ceremony where Belwynn played a central role, placing the crown on his head, for Elana had succeeded in making the Madrians the only religion left in Heractus. The Knights of Kalinth gave their loyal support to their former Grand Master as he was elevated to the throne, but it was far from a joyous occasion.

Even if few citizens voiced suspicions of foul play, the fact remained that Jonas had been confined to his rooms in the castle and had displayed no signs of ill health. But it wasn't only the circumstances of the king's death. The people of Kalinth, like everywhere else, held their customs and laws dear, and Theron had no connection to the royal family. A high-ranking nobleman, to be sure. A war leader, at a time when that was what the country needed above all else. But still, the lack of blue blood left a black mark hanging over his right to rule.

It was only when these rites were done that Soren informed his sister and friends that it was time for him to leave.

'You're not recovered enough,' Belwynn said, taking on the role of mother as she was wont to do.

Soren gave a sardonic smile. 'I rather think that this is as good as it's going to get, Belwynn. Onella's Staff will get me there.'

'What's the journey for?' Clarin asked, still somewhat behind the news since his poison-induced sleep.

'I need to know what has happened to the Krykkers,' Soren explained. 'The Drobax invasion came from their lands,' he added, referring to the battle with Siavash's shadow. 'From what you say, Herin believes that the Krykkers have been conquered. At the very least we need to know that Bolivar's Sword, the weapon that Rabigar carried, is safe. Then there is the question of the Giants' Spear and the Cloak of the Asrai. Without those three weapons we are lost.'

Clarin hung his head a little, as he tended to do when Herin and the weapons were discussed. Despite attempts to correct him, he still blamed himself for the loss of the Shield, and it reminded him of his brother's betrayal to boot.

The big man's forlorn face perked up a little as an idea crossed his mind. 'Maybe I should go with you?' he suggested.

'You said you would help me with the defences here,' Belwynn reminded him, strategically omitting the larger point that Clarin had only woken from his stupor three days ago and was hardly in a fit state himself.

'It makes sense for me to go with Soren,' said Gyrmund.

That was hard to object to, though the look he shared with Moneva made it clear that neither of them wanted it. After what happened to Elana, Moneva had sworn that she would never leave Belwynn's side, and Soren was grateful for her commitment. But Gyrmund was the best person to guide Soren through the dangers he would face travelling south, and that meant separating the two lovers.

'It won't be for long,' Soren said. 'Once I get the information I need, Gyrmund can return here.'

'Without you?' said Belwynn sharply, not missing a trick.

'That is entirely dependent on the situation I find.'

Belwynn looked at him, her mouth pressed into a thin line of dissatisfaction. But the logic of their decisions couldn't be challenged. Soren and Gyrmund would go south; Belwynn with her commitments here would remain in Heractus.

And anyway, Soren said privately to Belwynn, *it's not as if there's any certainty that Kalinth is going to be safer than our destination.*

The other reason for leaving at this moment was that Soren and Gyrmund could travel south with King Theron's entourage. Theron had always been intending to tour the south of Kalinth to raise supplies and troops, but the need was more pressing now. He had to present himself as the new monarch and receive oaths of allegiance from the major landholders. Meanwhile, the Knights had their own business to attend to. Leontios was to become Grand Master, and the ceremony would be performed at the High Tower, the home of the Order.

It was the High Tower that the group of approximately five hundred riders, knights and their servants, made their first destination. It was a frequently made journey in Kalinth and the road was well maintained. It was cool for late spring, a northerly breeze blowing down the open plains; good weather for travelling. The Kalinthian horses made light work of the journey and when they stopped on the outskirts of a village to make their evening camp, Leontios himself let Soren know that they were over half way to the Tower.

In a nice little patch where the grassland met a copse of trees, Soren sat himself down to rest. His lower back had started to complain for the last few hours, his body not used to riding for so long on horseback. Gyrmund was content to prepare their evening fire by himself; it was a task the ranger liked to do, and liked to do his own way.

Theron found them, wandering over by himself, no bodyguards in attendance. Really, Soren should have stood up for a king, but he thought Theron might not mind if he stayed on the ground.

Theron and Gyrmund shook hands.

'I'm not disturbing you?' he asked.

'Nearly done,' Gyrmund replied.

A slightly awkward silence followed. Clearly, Theron had come to talk with Soren.

'Anyway,' Gyrmund added, 'I'd better get on,' and he strode away, leaving them to it.

Theron walked back and forth a bit. He probably would have liked a walk and talk, but Soren really didn't feel up to it, and in the end, Theron sat down next to him.

'Will you be alright sleeping out here?' Theron asked him. 'I can get you a bed in the village if you would like.'

'I can't deny that sounds tempting, but staying here trumps it because I don't have to move. Anyway, it really should be you taking rooms in the village, Theron. That's what royal courts do.'

'Yes. I suppose I will have to get used to playing the part of the king.'

He paused, looking into the distance before he continued. 'I didn't want this, you know. I don't know what people think, what they're saying about me. Maybe they look at my actions and believe I was after the throne all along. But that's not true. I always wanted to retire from the Knights, go back home and start a family. Uncle Sebastian would have been a great king. But Kalinth is on the brink. We need a ruler, and we need everyone to know who it is. There was no-one else but me left to do it.'

Soren nodded. He believed it, or at least he believed that Theron believed it, which amounted to the same thing. No doubt history was full of men who took power with righteous intentions, believing they were the only ones who could rule. The human mind can be quick to justify its actions.

'Kalinth needs to be united. You need to stand up to the Isharites a while longer, until we take all Madria's weapons. Until we end this once and for all. That's what ultimately matters. You've made yourself king. There's no going back now. You'll have to grow a thick skin, not worry so much what people think. Because there will always be whispers now. Don't imagine they will ever stop.'

Theron nodded, a miserable look on his face.

'I can live with that, Soren. It's only Belwynn I care about. She crowned me yesterday, but she can't look at me anymore. Does she think me a monster?'

'Belwynn did what she had to do. You did the same. That's all there is to it. Belwynn's confused, she doesn't know what to think. So give her time. I'll speak frankly, Theron, even though I'm talking to a king. It doesn't matter. When the lives of every good soul in Dalriya are at stake, your relationship doesn't matter. If we destroy Diis, then it is worth your time. If we fail our task, it will never matter.'

Soren knew he could be harsh. He knew he lacked sympathy when it came to affairs of the heart, perhaps because he had never had one himself. But Belwynn and Theron had crucial roles to play in the coming days, and he needed them to be ready. They had to be ready to sacrifice everything else if it came to it. They all did.

They reached the High Tower at midday. Soren and Gyrmund received full hospitality from the Knights, and fresh horses. Theron also offered them the services of Philon, a knight who could guide them on their journey to the Krykker border. Gyrmund assured him that it wasn't necessary, and Soren was sure that the young knight would want to witness his friend's elevation to the head of their Order.

So five hundred became two, as Soren and Gyrmund took the road south. There had been no more incursions by the Drobax since their defeat at the Pineos, and they were able to enjoy the ride without worry. Yesterday's wind had started to blow itself out, and as the afternoon crept into evening, the sun made an appearance, encouraging them to stay in the saddle until it grew late.

They came upon a farm, where the husband and wife invited them in to take supper with the family. More children than Soren could count sat around the table. The farmer began the story of how they had hidden when the Drobax had come through their land, but he was soon interrupted by his wife and offspring, who between them finished it off.

Soren could tell that Gyrmund was taken with the family and let him tell them about the next chapter, when the Knights of Kalinth fought the Drobax off at the Pineos. He strung the Jalakh Bow and let the kids have a go with it, each waiting patiently for their turn. None of them really understood what it was that they held, but that just added to the charm of the evening. When the farmer's wife explained that they could have a bed each, Soren felt like he must be in heaven.

'It brings home what we're fighting for, to me at least,' Soren said to Gyrmund in their room at the back of the farmhouse, before settling himself under the blankets and laying Onella's Staff down at the side of the bed.

Gyrmund was sitting on the bed opposite. Without the staff he had become little more than a fuzzy shape.

'I would dearly like it for myself,' said the ranger at last.

Soren harrumphed. What was it with everyone at the moment? He knew that spring was in the air but all anybody talked about recently was their relationships.

'Well I'm sure that's a conversation you can have with Moneva. After all this is over.'

'Do you really think Moneva would be interested in starting a family?' Gyrmund asked him, sounding sceptical.

'Gyrmund, I think we've both witnessed stranger things, over the last year, than a woman of a certain age getting broody.'

Soren was relieved when the only response he got to that was a chuckle. For his belly was full, and he was ready for sleep.

The farmer's wife sent them off the next morning with cooked eggs for breakfast.

The terrain around them began to transform from the flat Kalinth Plain to the mountains of the Krykkers. Soon the roads became paths and tracks, and when those began to disappear they left their horses in a little hamlet that was perched at the bottom of a mountain. It was time to walk. Soren gripped Onella's Staff tight, hoping it would continue to give him the strength he needed.

Hour by hour they got higher. The upward climb was tough on the thigh muscles and on the leg joints; the sun beat down and the air got thinner, making it more difficult to breathe. Soren found himself having to stop and rest. Gyrmund never complained, either sitting down with him or scouting ahead.

At some point they must have crossed from Kalinth into the lands of the Krykkers, but it was impossible to tell. No humans lived up here, and if Krykkers had once patrolled these mountains, none came to intercept them now. The Drobax had invaded Kalinth from these borderlands, and while Gyrmund was careful to look for signs, he found little pointing to recent activity. It seemed they had wandered into a world that had been rejected by everyone else—a territory they could claim as their own, with no-one to dispute their ownership.

When Gyrmund did locate the Drobax it wasn't one or two of them, it was a thousand. And they were all dead.

Bodies lay strewn about a cave opening that was crowded with rocks of all sizes.

They approached tentatively, forcing a wake of vultures to reluctantly leave the scene. Gyrmund was wary, on the look out for survivors, though judging by the state of the bodies they had died some time ago.

'Rock slide?' Soren asked him, having noted that some of the bodies were trapped under the bigger rocks.

Gyrmund walked about, studying the corpses, a good proportion of which had been nearly picked clean by the feeding birds.

'No, I don't think so. Some have wounds from weapons. They were trying to get in.' He gestured towards the darkness of the cave. 'And they did.'

Soren walked into the interior of the cave. As he did so he raised Onella's Staff, casting a light that illuminated all but the darkest crevices.

More Drobax bodies littered the place. Another pile lay at the far wall of the cave. As he got close the stench of decay in the close confines of the cave became almost unbearable, and he pinched his nose to keep the worst of it at bay. He shone the light on the scene for Gyrmund to examine.

'There's no doubt the Krykkers were fighting here,' said Gyrmund. 'Some of them fell, but their bodies have been taken since.' He pressed against the wall of the cave, then shoved at it. Soren was unsure why. It had the jagged, uneven look of natural rock, no different from the rest of the cave.

'It seems they passed in and out here,' he said finally. 'Is that possible?'

'According to Belwynn, Rabigar and some of the other Krykkers displayed the ability to pass through rock. I had never heard of such a thing before. If you're telling me that is what it looks like, then that must be what happened.'

Soren now reached out to touch the wall. There was no magic to it that he could detect. 'I don't have such powers,' he said, in case Gyrmund was wondering that he could somehow get them through. 'But we have learned that there is a Krykker resistance of some kind. There must be a way to find them and learn what goes on here.'

They left the cave and walked a route around it, before Gyrmund led them upwards, until they stood above the roof of the cave, affording them a view of the surrounding territory. But even Gyrmund's sharp eyes found no secret entrances to the Krykkers' underground lair. The truth was that they didn't know what they were looking for, or even if there was anything to find. Soren grew weary and, as the sun began to go down, increasingly irritable. The thought that this could become a complete waste of time gnawed at him. There was little chance of them locating the Krykkers if, as seemed to be the case, the Krykkers didn't want to be found.

It was just as this thought was circling around in his head that two Krykkers approached. When they were content that they had been seen they stopped, waiting for Soren and Gyrmund to come to them. There was an aura of menace about the pair. Soren recognised the look in their eyes—he had seen it after the battle of Pineos. The eyes of a killer see everyone as their next victim.

Nonetheless, it was still a relief to see them instead of the empty landscape they had been searching for hours. Soren walked over, opening his mouth to speak, but one of the Krykkers got in before him.

'We are to bring you to chieftain Maragin.'

Relief flooded through Soren. Maragin, chieftain of the Grendal clan, had met them at the beginning of the spring, in Coldeberg. She was perhaps the most influential of the Krykker leaders. She was the ideal person to speak to.

They followed the two Krykkers down a slope, before they stopped at an inconspicuous looking, windswept spot. Tufts of vegetation struggled through loose rock that had stacked up against a formidably high rock face. The Krykkers looked around, checking whether they were seen. Perhaps the Drobax were still out there.

'Wait here,' one of them said, before placing his hands against the rock. Soren then saw the Krykker's hands disappearing into the rock, followed by his arms. The Krykker strained then, muscles bulging, before shoving his head into the rock, continuing though until he had gone.

The second Krykker bent down and began pulling loose stones away from a spot against the rock face, his hands like shovels. Eventually he exposed a hole in the wall of rock that had been hidden by the stones. It was small, however, and Soren hoped that they weren't expecting him to crawl through it. It didn't look possible and he felt nervous at the thought of trying to move through such a tight space.

Then, a hand appeared in the hole, clutching something, and the Krykker leant in and grabbed it. Pulling it outside, he spread it open, revealing a leather blanket that was attached to a rope.

'This is how we'll get you inside,' said the Krykker gesturing down.

Soren and Gyrmund shared a look. 'I'll go first,' Soren said, 'before I change my mind.'

The Krykker got him to lie on the blanket, head towards the wall. He then told Soren to hold on to each side of the blanket and wrap it around his body.

'Ready!' shouted the Krykker, and Soren lurched as the blanket was pulled under the wall of rock. The thought of all that rock pressing down from above filled him with a cold fear. He closed his eyes. Before he knew it, hands were on him, pulling the blanket open.

Soren opened his eyes, but it wasn't until he clutched Onella's Staff at his side that his surroundings were revealed. They were in a sizeable room, located under the rock. Lamps placed along its walls let out enough light to see it had a rectangular shape. In between the lamps Krykker warriors sat in small groups, many in their blankets, getting ready to sleep. As he got to his feet, using his staff to take his weight, he saw that the walls were smooth. The room had been excavated, perhaps extended from a natural cave. An opening at one end led into another room, with the same dim glow of artificial light. So this was where the Krykkers now lived? Hiding under rock, in the darkness and the damp. It told Soren, with no need for words, that a great catastrophe had befallen this people.

The Krykker reappeared and began pulling on the length of rope, until Gyrmund arrived through the same hole Soren had done. Once the Magnian had found his feet, the Krykker gestured to the opening Soren had noticed.

'Maragin is in there,' he explained.

They followed him, his colleague nowhere to be seen, probably replacing the stones outside to conceal the entrance to this place.

Through the opening they found themselves in a much more irregular, natural looking space. The roof was lower, and the floor of the cave sloped down quite sharply to the right. At the bottom of the slope Soren could just make out the shimmer of water.

On the left wall Soren spied Maragin. She sat alone, surrounded by the items you might find in a bedroom. She nodded at the Krykker as they approached, who turned around and left them to it.

Wordlessly, Soren and Gyrmund took a seat opposite the chieftain. She looked tired, but studied them with a keen eye.

'What happened?' Soren asked gently.

'The Drobax came through the lands of the Grand Caladri and into ours. I was away, in Halvia, when it happened. When I returned we were already defeated. Maybe if it had been only the Drobax we could have held out. But they had a dragon with them.'

'A dragon?' asked Gyrmund.

'What kind of dark magic brought it here, I don't know. Your medium knows more of such things than I,' she said, gesturing at Soren. 'We have always used the high places as defence points. Built fortresses in the passes, on mountain tops. The dragon rendered them all useless. The only places that were safe were underground. Places like this.'

'The dragon is still out there?' Gyrmund asked.

'It hasn't been seen for over two weeks now. You come from Kalinth? It still stands?'

'Yes,' Gyrmund replied. 'The Drobax invaded from these lands but we fought them off.'

A look of reluctant respect passed over Maragin's face. 'I had assumed the worst for Kalinth, I must admit. If the dragon was not sent there, the Isharites will be using it elsewhere. Your friend Farred was here. He left for Guivergne and Brasingia, to warn them of the monster's presence. If it has been sent into the lands of the humans, at least he may have given them some time to prepare for it.'

A chill ran down Soren's spine at the way Maragin talked of this dragon. If the Isharites had such a deadly weapon, they had even less time than he had feared.

'What of the rest of your people?' he asked her. 'Does Rabigar live?'

'Our people were evacuated, by the fleets of the Vismarians and the Sea Caladri, to our cousins in Halvia. Only a few hundred of us remain in Dalriya. I have had no news from them since they left. Rabigar went with them, to find the Giants' Spear.'

'You said you visited in Halvia with him?'

'The Vismarian leader, a man named Sevald, said he might know of people with information about the Giants. It was a vague lead at best. But if anything comes of it, Rabigar will find the spear.'

Soren nodded. 'I will put my faith in Rabigar returning with the sword and spear from Halvia. For there are other, equally difficult challenges. We have the Jalakh Bow,' he told her. Gyrmund passed it to the Krykker for her to examine. 'But we have lost the Persaleian Shield to Ishari,' he said.

Maragin's forehead creased into a frown, but she let him continue.

'At least we might guess where they have it. The Cloak of the Asrai, though. We have no way of knowing where to look.'

A sly smile came to the chieftain's face then, and Soren was both intrigued and pleased to see it.

'Not entirely,' Maragin said. 'Farred voyaged with a Caladri sea captain. He had the location of the Asrai marked on his charts.'

A glimmer of hope swelled in Soren's chest then. Maybe his task wasn't impossible. 'Where? Do you have them?' he asked.

Maragin held up a hand. 'Steady now, medium. I don't have the charts, nor have I seen them. But when I interrogated Farred he told me what they said. South of Halvia, west of Dalriya. One of the charts showed an island chain. That's all I know.'

Hope and despair warred in Soren then. He had a location for the Cloak. But it was so vague. The task of exploring the endless, featureless ocean, for a tiny island, felt overwhelming. An experienced sailor might spend a lifetime on it. With the Isharites on the offensive, he had mere days.

'Then that is my task,' he said, resigned to it. 'Maragin, hold out here, and be ready to tell Rabigar our news when he returns. For now, and unless you are told otherwise, the weapons should be taken to Kalinth. They must come together, soon. Gyrmund,' he said, turning to his friend. 'I must head south to find this Cloak. I will tell Belwynn what I intend, but you should return to Kalinth. I fear it will need protecting. And there is more,' he added. 'There is the Shield. I don't know what you can do, but speak with Belwynn; Moneva; Clarin. We need to somehow find out where the Isharites are keeping it.'

VII

A BRIDGE TOO FAR

RABIGAR KNEW THERE WAS SOMETHING wrong with his leg. The wyrm had sunk its teeth deep into him, either side of his knee, and he couldn't put his weight on it. He dug the tip of his blade into the ice as he walked to keep his balance. At first, sharp, hot pain lanced up and down the limb, but now he could feel it growing numb. He felt warm, too hot even; and in the icy wastes of Halvia, he knew that wasn't a good sign.

They had to reach the mountains by nightfall, he knew that much. He wouldn't survive a night out here. At least Stenk seemed well enough. The young Krykker had a sore head and a stiff neck from where he had landed on the ice, sent flying from a strike by the wyrm's tail. But Gunnhild had got him up and walking.

When Rabigar lost all feeling in his leg, he had to ask Gunnhild for help to carry on. There was a part of him that wanted to ask to be left, that said the other two should carry on alone. But he was never going to do that. He carried Bolivar's Sword, and he was the one who would find the Giants. He had no business dying here.

So he let the Vismarian woman support him, while he effectively hopped his way along the ice. Each time he landed on the ice he expected it to crack. One leg numb, his other leg soon tired from the exertion and the cold. It began to cramp. Gunnhild was virtually carrying him now. Her strength was incredible, but even her stamina must give out soon.

Time started to unhinge. Rabigar understood that he was delirious. He came in and out of consciousness, vaguely aware that he had been talking out loud. He had gone from being supported by Gunnhild to being carried. Then he was slung on the back of an animal, his head pressed into its woolly coat. They were no longer on the ice, instead travelling up a mountain trail of some kind, the animal's hooves clacking on the ground. It was no longer just the three of them, either. A fourth was with them—a man. The man talked with Gunnhild and Stenk, even with Rabigar, though he couldn't retain the words the man said, or his face. All he could really see, and smell, was the woolly coat of the animal. All he could hear was the clopping of its hooves on the hard ground; and finally, Rabigar went to sleep.

He woke in a bed, in what looked like a stone-built house. Something felt wrong. He didn't feel well. He struggled to get himself up to a sitting position. Something stirred to his right. A girl, or a young woman more likely. She had the looks of a Vismarian, her red hair braided. She was seated on a chair by the bed. Her eyes went wide when she saw him studying her.

'Master Rabigar!' she exclaimed. 'I am happy to see you awake.'

I don't know this person, or this place, Rabigar said to himself. He felt the dream world calling him back, and it was easier to surrender to it.

The next time he woke, a trio of faces were looking down at him from the other end of the bed. The young woman from before; an older man, a big black beard flecked with grey, who looked like he could be her father; and Stenk. It was a relief to see the young Krykker, and it encouraged Rabigar to try to sit. As he did so, Stenk and the man rushed to either side of the bed and helped him up. He tried shrugging them off and doing it himself, but his legs felt strangely numb.

He had been lying here for too long, that was the problem. He needed to be up and out. They had to find the Giants' Spear.

The man put a restraining hand on his shoulder.

'Master Rabigar, you must take care, you are still recovering. My name is Nemyr, this is my daughter, Dalla. We have been treating you here.'

'What is this place?' Rabigar demanded, slapping the man's hand from his shoulder. 'Stenk, what are we doing here?'

'Listen, Rabigar,' Stenk said simply, and something in his friend's voice made him settle, though he folded his arms to express his displeasure.

'Master Rabigar, my oldest son, Ketil, found you and your friends out on the ice. When he saw your injuries, he took you here as soon as possible. You were bitten by a white wyrm. The arteries in your leg were severed. Infection had set in and it is not possible to repair that kind of damage.'

Rabigar felt a strange sensation as he heard these words. It was like he was floating above the conversation. He could see the serious face of Nemyr, the concerned looks of Dalla and Stenk. He could even see himself, a patch over one eye, a pained expression. He didn't like what he saw. *I look so old.*

'I am afraid we had to take the leg from above the knee.'

Rabigar watched himself frown, saw himself processing the information.

'What do you mean?' he bellowed, ripping away the blankets.

And there it was. A bandaged stump where his leg had been. But he could still feel it. This wasn't right.

Rabigar shouted, trying to wake himself from the nightmare. A hundred thoughts rolled around in his head, competing for his attention. The strongest was about the sword. *I carry the sword of Bolivar the Bold, but I have one eye and one leg. This is a cruel jest.*

He grabbed Nemyr's tunic. 'What have you done to me?' he shouted at him.

But for all his shouting, Rabigar didn't wake up, and his leg was still gone.

***

GUSTAV LIVED, though he suffered great pain. Farred had come to visit once, retracing the route to the top room in the tallest tower of the Emperor's Keep. He had come here several times during last year's siege, helping Gustav with his transformation into the hawk. He had been a stand-in for the wizard's apprentice, Inge, who had been allocated the task of protecting the emperor.

The witch now worked day and night to help her master, cooling his skin with water, applying salves. This was the Inge he had first met, tending to Prince Ashere's injuries. His attitude towards her couldn't help but change. He had seen her save the archmage's life with his own eyes, cushioning his fall from the sky after he was burned with dragon fire.

He had his suspicions that she had helped *him*, too. Some force had helped to release the great boulder from its buttress, for example. Still. That didn't mean that he suddenly enjoyed her company. He had given his regards to Gustav and left her to it.

Outside, the daily grind of defending the fortress continued unabated, albeit with no dragon to worry about. Coen's Thessians manned the Emperor's Crag, forming a ring of steel around the thick rock. With no path here, the Drobax came clambering up all sides of the rock face. There were many, but the Thessians stood behind a wall that circled the crag, and the height advantage gave them superiority.

Baldwin had directed his Kellish soldiers to the Duke's Crag, giving them the task of stopping the Drobax from forcing their way up the path. This hard task had got harder since the dragon had destroyed all of Walter's wooden gates. Each day they got farther up the crag. The Kellish pushed back, the tired and injured at the front having to be replaced by the fresher troops.

But it was the third day now, and no-one was fresh. Farred peered down. Bodies littered the path, sliding down to the bottom. They baked in the sun; the air was thick with flies and carried the stink of disease.

Shouts came from the battlements of the keep. Looking up, Farred saw a head leaning over the edge. Walter.

'Farred!' he shouted.

'What is it?' Farred shouted up.

'It's back.'

Farred felt his jaw drop open, felt his legs turn to jelly. Two days. That was all Gustav's bravery had bought them. As a hawk, he had ripped a hole in one of the dragon's wings. But it was back again now—healed, or somehow repaired by the Isharites.

'Will you tell Gustav and Inge?'

'Yes,' Farred replied.

He turned and ran. First towards the bridge that separated the two crags. He would never get used to it, suspended in thin air so high up, but he ran over it now, desperate to pass on his warning. Once over the bridge he made for the Emperor's Keep, the larger of the fortifications. A guard on the gate gave him a puzzled look, but when he shouted 'dragon' he quickly stepped aside. Then Farred made for the stairwell of Gustav's tower and began the ascent. His thighs ached with the exertion, but he kept on going, until he emerged, breathless, into Gustav's room.

Inge turned around to look at him, gasping for air.

'It's back,' she said.

'Yes.'

She gave a little smile. 'I'm coming.'

Gustav struggled up from the table. He was a sight, his skin a patchwork of different colours, his hair and eyebrows singed off. 'Help me up.'

Inge gave him a firm push back down. 'You're staying here,' she said. 'You can't help now.'

'I'm needed,' said Gustav weakly.

Inge gave Farred a look.

'We need you alive, archmage,' he said. 'There are more fights to come. Save yourself for those.'

Defeated, Gustav remained where he was. Farred and Inge made for the stairs.

Farred ran down, Inge not far behind him. He wondered why she didn't fly over to the other crag, or some such. Maybe she couldn't, or maybe she needed to save her power. He didn't understand how magic worked, but for whatever reason, Inge ran behind, negotiating the steep twists of the stone steps until they were out of the tower, out of the keep, and running for the bridge.

Then they saw the beast above the Duke's Keep. The battlements steamed with fire, and as they watched, the dragon clattered into one of the towers, its powerful legs smashing it into pieces, the masonry landing on the crowd below.

'Walter was up there,' Farred said.

A stream of soldiers was making for the bridge, some coming from the keep, some from the path that led down the crag. It looked like a full retreat.

'We're not going to push our way through there,' Farred said as the soldiers ran towards them. They looked panic-stricken, and he worried that if no-one took control they would barge into one another and some would get pushed off the edge.

'Come,' said Inge, taking Farred by the hand. She stretched her other arm out in front of her, towards the bridge, and they walked towards the oncoming soldiers. Without Farred realising it at first, he found that they were walking upwards as well as forwards, so that they began to rise above the men coming towards them. When he looked down, Farred saw his feet standing on nothing—it was worse than walking across that bridge, and he resolved not to look down again.

Once they reached the bridge, Inge's invisible pathway levelled out, and Farred found himself walking above the soldiers streaming the other way. Some of them looked up at him in horror, though others ignored the sight: when you have a dragon at your back, a witch hovering above you is of secondary importance.

They got to the far end of the bridge. Inge took them down, lowering her outstretched arm and releasing Farred's hand.

They were on the Duke's Crag, but that didn't mean Farred knew what to do. He could see the dragon in the sky, probably circling around for another attack. They didn't have long.

A group of soldiers exited the keep, carrying broken bits of furniture. Among them was Walter, and Farred felt a flood of relief at the sight of the duke.

'Come!' Walter called out to his men, the soldiers who had served him for years as Marshal of the Empire, and Farred found some belief that there might be a way out of the situation.

Walter saw them and came over. He looked at them both for a moment, weighing them up.

'The keep is lost,' he said finally. 'We need to evacuate everyone across to the other crag. I will hold the Drobax up at the bridge. Can you keep them away for a while?' he asked, pointing at the path where the Kellish kept coming, and from where Farred heard the screams of the Drobax, not far away.

'I can hold them for a while,' Inge said. 'Not long.'

'I will stay with her,' Farred agreed.

'Thank you,' said Walter. The duke had no time for more talk and began barking out instructions to his men.

Farred and Inge moved to one side of the path, out of the way of Baldwin's soldiers. It looked like they were amongst the last to come up, the tired and the injured being helped along as they escaped the Drobax chasing them, some daring to look up into the sky to see if the dragon had come for them.

Farred made his way up to the wall that overlooked the path. This part of the defences should have been occupied by soldiers, but it lay deserted, stockpiles of stones unused. Looking down, he saw that the Drobax were nearly at the top. The Kellish, to give them their due, were still fighting a rearguard action. A core group walked backwards, fighting off any Drobax attempts to smash through their wall of steel and overrun them.

Farred looked down to Inge. 'I can see them,' he shouted. 'I will tell you when it's time. I'll stay here, stop them overrunning this wall.'

She nodded back. In that moment she looked like a scared child to Farred: the worry plain to see on her face, the bravado and delight of her romps with the emperor seemingly long gone.

Looking back, he saw the Kellish had reached the point where the path branched into three options. The Kellish took the right one, while the Drobax ran screaming down the other two, thinking they had at last found a way to get by the defenders. They were running straight for Farred's position, not knowing that the paths simply met each other just below where he stood, going nowhere.

He grabbed one of the stones from its container. He had always fancied he had a good arm. It was time to find out.

The first one hurtled in the direction of the Drobax. It had power but poor direction, missing by yards. The second one connected with the chest of the first Drobax, knocking it to the ground. Farred allowed himself a smile. This was close to being fun.

The Drobax saw him atop the wall, and ran at him. That made things easier. He threw the stones, striking one head then another, as they surged beneath him, the wall too high for them to climb. Farred glanced across at the Kellish soldiers, who had found some relief from the pressure the Drobax had been exerting. The last of them were just about to leave the path and come out on top of the crag.

'Very soon!' he shouted down to Inge.

He watched as the Kellish backed towards her, as she threw up a protective wall where they passed. A few of the Drobax got through with them, but the Kellish made short work of them. Then they could see where the creatures shoved, slashed with their weapons, but couldn't get past. Turning around, they ran for the bridge. Inge just had to hold her barrier for a while longer. But Farred had no idea how long she could last.

He turned his attention down to the seething mass of Drobax beneath him. Just in time, as one of them threw a wooden club at him. He had to block it with his arm, the chain mail he wore protecting him from a blow that might otherwise have been serious. The Drobax were now helping each other up, threatening to climb the wall he stood on. Farred threw a few more stones at those who threatened to reach him but decided that was taking too long. He drew his sword and began to march along his wall, chopping down at those who got within reach.

He turned around to look at the bridge. All the Kellish were on it now. It was time to go.

He jumped down to the ground and ran over to Inge. The magic shield she had created was still working, but the strain it placed on her was visible. Unsure whether it was the right thing to do or not, Farred placed his hands on her shoulders and began to slowly guide her backwards. She responded, moving with him while maintaining her concentration on her magic.

Farred saw a hand appear on the wall where he had been standing, then a second.

'Come on,' he said to Inge. 'It's time to go!'

They turned and ran. He could hear the roars of the Drobax behind them, suddenly released. Then he heard the whipping sound of arrows. From the Emperor's Crag, archers were firing into the Drobax, giving them a chance to make it to the bridge.

Inge was tiring; she stumbled. Farred grabbed her around the waist and half-carried her to the bridge. On this side, half the width of the bridge had been piled up with the furniture that Walter's men had been carrying, but they had left a gap for them to get through. Farred pushed Inge ahead, then looked behind him. The Drobax were some way off, the shower of arrows doing enough to distract them.

As he and Inge got off the bridge onto the Emperor's Crag, Walter's men moved. Farred watched them carry more items onto the bridge, stacking them up into a pile. He supposed it might hold the Drobax off for a while, but it was hardly a strong defence. Then he realised what they were doing. Barrels of ale were poured onto the stack and it was set alight, bursting into flames.

The Drobax who had been approaching retreated from the heat. They turned their attention away from the bridge to the Duke's Keep, defenceless and free for them to ransack.

They had lost the keep and the crag, and the Drobax were now only a bridge away from the top of the Emperor's Crag as well. Men looked at one another, dazed by the speed of the collapse. Farred looked to the sky, but the dragon was gone, its revenge complete.

Baldwin stood with them on the crag, commiserating with his men; praising them; bringing some order to what had come close to a capitulation. In the end, they had held their nerve and performed a full retreat. But there was nowhere else to retreat to now, and the Drobax were half way up this crag, still trying to force their way to the top.

Baldwin saw Inge, exhausted, swaying on her feet. He lifted her up into his arms and walked with her back to his keep. Farred saw the looks his men gave the pair as they departed. Baldwin would have to be careful. The blame game begins when armies start to lose, and a witch always makes a fine choice for those who wish to play.

With Baldwin gone, Walter giving his full attention to the fire he had set on the bridge, Coen further down the crag fighting with his men, it fell to Archbishop Godfrey to begin organising things. Men had lost their beds when the Duke's Keep fell, and many of them had injuries. He and a small group of his priests began rounding people up and telling them where to go, until Farred found that the top of the crag had been stripped of men.

Walter and his men waited, watching the opposite crag. Farred sat on the ground and did the same. The Drobax were swarming over the keep like a plague of insects, seemingly intent on destroying the building. He could see chunks of stone being thrown down from the battlements, and then a whole wall collapsed to the ground, throwing up a cloud of dust. All the while more and more Drobax found their way to the top of the crag.

Something changed then. It wasn't clear to Farred how the Drobax received their orders, though he remembered about the taller type in their ranks—those who could speak. Perhaps it came from them, perhaps from some form of unseen magic, but the Drobax turned to the bridge, all heading towards it at once. The idea of insects persisted in Farred's mind as he watched them come. The fire that Walter set still blazed just as fiercely, but now the Drobax willingly walked into it, striking the burning material with their weapons so that it spun away, over the void.

Walter gave a signal and a dozen of his men moved over to the bridge. On their hands and knees, they began working at it.

Intrigued, Farred walked over to the duke. The Drobax had already cleared half of the fire now, the fierceness of the conflagration tamed. Some of them staggered away, burned by the flames or suffocating from the smoke, but there were always more to replace them.

'Yet another trick up your sleeve?' he asked Walter.

Walter gave him a fierce smile. 'I think you will enjoy this, Farred—maybe as much as the boulder.'

The Drobax had now cleared away enough of the fire to get past it. They came across the bridge, first a few, then their numbers grew, and their pace quickened.

'Hold!' Walter shouted over to his men.

They were past half way now, filling the bridge, and still nothing happened. Farred began to get anxious. If something went wrong, if the Drobax claimed this side of the bridge, then the whole horde would be able to cross.

Two thirds of the way.

Four fifths.

'Now!' shouted Walter.

A grinding, screeching noise of metal on metal came from their side of the bridge. And then it gave way. The bridge came away from the Emperor's Crag and swung down, Drobax screaming and falling off into the great drop below, the remains of the fire drifting down more slowly. It swung all the way until it crashed into the rock of the Duke's Crag, dangling, held there by the fastenings on the opposite crag.

Somehow, some of the Drobax remained on the bridge, clinging onto the structure. Then a grinding noise echoed out from the Duke's Crag. A jolt, shaking the bridge, and then the whole thing came loose, spiralling down to the ground below.

A bridge full of Drobax wasn't quite so many as the boulder had crushed, but still—Walter had been right. Farred had enjoyed it.

Here on Burkhard Castle, you had to take whatever pleasure you could find.

VIII

FOREIGN SOIL

IT WAS MORE LIKE A SUMMER'S DAY than spring. Edgar's army lounged around on the grass, their laughter carrying on the breeze as they relaxed. Well fed; no injuries; no lost comrades. Not yet. May this last as long as possible, Edgar prayed.

'That's them,' said Elfled, pointing into the distance.

They sat together in the grass, stealing a final sliver of time before it was time to part. Edgar made a face.

'What is it?' his wife asked.

'Much as I like your brother, I wish he hadn't got here so soon.'

'The sooner you go, the sooner you'll be back,' she said.

'I'm not sure it works like that,' Edgar replied.

She smiled at him.

'You grow prettier every day,' he said. Yes, it sounded like flattery. But he meant it.

'Don't be soppy,' Elfled said, but she leaned over for a kiss anyway. 'You may not think so when the morning sickness starts. It's meant to start soon.'

'Huh. Maybe it's just as well I'm leaving now then.'

She slapped his arm. And that was that, because Cerdda and Irmgard were dismounting.

Edgar got to his feet and helped Elfled up, before they walked over to see his in-laws.

Edgar reached out a hand, but instead found himself being hugged, as Cerdda and then Irmgard grabbed him enthusiastically, before asking Elfled all about the pregnancy. Edgar had thought it might be awkward, since the pair had remained childless for years, but instead it was touching to see how happy they were for them.

Elfled had decided to return to North Magnia with Irmgard while Edgar was away. Her mother was there too, and it made sense for her. His bodyguard, Morlin, would go with her. It also made things simpler at home. His noble council would rule in his absence, men like Otha and Aescmar. It had not turned out so bad last year, and leaving them behind in South Magnia meant that they wouldn't get in his way on campaign.

Eventually, Cerdda detached himself from the women and they began to talk of military matters: numbers, supplies, all the decisions that had to be made to get a group of armed men from one part of the world to another.

'Ashere was always the more military minded,' the Prince of North Magnia admitted ruefully. 'He used to obsess over weapons and tactics. When training was done I was ready to go home for a hot drink and a bath. He would stay out for hours. Got bored if he wasn't doing something physical.'

'We'll be fine,' Edgar said reassuringly. What else was there to say? The horror of war wasn't something you could ever really prepare someone for anyway.

The Princes of North and South eventually made their farewells to their wives. They made them quickly, since both Elfled and Irmgard looked tearful from the first word. Then they gave the orders to march.

The rendezvous had been set at the point where three borders met: the two principalities of Magnia, and the Midder Steppe. As soon as they marched east, therefore, they were on foreign soil.

A summer's day was all very well for sitting about, but for travelling it made things harder. Man and beast had to stop for water, and there wasn't so much of that about on the steppe. Scouts had to be sent out to cover a wide swathe of territory, and when they found a stream that was still full the whole army would make a detour for it.

Marching through someone else's lands is not generally advisable. But this southernmost patch of the Midder Steppe belonged to Frayne's tribe, the chieftain who had fought with Edgar in Brasingia last year, and he had given his consent to the crossing. Thus, when Wilchard rode up to report that a large army of Middians had been spotted on their route east, it came as something of a surprise.

'How big?' Edgar asked him.

'According to the scouts, smaller than our army, but not by much.'

Edgar and Cerdda looked at one another.

'I'm not sure we should be heading towards another army without knowing who they are,' Cerdda offered.

'It might be wise for Your Highnesses to go and speak with them,' Wilchard suggested.

Ordering their armies to stop and rest, Edgar and Cerdda let Wilchard lead them towards the army. The grass stretched out for miles around them, though to the south Edgar could see a treeline that was the beginnings of the Wilderness. The flatness of the terrain meant that they could see the Middian army ahead of them for a while before they got close enough to make out the details.

Some of the Middians had put up tents to shelter from the sun, others lazed in it, their dark skin protecting them from the kind of burn a Magnian might receive. Some had the job of shepherding animals, the bleating of sheep and the lowing of cattle making it sound more like a market than an army camp.

'They must have seen us coming for a while,' Edgar muttered, and sure enough, three riders detached themselves and came to meet them.

As they neared, Edgar could distinguish each of the riders. 'Brock and Frayne, the Middian chiefs,' he said, though Cerdda had met them himself before. Indeed, Brock was the chief who had served under Ashere last year, fighting the dreaded Drobax with him. 'And Lord Kass, Baldwin's diplomat. An interesting development.'

Brock and Frayne smiled good-naturedly as they approached, and they reached over to grasp hands in greeting. Kass's moustache wiggled with pleasure.

'Well met,' said the Brasingian. 'You have made excellent time.'

'We weren't expecting to find an army here,' Edgar said.

'No, well, discussions with chiefs Brock and Frayne have resulted in an outcome that meets everyone's interests.'

Edgar had to smile at that, recalling the tortuous negotiations between Rosmont of Cordence and the Middians last year.

'So, you squeezed all the money out of him?' he asked the two chiefs, who smiled slyly, but said nothing.

'I'm not sure why we don't get any,' said Cerdda, perhaps only half joking.

'Come, come, my lords,' said Kass, looking a little flustered, 'let's not spoil such a fine moment. The Emperor and his people are eternally in your debt.'

'Yes,' agreed Frayne, 'my tent is waiting, bulging with food and drink and serving girls,' he said, then noted Edgar's expression. 'But of course, you are newly married, Prince Edgar. It will be another few months before you are tempted by serving girls.'

Brock laughed enthusiastically at the joke, though Edgar produced something between a smile and a grimace, not least because Elfled's brother was sitting right next to him.

'We'll have to go back to fetch our army,' he said.

'Don't worry, Your Highnesses,' Wilchard said. 'I'll go back and give the order. You enjoy yourselves.'

'Very well,' Cerdda agreed. 'I shan't refuse the offer of hospitality in this weather.'

They fell in with the two Middians and the Brasingian, making their way to the camp.

'I must know,' said Frayne to Edgar, keeping his voice quiet. He wore a serious expression on his face now and nodded over to Kass. 'Did you even ask him for any money?'

***

IT WAS A good day for forgetting. The early morning sun shone through a cloudless sky and the grass outside Heractus smelled sweet. Theron and the Knights were gone to the High Tower, so Belwynn didn't have the stress of avoiding him, of examining her feelings once more. Soren was gone visiting the Krykkers, so she didn't have her brother's constant references to the weapons they hadn't yet found, or his warnings about Madria. Those worries weren't gone, but they could be put to the back of her mind for a while. Instead she could focus on the here and now.

The here and now was training the Kalinthian infantry. The core of it remained the Madrians who took their orders directly from her. For most of her life Belwynn believed her telepathic power had been a special link with her brother, stemming from his powers more than her own. Only now had Madria taught her that it was from her—that she could communicate with others in the same way. She had established a link with her Madrians, and at the battle against the army of Siavash at the River Pineos, she had used it to turn them into an efficient unit, all receiving the same set of orders at the same time.

Now those Madrians, once the ordinary citizens of Heractus, were the veterans of the Kalinthian infantry. Others had fought at the Pineos too, and more had been recruited since: townsmen, villagers, farmers, noble retinues. They needed to be melded into a force that could hold their ground, while the cavalry of Kalinth—the Knights—did the killing.

It was Clarin who now emerged as the commander of this disparate force. He was throwing himself into the task of training, drilling, organising. Belwynn hadn't seen this disciplined side to him before. His own strength and experience demanded respect. But more than that, he had a good nature about him, was quick with a smile, and that meant he was able to get through to the trained fighter and the complete novice with equal success.

He strode around now, bare-chested in the sun, waving around the crystal sword he had returned with from Samir Durg, cajoling and praising where needed. But Belwynn knew that he had also begun to make decisions: who would fit where in which unit; who his leaders were.

A couple of miles away, in the woods, Moneva had taken a much smaller group. Standing in for Gyrmund, she had taken those who could use a bow or sling, and they hunted together.

Belwynn herself, well she currently sat to one side, watching, along with anyone else who was excused. Not far away the two Dog-men lay snoozing on the grass, occasionally flapping an ear to ward off a buzzing insect, or opening one eye when there was a loud shout from the training grounds. Belwynn knew nothing of Dog-men, but it was clear that they didn't train. Despite that, she had no doubts that they would be amongst the fiercest in battle.

Next to her was Jurgen. His cousin, Rudy, was out there, working with the recruits that Theron had brought in from the north of the country. Jurgen had been lamed in the fighting in Samir Durg and, despite that, had done a lot of walking over recent weeks, first escaping from Samir Durg and then following Clarin into Persala. He needed rest. He shouldn't have been asked to fight at all, but they needed everyone they could get.

'What became of the rest of your friends from Samir Durg?' she asked him. 'Those who didn't return here with Clarin?'

'Well of course it turned out we had a prince in our midst all that time,' Jurgen said. 'With his father killed, by Herin, Zared and the rest of the Persaleians stayed behind. He is needed there, to carry on the resistance.'

An unpleasant tightening in Belwynn's gut came at the mention of Herin's involvement. She had never been under the illusion that he was a hero. But what was he doing, joining the Isharites, killing the exiled King of Persala?

Something must have happened to him in Samir Durg. But Clarin and Gyrmund had returned to fight the Isharites, so what made Herin so different?

'Then there was Tamir and the Barbarians,' continued Jurgen. 'When Herin confronted us, he had a Drobax with him, but it was different to the others we had seen. Taller and more human-like, to my eyes. It could speak. Herin told us that it was a new type, that had been—' he paused, suddenly looking embarrassed. 'Herin said they had been bred from women captives. He called them the new officer class of the Drobax army. Tamir and the Barbarians felt the need to go home, to find out what happened to their womenfolk.'

'I see,' said Belwynn, disgusted by the story.

She had to use it. Use it to give her the will to do what Madria and Soren both wanted of her. To kill Diis. To break the power of the Isharites for good.

The evening meal in the castle hall required Belwynn's presence. With the new king and the future grand master gone, the castle needed someone to sit at the top table. Belwynn, with her long list of informal titles—Lady of the Knights, Voice of Madria—was expected to do it. All the officials agreed that it just couldn't be done without her, and so she was persuaded to perform the role of master of ceremonies once more, leading the toasts and mixing with those who were lucky enough to be invited.

It wasn't until late, therefore, when she was able to summon Clarin to her room. Moneva was already there, having taken Soren's bed for herself. She was taking the role of Belwynn's bodyguard very seriously, and Belwynn did her best not to complain about it. Lyssa was already there too, pretending not to be excited that she was staying up past her usual bed time.

'You look tired,' she greeted him as he sat down on the bed next to the girl, making Lyssa's side of the mattress rise several inches into the air.

'I always used to think the officers had it easy, giving us all the shitty jobs to do,' Clarin said. 'I'm not so sure any more.'

'Come then, Belwynn,' said Moneva. 'Explain yourself.'

'Alright. I was thinking today about my link to the Madrians, and how important it would be to extend that to other people. So, I will start to try to make a connection with other people, especially those who might need to communicate with me on the battlefield. Since I am closest to you three, I wanted to start with you. So I can test out how to do it.'

'How to do what?' Lyssa asked, not following.

How to speak to me using your mind, not your mouth.

Poor Lyssa's eyes nearly bulged right out of her head. Moneva gave a little smile; Clarin frowned. They had all heard her.

'I thought you could only do that with Soren?' Clarin asked, uneasy.

Hello!

Lyssa, taking to the idea naturally, as children often do.

Hello, Lyssa.

'That's what I thought too, Clarin. But it's not the case anymore. Think how useful it would be to communicate between each other on the battlefield. Just concentrate on passing a sentence to me, saying the words in your head for me to hear.'

Get out of my head, witch.

Thank you, Moneva. That worked.

Clarin still looked uncomfortable.

'I don't know what to say.'

Belwynn rolled her eyes.

There was a knock at the door.

Moneva, alert to trouble, went to open it.

It was only Coronos.

'Apologies for disturbing so late,' he said, as Moneva ushered him into the room, looking beyond him into the corridor, just in case.

'The city watch let a rider in just now and brought him straight to the castle. Says he has ridden here with haste from the northern border. Says there will be many more coming tomorrow. I thought you should know immediately.'

'Of course, Coronos,' Belwynn said. 'I'll see him.' This didn't sound good.

'Has he told you what it is?' Clarin asked.

Coronos looked at Belwynn. She nodded.

'He says the Isharites have crossed the border into Kalinth. They came from Masada. Drobax, Haskans—the lot. His people saw thousands of them, he told me. Thousands upon thousands.'

IX

LEGACY

RABIGAR SAT STILL, ALLOWING Nemyr, the man who had taken his leg, to check the stump, before putting a fresh bandage on.

His anger was gone. Instead a kind of emptiness, a mild melancholy, had settled on him. He had done his best, fought as hard as he could. Here he was, a cripple at the edge of the world. So be it. He couldn't complain that he deserved better.

'It's healing well,' Nemyr murmured quietly, tying up the bandage.

Rabigar said nothing.

'I had to do this once before. Four years ago. For my wife. It didn't work. But you are strong.'

Rabigar didn't want to say a word to this man. But he had forced Rabigar to say something by mentioning his dead wife.

'I am sorry for your loss,' Rabigar growled.

'Thank you. I have a lot to thank you for, Master Rabigar,' Nemyr continued. 'My ancestors came here with the Orias—The Giants. They had the honour of guarding their resting place, keeping alive the memory of its location, until a great Krykker hero would come to wake the Giants from their slumber. From one generation to the next, this secret was passed down. When my father died, I became responsible. I told my children that when I died, the responsibility would pass to them.'

Nemyr paused, his eyes staring into the distance at something only he could see.

'My older son, Ketil, found you and your companions. He brought you here. He lives down near the foot of the mountain, with his wife and child. He never said as much to my face, but I knew. He didn't believe the stories I told him. That our family held a secret trust.'

Nemyr looked at Rabigar now, grey eyes holding him. 'It was beginning to die, you see. The memory; the belief, in our duty. Such a thing cannot last forever. It must be forgotten eventually. I worried, in my old age, that we would let you down. That my line would fail. Now I know that we didn't. My parents, grandparents, all those ancestors, stretching back I don't know how long. We kept it alive. We fulfilled our duty.'

A spark of hope came to life in Rabigar then, when he thought there was none left.

'You know where the Giants' Spear is located?'

'The resting place of the Giants is on this mountain, a hard climb away. My younger son has taken your friend Gunnhild to show it to her. They will be back soon.'

'The spear is there?' Rabigar asked, pursuing his line of questioning.

Nemyr gave him a slight frown. 'My family was entrusted with the knowledge of the resting place. We do not know what is inside. We cannot access it.'

He raised his hand and pointed a finger at Rabigar.

'That is why you are here.'

'The last few hundred yards are a bit tricky, but we'll be fine,' Gunnhild reassured him. 'I'll just drag you up that bit.'

They had wrapped him in furs, Nemyr and his children going out of their way to show him respect. It was a respect he wasn't entirely comfortable with. To them he was a hero that they had been waiting for—waiting for several lifetimes. He was pleased to have Gunnhild's rough and ready ways to provide a counterbalance to the reverence with which they handled him.

It was Gunnhild who carried him out of Nemyr's house and deposited him on the sled they would use to take him up the mountain. They were all ready, packs over their shoulders, breath visible in the cold air. As well as Rabigar, Gunnhild and Stenk, Nemyr and his three children were all going. Ketil, broad-shouldered and stern looking, had left his home in the foothills to accompany them. Dalla, her red hair hidden in a hood, stood next to her younger brother Jesper. He was slim, athletic looking, only the beginnings of a beard on his face.

They looked at one another, drinking in the moment, as if they were about to embark on some great, historic journey.

Maybe they were, but Rabigar didn't feel it. He had no goose bumps, no weighty feelings of destiny in his bones. He grasped the hilt of Bolivar's Sword, but it didn't communicate a momentous message to him. He wondered about the great man then, revered by all Krykkers, who had stood against the terrible power of the Isharites. Had *he* felt a sense of history? Known that his actions would reverberate down the years, that his name would never be forgotten? Perhaps not.

'This way,' Nemyr said, gesturing towards a path that curved upwards.

Nemyr and Ketil led the way, followed by Jesper, Dalla and Stenk. Gunnhild pulled on the rope of the sled. It tightened, and Rabigar began to move, the wood scraping over the rock and ice beneath.

***

COEN'S THESSIANS defended the Emperor's Crag once more. The Drobax swarmed towards them, focused now on taking the second fortress. But so far the dragon had not come, and the Thessians held their line.

Across a chasm that until yesterday had been spanned by a bridge, the Drobax ruled over the Duke's Crag. They seemed aimless, the previous days of bloodshed somehow pointless, since they were separated from their target and all they had won was a rock.

Walter led Farred down from the hall of the Emperor's Keep to the storerooms that had been built from the rock underneath. Here the Marshal managed the precious supplies that kept the army fed. Feeding thousands of warriors was a tall order, but looking about, Farred saw they had more food here than they would ever need. It wasn't just that their numbers had fallen over the last few days, the Luderians and Kellish taking heavy losses. Walter had prepared for a siege that would last weeks, and it felt like they could lose at any moment. Whenever the dragon came back.

Through a store room Walter took Farred to the well room. He greeted two soldiers, both of whom looked more like boys than men. The huge opening in the middle of the floor dominated the room, a massive wooden bucket tied to the top was empty now, but capable of holding gallons of water. Around the sides of the room containers of all shapes and sizes had been filled with water.

Walter gestured at the bucket.

'This is what I wanted to show you,' he said, swinging one leg over the side and climbing in.

Farred was surprised to see the duke standing inside a wooden bucket. 'I wondered if you had another surprise up your sleeve.'

'I suppose I do. This one is different to the bridge, though. And it's the last trick I have. Come on, Farred—get in!'

Rather reluctantly, Farred clambered inside the bucket with Walter. It was massive, with room for at least half a dozen men to stand in with comfort.

Walter nodded to his two young soldiers, who went through an archway into the next room.

'We've got a mule in there,' Walter said when he saw Farred's eyes follow the two soldiers.

A thick length of rope passed from a complex looking pulley system above them, along the roof and into the room next door.

The bucket jerked, making Farred grip the side, before beginning to move downwards at a steadier pace.

They descended a roughly circular, vertical stone tunnel, before it disappeared, opening into a dark expanse all around them. Farred could hardly see, though enough light came in for him to get a sense of the size of the space all around him. As his eyes adjusted, he could make out the glistening of the pool of water beneath them, from where the fortress took its water supply.

The bucket shuddered to a stop before they reached the pool, leaving them suspended in mid-air. Walter reached over, his hands waving about, until he found a wide stone ledge. He climbed out onto the ledge and Farred followed behind, making sure his arms could take his weight on the ledge before swinging his legs over. It felt a little better to be on a firm piece of stone than in a wooden bucket, but his vision of the cave around him was still limited.

Walter now fiddled with a metal torch. When he got it lit, it threw a bit more light out, casting eerie shadows about the cave. Farred could see the roof not far above them, from which stalactites hung down, like stone fingers.

'You can follow this ledge down to the floor of the cave over there,' Walter said, pointing off to the left. 'It leads to a whole network of tunnels and caves.'

So, this was more than a source of water for the garrison.

'A way out?' said Farred, almost not daring to ask.

'We've explored the passages, put torches up on the roof along the way. They go on for miles. We can get people out, Farred. Now is the time to start, before this crag falls to the Drobax and we miss our chance.'

'How long have you known?'

'It's a secret made known to emperors and marshals. Baldwin and I have always been aware that it's an option. But it's best not to reveal it to others until it's time for it to be used. I have supplies ready. We can start to send soldiers down. They will have to wait in the caves until the evacuation is complete.'

'What a place this is. Old Duke Burkhard did the Empire proud when he built it.'

Walter made a face. 'The stories say that Burkhard built this place, with the help of some Krykkers. The more I've thought about that, the more I think that it already existed long before his time. Perhaps the Krykkers once owned it. Maybe some other race of people before them. But yes, whoever we should thank, I most certainly do.'

Farred considered the logistics of it. 'How fast can you get people down here?'

'I've calculated it to be at least six thousand a day, if we work all hours.'

'How many—'

'There's about fifty thousand of us on this rock.'

Farred looked at Walter. That didn't go, it wasn't even close, and Walter knew it as much as Farred. It would take a week to get everyone down here. Neither of them knew exactly how long they had, but they knew they wouldn't get that long.

'I need someone to manage it,' Walter said.

Here it came. Farred knew he hadn't been brought down here so they could share the view.

'I'm needed up top. So is Baldwin,; so is Coen. Please?'

Farred understood. Everyone else had men to lead. Farred was spare.

'Alright, Walter,' he said, conceding to the logic of it. 'I suggest we get started straight away.'

***

BALDWIN STOOD shoulder to shoulder with his brother as they stared across the divide between the Emperor's Crag and the Duke's Crag. Something was happening over there: the Drobax gathering together in units, looking more organised. Something was happening, and whatever it was couldn't be good.

He looked away, the sight of the crag occupied by those monsters like a knife twisting in his gut. He had lost the Duke's Crag. They were barely clinging on to this one. He would be remembered as the emperor who lost Burkhard Castle. Maybe as the last emperor, the man who let his enemies into Brasingia. Baldwin the Last.

He shook his head, trying to rid himself of these thoughts. He looked at the men of Kelland, stood all around him, men who needed him to lead, now more than ever. The Eagle of Kelland fluttered by his side, the flag of his homeland; of his father. That tough old bastard wouldn't have flinched from this fight. Lower, about half way down the crag where the wall circled it, the Mace of Gotbeck was displayed. Coen's Thessians had been badly mauled yesterday, but they had not let the Drobax take the wall. He had to hope that the Gotbeckers would be equally resolute.

'How does Farred's evacuation go?' he asked his brother.

Once, he had told himself never to think of the escape route under the crag. He had told himself they would all die trying to hold this castle. Now, he couldn't stop thinking about it.

'Farred's doing a good job. They're picking up speed now that he has his systems in place. The men of Rotelegen and Luderia are already down there, along with all the wounded. We persuaded Jeremias to go down with them. He started moving the Barissians down today.'

Baldwin made a grimace. He didn't have to spell out what he thought of that. The Barissians should be the last ones to be taken to safety. On the other hand, he didn't trust them to stand here and fight for the Empire, either. The only people he despised more were the Atrabians, who had ignored his war summons once again.

Movement opposite drew his attention. The Drobax were throwing rocks off the edge of the crag. Something odd was happening, and it took his mind a moment to understand what he saw. Instead of the rocks falling to the ground far below, they stopped in mid-air. They all stopped at the same height, too. It was the strangest sight, but he knew what it meant.

The Isharite sorcerers were at work. They had created a bridge of their own, an invisible one, to replace the one that Walter had destroyed. And, now that the Drobax could see that it held the rocks they had thrown, that it could be crossed, they began to walk onto it.

It only took a few of them to demonstrate that it was safe before a tentative handful became a horde, running across to take the Emperor's Crag and finish the siege. They charged, now only yards from where Baldwin stood.

'For the Emperor!' Walter bellowed. 'For Kelland!'

Kellish shields rammed into the charging Drobax. Yes, the Isharites had somehow formed a bridge with their magic; it was wider than the one it replaced, but it still had two edges—and the shield bearers were quick to find them, pushing the creatures off into the terrible drop below.

Then the weight of the Drobax was on the shields, pushing them back, and it became a scrum. Shoving, pulling, short blades thrusting.

Baldwin found himself amongst the melee. With one arm he shoved forward with his shield, pushing the enemy back, not letting them get close. Then, when an opening came, his hammer came down. He caved in skulls, broke bones so that the Drobax dropped their weapons. Once they were defenceless, he finished them.

He was grinning, he knew. Locked away in the keep, protected from harm, he had been forced to watch others lead the Brasingians into battle. He knew it had been necessary, that his death could see the morale of the army crack. But that didn't seem to matter so much anymore. All his pent-up frustration was getting a release, and his body flowed with energy.

And Baldwin was just one man among many. His soldiers gripped the sharper, stronger weapons; they wore armour and carried shields that could protect against what the Drobax offered; and they had the better of it. A pile of Drobax corpses was created where the bridge met the crag. It grew and grew, until the Drobax that came behind had to scramble over their fallen to reach the Kellish line, and when they did there was a competition over who would skewer them first.

The Drobax stopped coming. The bridge suddenly disappeared, the bodies that had been lying on it tumbling down into the chasm. Baldwin's men began pushing the Drobax that had fallen on the crag off the edge with their feet. It was satisfying—sensible, too. That many corpses could quickly spread disease.

Baldwin walked to the edge of his crag and peered over. He was looking for the corpses of the Drobax down below, but it was too far to make anything out clearly.

'Careful, brother,' Walter said next to him, grabbing his arm. 'We know there are sorcerers about.'

'How many have we lost, Walter?'

'Fifteen thousand.'

'What about them?' Baldwin asked. 'The Drobax?'

He could see Walter thinking. His brother hadn't considered the question before. 'I would estimate five for every one of ours.'

'So seventy-five thousand, if not more. Do you think we will get to a round hundred?'

'Why not?' Walter replied, a quizzical smile on his face.

'And last year?'

'The same, at least.'

'So we will kill two hundred thousand altogether.' It was an impressive number. 'Do you think any other emperor has killed so many enemies?'

'No-one has come close,' said Walter, allowing himself a full smile now that he could see why Baldwin was asking. 'That's a rather morbid record to celebrate.'

'Mmm. But I have to take what I can get. Perhaps people will remember me as Bloody Baldwin, or some such.'

'Perhaps,' said Walter, sounding dubious.

Baldwin smiled at that, and so it was with a smile on his face that he greeted the arrival of the dragon.

It appeared behind the ruins of the Duke's Keep, beating its great wings to gain more height. Baldwin had never seen it up close before. There was something shocking and repulsive about seeing its long green tail and wings in the blue sky; a sensation that made you want to run and hide.

It came for them then, roaring in anger. *How dare you*, Baldwin thought. *This is my castle. I'm the one who should be angry.* He roared his defiance out, as the monster dived at him, opened its maw, and released its flame.

He felt the heat coming for him, but a barrier appeared, protecting Baldwin and his men from the fire.

He turned to see Gustav, arms outstretched, shielding this part of the crag from the dragon's attack. He hadn't even known his archmage was here. Many had protested about his employment of a sorcerer, and yet again they had proven to be fools.

The dragon peeled away, roaring in frustration. Arrows flew towards it from the battlements of Baldwin's keep, and he heard the crack from their last remaining ballista, as it sent a bolt speeding towards the monster.

The dragon manoeuvred itself away from the missiles, before heading for the battlements. Again, a deafening roar preceded its attack, before it blasted the top of the keep. And again, its flames were deflected by a barrier, this time covering the battlements.

Inge was there.

The dragon poured its flame out. Baldwin could see Inge's barrier retreat and falter; but somehow it held, and the dragon flew away as the next wave of arrows were sent, some of them finding their mark.

Baldwin felt a pang of fear for his lover, quickly followed by shame. He thought then of his family back in Essenberg. He imagined having to tell Hannelore that her brother had died defending the castle. He thought of his daughters: Katrina, old enough now that he would have to start thinking about marriage plans, though he didn't want to give her away. Liesel, her head still full of stories and daydreams. His son and heir, Leopold. He had not spent enough time with the boy, not prepared him at all to be a ruler. But he had assumed that he still had plenty of time for that.

Ahead of him, the sorcerous bridge had reappeared. The Drobax began to cross. Baldwin hefted his hammer. He would fight and kill today, for his children and his empire.

'Come on,' he said to the monsters, under his breath. 'I can still reach two hundred thousand.'

X

THE BATTLE OF HERACTUS

THE TRICKLE OF REFUGEES COMING from the north was now threatening to become a flood. Whole villages had taken whatever possessions they could carry and fled, ahead of the advancing army. All the reports were the same. The enemy numbered in the tens of thousands. The only good thing was that the Isharite army was so large, it travelled slower than those who fled from it.

They were all coming to Heractus for protection. The hardest part for Belwynn was the faces of the parents when they realised what they had come to. The king they knew was dead. The new one was gone, along with the Knights. She persuaded some of them to continue south, where they would be safer. But most of them knew that the south of the country had been invaded by Drobax only weeks ago. Most of them stayed in Heractus, putting their faith in the city walls.

She agonised over what to do with Lyssa. She could send the girl away with someone—place her with a family that was heading for the south. But when it came to it, she didn't go through with it. She wanted to keep her close.

Belwynn found herself staring at the grey walls of Heractus. She had never been impressed by them. She had little faith that they could hold against the kind of army that was coming here.

Clarin, on the other hand, was busy seeing to the city's defences. He had divided the soldiers he had into units and given each of them a captain and a stretch of wall to maintain and defend. He ordered cauldrons of oil and sand to be placed on the walls of the city and of the castle. Any spare bodies were put to work for the smiths and fletchers. Food and drink were commandeered and managed centrally. He was doing his best to prepare the city for a siege.

Belwynn found him inside the northern gates of the city, talking with a group of his captains. The gates were large; vulnerable. They would have to think of some way to protect them.

Clarin saw her waiting for him and excused himself.

'You've been busy,' she said.

He smiled. 'I've delegated all the work. That's one advantage when you're in charge.'

'You know, we never got to practise the telepathy, Clarin.'

He made a face.

'It could be important.'

'Alright, Belwynn.'

He gestured to the gates and they walked out of the city. Outside the walls lay the tents and more permanent wooden structures built to accommodate the influx of soldiers. Now they were mixed in with the wagons, animals, and other paraphernalia of the refugees. More were still arriving, and it was becoming a chaotic mess. Belwynn shuddered to think what would happen should the Isharite army arrive with things still like this.

Try to speak to me, Belwynn said to Clarin.

He looked at her for a while. She wasn't sure whether he was trying to communicate or not.

I love you.

The words took Belwynn by surprise. She felt her cheeks go red. She knew that Clarin felt that way—he had made it more than clear before he had left for Persala. But he had said nothing since he returned.

She also knew that he thought little of Theron. At the time she had put it down to jealousy, not willing to listen to his criticism. Now she wasn't so sure. Clarin had objected to the execution of Ampelios. Since then, Belwynn had witnessed Theron kill both Straton and King Jonas, in cold blood. She had seen him seize the throne, in a ruthless manoeuvre. Was he just doing what he believed was right for Kalinth? And even if he was, how much had it changed what she felt about him?

Did you hear me? Clarin asked.

Yes, I heard you Clarin. She smiled. *Well done. I don't know what you want me to say.*

Clarin shrugged. 'I'm not asking you to say anything.'

'Soren told me to forget about all this stuff. Until it's over.' She gestured at the camp around them. 'There is too much else to worry about.'

'I just want you to know. That's all.'

She nodded. 'Thank you. I know.'

They both turned simultaneously at the sound of horses being ridden hard in their direction. They were coming from the south. It was half a dozen knights, and they pulled up a few feet away from where Belwynn and Clarin were standing.

One of the knights dismounted and Belwynn saw that it was Philon. He strode over.

'My lady,' he said to Belwynn, his head dipping. He gripped Clarin in a handshake.

'Theron is on his way?' Belwynn asked.

'The king leads the Knights back to Heractus. They will arrive tomorrow.'

Belwynn still had to get used to calling Theron 'king'. He hadn't told her he was coming back. The new distance between them meant that they had stopped using telepathy. That wasn't wise, especially in the current circumstances.

'You've heard about the Isharites?' Clarin asked.

'Yes. We're going to ride north now so we can report back to the king as soon as possible. How are things here?' Philon asked, looking around at the rather chaotic situation outside the city. Something in the look made Belwynn think he was less than impressed.

'We're getting ready as best we can,' Clarin answered.

'Did you enjoy the ceremony for Leontios?' Belwynn asked him.

Philon allowed himself a smile. 'Very much so. It doesn't seem so long ago that Leontios and I were nervously asking you for your blessing.'

Indeed. It had been less than a year since the army of the Knights, then led by Sebastian, had marched to Heractus. They had taken the capital without a fight. If they were to lose it now, they would have held it for less than a year.

Whatever Belwynn now thought of Theron, they needed him here.

Theron arrived mid-morning of the next day. He had stripped the High Tower of men, bringing knights, squires and anyone else who could fight. He wasted no time in calling a war meeting in the hall of Heractus castle.

Clarin and Belwynn attended as the leaders of the infantry forces. For the Knights, there was Leontios and Tycho. Moneva was there too, still in charge of the archers in Gyrmund's absence. Soren had told Belwynn that the ranger had left the lands of the Krykkers yesterday, meaning they could expect him back tomorrow.

'We need to fight them in the open,' Theron said with no preamble.

Clarin bristled. 'I've organised the defence of the walls, given out orders already.'

Theron turned to him. 'The strength of the Knights is as a cavalry. We'd be giving it up if I stuck them behind the walls.'

'What about the infantry?' Clarin demanded. 'You'd stand them out in the open where they'll have no protection? The Knights can escape on their horses. The rest of us can't. They'll be butchered.'

Everyone else in the room gazed away somewhere as the verbal confrontation between the two men threatened to boil up. Even Tycho, hardly the most diplomatic of men, seemed to find something intensely interesting about the rafters of the hall.

'Heractus would be a death-trap,' Theron countered, retaining his composure. 'We'd be surrounded, with no escape. How long will it take the Drobax to get inside? A day or two? There's no ally coming to the rescue, Clarin. We're on our own. We need to fight them the best way we can. That's fighting on horseback. It's what we do.'

Do you agree with this? Clarin asked her.

Toric's arse, why did *she* have to decide between them? She thought Theron was right. And anyway, he was the king. It was his decision. Couldn't Clarin see that?

I think you'll have to go along with it, Clarin, she said, trying not to offend him.

She saw him clench his teeth. He looked ready to storm away.

'Very well,' he managed to get out.

'What of the people inside?' Moneva asked. 'Many have sought shelter in the city.'

'They need to be told to leave,' Theron answered her.

'Some won't go.'

'I can't spare soldiers to forcibly remove people,' Theron said. Now Belwynn could hear the edge in his voice. 'We tell them they must leave. Heractus must be evacuated. Everything and everyone. Those who can fight stand with us, those who can't are sent away. We choose a place to fight: dig trenches, put in spikes, do what we can to protect the infantry. We ready the cavalry. We fight for Kalinth. That's all we can do now.'

'I agree, Your Majesty,' said Leontios.

The Grand Master's jaw was firmly set now. The Knights knew what they were about. They had been created to fight for Kalinth. Belwynn knew that's what they would do, even if there seemed to be only one possible outcome.

***

COMING FROM the south, Gyrmund could see the supply train of the army ahead of him and nudged his horse in that direction. He had been told the location of the Kalinthian army at the gates of Heractus, by a man he didn't know. Reluctant to open the gates to him, the man had shouted down, explaining that Theron had led all his soldiers north to face the invading armies. Who had been left in charge of Heractus, and why they weren't opening the gates, was left unclear. Gyrmund assumed that Moneva, Belwynn and Clarin would be with the army.

As he approached, he could see the accoutrements of war being readied: horses cared for, wooden stakes unloaded, food and drink organised. He was pleased to see a cart loaded up with bundles of arrows. Those who worked here were a diverse bunch: older men who held some office or another; tradesmen; women and young boys. All were busy with one job or another. Gyrmund recognised young Alpin, who had been squire to Sebastian. He was organising a team of youngsters who managed the horses.

'Greetings Alpin,' he called.

Alpin wandered over and gave Gyrmund's horse a scratch.

'You're looking for the king and the others?'

'Everyone is here?'

'Yes, they're at the front,' Alpin said, pointing to a hill that rose out of the plain some distance to the north. 'Scouts came in a few minutes ago. If you hurry, you'll likely get to hear what they have to say.'

'Will I like it?'

Alpin gave him a sombre look. 'I don't think so, Gyrmund. Here, I'll look after him for you.'

'Many thanks,' said Gyrmund, dismounting. He gave the beast a pat before striding off.

This side of the hill rose at a gentle gradient, though he could see that the sides to the west and east were steeper and rocky. The Kalinthian soldiers he passed were not yet set up for battle, sitting around in small groups, waiting to be told by their superiors where to go. Some shouted out a greeting to Gyrmund as he passed them, but he didn't stop to talk, keen to reach his friends as soon as possible.

He saw them standing at the top of the slope. The large forms of the Knights, and Clarin, already wearing some armour, contrasted with the slighter figures of Moneva and Belwynn. An even smaller figure sat to one side. What was Belwynn thinking bringing Lyssa here?

They each turned to see him approach, but Gyrmund only had eyes for Moneva. Her smile had a good deal of relief mixed in with it. He felt himself break into a big grin, aware that he probably looked very stupid, but not really caring.

When he reached them, he looked down the other side of the hill. Again, the slope was gentler this side, not ideal if this was where the infantry would stand. Grassland stretched out around the hill on all sides, almost as far as the eye could see, giving the Knights the freedom to roam around as they wished.

'A good spot,' he suggested. His comment was met with some dark looks. Perhaps it was better if he kept quiet.

'Welcome, Gyrmund,' said Theron. 'Thank you for coming to help.'

'Your Majesty,' Gyrmund replied, giving him a slight nod.

'Philon,' Theron said, 'you won't mind giving a brief recap for Gyrmund's benefit, will you?'

'Of course not,' said the knight. Gyrmund knew Philon as an able scout with a good eye.

'Siavash has sent four armies into Kalinth. They are organised identically, suggesting that he has introduced a common system to his forces. Most of each army, something like four fifths, are made up of Drobax. They are led by the new class of Drobax Clarin told us about.'

Gyrmund glanced at Clarin who wore an unusually grim expression; perhaps recalling his encounter with Herin.

'Then each army has a range of human soldiers: we have identified Haskans, Persaleians and Kharovians amongst them. These units are well armed and include specialists such as archers and cavalry units. Finally, there are the Isharites themselves.'

Gyrmund knew all about the Isharites from his time in Samir Durg. They were dangerous, and if some of them were wizards, they would be in trouble. Pentas was dead and Soren was gone, looking for the Asrai.

'Two of the armies entered Kalinth from Haskany, via the fort of Masada. They are marching directly for Heractus and are approximately two hours away. A third invaded from the lands of the Drobax and is approaching our position from the west. The fourth invaded from Persala. It has taken the town of Korkis but is still some distance away.'

Gyrmund blew out a breath. Siavash was certainly trying to make sure of his conquest this time. 'What are the numbers in each army?' he asked.

'At least fifty thousand in each.'

Gyrmund looked at the faces around him, watching for his reaction. He glanced around him at the soldiers Theron had brought here. Had he missed something? No. There were less than twenty thousand here. Ten times that number were on their way.

Say nothing, Gyrmund, he advised himself. *Best to just keep quiet.*

Unfortunately, Philon had been correct. The enemy to the north came into view not long after midday. By then the Kalinthians were just about ready.

Gyrmund led just under a thousand archers and slingers. They were positioned together in a line at the front, with a clear view down the slope at the approaching enemy. He could see them quite clearly. Riders went to and fro, giving out orders, as the Isharites readied their forces. Slowly, two blocks began to form up, a few hundred yards from where the slope flattened out. Philon confirmed that these were the two armies, both lining up to face Theron's position. That meant that there were in the region of eighty thousand Drobax ahead of them, not to mention the other supporting soldiers.

Sharpened stakes and other unpleasant things had been placed all over the slope, designed to slow an attack, and a full line of them stuck out in front of Gyrmund's troops, affording them some protection.

Behind Gyrmund's position stood the infantry. A wide channel separated them into two divisions, allowing Gyrmund to withdraw his bowmen to safety. On the right, Clarin led one half of the infantry. He commanded a diverse group, trained men-at-arms at the front, untrained villagers at the back. On the left, Belwynn led the Madrians. Moneva was by her side. She had explained again why she felt the need to be with Belwynn and not him. But she needn't have. Elana's death had hurt him, too. And if there was anything to this business with the weapons and Madria, then keeping Belwynn alive was their priority. Lyssa was somewhere at the back with the train. Gyrmund just hoped that wasn't a complication they would regret.

Out on the wings were the Knights. Theron commanded the left and Leontios the right. They would have to watch for the other two armies that Philon advised were coming their way from the flanks.

Gyrmund wondered whether Theron would be tempted to harry the enemy down below while they were organising themselves. Normally it might make good sense. But what were their goals here? They were buying time, time for Rabigar to find the Spear and for Soren to find the Cloak. Soren had wanted him to discuss with Belwynn and the others how to get the Shield. That seemed far beyond their capabilities now. But they were slowing the pace of the Isharite advance. Maybe they were buying a day, maybe two. More time for the Kalinthian civilians to retreat south. More time for Rabigar and Soren.

So instead of taking the initiative, Theron waited for the Isharites to make the first move. It is not easy to get one hundred thousand men to stand exactly where you want them to, never mind beasts like the Drobax. The afternoon passed into evening, and still Gyrmund looked down on an enemy that wasn't attacking. It crossed his mind that they had orders to wait for the other two armies to arrive. According to Philon, that wouldn't be until tomorrow.

As evening came, the women and boys from the supply train came to hand out food and drink. The Kalinthians sat and ate as the sun began to set. There was enough to go around tonight, but Gyrmund thought they would struggle to feed everyone tomorrow.

Still, what about their enemy? They had marched all this way, and Gyrmund doubted that they were all well fed.

He remembered Farred telling him about the siege of Burkhard Castle. The Isharites had not even attempted to provide for the Drobax. When they got hungry the creatures resorted to eating each other. It was a grim thought, but down the slope their Drobax enemies would either be hungry, or there would be less of them come morning. How long could the Isharites sustain such an army without food? And if the attrition of the Drobax was really so high, why did they not attack immediately?

As night came, the soldiers tried to settle down as best they could. It wasn't easy. People had to relieve themselves. Gyrmund sent them down the slope to do it—another little treat for their enemies—but they had to negotiate their way past the wooden stakes to get there. There was a chill to the air too. They were dressed for fighting, not sleeping. Some people managed to nod off but Gyrmund, like most, stared down into the growing gloom. His eyes adjusted to the reduction of light and he could still see the shadowy shapes of the enemy.

At the point when Gyrmund felt sure there would be no attack until morning, it began. Drums thudded, and the shadowy lines of the enemy began to move towards the slope.

From all about, Kalinthians shouted a warning to their comrades, fear in many voices. Fighting in the dark of night seemed even more terrifying. Some men complained they could see nothing in the darkness. Others got to their feet bleary-eyed and groggy, their brains struggling to process that a battle was coming in the dark. Gyrmund shouted at his bowmen, calling for quiet, until his voice was hoarse. He needed them to focus on his orders, that those around him would relay, not engage in a hundred private conversations.

Eventually, the soldiers calmed, and focused their attention on the enemy. No-one could be surprised to see that it was the Drobax who came for them. Grim smiles were shared when they heard the scream of a creature when it stood on a buried spike. But for every injured Drobax, hundreds more ascended the slope, getting closer.

'Ready!' Gyrmund shouted. His archers picked up their first arrows and slotted them to their strings. Meanwhile, the small group of slingers, stood to one side, released their first volley. Their stones travelled farther, and they had more ammunition. Gyrmund needed to be stingier with the arrows.

Screams of pain reached them as stones hit the unarmoured Drobax, shattering bones. The slingers released again.

'Aim!' Gyrmund shouted. The order spread through the bowmen. The darkness didn't matter much, because like the slingers, they weren't aiming at individual targets. They were aiming into the sky.

'Release!' The arrows flew up and then came down in an arc. There were so many Drobax, so thick on the ground, that when the arrows came down on them most would find a target, with the velocity to puncture great wounds in the enemy, incapacitating or killing.

'Ready!'

The drums beat faster now, and Gyrmund could hear orders from the slope below, from the new breed of Drobax. Shouts of 'Run!', 'Don't stop!' carried to him.

96

'Aim!'

Gyrmund pulled back the string of the Jalakh Bow to his ear, and tipped his upper body back to the position he wanted to shoot from. The men around him followed his lead, and it spread throughout the bowmen.

'Release!'

Some of the arrows went farther and faster than others, but they all landed where there were Drobax. Indeed, as the drums continued to pound, it was hard to locate a spot where there weren't Drobax.

Once Gyrmund could make out individual shapes coming towards their position, things changed. No more shooting as a unit; no more firing into the air. Now they had targets to aim at. Should a Drobax dare to come faster than the others, dare to draw attention to itself, it would soon be downed by a missile.

Now Gyrmund fired fast. The Jalakh Bow made a cracking noise that echoed over the battlefield every time an arrow was released. And the arrows left the bow at such a velocity that he saw more than one Drobax thrown backwards into the air when it was struck.

Hundreds lay dead or dying on the slope. But there were thousands of Drobax in the charge, and in the end, they came faster than Gyrmund's bowmen and slingers could kill them. It was tempting to stay and kill a few more. But the infantry needed to move into position along the line of wooden stakes, and that would take some time. Reluctantly, Gyrmund gave the order to retreat.

Away his men went, funnelling down the gap between the two divisions of Kalinthian infantry. Gyrmund stayed for as long as he could, using the Jalakh Bow to full effect, keeping the Drobax at bay. At last it was his turn. Fingers and shoulder aching from pulling the string so many times, he followed his men away from the slope, while the rows of infantry marched towards it. He caught a glimpse of the unmissable form of Clarin, stood in the front row, armed with shield and spear. He looked across in the other direction but couldn't see Moneva or Belwynn. That was a good sign. It suggested they had placed themselves in a sensible spot not too close to the front.

Gyrmund reorganised his unit, spreading them out behind the lines of infantry. He heard the almighty clash as the shield wall of the infantry met the attacking Drobax. He gave his archers their orders. It was easy work for the moment. They would fire high into the sky, so their arrows would land down the slope, far away from the front line.

Gyrmund himself, meanwhile, needed to take a look at the battlefield. The situation could change quickly, and he had to be able to respond.

He ran to the eastern end of the hill and looked down. It was darker down there, in the shadow of the hill. The Drobax had come, and would have been able to ascend the hill, flanking the Kalinthian infantry, were it not for the Knights. Leontios had been forced to intervene and his unit was now fully engaged with the enemy. For now, they were keeping them at bay.

Gyrmund realised the urgency of checking the other side of the hill and ran across, past his archers still firing into the sky. Once there he stopped, lungs heaving, and looked out. It wasn't the same here. The Drobax had got closer, had already begun the climb up. Where was Theron with his knights? Gyrmund looked farther out, beyond the hill, and his eyes detected movement. He could see a column of riders out there, and past them, a shifting landscape. He screwed his eyes up, urging them to tell him what he was seeing. And then he realised. The third army had arrived. Theron had taken his knights and was attempting to hold it off. But that left the western side of the hill undefended.

Gyrmund ran back to his men. Leaving the archers to it for now, he called over the slingers. Not so effective stuck behind the infantry, they would do a perfect job of slowing down the approaching Drobax on the west face. They spread out, enjoying the space they had to operate in, and soon their stones were flinging down the side of the hill. Many Drobax carried weapons, but few had shields or armour, and when the stones hit they did terrible damage. Gyrmund joined in, able to find individual targets here where he couldn't with the rest of the bowmen.

The Kalinthian position held that way for a while. It was hard to say how long it lasted in the gloom of night-time. The infantry held at the front, while the archers softened up the Drobax who approached. Leontios kept them away from the eastern approach, while on the west Gyrmund and the slingers tried to do the same. Out beyond the hill, Theron's knights kept the third army away.

It was a mighty effort. Everyone played their part. But the problem at the beginning of the battle remained the problem at the end. Despite the numbers they had killed, there were simply too many Drobax.

Gyrmund had to order his bowmen to the west side of the hill, as the Drobax swarmed closer. They now threatened to circle around the hill altogether, and if they were allowed to do that, the Kalinthians would become trapped and overwhelmed. Belwynn must also have become aware of this threat, as the Madrians began to move around to protect the western side as well as the northern. But almost as soon as they did, Gyrmund could see the infantry ahead of him begin to be pushed back. It looked like the Drobax had finally gained the upper hand and broken through the line of stakes that had held them back.

All about him Gyrmund could see the Kalinthians begin a retreat. It wasn't the retreat itself that was the problem. It was the danger that their position would be totally overrun, with no means of escape. A retreat here would soon become a massacre.

Then suddenly, all the Madrians around him, every man and woman, turned around. It was a strange, almost inhuman sight; but Gyrmund knew that Belwynn was behind it, passing orders to all her followers simultaneously. They began to march off the hill.

Gyrmund had little choice. His soldiers had to move as well. He shouted at his bowmen to move with the infantry. Some of them heard him. But it was now becoming difficult to keep his men united: in the darkness it was hard to see each other, and as the infantry streamed down past them, and the screams of the Drobax got louder as they closed in, it was difficult to be heard. Gyrmund left his position, mixing in with the retreating Madrians. He looked around for Moneva and Belwynn but couldn't see them.

When they reached the bottom of the hill, the Madrians streamed to the left and right. Gyrmund realised that Belwynn had ordered them to hold off the Drobax while the rest of the infantry made their way off the hill.

Knowing that the threat from the western side of the hill was more serious, Gyrmund went in that direction. The Madrians hadn't got far before the Drobax were onto them, trying to push them back—trying to close off the south side of the hill.

Gyrmund ran to the end of the Madrian line. Here he had a clear enough view of the Drobax coming at them. They emerged from the darkness like creatures from a nightmare. Gyrmund was used to nightmares. He'd fought the Drobax before. But even he wavered at the sight of so many of them.

Then he was drawing his bow and he was working on instinct, not needing to think any more. The Jalakh Bow seemed to work with him. They found their targets together, and when Gyrmund released his arrow the bow flung it with unerring accuracy, striking the heads and chests of the enemy. It helped to keep the Drobax back, buying a little more time for the infantry to evacuate the hill.

But the Drobax didn't stop. They got close to Gyrmund, and he knew he would have to put aside the bow and draw his sword. Then, a thundering noise came from his left. He saw the Drobax turn and look in that direction, and he did the same.

It was the Knights. He saw Theron at the front, leading the charge, his sword drawn. Not far behind was Tycho, and the rest of the Knights followed. None carried lances anymore; they must have lost them earlier in the battle. Nonetheless, it was a breath-taking charge. Gyrmund could see their lips moving: they were shouting, though the words didn't carry to him.

The Drobax stood transfixed as the war horses thundered towards them. The Madrians turned and ran south, again following some silent order from Belwynn. Looking across, Gyrmund could see the last of the infantry coming off the hill. They had turned their backs and were running too, the Drobax behind, catching those who were too slow. It was perhaps time for Gyrmund to run himself. Instead, he turned to watch the Knights.

Theron led his cavalry force towards the Drobax. Terrified, those at the front tried to move out of the way, while those behind continued to surge forwards. It made it easy for Theron and those who followed to get close, to launch a swing at the nearest creature, and then veer out of the way to safety.

It seemed like they had timed it to perfection, occupying the Drobax and giving the infantry a chance to escape. But there were other threats than the Drobax.

A burst of power hit the Knights. It carried to where Gyrmund stood, feeling like a strong gust of wind. But to the Knights, it proved deadly. The magic blast sent their horses tumbling over, crushing the riders who were too slow to extricate themselves, smashing into those unlucky enough to find themselves in the path of one of the great stallions.

Barely a handful of knights stayed mounted, and Gyrmund could see that Theron and the others in the van had taken the full force of the strike.

He strode forwards, as an animal howl poured from the throats of the Drobax in their excitement to destroy the Knights.

Gyrmund nocked an arrow and drew back the string of the Jalakh Bow. But he wasn't hunting for Drobax—not just yet.

Gyrmund was looking for the Isharite wizards who had attacked the Knights, and the Jalakh Bow helped him to find them. There were four of them, standing in the shadow of the hill, watching as the Drobax moved in for the kill. The Drobax stayed clear of them, so they were given their own circle of space on the battlefield.

That gave Gyrmund a cleaner sight.

He released his arrow. It struck his target in the eye and the Isharite collapsed to the ground. By the time the other three began to realise what had happened, he had already put a second arrow to his string. The bow sent it straight into the forehead of the second wizard.

Somehow, one of the two remaining wizards had seen him. They locked eyes and the wizard pointed in his direction, before launching a blast of magic.

Gyrmund ran a few steps to the side then rolled, keeping a grip on the bow. He came up on one knee, grabbed an arrow, nocked it, and fired. He caught his enemy in the neck. He saw the Isharite move its hands to the shaft, before it slumped to the ground.

The fourth wizard abruptly changed tactics, turning and running in the opposite direction. Without even thinking about it, Gyrmund found a fourth arrow in his hand. He aimed, allowing for the fact that his quarry would be slightly further away when the arrow reached him. He released, watching the flight of the missile. It came down on the back of the wizard's head, dropping him to the ground.

There was little time for relief. Gyrmund turned his attention to the fallen knights. Some had made it onto their feet and held their swords, while a few more scrabbled about in the darkness, looking for a weapon. Many lay prone and lifeless. All about them horses kicked out in agony, some of them making a horrible sounding scream. Most mounts that made it to their feet had run off, while a few stood dutifully, waiting for their owners.

Gyrmund grabbed another arrow, intent on targeting the Drobax who now began to swarm over this scene. He checked, looking down at his quiver. He had less than a dozen left.

He decided to walk closer, looking for Theron. A knot of knights drew his attention. Moving towards them, he recognised the king. He was on his hands and knees, removing the helm of a knight. Gyrmund peered down. It was Tycho. Theron was talking to him, putting his fingers to his neck to find a pulse.

The king looked up, face red. When they met eyes Gyrmund could see a murderous rage there. With a snarl, Theron grabbed a sword that lay by Tycho's side. He stood, faced the Drobax that were coming for them, and went for them, swinging his weapon in wide arcs, eager for bloodshed. The small group of knights that had gathered around their king went with him, and the first line of Drobax fell.

But more came behind them. The king and his knights would soon tire and be overwhelmed.

Gyrmund followed. He grabbed Theron by the arm, risking the king striking out at him. Theron turned to him.

'You must go,' Gyrmund shouted at Theron.

A snarl returned to the king's face. A madness had overcome him, and he stared through Gyrmund.

'You're the king!' Gyrmund shouted, trying to remind him of his duty. 'You must go!'

He thought Theron would ignore him and give his life away cheaply. But a rider approached, leading a horse. When Gyrmund looked up he could see it was Evander.

Theron looked up at his former squire and tears came to his eyes. That was a good sign. Gyrmund signalled to a couple of the knights and they grabbed Theron. Gyrmund guided his foot into the stirrup and they pushed him up into the saddle. A knight wearing all that heavy armour, making a clanking noise, was unlikely to out run the Drobax. A knight on horseback had a chance.

Evander, one hand still on the reins of Theron's horse, began to lead him away. Theron looked down at Gyrmund.

'Belwynn and Moneva live,' he said.

Gyrmund nodded. He took an arrow and fitted it to his bow.

'Go with them!' he shouted at the knights.

He released an arrow at the Drobax and pulled out another.

Some of the knights went for the spare horses, trying to heave themselves up into the saddle. Some turned and ran, as fast as they could. Others turned to face the Drobax, ready to lay down their lives.

Gyrmund walked backwards, using the last of his arrows, making sure he didn't waste any—didn't miss.

Some of the knights got away. The rest were knocked to the floor by the heaving mass of the Drobax.

When Gyrmund had used his last arrow, he turned away and ran into the night.

XI

THE GIANTS' SPEAR

EVEN BENEATH ALL THE FURS, the cold of the mountain got its claws into him. While his companions trudged up the steep climb, the exercise keeping them warm, Rabigar had to sit on his sled, pulled along by Gunnhild, like a baby by its mother. *Stop feeling sorry for yourself, Rabigar,* he lectured. *You're lucky to be alive. Remember Ignac, who took himself under the ice to save you. Remember the Krykkers and Vismarians you left, stranded miles from the Drang. Remember Guremar and the warriors of the Plengas clan, turned to ash by dragon fire. Feel sorry for them, if you must waste your energy bemoaning events that have already happened.*

As they climbed higher, the path became narrower and more treacherous. Gunnhild, puffing heavily in the thin mountain air, was persuaded to take a break. The brothers, Ketil and Jesper, pulled the sled. They pulled Rabigar up the mountain until the path ended. He got out then, and they left the sled for the return journey. Rabigar put one arm around Stenk, and part-hopped, part-climbed his way over the rock and ice of the mountain.

It's strange how unprepared your body is for a new movement. After a few minutes of this, Rabigar's leg muscles began to fail.

'Sit me down here, Stenk,' he gasped.

The others stopped and turned to look.

'Alright, Gunnhild,' he said, admitting defeat. 'You'll have to carry me the rest of the way.'

'It's not far now,' said Jesper.

The lad helped Rabigar to his feet. Gunnhild crouched down and Rabigar linked his arms around her neck. Jesper and Stenk grabbed an arm each and pulled her to her feet. Rabigar felt the Vismarian tuck her hands beneath his arse and lift him up.

'Comfy?' she asked him.

'Just get on with it,' he growled.

Gunnhild took him to the place where Nemyr believed the Giants rested. It was a wall of rock. Even before he put his hands to it, Rabigar somehow knew it was Krykker rock. What it was doing all the way here, at the far end of

Halvia, he couldn't know. It was clear that Nemyr didn't either. If his ancestors had once known, it had been lost: all extraneous information had been discarded over the years, save for the core fact that the Giants, or Orias as Nemyr called them, had come here. Rabigar was about to find out if that was truth or myth.

He pushed one hand, then the arm, into the rock, testing its depth. Dalla gasped as she saw his limb disappear. Rabigar pulled it out again.

'It's thick,' he said, grunting with the effort. 'I may need some help.'

Gunnhild and Stenk stood to each side of him. Rabigar took in a few deep breaths. 'Now,' he said.

He pushed his hands into the rock, then used them to pull his head inside. Pushing one arm then the next forwards, he felt Gunnhild and Stenk lift his torso and leg, then shove him into the rock. Rabigar kept using his powerful arms to pull deeper, until his whole body was inside. Just as he started to worry that it might be too thick, one hand pushed out of the rock into air. Relaxing, he wriggled further, then pulled his head out. It was pitch black inside. He lay, half-in and half-out of the rock, catching his breath, before forcing his way completely free, dragging himself onto the floor.

Rabigar sat himself up but didn't move for a while. He didn't know what might be inside, or even where he was, though logic told him it must be an underground cave. He let his eyes slowly adjust. Krykkers were used to being underground, and their eyes could operate even with the faintest of light sources.

Rabigar soon became aware that there was a source of light. Daylight came in from very high up, which gave him a sense of the space he was in. While he began to see the walls of the room, irregular in shape, about thirty feet wide in most places, the roof was far above, as if it rose to the very top of the mountain. Dangling down from the roof was a thick piece of rope, on which was attached a chandelier.

Rabigar got up to investigate. It held candles, about twenty in all. He looked around the room for something to light them with. Nearby was a wooden stand on which sat a large metal tinderbox. He traced a finger over the decorative lid, admiring the craftsmanship. Opening the lid, he took out the steel, flint and a half dozen wooden sticks. Once he made the flames, he took a lighted stick over to the chandelier. The first stick held the flame long enough to light all the candles.

Now that the chandelier was lit, he could see around the room much more clearly. A large wooden door was set in the wall opposite the one he had climbed through. But a sight to his right arrested him.

Against the wall lay three stone coffins. Each was giant-sized. Curiosity drew Rabigar towards them. Could it be? Nemyr had called this the resting place of the Giants. He had to look.

The stone slab on top of the first coffin was heavy. Rabigar needed several goes to slide it away enough to peer inside. It was empty. He tried to stave off a sense of disappointment. If they had come all this way for nothing it would be difficult to take.

He pulled the lid back on to the coffin and moved to the second, the one in the middle. This time, as soon as he swung the lid over a little, he noticed the difference. A musty smell hit him. Peering inside, Rabigar could see a green face, covered in thick beard, with coils of long hair around it. The giant was wrapped in blankets. Tentatively, Rabigar pulled aside a bit of the blanket, to reveal the giant's hand. It was green, too. So, the statue they had seen on the Nasvarl had been lifelike in more ways than he had known.

Rabigar pulled the lid completely off the coffin, letting it clunk onto the floor. He moved around to the third coffin and looked inside. Empty. But still, he had found a giant. That was something. He put his weight on the side of the centre coffin and leaned down, putting his ear to the face of the bearded man. Perhaps he was fooling himself, but Rabigar thought he heard breathing.

The giant stirred. Rabigar backed away a few steps, fearful that should it wake from its slumber with a stranger's face peering at it, it might react with violence.

He didn't, therefore, see the giant wake, until it sat up in its coffin. Seated, it was already taller than Rabigar. It rubbed at its face, then opened its eyes. Bright green like freshly watered grass, they focused on Rabigar.

'A Krykker come to my hall,' he said, his deep voice booming and echoing around the space. 'That means it is time to rise.'

The Giant put a hand on each side of the coffin and began to push himself up. Standing to his full height, he was an intimidating sight, at least the twelve feet of the statue they had found by the Nasvarl. He tied one of the blankets around his waist. Everywhere else was pale green skin, his muscular body decorated with blue tattoos in swirling geometric patterns. The giant stepped out of the coffin.

'I am Rabigar, of Clan Grendal,' he greeted the giant, offering a hand.

'Oisin, King of the Orias,' the giant responded, his huge hand swallowing Rabigar's. 'We have been asleep a long time, dear Rabigar. My family must need some help with their waking.'

Oisin turned to the coffin on his right, a gentle smile on his face.

'Your Majesty,' Rabigar said, uncomfortable. 'I found the other two coffins empty.'

Oisin frowned. 'That cannot be.' He slid the lid of the coffin aside with ease. Peering in, his frown grew deeper. 'I don't understand,' he said, moving to the third coffin to check that Rabigar's words were true.

He looked at Rabigar then, worry evident on his face. 'Here beside me lay my wife, Niamh, and my brother, Cillian. We came here to rest, so that we would be ready to give aid if needed again. That is why you are here?'

'Yes. The Isharites have taken our home, they are close to defeating all Dalriyans who stand against them. Here I have Bolivar's Sword,' he added, drawing the blade for King Oisin to see. 'I have come here looking for a spear.'

'I know that sword and remember well the Krykker who wielded it. You must understand that I have slept for a long time, Rabigar. To me, it seems like mere days ago that I was fighting by Bolivar's side. But that is not the case, I'm sure you will tell me.'

Rabigar studied the face of Oisin, searching for some sign that this was a jest. But he found none. 'You mean to tell me that you have slept here since the days of Bolivar?'

'Indeed. Will you tell me how long it has been?'

'I don't know exactly. We Krykkers have preserved our history as best we can. It has been hundreds of years. How can that be, Oisin?'

'The Krykkers have forgotten us?' asked Oisin, a note of sadness in his voice. 'The Orias can sleep for many years if need be. We fought with your kind and the other peoples of Dalriya against the Isharites. Fought them to a standstill. We lost all of our people in that war, save for the three of us. I agreed that we would return here to sleep, and be ready should we be called on again.'

'Only fragments of that story remain,' Rabigar explained. 'I came here looking for the Giants' Spear. We have been told that all the weapons of Madria are needed. I did not expect to find you here.'

'I see,' Oisin said, pushing his lips together. 'I must look for my wife and brother. You want the spear. Perhaps we will find our answers in there.'

He pointed to the large wooden door in the cave wall and walked towards it. When he pushed it the door resisted, but Oisin put his weight into it, scraping the wood along the stone floor until it was open.

Following behind, using his scabbard to help him walk, Rabigar emerged into a large living room. Frozen in time, it felt like he was intruding into a private space. Wooden furniture lined the walls, all items huge in size. To the right a fireplace took up much of one wall, a sink with crockery and utensils to the side of it. There was a door opposite the one they had come through, but this was bolted from the inside, suggesting that this door led somewhere outside. By the door was a weapons rack. It was here that Rabigar's eyes were drawn. A variety of super-sized weapons hung on the rack. Pride of place was a spear, perhaps fifteen feet in length. The metal spear head took up approximately the final third of the length, ending in a broad, leaf-shaped blade that was about the same length as the blade of Bolivar's Sword. Rabigar knew he had found the Giants' Spear.

But if Rabigar's eyes were drawn to the weapon that he had been searching for for so long, Oisin had instead walked over to the massive bed that took up the left wall of the room. The giant made a keening noise that took Rabigar's attention from the spear. Glancing over, he saw why. Poking out from the tattered blankets were two heads. Their size made it clear that they were Giants, and that they must be Oisin's family.

'What? What happened here?' the king demanded.

His hands hovered, shaking, over what he had found. He pulled aside the blankets to reveal the bodies. It looked like they had died recently. But Rabigar knew that the cold mountain air could have preserved them intact for a long time. Even for centuries.

'What are you doing, laying down together in this bed?' Oisin asked them. But his wife and brother had departed from this world and gave him no answers.

Or did they?

Turning away from the scene, Rabigar saw a clay pot sitting on the hearth. Inside it were rolls of parchment. He took out the parchment. He could see it was filled with lines of writing. Perhaps he could have read it, but it wasn't for him.

'Oisin,' he said softly, holding it out.

The King of the Giants took it from him and began to read. Tears began to roll softly down his face as he did so.

'My wife and brother were in love,' he said after a while, though whether he was speaking aloud for Rabigar's benefit or not, the Krykker wasn't sure. 'They say they weren't as strong as me. The thought of sleeping for hundreds of years, waking up again in a strange land, scared them. So they pretended to go to sleep. When they were sure I was under, they quietly climbed out of their coffins and came here. They—'

Oisin's voice was emotional now, and he began to choke on his words. 'They lived a quiet life, spending the years they had left together. They wanted me to know—' a wail came from the giant now, a wrenching sound of heartache. 'They wanted me to know that they were happy. That they were sorry for their weakness.'

Rabigar felt lost. How could he comfort this creature? Should he even try?
'I am sorry, Oisin. Truly.'

Oisin put a hand to his forehead. He wept, his body wracked by miserable sobs. 'How strong did they think me? That I could wake to this and not be crushed? That I could wake alone and friendless in the world, the last of my kind, my wife and brother dead, and carry on regardless?'

'They must have thought you strong enough, Oisin. Because we need you. We need the Giants' Spear. I see it there, and I realise now that you are the only one who can wield it. I am not sure that any of us could even carry it.'

'Us? There are others?'

'I came with others. They wait outside the walls. Another Krykker. Humans, the descendants of those you set to protect this place, they kept their vow. And one other who I think must be related to you in some way: because although she calls herself a Vismarian, she is eight feet tall and hugely strong with it. So you see, you are not alone. We have come for you.'

Oisin wiped his tears away. 'You speak well, dear Rabigar, but I fear you have found a broken thing. The Orias died out a long time ago. I see that now. I am not meant to be here. I should have died in my sleep.'

'I have lost things too, Your Majesty,' Rabigar said. 'You can see that well enough just by looking at me. But I too have lost time, years I will never get back. I have seen my people defeated and exiled. But I have come all this way, to the edge of the world. I have found the Giants' Spear, and I have found you. And I need to get both down from this mountain.'

Oisin looked at Rabigar for a while, his deep green eyes sparkling, his face unreadable. Then he turned and went to the weapons rack behind him. He picked up the spear, turned back, twirled it around in his hands.

'Very well, dear Rabigar. You are right.' He slid the bolts free on the door and opened it. 'We are only gifted with one life, and none of us know how long it will last. We don't have time to waste feeling sorry for ourselves, do we?'

Rabigar wondered at Oisin's words, for he had said as much to himself just a couple of hours past.

'Come,' said the King of the Giants, the last of his kind. 'Come and show me my new friends.'

XII

ESCAPE

THE HALL OF THE EMPEROR'S KEEP was so much quieter now. The last time Farred had been here it had been crammed with bodies: those soldiers who had escaped from the Duke's Keep adding to the numbers already allocated a space to rest their heads. Some had fallen in the intervening days. Fortunately, most had been evacuated down into the caves underneath the crag. Caves they hadn't even known had existed.

'We are ready for you, Your Majesty,' Farred announced.

Baldwin and Godfrey turned to look at him as he approached. The Emperor's face was impassive. Farred wondered what he really thought about abandoning Burkhard Castle. He understood that the weight of leadership rested heavily on his shoulders. But he still bore it.

As for the second man, Archbishop Godfrey of Gotbeck, Farred's view of him had now completely reversed. For Godfrey was to stay behind in the Emperor's Keep, holding out for as long as possible. A few thousand men stayed with him, volunteers all. That so many chose to stay had surprised Farred. Most were men of Godfrey's duchy, but not all. It was impossible to know all the reasons that had made men stay. Heroism, certainly. Loyalty to the Empire, to its gods, played no small part. Perhaps they thought this was as good a place to die as any other, for there seemed to be nowhere safer in the Empire for anyone to escape to. The fact that Baldwin's Archmage, Gustav, was staying too, might have persuaded some. Another man to admire, though Gustav's bravery was tempered a little in Farred's eyes. He always had the option of flying away, after all.

Farred offered his hand to the Archbishop, who took it.

'May the gods of Brasingia bless you,' he said.

Godfrey smiled. 'And you, Farred. I am sure they watch what we do. I will pray they keep Magnia safe.'

Baldwin and Godfrey embraced, then Farred was leading the Emperor down to the lowest rooms of his keep. From out of the shadows somewhere, Inge joined them, unspeaking.

In the well room, two of Godfrey's men were ready to lower the bucket one last time. Down below, dukes Walter, Coen and Jeremias had already begun to lead the Brasingian soldiers through the tunnels that would eventually take them out into the open.

Farred climbed in first, then helped Baldwin and Inge into the bucket. They began to move, leaving the keep behind, dropping into the hollow insides of the crag. Inge latched onto Baldwin's arm. She placed a hand on his chest and began to run it down to his belly, then to his groin. Baldwin pushed her off him. The witch gave Farred a look full of hatred, for witnessing her rejection.

'Lars the Creator!' Baldwin exclaimed.

Lanterns now adorned the network of caves, placed at regular intervals along the roof, signalling the way to the first tunnel. The pool of water at the bottom shimmered eerily. They descended into this underworld realm, as if passing through some portal into another world. Inge stared at it all. Farred could see her eyes light up. A thin smile came to her face.

'Never mind Lars,' she whispered. 'This is the Kingdom of Justus. God of Death.' She gave a tinkle of laughter, the sound grating on Farred's nerves. 'We have escaped the death that waits above, only to enter the Realm of the Dead.'

***

WE'RE DOWN, Belwynn said to him, using her telepathy. *Come now.*

It was strange—unpleasant, really, having a voice in your head. Even if it was Belwynn's.

Still, it had its uses, especially when it was too dark to see more than a few feet in front of you. Belwynn had received a warning from Theron that the hill they defended was close to being surrounded, that they had to retreat immediately. Her infantry force had gone first, each of the Madrians given instructions, from her mind to theirs. Now it was time for Clarin's force, spread thinly along the top of the hill, to follow. But this wasn't going to be so easy.

For Clarin couldn't speak into his soldiers' minds. What was more, his was a force that hadn't fought together before. They were from different corners of Kalinth, townsfolk mixed with farmers, noblemen with peasants. That lack of cohesion, not knowing what your job was and not being able to rely on those you fought with—all that mattered when you tried to implement a fighting retreat.

It would have been nice to have had Gyrmund's archers to help, but Clarin had no idea where they were. For a while their arrows had sailed over the heads of his lines, peppering the Drobax that came up the slope. But that had stopped some time ago now.

He shouted out the orders. Leading by example, he punched his shield forwards, shoving the Drobax ahead of him off balance, before taking a few steps backwards. But it soon became clear that this would become a mess. Some followed his lead, others didn't. In some places, the rows behind had moved out of the way of Clarin's front line, giving them space to move back into. In others, they were still there, constricting their movement. Some soldiers even tried to overlap to the front, attempting a manoeuvre that was simply beyond this ragtag force. Then there were those who had simply turned and run.

Gaps emerged up and down the Kalinthian line, and even the mindless Drobax were able to exploit that. There was nothing Clarin could do but carry on, pushing forwards before falling back, hoping that enough of his soldiers stayed with him. By the second, however, Clarin's line began to disintegrate before his eyes.

He met eyes with his two Dog-men, positioned behind him. They didn't carry shields or swords, and had no place in his front line. They slashed with their claws and bit with their teeth, and now they were needed.

'Go!' he ordered them, pointing at the enemy.

Obedient to the last, the Dog-men launched themselves high into the air and came crashing down onto the Drobax, tearing into their ranks, cutting faces and savaging necks.

'Run!' he shouted to his soldiers. 'Run!'

That was it. The battle was over, the Kalinthians streaming down the hill, Clarin with them. The battle was over, and the flight had begun. He had sent the Dog-men to their deaths, but it would buy them a valuable head start on the Drobax. And while the night-time attack by the Isharites had left his inexperienced soldiers less able to withstand the Drobax attack, it now gave them a chance to escape.

Clarin ran hard, his crystal sword, Cutter, still in his right hand, his shield still attached to his left arm. To his right he saw some of Belwynn's Madrians holding off groups of Drobax, who had nearly made it to the bottom of the hill. They had got off just in time.

Clarin ran, and he passed others running, coming in and out of his vision in the dark of the night—and he didn't stop for them. It was a game of survival now. They had fought together as an army, but now they escaped as individuals.

Clarin!

Belwynn, we're off the hill. We're scattered. Tell your soldiers to get out of here.

Clarin, it's Lyssa. Belwynn sounded anxious. *She says she needs our help.*

Maybe Clarin was wrong. He wasn't just an individual after all.

What do you want me to do?

***

LYSSA FELT a little worried about the battle being fought up on the hill. Belwynn was there, and Theron and Gyrmund, and lots of her other friends. But she knew that the Knights were the strongest fighters in Dalriya, so there really wasn't any need to be frightened.

Of course, she had to wait at the camp, with the carts and the crates and all the other people who weren't good at fighting. Some, like her, were too young to be good at fighting. Others had got too old. Still, being near a battle was exciting. At least, she had thought it would be. But after a while of nothing happening, it actually got pretty boring. Things livened up a little bit when Alpin brought her supper. After that, with the sun going down, Lyssa decided she would rest her eyes a little, so she would be ready for when the action really started.

'Lyssa!'

She opened her eyes. Alpin's face loomed over her.

'Keep quiet!' he hissed.

His hand was over her mouth, gripping her much harder than he needed to.

She nodded.

Alpin withdrew his hand. 'They've sent soldiers into the camp,' he whispered. 'You need to get out of here.'

She heard shouting and the clang of metal on metal. Alpin got her on to her hands and knees and they crawled behind a cart. They both peered around the side of the cart. A group of men were moving about in the darkness. Flames licked into the sky from more than one place. They were burning the carts.

Lyssa could see a strange looking man shouting out orders to the other soldiers. He wore no armour on his chest.

'Oh,' she said, remembering to whisper. 'It's a Krykker, like Rabigar.'

Alpin looked over. 'Yes. But it's not Rabigar. This one is working with the Isharites. They suddenly appeared in the camp and started killing people. They must have been sent here by their mages.'

'So our army is still fighting?'

'I think so. They are burning the carts, we can't risk hiding. Come, we must get out of here.'

'Where?'

'South.'

'But where?' Lyssa knew that she sounded a bit stubborn. But just saying 'south' didn't seem like much of a plan.

'As far away from here as possible. As quick as we can.'

Alpin turned, and staying in a crouch to avoid being seen, began to walk over to the next cart, a few feet away. Lyssa, too small to be seen above the cart, ran next to him. Alpin dived under it, then began to crawl to the other side, pulling himself along using his elbows. Lyssa followed him. Alpin put a restraining hand out when they got to the far side. He looked around from under the cart before he was satisfied that it was safe to come out.

They crawled out and looked around again. Alpin pointed into the darkness. 'South,' he whispered. 'The survivors will keep going south until they reach the fortress of Chalios. That is where King Theron and the others will gather.'

There were no more obstacles to hide behind now. They ran for it, legs whipping against the long grass. Lyssa's foot landed in a patch of heather and she sprawled over onto the ground. Alpin picked her up.

They both turned at the sound of footsteps behind them. Two men, coming for them silently through the night. Lyssa had never felt so scared.

Alpin drew his sword. 'Run, Lyssa,' he said. 'Run and don't look back.'

Lyssa did what she was told, running into the night. Tears ran down her face as she did. She heard the grunts and crashes of the fight, heard Alpin's cry of agony as he was cut down. That wasn't fair. Two men against one boy. She heard them coming after her.

She wasn't going to outrun them, she knew that. She was better at hiding than running. It was just that there weren't many places to hide out here. Seeing a patch of gorse, she made her decision, burrowing underneath, ignoring the scratches. Then she stayed still, because she knew that the men had been able to follow the sound of her movement before. It wouldn't be so easy for them now.

Belwynn had told her that she needed to concentrate during the battle. She was only supposed to contact her in an emergency. But Lyssa thought that this situation was bad enough to warrant it.

Belwynn? I'm in trouble. Alpin's dead and now they're coming after me.

***

BELWYNN MOVED with her soldiers, the Madrians, away from the hill. Behind them, and on each flank, the Drobax were not far behind, threatening to catch them, drag them back into a fight they couldn't win.

Moneva, ever present at her side, grabbed her arm.

'Ahead,' Moneva warned her, pointing into the distance. 'Fire.'

The baggage area was alight. The Isharites had somehow slipped a force behind them. Were they now trapped? This was what she had feared the most. At the Pineos, they had Soren and Pentas to help them get the better of Siavash. Now they had no-one, and it looked very much like the Isharite wizards had used their powers to teleport a force where it could cause them a serious problem.

Then it hit her. Lyssa was there. She panicked, not knowing what to do. Should she send her soldiers at the enemy ahead of them, not knowing their numbers, to help Lyssa and the others at the camp? Engaging the enemy might tie her soldiers up and allow the Drobax, not far behind, to catch and destroy her force. Sacrificing her soldiers for the sake of one child couldn't be right. Even if that child was Lyssa.

Of course, it was her own stupidity that had led her to take Lyssa with them. But she hadn't been willing to send the girl away with strangers. She had decided that Lyssa would be better off near her. That she and Madria and

Theron and the Knights could protect her. What a foolish decision that now seemed.

Belwynn? It was Lyssa! *I'm in trouble. Alpin's dead and now they're coming after me. Where are you?*

Hiding in a bush. We ran away to the south. Two men came after us. I can hear them looking for me.

Stay there, Lyssa. We're coming for you.

'It's Lyssa,' she said to Moneva. 'She's run away from the camp, she thinks to the south. There are men after her. She's hiding from them.'

She saw Moneva thinking the situation over. The enemy ahead and behind, Clarin's infantry behind theirs, the Knights fighting on the flanks, a third enemy army coming from the west. There was a lot to think about.

'We have to attack,' Moneva decided. 'If we try to go around they'll see it and slow us down. Send the Madrians straight at them, Belwynn.'

'What about Lyssa?'

'We'll try to find her when we break through. Tell Clarin.'

Belwynn nodded.

Forwards! She ordered the Madrians. *Hit the enemies in the camp! Clarin!*

Belwynn, we're off the hill. We're scattered. Tell your soldiers to get out of here.

Clarin, it's Lyssa. She says she needs our help.

What do you want me to do?

There are enemies in our supply camp. We're engaging them. If you get a chance, please look for Lyssa for me. She thinks she's run away to the south of the camp. But she could be wrong. She says there are two soldiers on her trail. If they catch her, they—

Belwynn found it hard to continue. She didn't want to think about what might happen to her. *They might bring her back to the camp.*

Of course. Stay in touch.

The Madrians at the front had reached the outskirts of the camp. Belwynn had allowed Moneva to guide her forwards with the rest of the soldiers. Concentrating ahead of her now, she could see that many of the carts were on fire, and the flames took away any night vision her soldiers had built up. Beyond the fires was darkness. If there was a line of soldiers waiting for them, they wouldn't know until they were on top of them.

They crept forwards, on the look out for the enemy, gaps in the line a necessity where they had to walk either side of a burning vehicle, but otherwise holding their formation.

Belwynn. We've had to retreat.

It was Theron. Something sounded wrong.

Are you alright?

Their magi attacked us. I lost most of my men. Tycho's dead.

Belwynn went cold. She knew something like this was likely. They had been so heavily outnumbered. But a part of her had believed that they would somehow get through it unharmed. Now she realised that anyone who escaped would be one of the lucky few.

Evander? She dared to ask.

He's with me. I saw Gyrmund, too. He's fine.

'Theron says Gyrmund is safe,' she told Moneva immediately, knowing that her friend would be desperate for news of him.

But what should she tell Theron now? That she was about to be ambushed? That Lyssa was missing? He was in no fit state to help, he'd just lost his best friend. He'd likely get himself killed. No. The King of Kalinth had to live.

Alright, she said. *We got off the hill. We're heading south.*

Good. Go to the fortress at Chalios, Belwynn. You remember it? Get yourself and as many as you can to Chalios.

Yes, Theron, she replied. *We're on our way. We're all going to Chalios.*

***

WHAT DO you want me to do? Clarin asked Belwynn.

There are enemies in our supply camp, she said. *We're engaging them. If you get a chance, please look for Lyssa for me. She thinks she's run away to the south of the camp. But she could be wrong. She says there are two soldiers on her trail. If they catch her, they—*

Belwynn paused. She sounded emotional. *They might bring her back to the camp. Of course. Stay in touch.*

Clarin kept moving. Ahead he could see the ranks of the Madrians. He skirted around to the right, aiming to get past them and search the area south of the camp. Lyssa wasn't stupid. If she thought she had run away to the south, that was where she was likely to be.

He began to see the flicker of fires coming from the supply camp. It confirmed what Belwynn had said—the Isharites had teleported a force behind their lines, no doubt trying to cut off their retreat. He thought briefly about Herin then. His brother could be here, somewhere on the battlefield, leading his soldiers. Well, so what if he is, he told himself. If I see him, I'll kill him.

He began to pass the lines of Madrian infantry now, about twenty feet to his left. They had kept their discipline, still in formation. Belwynn had done a better job than he had in keeping her soldiers together. Of course, she had certain advantages that he didn't.

He heard the noise of fighting come from that direction. The Madrians must have engaged with the enemy in the camp, but he was too far away to see anything. His attention drawn to that area, it was only at the last second that he became aware of the figure coming towards him from the right. He swung around, ready to strike out.

'Toric's balls, Gyrmund! I was just getting ready to bring Cutter down on you.'

Gyrmund gave a tight smile. He had his sword drawn, the Jalakh Bow slung over his back. 'Any news?'

'Sure. Belwynn and Moneva are unharmed. They'll be over there, somewhere,' Clarin said, gesturing at the Madrians attempting to force their way into the camp. 'Those Isharite bastards have dropped a bunch of soldiers there. Little Lyssa has run off. Belwynn asked me to find her.'

Gyrmund grimaced. 'I wondered at the sense in bringing a child to a place like this. Anyway, I'll help you find her. Come,' he said, wasting no more time and moving ahead.

Clarin was glad to have the ranger along. He had some kind of sixth sense when it came to tracking, and that was just what was called for. He followed behind, ready with sword and shield should they be needed.

Gyrmund stopped abruptly, holding up a hand, before crouching down. Clarin got down next to him.

'Men coming,' Gyrmund whispered.

A line of half a dozen men filed out from the camp. They moved silently, and in the darkness, they looked like ghosts. They were leaving, perhaps driven out by the Madrians. Although they looked about them, ready for trouble, weapons drawn, they hadn't seen Clarin and Gyrmund.

Clarin heard Gyrmund take in a sharp intake of breath. 'Kaved.'

The name of the Krykker who had betrayed them all in Coldeberg sent a jolt through Clarin's body. Not satisfied with his evil work in Coldeberg, where Rabigar had lost an eye in the torture rooms of Duke Emeric, he had tried to assassinate Prince Edgar, only stopped by the heroism of Edgar's bodyguard, Leofwin.

He peered into the darkness. The figure in the lead had the broad chest of Kaved, alright. The more he studied him, the more he knew it was the Krykker.

'Take him down,' Clarin hissed, knuckles tightening on the hilt of Cutter.

'I would if I had any arrows left.'

Maybe their voices carried, or maybe it was just coincidence, but Kaved turned to look at them then. He frowned at first, then Clarin saw his eyebrows rise and a sardonic smile came to his lips when he realised who he was looking at. A hand gesture followed, part-wave, part-salute, and he was off, leading his men away.

Clarin got up to follow him. He would chase him down, kill all six of them if need be.

Gyrmund placed a restraining hand to his chest.

'We have Lyssa to find.'

'You find her.'

'Come on, Clarin. We'll have our chance to get Kaved another time.'

'How do you know?'

'I promise. Come on.'

They ran now, around the outskirts of the camp, then south, Gyrmund stopping every now and then to check the ground for signs of Lyssa's passing, or of the two men who chased her. Then he pointed into the distance, towards something lying in the grass. They ran over. Gyrmund turned the body over. It was young Alpin. He had been cut down.

Gyrmund left the body and looked around, reading the information left on the ground.

'This way,' he said curtly.

Clarin followed again, his mouth dry. He didn't want to find the dead body of a little girl. That would be too hard.

'Please Madria,' he whispered under his breath, trying to keep up with Gyrmund. 'Let her be alive.'

They ran, and two men came running the other way. Gyrmund was fighting the first before Clarin fully realised what was happening. He moved in towards the second man. He lunged at Clarin with a spear. Clarin caught the move with Cutter, blocking the spear aside, then he moved in with his shield, smashing it into his opponent's face. The blow felled the man. Clarin kicked the spear away to one side. Yes, he could have killed him. But maybe they needed him alive.

He looked up to see Gyrmund pulling his sword from the second man's chest. It didn't look like he would be able to tell them anything.

His attention returned to the man lying on the ground in front him. 'Where's the girl?' he demanded, moving the point of his crystal blade towards his face.

The sound of hoofbeats interrupted them before he got an answer.

Two knights appeared from the south. Theron was the first.

'Ah. You got them,' the new king said. 'Well done.'

The second knight pulled up. Evander. Behind him a little face poked out.

'Hi Gyrmund. Hi Clarin. Don't worry, I'm alright.'

'Did they hurt you?' he asked her.

'No. They didn't find me.'

Clarin thrust his sword into the neck of the man on the ground, slicing until he was dead. 'I'll give him a quick death, then.'

He could feel anger boiling inside him, so hot because it was partly aimed at his own pettiness. He should have been happy that Lyssa was alive and well. Of course, he was. But he had wanted to find Lyssa, and Theron had instead. It was always Theron.

'Let's go and help Belwynn,' Theron said. 'The Drobax will be closing in. We need to get out of here.'

Clarin turned and began marching back to the camp.

'Evander, please stay here with Lyssa,' he heard Theron say.

Gyrmund caught up with him.

'Are you alright, Clarin?'

Clarin grunted. He didn't want to talk to anyone.

There weren't so many of the enemy in the camp. They were men, not Isharites or Drobax. Haskans, maybe. Or Persaleians. They were barely holding off the Madrians, fighting desperately in the hope that the Drobax would reach the fight and relieve them. It was easy enough for Clarin, Theron and Gyrmund to come up behind them and finish off their resistance.

Clarin tore into them from behind. Something made him want to kill with Cutter; made him want to see the blood of his enemies on his blade. He hacked and stabbed with the crystal sword, only using his shield when he needed to defend himself. That wasn't often. The Madrians began to move past him but he stayed for as long as he could, until there was no-one left to kill.

Belwynn was lifted up to Theron's horse and they rode away together, leaving the rest of them to walk south.

Moneva and Gyrmund embraced, clinging to each other, the fear that the other was hurt now turned into relief.

Clarin wiped Cutter clean of blood and guts. He sheathed his sword and began to walk. Alone.

XIII

LEFT BEHIND

THEY MADE SMOOTH PASSAGE THROUGH the Brasingian Empire. Lord Emmett had met them on the Thessian border. It was another chance to reminisce about last summer's warfare. Emmett had commanded the right flank in what had since become known as the Battle of Lindhafen, and there was nothing soldiers liked to do more than to rehearse the details of a battle. Cerdda smiled along at the retelling, but it was grim stuff, and Edgar worried that they were making his brother-in-law more anxious than was wise. Emmett's news from the north didn't help, either. A huge Drobax army, as well as the dragon that had wreaked havoc in the Krykker lands, had come to Burkhard Castle. It was feared that the forces of the Emperor wouldn't be able to hold against such a combination for long.

Emmett oversaw the duchy in Coen's absence, and escorted them across the territory. The fields of Thesse were full of colour as spring began to move towards summer. The brief incursion of the Barissians last year had not done much to damage the economy here and Emmett was happy to feed their army from his own supplies. A mark of gratitude, he explained, for their willingness to help the Empire once again.

Once he had taken them to the eastern edge of the duchy, Emmett made his farewells. Here they could take the Great Road north towards Essenberg. The road had been built for the movement of armies and they made good time, crossing into Barissia. Edgar had visited the capital, Coldeberg, twice. Once to lay siege to it, resulting in the death of Duke Emeric. The second time, two months ago, to attend the coronation of his replacement, Duke Walter. There he had been reunited with Belwynn and Soren and been told about the significance of Toric's Dagger and the other weapons. He hoped that his cousins and their allies were close to completing their quest. For although parts of it sounded fanciful and strange, it remained the only plan that might end in the defeat of Ishari.

On this occasion they ignored the road to Coldeberg and stayed on the Great Road, which finally took them to Kelland, the duchy of Baldwin. Neither

Edgar or Cerdda had travelled this far north before, and while they wished it would have been in different circumstances, both agreed that they were excited to see Essenberg.

'I expect to learn a few things about civic organisation that I can apply when I return back home,' said Cerdda.

Edgar had his doubts. 'Nowhere in Magnia approaches Essenberg in size. Neither of us even has a capital, Cerdda.'

'Well, maybe we should.'

Edgar nodded along, more to avoid an argument than because he liked the idea.

It was no surprise that news of their coming would arrive in the city, and as Essenberg came into view, a small force rode out to meet them.

Edgar and Cerdda for the Magnians; Brock and Frayne for the Middians; Lord Kass, Baldwin's agent; all left the army behind. With them came Brictwin, Edgar's bodyguard. It was precautionary, but Edgar had already survived one assassination attempt. That kind of thing encouraged you to take precautions.

Breaking from the score of soldiers who had come from Essenberg, one man came to meet them.

'Lord Rainer,' Edgar greeted him, recognising Baldwin's chamberlain. He was the Emperor's chief official, the man who made the Empire work.

He impressed Edgar by greeting them all by name, those he was meeting for the first time as well as those he had met before.

'On behalf of the people of the Empire, I extend you all thanks for coming to our aid like this. Most of our soldiers are at Burkhard Castle, so there is room enough for all your men in our barracks. I have already seen to the arrangements. Even so, I must warn you that space is still at a premium. Essenberg has taken in many refugees from the north, putting pressure on our resources.'

'We are grateful for your attention,' said Cerdda.

Rainer paused then, as if unsure how to continue. A consummate politician, he looked suddenly uncomfortable.

'There is something else?' Edgar asked him.

'Yes, I'm afraid there is. When the Emperor left for Burkhard Castle, he left Empress Hannelore in charge of the duchy, including the defence of the city. Almost all our soldiers went with him. The Empress felt that left the city too vulnerable, so she decided to hire a mercenary captain to provide soldiers for the city's defence.'

Edgar wasn't sure what the problem was. Although they never described themselves as such, Brock and Frayne were really only one step removed from mercenary captains themselves. Then a thought crossed his mind. It was so outrageous that he almost rejected it out of hand, but there was clearly something unsettling Rainer.

'You're not trying to tell me that Gervase Salvinus and his crew are behind these walls?'

'I am afraid so, yes.'

A cold rage swallowed Edgar. He could feel his anger taking control, a series of violent actions running through his mind: striking Rainer down dead; breaking into Essenberg and tracking Salvinus down until he killed him. He had marched an army all the way here to be insulted like this?

Edgar wasn't the only one outraged by the revelation.

He looked at Brictwin first, who had been inside the tent with Edgar when Salvinus had killed his uncle Leofwin, stabbing him in the back while he defended Edgar. Brictwin's hand was on the hilt of his sword. Edgar moved over to him, grasping his arm. Brictwin looked at his prince then down at his hand, as if he hadn't even realised where it had gone. He took it away from his weapon, but Edgar couldn't mistake the look on his face.

Glancing at the others, he saw that Cerdda was shocked, Kass embarrassed. The two Middians looked ready for murder.

'Salvinus snuck into Prince Edgar's tent in the depth of night and tried to kill him!' Frayne declared angrily. '*Did* kill his councillor and bodyguard! He and his men fought for Emeric against us at Lindhafen. And what, you expect us to befriend him now? Work with him?'

'I am truly sorry,' said Rainer. The chamberlain held a hand out, ordering the soldiers he had come with to hold their position. Some of them had taken a few steps forward, concerned by the reactions of Edgar and his friends. 'All of Hannelore's councillors advised her against it. She let Salvinus into the city against our wishes. You must understand: she is the Empress. I can advise, but at the end of it all, I must obey.'

'So, what are you saying, Rainer?' Edgar asked him, his voice cold as he tried to maintain control.

'We are desperate for your help. But I can't let you in to Essenberg if it will lead to bloodshed in the streets. I must maintain order here. So I need your oath, Edgar. I need you to swear that you will work with Salvinus, that you won't seek revenge. If you can't do that, I understand. But I can't let you in.'

***

RIMMON LEFT his tent and strode out through the camp. The soldiers sat in groups, taking their time over their breakfast as only soldiers knew how, another day of doing nothing stretching out before them. He attracted suspicious looks as he passed, even from his own countrymen. One of the problems with being a red-headed mage was that everyone knew who you were. The mage who had followed Shira into rebellion and yet lived. Not trusted by those loyal to Ishari, for he was pardoned only because he was useful. Not trusted by the Haskans, who wondered what treachery he had committed in order to be spared. Not trusted by anyone.

Still, the suspicions of the soldiers meant little to him. It was Peroz, as the eyes of Siavash, who really mattered. If he decided that keeping Rimmon alive was a risk no longer worth taking, he would die. But Peroz had been called back to Samir Durg, and so the eyes of the Order of Diis were off him for a few days.

He left the camp behind, finding his own little part of the Kalinthian Plain. Dreadfully dull to look at, but empty of people. The air was fresh. It was damp, blowing in from the west. Sometimes Rimmon thought it carried the smell from the battlefield with it, the corpses of Drobax and Kalinthians left to rot in the open. Or perhaps it was just his imagination. Unlike some of the ghouls in the host, he had not gone to inspect the site. He took no pleasure from the deaths of Kalinthians. And the Drobax disgusted him when alive, never mind when dead.

He turned at the sound of footsteps behind him. So, there were still eyes on him, after all. Herin, the general of the host, along with the Drobax leader, Kull. The creature was never far from his side, Herin finding something infinitely amusing about a Drobax that could speak.

'I was told I might find you here,' Herin said, perhaps reminding him that the soldiers reported to him. It seemed true enough. The common soldiery liked Herin, no doubt recognising him as one of their own.

'Why do I need to be found?'

'I've been invited to a meeting of the generals. Not easy to decline. It would be useful to have a wizard with me. Might make the others a little nervous—that you might curse them or whatnot.'

Herin always used the term 'wizard' to describe his kind, a childish sounding word to Rimmon's ears. He also liked to pretend he knew nothing of magic, but Rimmon could tell that wasn't the case. Indeed, Herin liked to pretend he was far more stupid than he really was. It was a ruse that worked with most people, because they were predisposed to believe it. Not Rimmon, though. He knew that Herin was as dangerous as they came.

They walked south-west to a neutral meeting point, somewhere between the camps of the four hosts. From here they could see the walls of Heractus, just two miles to the south, a grey city under grey clouds.

Each general had come, as diverse a group as one could imagine leading the armies of Ishari. Etan of Haskany, Linus of Persala, Kaved the Krykker, and Herin of Magnia. This was Siavash's plan. All chosen for their military skills—and all powerless. For none were Isharites; none had a following of any note; none were a rival. Each useful, but easily removed if need be. Not only that, each host they commanded had a servant of Diis attached to it. These figures were the real power, and they reported directly to Siavash.

Like Herin, the other generals had brought a few henchmen each with them. Rimmon was quick to note that only one other was a mage. That was the key to his own survival. It was never discussed, but the Isharites had few mages left. Ever since their invasion of the Grand Caladri, their numbers had been reduced. The civil war between Siavash and Arioc had only made things worse. Apparently, four more had been killed in the battle two nights past. Found together, they each had an arrow in them. Targeted by the enemy. A double-edged sword for Rimmon. It meant that he was a target, too. But it also meant that his value increased.

'Well met colleagues,' said Herin, his persona relaxed, his smile and his words gently mocking. 'Are we to quickly discuss tactics while our masters are away?'

'Have a care with your words,' Linus warned him. He was big, muscular, every inch a soldier. Rumour had it that Linus was an old rival of King Mark of Persala. That he had been amongst the first in that country to bend the knee to the invader.

Jamie Edmundson

'Come now,' said the Krykker, 'no-one here doubts the loyalty of Herin, surely? Even despite the strange sights we have witnessed.'

A tension existed between these two, everyone could sense it. They had a history. It felt like at any moment they might drop the pretence and have their hands around each other's throat.

'Strange sights?' asked Herin. 'I'm sure you intend to share.'

'It would be hard to believe if I hadn't seen it with my own eyes,' said Kaved. 'Your brother, and his friend, Gyrmund. Fighting for the Kalinthians against us.'

All eyes were on Herin now. Kaved was playing it cool, not yet accusing him of anything.

'You saw him during the battle?' Herin asked.

'Aye. With my own eyes.'

'You killed him?'

'No. I didn't get the chance.'

Herin laughed. 'You were on the battlefield with him, you said. If that's not your chance, I don't know what is.'

'He was a good distance away,' Kaved replied, irritated.

'Close enough to see is close enough to kill in my book.' Herin held up his hands as an angry expression came to Kaved's face. 'I understand, Kaved. My brother is a big man. Most men would see their courage falter if they came across him on the battlefield. Though it is known that I bested him with a sword.'

'Saw it myself,' Kull confirmed.

A look of disgust and hatred crossed the faces of the men gathered at Kull's intervention. It was the same reaction he always got, but he didn't seem to mind.

'Bested him but set him free, that's what I heard,' said Kaved, returning to the offensive. 'Free to kill our soldiers.'

'Your point?' Herin asked, his turn now to let his irritation show.

'Take it as a friendly warning, Herin, that's all,' said Kaved, smiling as he sensed he had gained the upper hand. 'I'm sure there were good reasons why your host was late to the battle here, only arriving once it was all over.'

'We had to fight our way across Kalinth,' Herin hissed.

'Indeed. But you managed that with very few fatalities. Those of us in the battle took many losses.'

128

'My host, along with Kaved's, took the brunt of what Kalinth threw at us,' Linus now joining in. 'Wave after wave of arrows, charge after charge from the Knights. Etan's host had to press back their new king,' he added.

Etan kept quiet, non-committal. The most cautious of the generals. Rimmon knew why. He had fought for Shira too.

'What are you saying?' Herin demanded, turning on Linus, ignoring Kaved now. 'That my host should have to take Heractus alone?'

'And why not?' Linus threw back, looking over for support from the other two generals. 'Why not demonstrate your commitment?'

But the look Kaved gave the Persaleian was an unhappy one.

'Very well!' Herin said quickly. 'If you will excuse me, I will prepare immediately.'

He turned and left, not waiting for a reaction. Rimmon and Kull were quick to follow.

'What?' he heard Linus ask defensively as they left.

'Fools,' said Herin once they were out of earshot. 'We will take Heractus by ourselves, just as we killed King Mark and took the Shield of Persala. Then Siavash will be left in no doubt about who his most able servants are.'

***

ONCE THEY got Oisin down from the mountain and into Nemyr's house he needed feeding. It was hard to imagine how the king could have lasted hundreds of years without sustenance, but it was clear that it had left him with an appetite.

Word soon got around amongst this small community of his arrival and, without being asked to, everyone got to work on making dishes. Oisin sat at Nemyr's table and began to eat. Dalla had cut and washed his hair and his beard for him. Nonetheless, they were soon wet and greasy. Huge tureens of milky soup were carried in, requiring two people to grip the handles on either side of the dish, but Oisin raised them to his lips like a bowl, glugging down the hot liquid. He politely thanked every cook, praising their food, but showed no signs of stopping.

Nemyr wasn't the only herder who sacrificed one of their flock for the Giant. Roasted sheep, yak and goat came in on huge platters. Oisin wasted little of the animals, popping huge globules of dripping fat into his mouth as if it were sweetmeat, cracking bones so that he could suck out the marrow.

Finally, he was sated.

'Do you need to sleep now, Your Majesty?' Dalla asked him, a look of concern on her face as she looked at his distended belly.

Oisin chuckled. 'No, little lady, I have had my fill of sleep. But I need to rest while I digest that feast. A seat by your fire would be most welcome.'

'Would you be willing to pass the time with a tale of the last war against Ishari?' Rabigar asked him. 'Everyone likes a story of heroes, and there may be details of it that would be helpful.'

Nemyr's family and friends gathered about the King of the Giants, last of his kind, as he told them his story.

'It was said that Diis and his followers, the Isharites, came to Dalriya from another world, by magic. If so, they came to conquer it for themselves. Madria, the goddess of our lands, was hard pressed. The Orias fought and bled for her, most of our kind falling at the hands of the enemy, undone by their magic and cunning. The other races of Dalriya suffered too, I know, until it came to be that Madria called upon a champion from each race of Dalriya to come together.

'It was the Avakabi, Masego, who was the closest to Madria; though more distant with the rest of us, for the Avakabi have ever held on to their own language. He was given the dagger. Kaisa of the Caladri, a great witch, was given the staff. Four warriors were armed, too: Bolivar the Krykker with a sword; Cloelius of Persala with a shield; Turgen the Jalakh came with a bow; and, of course, King Oisin had the spear of the Orias. That just left the Queen of the Asrai, with her cloak.'

'And the Asrai Queen, she came from the Lantinen Sea?' Rabigar asked, knowing that they had yet to find this cloak. All they had to go on until now was what Farred had seen from the charts of a Sea Caladri captain.

'Aye, I believe so, though you must understand that few of us ever became close. The Queen of the Asrai was a fiery thing who had little time for the rest of us. I never learned her name. Many others of us hailed from races who considered each other enemies. We were allies out of necessity, you see. I formed a great friendship with your countryman, Bolivar. But with the others, the bonds of friendship were weaker. Perhaps, if we had more time, we could have become more of a team. I wonder if that was a cause of our failure.'

Rabigar had never heard the word failure used in relation to Bolivar's exploits before. But he had come to learn that the Krykker legends had not preserved the full story.

'We met Erkindrix and the Isharites at a location that is now on the island of Alta, though then there was no island. While the armies fought, we brought our weapons to kill Erkindrix, and thereby kill Diis. Diis had learned of us, and made his own weapons to stop us. Seven crystal swords, each of a different colour: sharper than obsidian, unbreakably strong.'

'I hear that the Isharites have many such swords now,' Rabigar said. 'My friends mined the diatine crystal for a while, in the prison mines of Samir Durg.'

'If that is true, then the Isharites have grown more powerful than in my day,' Oisin said unhappily. 'Back then, we fought our way past the seven Isharite warriors, though some of our number fell to their swords. When we reached Erkindrix, we should have been able to kill him. But something was wrong. Neither the Spear of my people nor Bolivar's Sword could finish him. There was something Madria had wanted us to do that day, and we failed her. Madria and Diis fought then, pouring all of their power against one another. But neither could win, and the more they clashed, the more the land about them became unstable. When it cracked, the sea came rushing in. The armies of both sides had to flee for their lives, neither leaving with a victory.

'Those champions who still lived, took up the weapons and returned them to their peoples, with tales of their fallen heroes. Bolivar and I returned the dagger to the Lippers, the staff to the Caladri, and the shield to the humans of Persala. Knowing that I might be needed again, I decided to take myself to the cold wastes of my homeland. Here, along with my wife Niamh and brother Cillian, I could sleep, ready to bring my spear again if I was needed.

'I had heard rumours that others of my kind still lived in the far north of Halvia, and I believe one of their descendants sits among us,' he said, gesturing to Gunnhild. 'Bolivar agreed with my plan, and ordered that Krykkers should settle in Halvia, with instructions to send for me should I be needed. Meanwhile, a small band of honourable Vismarians entered my service, and travelled west with me. To them I gave the duty of watching over our resting place, protecting us from any enemy while we slept. When one of Bolivar's people came to wake me, they would know my location, and take them to it.

So, the story finishes with the arrival of Rabigar and Stenk, and of all of you, Nemyr's folk, who have fulfilled the duties you were given.'

The people of the mountain clapped in appreciation and began asking Oisin questions about his story. Rabigar grew thoughtful about what the king had told them. His story filled in many of the gaps in his knowledge. And yet, one inescapable fact could not be ignored. Bolivar, Oisin and their allies had gathered all seven weapons of Madria—and still failed. Despite Rabigar's success, their chances of victory remained remote, and more sacrifices would need to be made.

The next day, Oisin was ready to travel. The brothers Ketil and Jesper would lead the group down the mountain. The time had come for Rabigar to tell them of his decision.

'I will not be coming with you,' he said. He saw the surprise in their faces. Although he had not known many of them for long, he still found the reaction moving; found what he had to say difficult.

'Last night Oisin told us of the significance of the sword and spear we carry. They must be taken to Dalriya as soon as possible. It is a difficult and perilous journey. If I try to make the journey with you now, in my condition, I will inevitably slow you down.'

'Nonsense!' Oisin exclaimed. 'Dearest Rabigar, I shall simply pull you along in the sled like I pulled you down this mountainside. It is nothing to me.'

'It is time wasted, Your Majesty. Every hour the monsters get closer to the homes of our kin, and so every hour counts. When you reach Dalriya, you must find Belwynn and Soren and any others who carry Madria's weapons. You must do this as quickly as possible. Bring the sled but carry the supplies on it. Should Stenk or Gunnhild pick up an injury, then use the sled to save them. But it would be foolish in the extreme, and selfish, for me to attempt this journey now. I am not healed from my injury. I am still too weak. I must not pretend otherwise, because there is far more at stake than my life and my pride.'

His friends bowed their heads, their looks of surprise turning to sadness.

Rabigar unbuckled Bolivar's Sword.

'Stenk, I name you Guardian of the Sword. I know you will keep it safe.'

Stenk had tears in his eyes as he took the weapon. 'I will fulfil this mission for you Rabigar.'

He told the young Krykker then what needed to be done with the weapon.

'I would humbly ask if I could take Master Rabigar's place,' said Jesper, Nemyr's youngest. 'I will put my shoulder to the paddle on the Nasvarl, and do anything else that is asked of me.'

He looked about him hopefully.

'You have my permission, son,' said Nemyr gravely. 'It would be an honour to my family if you think Jesper would provide some value to the expedition, Your Majesty.'

'But of course!' said Oisin. 'It tempers my sadness at leaving Rabigar behind with some joy.'

The Giant approached Rabigar and gave him a hug, careful not to squeeze too hard, before slapping Jesper on the back.

A sombre silence descended on them all then, as those who were leaving readied their packs and made their final preparations. When it was time to go, Dalla hung on to her youngest brother for a while before letting him go. Gunnhild came for Rabigar and gave him a crushing hug, far stronger than the one Oisin had delivered. She released him, giving him a nod.

'Don't worry,' she said, loud enough for Nemyr and Dalla to hear as well. 'I will look after them all.'

Then they left, making their way down the mountainside. The three who remained stayed to watch until they were gone. It did not take long for the forms of Ketil, Jesper and Stenk to disappear, a little longer for Gunnhild. Oisin disappeared and reappeared several times before they were sure they would see no more of him.

'It is much harder to be left behind,' said Rabigar, his heart heavy. He didn't have to look at Nemyr and Dalla to know they agreed. They already knew it. But it was a new experience for Rabigar. Until this moment, he had always been the one doing the leaving.

He didn't like it. Not one bit.

XIV

THE ASRAI

S OREN HAD BEEN GIVEN ALL THE LUCK he could have asked for, he knew that. Perhaps Madria was at work, in that way gods seemed to behave: leaving you in doubt as to whether they were responsible for all, some or none of the events in one's life.

The Duke of Martras, ruler of the ports that dotted the northwest coast of Guivergne, had been sympathetic to his cause once Farred's name was mentioned. The Magnian had come this way a month prior, full of warnings of Drobax and of the dragon. The dragon hadn't come to Guivergne, but the Drobax had, pouring across the country's borders with the Krykkers and the Grand Caladri. In Martras the creatures had been pushed back, the king raising an army and coming to fight. Further to the east, the duke had explained, there had not been such a complete success. The Guivergnais had retreated to the Cousel, leaving everything north of the river to the monsters.

Since the duke felt he owed Farred a debt of thanks, he had agreed to put Soren on a ship that would take him south. The captain insisted on sailing at night only, fearful of the Kharovians, who had started to seize Guivergnais shipping and even begun to raid the coastline. So it was, that they passed the eerie Forest of Morbaine at night. It acted much as the Wilderness did further south, separating the two states with miles of impenetrable woodland. Once past this it was Morbaine proper, ruled by the King of Guivergne's brother, before docking safely in North Magnia.

It was here that Soren had his second piece of good fortune. Not far from the harbour where he was dropped off lay Wincandon, an estate of the Prince of North Magnia. Warned of the presence of a foreign ship, he was visited by a delegation from the royal family, led by the two princesses of Magnia, Irmgard of the north, and Elfled of the south.

Soren learned that his cousin, Edgar, had not only got himself married to Cerdda's sister, but got her pregnant as well. Further, that he and Cerdda had led an army to the Empire. In the absence of their husbands, the two women were pleased to offer him help: his own private room upstairs in the hall, with his meals provided; and an escort to and from the beach, in the shape of Elfled's bodyguard, Morlin.

With this support in place, Soren could focus on his quest to find the Asrai. He was under no illusions about the difficulty of his task, but even so, the enormity of it struck him on the first day. Using Onella's Staff, he created a spherical shield around himself—a bubble of air. He walked into the waves. His shield kept the water away and he began to move into the sea.

There was a lot of trial and error at first, but there was such a large area to cover, he had to perfect the movement. At last, he was able to direct his bubble, pushing it in the direction he wanted to go, gathering speed as it went. Now he could scour the Lantinen, looking for signs of the Asrai. He didn't have much to go on—a story, passed from one mouth to another, of a Caladri map showing islands.

The cost of expending magic in this way, for hours at a time, was immense. Without Onella's Staff it would have been impossible. Even with it, he felt the damage it did to his body. But what choice did he have? He kept looking, kept using his magic, though careful not to overextend himself like he had done in the Wilderness. If he lost consciousness here, he would simply drown. The staff would be lost to the bottom of the sea, and the cloak never found. But the more he looked, the further away the Asrai seemed. There were no landmarks in the ocean to mark place or distance; just endless stretches of water. He tried looking down at the seabed to help him navigate, convinced that he was searching the same location over and over; but the water was murky and the depths of the Lantinen obscure and unhelpful.

He would return to the beach exhausted, dragging himself across the sand, until Morlin spied him. With unusual patience, the bodyguard would wait for him for hours at a time, then pick him up, put him on his horse, and take him back to Wincandon. It may have seemed a small service to some, but Soren couldn't have kept going without it.

He said as much to Morlin one morning, as they returned to the beach, their horses picking their way down along the now familiar route. The bodyguard raised an eyebrow at the compliment.

'I fought under Farred and Ashere at Burkhard Castle last summer,' he said, in his slow, quiet voice. 'We all thought we would die on that rock; the Drobax getting closer every day. Sitting on a beach all day doesn't feel like a hard job in comparison.'

'What was Prince Ashere like?' Soren asked, his curiosity piqued.

A subtle change came over Morlin then, as if only now was he fully awake.

'I've been very lucky,' he began, 'to have served under Farred, and now Prince Edgar and Princess Elfled. They are very generous lords. But there was something special about Ashere, I must admit. Something that made you want to fight with him; go to hell with him, just to see if he could lead you out again. I suppose in a way that's what happened.'

'You went to hell?'

'The last time he led us out, the Isharites set an ambush. They hid their army under a belt of fog. Used their magic,' he said, glancing nervously at Soren as he used the word. 'It was a massacre. Ashere never recovered his health.'

But Soren barely noticed, because Morlin's words had hit home in an unexpected way.

'Hid with magic,' he repeated, focusing on the idea. 'I think I've been a little foolish. What if the Asrai have been hiding their whereabouts?'

He was talking out loud, but Morlin understood he was really talking to himself, and left him to his thoughts. When they got to the beach, Soren readied himself with a bit more hope.

'Today may be the day,' he said to Morlin with enthusiasm.

'Good. I'll wait here anyway. Just in case.'

Soren headed out to sea again, to the area of the Lantinen Maragin had described to him: south of Halvia, west of Dalriya. This time he was aware of the need to search for magic, a spell that might be hiding the whereabouts of the islands. Using Onella's Staff he tuned in to the echoes of magic, the traces that remain when power is used. It drew him, so he thought. But all he could see was the same empty blue vista. He scanned the surface, looking for any sign.

A ripple of movement on the horizon ahead, the suggestion of a pair of legs, just for a moment, before they disappeared under the waves. Soren headed in that direction.

The aura of magic was unmistakeable now. It covered a large area, misleading his senses. But now that he was aware of it, its power over him faltered. Falling away in front of him, the vision of an empty sea disappeared, and a chain of islands was revealed.

He made for the nearest of them, a tiny parcel of land barely poking above the water: sand, rock and some vegetation all there was to see. Nonetheless, it felt good to put his feet on something solid, and it afforded him something of a view of the rest of the islands.

They spread out before him. Some were no larger than the one he stood on; others were simply vertical chunks of rock, an ideal nesting place for sea birds, maybe, but not capable of supporting much else. A few were more substantial looking. These were the ones where he might find the mysterious people he was looking for: the Asrai. His current vantage point, however, gave him no clues. He could see thick foliage, yellow sand, bare rock, but nothing that might indicate civilisation. No buildings, no agriculture—nothing.

Soren was tired, it was true, but he was so close now he decided it was worth spending more of his dwindling energy on the search. With so many islands, a search from the sea could conceivably go on for hours until he found a sign of habitation. From the air, however, he would make quicker progress.

Gripping Onella's Staff, drawing on the extra power it gave him, Soren floated several feet into the air. He then moved, guiding himself towards the nearest island that held some promise. When he arrived he floated even higher, until he reached a height that allowed him to inspect the whole island.

What he saw was a location that could have supported a small population. A rock pool in the middle of the island provided fresh water, and a variety of fruit bearing trees and bushes were thriving in different parts of the island. He could hear birds squawking in the trees and it was more than likely that small mammals also had their home here. But there were no signs of human or near-human life.

Doubt crept into Soren's mind. If the Asrai had once lived here, hundreds of years ago, it was surely possible that they had died out since. Some natural calamity could have occurred in that time. It didn't help, of course, that he didn't know what he was looking for. He had assumed until now that they would be creatures like the other races of Dalriya: two legs and two arms, like the humans, Caladri, Krykkers and Lippers. Some other creature, more alien in appearance, could be much harder to locate. But pushing those doubts aside was a simple fact. Some power had been at work here, hiding the islands from him. He had to find whoever or whatever was trying to protect the place.

He looked at the other islands, trying to decide where to explore next. A movement in the water caught his attention. Something was swimming towards one of the islands. He moved towards it, travelling as fast as he could. He held it in his sights. It was hard to make out at first, as different parts of the creature emerged and submerged into the sea. But it soon became clear it was human-like. Long, green-coloured hair trailed behind it. Human-like legs kicked in the water, making a splash. Human-like, Soren observed, but with webbed feet. Just as he made this observation, the creature dived under the water, disappearing from view.

Soren followed it, dropping from the sky. He formed his protective shield around himself as he entered the water. Desperately looking about, he saw two pale legs kicking, as the creature—he was sure now it must be an Asrai—continued to dive down. He followed, the spherical bubble around him keeping the water out and allowing him to breathe. He had enough air to last a while, but he would have to resurface eventually.

The pale legs he was following began to kick further away, and the murky sea water reduced the distance that Soren could see. He lost sight of his quarry but continued in the direction it had been taking, desperate not to lose this opportunity.

The sea became much darker. Looking up, he could see that he was now swimming underneath the rocky outcrops of the island. Fear gripped him. It was already getting more difficult to breathe. But he pressed on further, hoping that he might find answers if he did. Up ahead, further under the island, he could see a lighter patch of water. He struggled towards it, holding his breath as the air around him turned stale. When he reached it, he pushed straight up. He could see the surface of the water now. Then finally, he broke through, taking a gasp of air.

He was in a cavern of some kind, under the island. The seawater took up approximately half of the area. Beyond it, shafts of light from above revealed that the other half of the cavern consisted of a rocky floor that overlooked the water. Soren saw a few figures on the platform—pale-skinned, with green hair. He headed for the rocky floor of the cavern. Exhausted now, still gripping his staff, he pulled himself out of the water and lay there for a few moments, gasping as his lungs pulled in the damp cavern air.

Once he had recovered, Soren got to his feet. He was standing on what appeared to be a natural cavern floor. Much of it was bordered by a rocky wall, but at the far end was a gap plenty big enough to walk through. Sunlight came in from there, indicating that it was an entrance into the cavern, presumably easier than entering via the sea.

Five figures looked at him. Four of them were Asrai. They were female and wore no clothing. They shared the same pale skin, almost blue in this dim light; the same green hair and slim shape. Their hands and feet were webbed. He couldn't tell whether any of them was the one that he had followed here, but it was clear that they were creatures of the water as much as of the land.

The fifth figure he knew, and wished he hadn't found. Cautiously, he moved towards them. He passed three of the Asrai, giving them as wide a berth as possible. They looked at him, eyes dark, expressions hard to read. Their skin was damp and they smelt of the sea. He found them alluring and alien at the same time. He could sense the fear in them, like they were trapped animals, but they didn't move or make a sound as he passed.

He stopped in front of the fifth figure. Arioc was sitting on the rocky floor, back against the wall, legs stretched out. Between his legs was a collection of food, mostly fruit. In one hand he held a raw fish, half-eaten. Soren guessed, or sensed maybe, that some of the Asrai had brought Arioc his dinner. The end of a piece of rope was tied around the wizard's left wrist. It was made from some substance Soren had never seen before—smooth and lustrous, it shimmered in the half-light of the cavern, but at the same time it looked incredibly strong. The rope led to the fourth of the Asrai, crouched on the other side of Arioc. It was tied around one ankle. Soren looked at her. It was a sadness, more so than fear, that he felt when he did.

'I know you,' Arioc said, in a way that suggested he wasn't sure how.

'We met briefly in Edeleny,' Soren reminded him. 'You captured me and had me put in a box, taken to Samir Durg, where you delivered me to Siavash.'

'Of course,' said Arioc. 'From whom you somehow escaped, marched into the Throne Room of Samir Durg and helped me to kill Erkindrix.' He pointed. 'The staff of the Caladri? That's why you were in Edeleny?'

'Yes.'

'Your name?'

'Soren.'

'Ah. I remember now. Moneva told me about you. Well, it's all very impressive, I must say. I had thought if anybody would find me here, it would be the agents of Siavash, sent to kill me. Instead it is a follower of Madria. That would suggest either that the Isharite advance goes slowly, or that Siavash has already won. And you've come here to hide. Which is it?'

'Siavash hasn't won. And I'm not here to hide.'

'I see.'

'And what is the King of Haskany doing here?' Soren asked, waving a hand at the strange cavern, taking in the Asrai.

Arioc grunted, biting off a piece of the fish. He looked over at the seawater that lapped against the rock. 'I underestimated Siavash, that was my mistake. Wasted time killing Ardashir; fighting Pentas. When I look back now, back then in the Throne Room, I think Diis chose Siavash as soon as Erkindrix died. He saw my actions as treacherous. Maybe if I had chased Siavash down there and then, killed him, Diis would have seen that I was the natural successor. Would have joined with me. Instead, I let Siavash get too strong.' Arioc looked at Soren. 'You must know what happened. That Siavash and Dorjan destroyed my forces?'

Soren nodded.

'I took my army to defeat Pentas and Shira. Siavash was waiting for me. I barely escaped. Have you heard what happened to those two?'

'Pentas and Shira are both dead,' Soren said, not wishing to waste time on the details.

Arioc blew out some air. 'Have a heart, Soren. That's my wife you're talking about. I'm serious. Never really appreciated her at the time, but what I wouldn't give now for one last fuck with Queen Shira. Instead all I have are these creatures to entertain me.' All of a sudden, he tugged the rope around his wrist. The Asrai tied to the other end had her leg taken from under her and was dragged to the floor. 'The Queen of the Asrai, you know?' Arioc said, pointing at her with his fish. 'A bit of a let-down, wouldn't you say?'

There was something so wrong with Arioc's treatment of the Asrai that Soren had to force himself to suppress his natural reaction. Arioc was one of the most powerful wizards of Dalriya. For some reason, he was telling Soren things he needed to know. He had to bide his time: wait, to find out what his best strategy should be.

'So, you came here?' he prompted Arioc.

'Yes. Ardashir, useless though he proved to be, had at least identified who each of Madria's weapons belonged to. We all agreed that it was that staff you hold that was key. Defeating the Grand Caladri and getting our hands on it would be the biggest obstacle. Whichever one of us wielded the staff would see their power enhanced. Naturally, I made sure that it would be me. I did the hard part, broke the Caladri. But Pentas spirited the weapon away at the last minute. That's when things started to go awry. Anyway, to answer your question. I needed a place to hide from Siavash. He would be desperate to have me caught, to secure his position. But where in Dalriya is beyond the reach of Ishari, Soren? Not many places. I chose this one. If Siavash stopped to think, he would have sent his followers here. But they never came. Looks like he's had other things on his mind.'

Like sending his shadow to Kalinth, Soren thought to himself. But Arioc would be oblivious of this.

'I've been stuck down here for the last two months. The first thing I did was find their queen. She can't escape from this bond,' Arioc said, waving the piece of smooth rope. 'Guarantees me my food and drink. I'm sure the bitches would like to see me dead, but it would only take me seconds to kill her.'

Arioc studied Soren now. 'Ardashir didn't know what all the weapons were. But he knew that one of them belonged to the Asrai. I told them to bring it to me, but they said they couldn't. I had to kill one of them to make sure they weren't lying to me.'

Soren felt the Asrai around him stir at this, but they remained silent.

'I was beginning to assume that the creatures had lost it long ago, that surely there was nothing of any value in this hovel of a place. But then you show up, Soren. Why else would you be here, but to claim the weapon?'

Soren shrugged. 'Maybe I like exploring.'

Arioc smiled at that. 'Maybe. I am impressed that you found this place, but you must be very tired now, and you must know that I would find it easy to strike you down.'

Soren allowed himself a look at the Asrai Queen. He saw something different now. What he had taken at first glance to be a watery wetness about her, was perhaps something else. Was she wearing the cloak? If so, it seemed odd that Arioc had not noticed it. But if he had been expecting a sword or dagger or some other hand-held weapon, he may have thought nothing of the watery clothes that the queen wore.

'But you know the saying,' Arioc continued, 'the enemy of my enemy is my friend? Think about that. You know that I want Siavash dead. If I had the weapon of the Asrai, I could fight with you. With my help you could destroy Siavash; destroy Diis once and for all. In return I would become the ruler of my people, but we would hardly be a threat to you any more without Diis in Dalriya. You won't get a better chance, Soren.'

Jamie Edmundson

Soren pretended to think about it. *I'm hardly going to fall for that,* he told himself. *As soon as he gets his hands on the cloak he will kill me and take the staff as well. Yes, maybe then he would go to find and kill Siavash. But only to replace him—bond with Diis himself.* But just because he saw through Arioc's offer, it didn't mean he had some way out of the situation. Because he knew that Arioc was right. He didn't have the strength to defeat the Isharite.

'It is a persuasive offer,' he said, desperate now to buy some time, to think of a way out.

Neither he nor Arioc saw the Queen of the Asrai move until they heard the splash in the water.

Arioc was on his feet in an instant, moving to the edge of the water, hand raised as if ready to send some terrible blast of magic at the queen.

'Not possible!' he shouted.

Soren peered down into the depths. Expecting to see the pale form of the queen, still tied to Arioc's rope, instead he saw nothing but the rope drifting under the water. Somehow, she had gone.

The patter of feet on rock made Arioc look back up. The three Asrai were running for the water. Face full of rage, Arioc threw a bolt of deadly magic in their direction with one hand, a second with his other. Acting on instinct, Soren blocked both strikes, negating them with his own magic. Three splashes followed, as the Asrai dived into the sea.

Arioc looked at Soren now, eyes burning with anger.

'That was a very stupid thing to do.'

He stretched both arms out towards Soren and directed a blast of magic at him. Raising Onella's Staff, Soren defended as best he could. But the blast kept coming, an endless charge of magic coming from the powerful Isharite. Soren stumbled backwards from the force, until his back was against the wall of the cavern. Arioc stepped towards him, keeping the strength of the magic constant, pinning him against the wall. Soren couldn't hold it back for much longer. The charge would soon reach him, and destroy him.

Then suddenly, Arioc was flying backwards. His left arm, still tied to the length of rope, was pulled towards the sea with such a force that he went with it, dragged into the water. There was a splash, the sound of struggling, and then silence.

Soren, sagging against the wall of the cavern, got to his feet, using Onella's Staff to hold his weight. Then, in front of him, four heads emerged from the

142

water, green hair floating on the surface. The Asrai pulled themselves out, dark eyes trained on him.

The queen approached him, while the other three stayed back. A line of blood ran from the corner of her mouth down her chin. She stopped in front of him, the salty tang of seawater hitting his nostrils. She opened her mouth, showing him two rows of sharp-looking, bloody teeth. Soren didn't need to ask what had happened to Arioc. What might happen to him.

He kneeled down, resting his staff on the floor. His eyesight instantly disappeared, leaving him virtually blind. He took the smooth rope, still tied around the queen's ankle, in his hands. It pulsed with a kind of magic, that would keep the knot tied forever. But it was a faint magic, perhaps because Arioc was now dead. Breaking the spell with his own, Soren untied the knot. He grabbed his staff, re-imaging his surroundings so that he could see again, and got to his feet.

He swayed, close to collapsing now. He had expended too much magic today, and desperately needed rest. He looked the Queen of the Asrai in the eye.

'My name is Soren. I have come on behalf of Madria. We are gathering her weapons once more,' he said, eyeing the almost translucent cloak around her shoulders.

'I am Tana,' she said, her voice a soft murmur. 'You know that I wear the Cloak of our people, don't you?'

'I guessed as much.'

'Do you know what it does?' she asked. She pressed the cloak to her body, lithe and pale beneath the watery shimmer. Soren felt the urge to pull the cloak away, to touch her body; and yet at the same time, there was something about the creature that repulsed him.

'You disappeared when you hit the water.'

'Yes. It allows the wearer to go invisible. If I had used it once Arioc caught me, he would have realised that the weapon was in front of him all the time. I took a risk using it when you came. But you helped us,' she said, waving a hand at the Asrai behind her.

'Arioc and the Isharites are our enemies.'

'And the enemy of my enemy is my friend, right?' replied the Queen, repeating Arioc's words. It wasn't hard to miss the sarcasm in her voice.

Soren shrugged. 'I have not come here to steal the Cloak from you. I am here to ask you whether you can help us—like the Asrai did once before. You could choose not to, and I would leave. But one of the Isharites has already found your realm,' he said, gesturing to the water, where Arioc's body had perhaps now sunk to the seabed.

He sagged, the argument gone out of him.

Tana grabbed his arm, holding him up.

'You will rest now. My people will care for you. Then the Asrai must decide what is to be done.'

XV

THE REALM OF THE DEAD

I T FELT LIKE AN ODD THING TO BE DOING. At the rear of the army, Farred was extinguishing each lantern he came to. Somewhere up above, Godfrey and the brave souls who had stayed on the Emperor's Crag were holding out for as long as they could. If anyone followed them down here, it would be the enemy, and Farred didn't want to leave potential pursuers a glowing sign of the route they had taken.

At the front of the army, Walter was leading their force through the tunnels. Farred didn't envy him. The marshal, meticulous as ever, had explored the area underneath the crag. But even so, it was not an easy job picking the right direction, in the darkness of these caves, with nearly forty thousand men behind you to notice if you got it wrong.

Walter ordered a halt on the first night, for the soldiers to get some sleep, even though every hour of the day seemed like night-time. Farred estimated that he must be at least a mile behind Walter's position. He settled down, too nervous to sleep, and kept a watch out in case they were followed.

He tried to ignore Baldwin and Inge sneaking off together to an unexplored part of the cave network. He tried not to think about what they were doing, but the tinkle of her laughter echoed around the tunnels and Baldwin's men sniggered and raised their eyebrows.

How Walter decided it was time to move, Farred didn't know. He just knew that the men ahead got to their feet and started walking, so he did the same. Nervous muttering carried back to him. Baldwin and Inge stood waiting for him to catch up.

'Did anyone pass you in the night?' the Emperor asked him.

'No. I'm certain. I was awake all night.'

'Me too,' leered Inge.

Baldwin ignored her. 'Some of the men are saying they've lost comrades since we stopped. I suppose they may have wandered about and got lost.'

'They could have moved further up the line,' Farred suggested.

'If you bring the living into the Realm of the Dead, don't be surprised if some don't make it out,' Inge said.

Farred couldn't tell whether it was one of her jokes or not. Baldwin ignored her, and so he did the same.

They kept walking, hour upon hour. The faces of the soldiers around him became increasingly careworn. Farred began to hear complaints. Faint mutterings at first, but increasingly bold. He understood it. After a while it felt like the rock was closing in on you. The dampness of the air was cloying, and it felt like you couldn't get enough into your lungs to breathe properly. The constant drip of water hitting the ground began to fill his ears. Farred was desperate to get out, to get fresh air. He began to wonder if staying on the crag to fight wouldn't have been the better option than wandering in these tunnels.

As these thoughts began to enter his head, some of the soldiers began to express them out loud.

'Quiet!' Baldwin's voice boomed suddenly. 'No-one's asked for your opinion.'

'Fuck you,' someone shouted. 'Go fuck your witch!'

'Who said that?' Baldwin demanded.

Farred could hear the rage in his voice. The emperor unbuckled his hammer and began moving forwards, pushing men aside. Surely this wasn't the best idea. Better to have laughed it off.

'Someone tell me who said that,' Baldwin repeated.

Farred and Inge shared a look and followed behind him.

His soldiers were looking at him blankly. He was met with frowns, dull faces. No-one seemed able to identify the culprit.

'Tell me!'

This was getting difficult. Baldwin wasn't backing down, but he wasn't getting anywhere either. If he wasn't careful, his authority would start to leach away right in front of his soldiers.

'It was him!' Inge shouted, pointing at one of the men.

The soldier looked at her in horror. 'No! It weren't, Your Majesty! It weren't me.'

'On your knees!' Baldwin seethed, his face red.

'Please!'

Inge waved a hand. The man sank to his knees, trembling. 'It weren't—'

Baldwin's hammer came down, hard. It needed two more blows until he was dead. The men of Kelland looked at the body of their comrade and at their emperor, hammer in hand. No-one spoke into the silence, but Farred somehow read their collective thoughts. They were going to kill Baldwin, kill his witch adulteress. Kill Farred too, his foreign favourite.

'Your Majesty!' came a shout into the silence. Walter's voice.

Baldwin's brother appeared, just in time. His eyes blazed with fury as he took in the scene, looking at everyone, Farred included—Baldwin even—with the same anger. 'You're needed at the front,' he said curtly.

Baldwin shook himself, as if waking from a dream, and moved forwards. Inge went with him. Farred followed close behind, not wishing to remain with the men of Kelland any longer.

Walter led them past the long line of soldiers, making them move awkwardly to one side where the passage narrowed. In those places the stink was oppressive—days of sweat lay on them; the stink of piss; the reek of Drobax innards; the smell of illness. Farred put his hand to his nose as he followed the two brothers, further down the tunnel, towards a cave opening, and then at last—thank Toric—outside, into sunshine and fresh air.

The four of them stood breathing in the fresh air, as the army slowly filed out of the cave. The madness of minutes ago, when Baldwin had attacked one of his own soldiers, seemed like a distant dream, as if it hadn't happened.

'There are creatures in those tunnels,' Inge said slowly, as if she too were awakening from a dream. 'They didn't reveal themselves, but they are dangerous nonetheless.'

'Yes,' agreed Walter. 'I think we were lucky not to lose more men than we did. But let's speak no more of it,' he added, a pained expression on his face.

An image hit Farred then, of the soldier pleading, *it weren't me*. Then of his head, a bloody pulp on the floor of the tunnel. He glanced at Baldwin. Had some hidden creatures in the dark cast a spell on them? Or had Baldwin given in to madness?

Walter pointed to the north. Burkhard Castle rose before them. The secret tunnels had brought them out only a few miles from the Emperor's Crag. Lines of Drobax still surrounded it. The Emperor's Keep, perched on top of the crag, looked like a toy house. From this distance Farred couldn't make it out clearly. It looked to be intact, but he could see smoke rising from it. He scanned the skies, looking for the dragon, but he couldn't see it.

'It's hard to tell for sure,' said Walter, echoing his own thoughts, 'but it's possible that Godfrey still holds out. We must assume that we have now been seen, and that the Isharites will come for us. I have sent some men on to Essenberg, to warn them of our arrival. I have a few horses spare, should you wish to reach the city early, Baldwin,' he offered.

'I'll stay with the army,' said the Emperor firmly.

'Very well. I suggest we continue to the Great Road. When everyone is out of the cave, we will march. If we keep a good pace, we will arrive tomorrow.'

Walter led the Brasingian army south along the Great Road. The Barissians were at the front, the Thessians in the middle and the Kellish at the rear, though Baldwin remained at the front, away from his soldiers.

Walter made them march through the night. It wasn't difficult in one sense, since on the Great Road all the soldiers needed to do was put one foot in front of the other. But this was the second night they had gone without sleep.

Farred understood why Walter had marched them through the caves after the first night, when some of the soldiers had gone missing. But now he wasn't so sure it made sense. They were all tired and irritable. If the Isharite army did catch up to them, they would be in no condition to fight. He found the marshal talking with one of his men, who was riding one of the few horses they had left.

'Are you worried they'll hit us in the night?' Farred asked, his words sounding slurred.

'Yes. It's impossible to know how quickly they'll catch us. But if we stop for the night we'll shed soldiers.'

'What do you mean?'

Walter exchanged a look with his officer. 'Some of them have already slipped away, others have been caught trying. The Luderians, especially, are keen to return to their homes. Once Burkhard falls, Luderia is completely exposed. But everyone feels it. The Empire is on the cusp of collapse. When that happens, men want to get back to their families. I need to get these soldiers behind the walls of Essenberg as soon as possible, Farred. For many reasons.'

Farred understood. He was surprised he hadn't realised it before. Essenberg was the last stand. After the capital fell, the Empire would disintegrate into its collective parts, easy to pick off one by one by the Isharites. Walter wanted to hold out for as long as possible before that happened. But realistically, if the formidable Burkhard Castle had only lasted for two weeks, how long could they expect Essenberg to hold out?

The army marched through the night, the soldiers too tired to complain now, just focusing on putting one foot in front of the other. As dawn came, Farred could see that the army had lost its shape. The stragglers: the exhausted, the ill and the injured, spread out miles behind them. Apparently, that wasn't the only problem.

'The enemy have been seen,' Walter advised him. 'We are meeting to discuss what we should do if you want to come?'

Wordlessly, Farred followed him down the line, as the soldiers continued to march the other way, inching slowly towards Essenberg. Baldwin and Inge joined them. When they got to the rear, the remaining leaders of the army waited for them: Coen of Thesse and Jeremias of Rotelegen. One after the other they all sat on the ground, an acknowledgement that standing, talking and thinking all at once had become too much.

Farred observed the tired faces. Even the usually energetic Coen looked old and haggard. He worried that they were in no condition now to make sound decisions.

Coen waved a hand to the north. 'I've just had a look for myself. It's a sizeable cavalry force. While the Isharites used the Drobax to take Burkhard, they've kept their Haskan soldiers fresh. It's going to be difficult for us to repel them. Meanwhile, all they need to do is tie us down until their infantry arrive and overwhelm us.'

Walter sighed. 'I thought we might make it to Essenberg, but it seems not. I don't see that we have many options. We must leave a force here to occupy the Haskans while the rest of the army continues south. The only questions is, who?'

To their credit, the leaders of the army volunteered themselves. Coen said the Thessians should stay, Walter argued for the Barissians, and Baldwin for the Kellish. There was little in the way of rational argument that Farred could hang onto.

He found it impossible to concentrate on the issue. He hardly cared any more. He gazed to the north, expecting to see the lines of cavalry descend upon them as they debated with one another. Instead, his attention was caught by movement to his right. He looked away to the east. A small mounted force approached the Great Road.

'Who are they?' he asked, interrupting Baldwin's flow.

All heads turned to look. Farred could see that the cavalry force carried flags, but the Leaping Fish design wasn't one he recognised.

Baldwin got to his feet. 'The Atrabians,' he said, his voice a mix of emotions. 'What brings them here?'

Everyone got to their feet, watching, as the Atrabians approached the Great Road. Then, to the north, Coen pointed out glints on the horizon. Ranks of Haskan cavalry came into view, the sunlight catching their armour. The flatness of the terrain allowed them to see both forces approach, one from the north, one from the east. The last of the stragglers from their own army passed them, and still they watched and waited, too tired to do anything else. It became clear that the Atrabians weren't heading in their direction. Instead they would meet the Great Road about a mile to the north.

'They're heading towards the Haskans,' said Walter, disbelief in his voice. 'Prince Gavan is buying us some time.'

'Or bowing the knee to the enemy,' Baldwin growled. 'Twice I have summoned them to Burkhard Castle and twice they have ignored my call. What makes you think they are acting with honour now?'

'The Atrabians have their own grievances,' Walter said carefully. 'That doesn't mean they've allied with Ishari.'

Baldwin grunted. 'Don't forget Emeric, brother. If the Barissians can be turned, treachery from Atrabia should come as no surprise.'

But the Emperor had it wrong. The Haskans stopped their advance down the Great Road and turned to meet the advancing Atrabians. Suddenly the Atrabians had turned their horses and the Haskans were giving chase, thundering off the road, their greater numbers giving them confidence. Then those in the lead fell, arrows coming at them from all angles as the Atrabians executed their ambush.

They all looked at one another.

'Well,' Baldwin said finally. 'I got that wrong.'

He smiled then, and Walter smiled with him, and then without warning the two brothers were laughing, tears rolling down their eyes. Hysteria had come, and Farred wasn't surprised: two weeks of uninterrupted pressure and two nights with no sleep would do that to anyone.

'Come on,' said Coen gruffly, though like everyone else he was finding it hard not to smile. 'We need to get this army to Essenberg.'

***

IT HAD been agreed that the less combustible of them would attend the meeting with Empress Hannelore. That meant Brock and Frayne were out, for the two of them had done nothing much but conspire over how they would kill Gervase Salvinus. Edgar had also explained to Brictwin that he didn't want him there, either. That left Prince Cerdda, Wilchard, and himself. In truth, he was no less angry than anyone else, but he thought he had the self-control to cope with seeing the mercenary captain again. If he didn't, well then; he would be the one to wield the sword and kill the bastard.

They left the barracks, known in the city as the Imps. It was where they had set up their headquarters and stationed most of their troops. It had been a difficult decision to give his oath to Rainer, a promise not to spill blood inside Essenberg. Rainer had helped to make it possible by suggesting a division of the city. It meant that the Magnian and Middian soldiers were given the city west of the Cousel, forbidden to cross the river. Likewise, Salvinus had agreed that the men under his command would have control over the eastern half, with the same penalty should they stray. Death.

Lord Kass had come to fetch them and he led the three of them towards the First Bridge. He gave them a commentary on the history of the city as he did so, which Edgar only half listened to. He wasn't in the mood for it, his excitement at seeing Essenberg completely gone. He wasn't here on a sightseeing trip. He was here to fight the Isharites, quite possibly leading his men to their deaths in a foreign land.

They crossed to Margaret Island, and then to the eastern side of the Cousel. Kass called it the Cathedral Quarter, before describing the building that dominated the skyline of the city. They weren't heading there, though. Kass was taking them north now, to Essenberg Castle. They passed the grand houses of the richer citizens, that stood in stark contrast to the crammed, ramshackle plots that could be found near the Imps.

'I've not seen anything like it,' Cerdda said, as they passed one mansion after another.

The Great Road had helped to make Essenberg the richest city of Dalriya. Clearly, it wasn't just the emperor who benefited.

'Even the merchants of Essenberg have nicer houses than we do,' Edgar agreed.

Everyone smiled at him, though the comment had come out sharper than he had intended. Still, it did make him wonder why they needed Magnians to come and fight for them. What had the men who lived here done with all their riches? Then he realised that they were probably paying Salvinus, and he wished he hadn't asked himself the question.

They turned into a square, the gleaming white walls of the castle appearing before them. Soldiers sat outside in groups, presumably Salvinus's men. Some sat smoking and drinking, others diced. Of course, it had occurred to Edgar that Salvinus might order his men to cut both Cerdda and he down. If he did, there was little they could do about it. But the Magnians would come storming across the bridges to avenge them, and they outnumbered the mercenaries, by at least two to one.

All they got in the end was half-interested looks, the guards at the gate standing aside to let them through. Edgar took a good look at the castle defences as Kass led them through the courtyard. It was a nice-looking castle, with clean, straight lines everywhere. But its walls were not as tall or as thick as the hulking castle in Coldeberg. Once the enemy got inside the city, it wouldn't keep them out for very long.

The doors to the castle hall were open and Kass led them inside. It was a large, rectangular space. Huge, colourful tapestries, depicting the emperors of Brasingia, past and present, hung along the walls. They walked past them, past two sets of pillars, to the far end of the space, where a small group waited for them by a table and chairs, some standing, some seated.

Lord Kass, eager to take the credit for his diplomatic success, introduced Edgar, Cerdda and Wilchard.

Rainer, smooth as ever, did the rest of the introductions. Edgar had met Empress Hannelore once before, at Duke Walter's coronation in Coldeberg. She wore a sleeveless gown, deep blue in colour. She was a striking figure, tall and handsome, broad-shouldered and shapely. She nodded politely at each of them, but she remained reserved, nervous looking.

Gervase Salvinus was the opposite, all confidence and smiles. Edgar had expected nothing else. He had first seen the man coming out of Toric's Temple in Ecgworth, after he had killed and tortured the priests inside, hoping to find Toric's Dagger. Then at the Battle of Lindhafen, where Salvinus had led his wing of the Barissian army against Edgar's South Magnians, aiming to kill him and drive them all from the field of battle. Soon afterwards, he had murdered Edgar's chancellor, Ealdnoth, before attempting to murder him too, entering his tent with the Isharite wizard and the Krykker. Finally, Edgar had watched him surrender Coldeberg to Duke Coen, giving them the head of Duke Emeric in exchange for walking away from the siege a free man. They had tussled so many times it was remarkable that they were both still alive. Now, they appeared to be on the same side.

Adalheid, dowager Duchess of Rotelegen, was seated. The widow of Duke Ellard and mother of Duke Jeremias, who had taken his army to Burkhard, she was a high-status guest of the Empress. She briefly turned her attention to Edgar, an unimpressed look on her face. Her son's duchy was little more than a name on a map now, its people dead or fled. She had a right to look miserable and she was exercising it.

Next to her sat the Archbishop of Essenberg, Decker. He looked old enough to have held the office since the empire was born, but by all accounts, he was still one of Baldwin's chief advisers.

'The Empress has received a message from the Emperor,' Rainer began, 'and thought it wise to pass it on to all of you. He has escaped from Burkhard Castle, with a force of some thirty-five thousand soldiers. The Duke's Crag has fallen. Archbishop Godfrey was brave enough to stay behind and hold the Emperor's Crag for as long as he might. We fear it won't be long, since the Isharites control a dragon, as well as countless numbers of Drobax, and it has proven to be impossible to resist the creature. To reassure you all, I should say immediately that dukes Jeremias, Walter and Coen all live and are with the Emperor, as is your man Farred, Prince Edgar.'

'Thank you,' said Edgar, grateful that Rainer remembered Farred amidst all the other facts he had to juggle.

'How did they manage to get out of there?' Salvinus asked.

Edgar wondered if the mercenary had hoped they wouldn't.

'I don't know the details of the escape,' said Rainer, 'but I need to pass on a warning. The Emperor is marching to Essenberg. Duke Walter was apparently keen to warn us that the Isharites may not be far behind them—they could even catch them before they make it here. He asked us to begin preparations for a siege. We must proceed on a worst-case scenario, that being that the army doesn't make it here at all.'

'A siege?' Salvinus asked. 'What chance do we have of holding out here, if Baldwin's army cannot hold Burkhard Castle?'

'I thought you were getting paid to defend the capital,' Edgar snapped at him, unable to resist.

Hannelore gave Rainer a look, who turned his blue-eyed gaze on Edgar— a silent warning.

'Defend it I shall, if those are my orders,' Salvinus said mildly. 'It's no secret I worked for Emeric, and some people will always hold that against me, but no-one can say I didn't serve him well.'

'Until you chopped off his head,' said Cerdda.

Edgar smiled, surprised that the prince had joined in.

Salvinus also gave a smile, but there was little humour in it. 'My men expect me to pay their wages. If I don't, they leave. They don't expect me to get them killed. That's the life of a mercenary, Prince Cerdda. We don't all have the luxury of leading soldiers who lay down their lives in exchange for a kind word from their prince.'

'Will the dragon come here?' Hannelore asked, fear apparent in her voice.

'If it does, no amount of preparations will make a difference,' said Salvinus. 'I think we should consider evacuating the empress and her children now.'

'I'm not leaving if Baldwin is coming here,' she said. 'If he's asked us to prepare for a siege, that's what we do.'

'I agree, Your Majesty,' said Decker. 'However, I think we should consider an evacuation of civilians. If they cannot help in the defence, and are merely a drain on the city's supplies, we would be better off sending them south to be looked after. I will be happy to organise this.'

'Thank you, Your Grace,' said Hannelore.

'Vital supplies must be managed centrally,' said Rainer. 'If Baldwin brings thousands more men into the city, our food stores will be consumed at a rate that will be difficult to sustain. From now on, we'll have to insist on strict rationing.'

'I can help you manage this on our side of the city,' offered Wilchard.

'Thank you,' said Rainer. 'Perhaps we can put our heads together after this meeting?'

'Of course.'

'Anything else from a military perspective?' Hannelore asked.

'Baldwin's Bridge,' said Edgar.

'What of it?'

'It will need to be manned just like the city walls. Our agreement forbids our soldiers from stepping foot on it.'

Salvinus shrugged. 'You're welcome to it. My men have the city walls and the castle to worry about.'

'If that is all,' said Hannelore, 'I will let you leave and proceed with your work. I would like to finish by expressing my personal gratitude to all of you, as well as on behalf of my husband and people. What you are doing here will not be soon forgotten.'

***

'YOUR MAJESTY!' came the shout.

The soldiers pointed to the sky. Baldwin's eyes flashed upwards, his gut wrenching, as he looked for the dragon. If it took them here, there was nowhere to hide. They would be eviscerated. The relief when he saw a hawk instead was palpable. His heartbeat recovered to a normal rate and he breathed once more.

The hawk flew in a circle—looking for him, he knew. He was joined by Walter and Inge, and they waved up at Gustav, until he made his descent. The hawk flew to the ground in front of them. It was a sorry-looking thing, and when it transformed into the archmage before their eyes, it revealed a broken man.

Naked, ravaged by dragon fire, Gustav lay before them, too exhausted to move. They knelt by his side for a good while. The only sound was the desperate wheezing of his lungs, as he fought to take in enough air. Finally, he was able to speak.

'Burkhard is taken, the keep destroyed. All who sheltered there are dead, Archbishop Godfrey included. They fought bravely to the end, but we couldn't stop the dragon.'

He stopped, his account interrupted by a coughing fit that wracked his body.

'I don't know whether the dragon will be sent on to complete its work here. But even if it is just the Drobax, there are still too many of them to resist.'

He met Baldwin's eyes then. Baldwin could see the pain in them, but also the strength and pride there had always been. 'We have done good work, Your

Majesty. Held back the tide for as long as we could. The burden of stopping Siavash is carried by others, not you. You must decide what is best for Brasingia now.'

Baldwin took Gustav's hand and Inge took the other. Gustav had no words for his apprentice, though tears ran freely down her face. They waited with him until he took his final breath.

'I will see to his burial,' Walter murmured, ready as ever to help shoulder Baldwin's burdens.

Baldwin nodded. He got to his feet and walked away from them all, away from the road. He needed a measure of time and space to think. Burkhard was gone. Gustav was gone. It was time to consider their situation afresh. As his archmage had counselled him, he must do what was best for Brasingia.

Baldwin could see Essenberg on the horizon, the place where the Great Road of Dalriya met the continent's greatest river—the city he called home. A message from Hannelore had arrived, telling him how well she had done in his absence. According to his wife, Essenberg was full of defenders—Magnian princes, Middian chiefs, mercenary captains. But something was wrong, a feeling that had been growing in his gut as they closed on their destination. He couldn't ignore it any longer.

Baldwin told his soldiers they should stop and rest. He called a meeting of his captains and advisers. Coen of Thesse, who had proven himself to be a fine leader of men. Young Jeremias, growing into the role of duke; Farred the Magnian; and the sorcerer, Inge. Most important of all, the Marshal of the Empire, his brother Walter.

'We are close to the capital,' he began, 'but what are we doing? My children are in Essenberg. I don't want to lead the Isharites there.'

They looked at one another.

'We can hold them up in Essenberg,' said Walter. 'It is the last place the Empire can make a stand.'

'I agree,' said Baldwin, 'but we are hastening that last stand. Pouring thirty thousand men into the city won't stop the Drobax from tearing the walls down.'

Walter shrugged. He looked tired, bereft of ideas.

'We've done our best. You most of all, brother. But I won't be going to Essenberg. I will lead my men east, get as far as I can to the Luderian border.

Walter, you could head west, cross the Cousel at Vordorf. The Isharites will be forced to follow us, they won't just ignore armies this large in the field. It will buy Essenberg some time.'

'Time for what?' asked Coen.

Baldwin pointed at Farred. 'His friends. Gustav believed they have a chance of stopping the Isharites. Maybe soon. I certainly won't forget the moment last summer, when the horde of Drobax surrounding Burkhard Castle turned around and marched back home. It's possible that they can do something again—kill Siavash, perhaps.'

Coen looked dubious.

'What is it, Your Grace? Now is the time to speak freely.'

'The Isharites have brought enough men into the Empire to follow your armies *and* send troops to Essenberg. Let's say they waste a couple of days chasing you around the Empire and it takes them as long to enter Essenberg. Then what?'

'Then you lead whoever is left in Essenberg to Lindhafen. We resist for as long as we can, as hard as we can. Putting all of our soldiers in Essenberg and waiting for them to finish us makes no sense. Until now our strategy has been to hold them up. We put all our forces in Burkhard to do it. But we've lost Burkhard. Our strategy needs to change. We use the size of the Empire. Spread out to the corners. Make the war last for as long as possible.'

Uncertain faces stared back at him.

'So far, the dragon hasn't come for us, but that could change. If it found us all in the same place, we'd be finished. This way, some of us can fight on for longer. Should Essenberg fall, there would still be Walter in Barissia, Arne in Luderia, Gavan in Atrabia, Coen in Thesse. Our forces are divided, yes. But we are harder to finish.'

Walter and Coen both nodded slowly. Baldwin knew he was right, he just hadn't been sure that they would see it.

'Then let *me* lead the *Thessians* east,' said Coen. 'You belong in Essenberg, Baldwin.'

Baldwin smiled. 'Tempting, but no. The enemy is in Kelland. Our land. We are the ones who need to stay and fight. Besides, the Isharites want me dead. They'll follow me east. I know it.'

'I could pretend to be you, wear your armour,' Farred suggested. 'You could get into Essenberg unseen.'

'A valiant offer, Farred. But I have made my decision. I've had my fill of hiding; of being protected by others. I'm tired of all that. And while you may think it vulgar, I'm minded to pull rank and give you your orders now. Walter and Jeremias take the Barissians and men of Rotelegen to Coldeberg. The Luderians I will allow to go home. Coen to Essenberg and on to Lindhafen if need be. Inge to Essenberg as well, to defend my capital and my family.'

'One of us should stay with you,' Walter protested.

Baldwin held up a hand and gave his brother a stern look. He noted that Inge didn't volunteer to go with him. He would perhaps have agreed to that.

'Farred will likely choose to go to Essenberg too, to be with his prince. But that is his decision, since I am not his liege lord. I *am* lord to the rest of you, though, and these are my orders. They could be the last ones I give, so I expect to see them followed.'

XVI

MUSTER

THE SERVANTS OF DIIS GATHERED before him in the Throne Room of Samir Durg. Siavash gazed out at them, and he felt Diis looking at them too. His eyes were hot black coals that made even the most loyal and resolute follower shake and shudder in fear.

'Tell me we are close to crushing Kalinth,' he began, keen to hear about the fate of the kingdom he despised most of all.

Peroz chose to answer. He was always prone to self-importance. 'We smashed the army they fielded, sent the Knights scurrying away.'

Siavash flicked his eyes to Harith, a servant attached to one of the other hosts he had sent to the kingdom. Harith gave a brief nod, confirming the statement.

'The Knights scurried away where?'

'To the south. We also learned that King Jonas was removed from the throne. Killed and replaced by the knight, Theron.'

Siavash nodded. That didn't surprise him. 'Heractus?'

'We will soon take the city.'

'See that you do. The Knights left for the south because they have a fortress there. Chalios, it is called. After Heractus you must proceed there. Kalinth isn't defeated until Chalios is taken.'

He turned his attention to Roshanak. 'What of the Krykkers?'

'We have won some victories,' Roshanak murmured, 'but they remain locked away underground. It is difficult. When we succeed in breaking into one of their tunnel networks, they abandon it, collapsing the walls behind them. Meanwhile, the attrition rate of the Drobax is becoming catastrophic. I need reinforcements.'

'There are no reinforcements,' Siavash exclaimed, fuming at the comment. 'The lands of the Drobax were emptied to supply the hosts that have gone into Kalinth. Once Kalinth is taken more will be sent south.'

The truth was, Siavash didn't care too much about the losses in the Krykker mountains. It was a price he was prepared to pay to keep the Krykkers out of the conflict.

'And Brasingia?' Siavash asked, turning finally to Mehrab, his commander there.

'Burkhard Castle is taken,' said the sorcerer, smiling with pleasure and pride. He was a fool, Siavash assessed, though a useful one, since he had observed the siege of Burkhard last year. He had done a reasonable job, but if he thought anyone believed the victory was down to him rather than the dragon, he was a bigger fool than Siavash had thought.

'I wanted to see it for myself before I came here,' Mehrab continued. 'Standing on top of the crag with out enemies crushed was a special moment,' he crowed, oblivious of the contempt he was held in.

'The Emperor?'

'Well,' he began, faltering a bit. 'Much of the Brasingian army did escape. We have discovered caves under the larger crag which we were unaware of. They knew they would die if they stayed any longer—'

'The Emperor!' Siavash repeated, his patience wearing thin.

'He still lives, Lord, and commands his army. I can confirm we have killed the Archbishop of Gotbeck, however—'

'The Archbishop of Gotbeck?' Siavash repeated, his voice dripping with derision. 'All Powerful Diis doesn't care about archbishops!'

He felt Diis stir within him at the mention of his name.

Mehrab went white and stared at the floor. 'Apologies, Lord. But now that Burkhard Castle is taken, Baldwin and the other Brasingian leaders have nowhere else that can delay us. It will be days before they are all taken, at most.'

'Of course it will be days,' Siavash spat. 'See that it is done, or I will find someone else to do the job. If there is nowhere left for the Brasingians to hide, your force no longer needs the dragon. See that it is transferred to Kalinth. I want to ensure that Chalios is taken, that Kalinth is destroyed once and for all. And I want to see it for myself.'

Most of all, he thought to himself, though his master Diis could read his thoughts if he so chose, *there is Soren the wizard and his filthy sister, the new champion of Madria; We must see them both dead with Our own eyes.*

***

EXHAUSTED IN body and mind, it took everything Belwynn had left just to hold on to Theron as he led the mount they shared south, through the night and into the day. Lyssa soon fell asleep, leaving Evander to ride whilst ensuring she didn't fall off. It was a sorry group of knights who sped across the Kalinthian countryside, leaving the rest of the army who followed on foot behind, leaving their fallen even further. Those knights who had fallen outside Heractus were like ghosts, riding amongst them; reminding them of their passing and stealing from them the ability to smile or to speak.

Their route took them through a village, and although there was a couple of hours of daylight left, Theron decided that they should stop and take beds amongst the villagers. Devoid of supplies, they accepted the offer from the village elders of a much-needed supper outdoors on the common, before Theron retired for the night. In hushed voices, his knights told the village about the horror that had descended on Kalinth. The villagers prayed to their gods, some invoking the name of Madria. When the knights turned to look at her, Belwynn gently shook her head, and led Lyssa away to their room.

It was another day of hard riding before they reached Chalios. Theron had taken her to see it last summer, just before they had left the High Tower with Sebastian's army to march on Heractus. It felt like a long time ago. She had been desperately unhappy then, not knowing the fate of Soren and her friends who had been captured in Edeleny. Theron had provided a welcome distraction. She wondered now how she could help him. He was quiet and withdrawn, gently ignoring any attempt at conversation, whether it was from Belwynn, his knights, or even little Lyssa.

They found the gates of the barbican closed to them, and it took a while for those inside to let them in. When Belwynn had come before, the place had been deserted, free for Theron to show her around at their leisure. Now it was occupied, principally by those refugees from the north who had heeded Theron's orders to flee south. When the gates were opened, they passed along the fortified approach to the cliff, the path wide enough for them to stay on horseback. The inside of the fortress was little more than a hollowed-out slab of rock. There were stables, however—a prerequisite in Kalinth—and so they now dismounted. Evander and a few other knights led their mounts away. They were even more precious possessions now, since they had lost many horses as well as men in the battle.

The fortress was occupied by a small number of families. There were few men of fighting age—most of those had been recruited to fight in the battle. Instead there were the old and the young and there were wives and mothers, desperate for news of what had befallen their men when the Isharites had come for them. Unable to speak or look them in the eye, Theron left for the stairs that led up to the cliff top. Belwynn stayed to explain what had happened as best she could. Their menfolk had fought under Clarin, and his retreat had not been orderly. The soldiers had scattered, running away in all directions in small groups or alone. It was impossible to know how many would make it to the fortress. Some may have headed for the walls of Heractus. Belwynn didn't try to hide the truth from the women she spoke to. She calmed them as best she could, and then helped Lyssa to befriend a young girl who looked about the same age. When all this was done, she took the stairs up to the cliff top.

Four young girls had been sent up to the battlements of Chalios, that lined the full perimeter of the cliff top. They had been given lookout duty, perhaps because their eyes were good. Theron, meanwhile, stood in the middle of the battlements, that afforded a view to the west. It didn't look like the girls had taken much interest in him. Belwynn doubted they knew he was their king.

She approached, wary of his mood.

'I'm sorry about Tycho,' she said.

He pulled a ragged breath in, fighting to control his emotions, keeping his gaze fixed ahead rather than turning to look at her.

'He didn't suffer,' he said finally. 'I think he died the moment he hit the ground.'

'I'm sorry you've lost him.'

'I wish I could take it all back,' he said.

Belwynn frowned, unsure what he meant. But she let him speak in his own time.

'Jonas was right. Straton, too. Kalinth would be better off if I had kept quiet. Bending the knee to the Isharites seemed wrong at the time. I was so sure I was right; that my cause was just. But if we hadn't acted as we did, the royal family would be alive. Sebastian would be alive. Tycho; Galenos; the list goes on. Thousands dead. Men and women and children. Their blood is on my hands,' he said, his voice shaking.

He turned to look at her at last. 'I didn't do it to become king, you know. I never wanted that. I know that no-one believes me.'

Belwynn's heart ached for him. He seemed so lost all of a sudden. So lonely, when before he had been so full of confidence.

'I know that, Theron,' she said. 'And you're wrong. If you hadn't resisted, those people might be alive, but where would they be now? Serving in the armies of Ishari, destroying other peoples the same way that the Haskans and Persaleians have come to Kalinth. Becoming the tool of the Isharites. That was the alternative.'

'Would that have been worse?'

'Yes,' Belwynn said. 'Absolutely.'

But Theron didn't look convinced. His gaze returned to the far horizon, and he said no more.

They achieved little over the next two days. Theron remained in a state of despondency, and it hung over everything they did. Evander and the other knights who had come to Chalios rode out to the surrounding estates, requisitioning food, recruiting soldiers to come and defend the fortress. But there were too few of them to make much of an impact. Chalios remained lightly defended. The Isharites would not take long to storm the place and end the war.

Belwynn kept in contact with whoever she could. Soren was unreachable; she didn't know why. Her Madrians were hard to reach, though with Madria's help she found she could get through to them, reminding them that their orders were to come to Chalios. Clarin and Moneva were the only ones she could get a reply from. They told her that they were going as fast as they could, but that the enemy cavalry were not far behind, shadowing their progress.

Then things got a little better.

First, Soren contacted her. Somehow, he had found the Asrai, out in the vast expanse of the Lantinen. He had the cloak. Belwynn felt like she needed her brother by her side now more than ever, and told him to get himself to Chalios as soon as possible.

She told Theron of Soren's success. He summoned a smile for her, but the news didn't cut through the gloom that hung over him.

Second, more good news.

So, this is Chalios.

It was Clarin.

Smiling with delight, Belwynn rushed to find Lyssa and dragged the girl up the stairs to look out from the cliff top.

'There,' she said to the girl, pointing.

The survivors from the Battle of Heractus were visible, marching for the fortress. They were together, and there were far more of them than she had feared. Her Madrian infantry marched in formation. Clarin's infantry forces were spread out all over the place in small groups, but they had somehow escaped the chasing enemy forces.

Then Belwynn could see one of the reasons why. Not far behind the infantry the sunlight glinted off the armour of neat rows of Kalinthian cavalry.

Is Leontios with you? She asked Clarin.

Yes. He's been doing a good job of shielding us from the mounted Haskans that are following us. The Knights drove them off a couple of times. Since then they've kept their distance.

Theron, she said, using her telepathy to contact him. *Grand Master Leontios and the rest of the army is approaching. The Knights of Kalinth are very much alive!*

It didn't take long for Theron to arrive. Evander came with him. The four of them looked out as the figures got closer, approaching the gates of the fortress.

Less than a hundred knights from Theron's unit had made it to Chalios with them. With Leontios' force, it looked like they would have over five hundred. Compared to the numbers that the Isharites had brought to Kalinth it was negligible. But it was enough. Enough to bring a smile to the King of Kalinth's face.

'Thank the gods!' he said, letting out a sigh of relief. 'Leontios has done well to keep his force intact. Kalinth is not defeated quite yet.'

'Thank *Madria*,' Belwynn responded archly. 'Anyway, Leontios didn't have a third army bearing down on his flank like you did. You held them off long enough to allow all these soldiers to get away. Now there are enough of us to defend the fortress. So, stop beating yourself up now, Theron.'

Evander's eyes went wide, and he grinned foolishly at witnessing his king getting a telling off.

'Alright, Belwynn. Point taken. I lost a little control for a while. I'm sorry. And you can knock that smile off your face right now,' he added, frowning at Evander.

Evander closed his mouth and returned his attention to the arrival of his brothers-in-arms. Lyssa began asking him whether he could see Gyrmund or Clarin or Moneva, even though it was impossible to make out who was who from this distance.

Belwynn felt a light touch on her fingers. Looking down, she saw Theron's hand and she took it.

The arrival of the rest of the Kalinthian army galvanised everybody into action. The wounded were treated in the main chamber of the fortress. Some had walked all the way from Heractus with serious wounds and now, having finally reached their destination, their bodies gave up. A few lost the fight completely. Some had wounds that were too serious to get them back on their feet. But many would be able to fight again with a few days of rest.

Leontios' knights had generally fared better than Theron's, and many were soon able to roam around the surrounding countryside, bringing in supplies, fresh fighters and craftsmen. His close friend Philon organised regular scouting missions north, reporting on the activities of the enemy, and on where it was safe to travel. The Haskan cavalry raided the surrounding territory to bring in food. Their actions sent a stream of Kalinthians to the fortress for safety. But the Haskans didn't have the numbers to threaten the fortress and seemed content to wait for reinforcements.

Gyrmund and Moneva organised the archers and slingers. The latter group found it easy enough to replenish their ammunition, but the archers had few arrows left and this was hard to address. Their shafts lay on the site of the Battle of Heractus and were lost to them. Gyrmund got a production line going involving those with the skills to help, who were supplemented by fletchers and smiths brought to Chalios by the knights. Each day they managed to increase the numbers they produced, but it was far from enough. When Theron arrived for an inspection, he took several archers off duty and gave them spears instead. He also made sure Gyrmund got all the arrows he could use: he had seen the impact of the Jalakh Bow at first hand, and was determined that they made the most of its power.

That left Belwynn and Clarin to organise the infantry who would defend the barbican, towers and battlements of Chalios. Most of them were located in the two rows of walled defences, running either side of the path that led from the barbican to the main fortress, which they had to defend at all costs.

Inside, thousands of Kalinthians had now gathered, relying on the fortress of the Knights to keep them safe.

The two large towers that supported the gates of the barbican each had a catapult on top. Elsewhere, they had to make do. Large rocks and anything else worth throwing or tipping over the walls were hauled up to the top of the structures. Should the enemy smash through the gates, they would have to pass through a tunnel of death to get to the cliff. They also had to prepare for the Isharites deciding against the front entrance and instead using ladders and siege equipment to scale the walls. Clarin and Belwynn divided up the soldiers available to them carefully, preparing as best they could for all possibilities. Belwynn's Madrians could be given orders and, to some extent, controlled during the battle. Clarin didn't have such an option. He was careful to appoint leaders to each tower or stretch of wall who would follow his instructions and have the initiative to react to events.

Clarin spoke no more of his feelings for her. For her part, Belwynn remained confused. Clarin was more natural company for her. He reminded her of home, and their relationship was relaxed. With Theron it was different. He burned with strong emotions, whether he was down, as he had been recently, or his more usual energetic self. After his violent seizure of the throne, she wondered whether she could trust him. But she couldn't deny that she still felt an attraction to him, that she hadn't experienced with anyone else.

When she and Clarin were done, they climbed the stairs of the cliff together to survey the defences from the vantage point of the cliff top. Up here they had placed those less able to fight: the wounded, the less experienced or more lightly armed. It was possible that the Isharites had sent a force on a detour around to the other side of the cliff, and had them scale its heights to attack them from the rear. But not likely. When the enemy had such superior numbers, it seemed pointless for them to do anything other than bring their army straight here.

'You can see the gaps from here,' Clarin commented.

He was right. The fortress had been designed as the last refuge of Kalinth. But far fewer soldiers had made it to Chalios than the Knights would have planned for. They both knew that compared to the numbers that were coming for them, they were seriously undermanned.

'I think this is all we will get,' she replied, wishing it wasn't so.

A brief look of pain passed across his face.

'Clarin? What is it?'

'I sent the Dog-men to their deaths, I know. But I had hoped that Rudy and Jurgen would find their way here. It seems that I have now lost all of my little band from Samir Durg.'

Belwynn understood his sadness. She had always been wary of the Dog-men, but she had developed an affection of her own for the two cousins from Rotelegen.

'They may have escaped the battle in some other direction. Don't assume the worst.'

'True,' Clarin agreed. 'They've proven themselves to be survivors. It is better to believe they are out there somewhere.'

Movement on the western horizon drew Belwynn's attention. She could see soldiers, and they were marching this way. They weren't the Knights or the Haskans, for they mostly marched on foot, though she could see some riders, and even horse driven carts, too.

She pointed in the direction of the force. 'Who are they?'

Clarin looked out. 'Hard to say. But friend or foe, we need to find out.'

It didn't take long for them to assemble a small force. Theron and Evander rode out with them, with a small group of knights for company. They chose the freshest of the horses and ate up the distance, so that the force soon came into view. They were dressed in the Kalinthian style, muted grey and brown furs and cloth, mixed in with the chain mail and leather armour of soldiers.

When the force saw them, a few horsemen rode ahead. One of their number detached to come and speak with them, and Belwynn got a strange sense of life repeating itself, because it was Count Diodorus, the Kalinthian general who had met them like this twice before. The first time he had commanded King Jonas's army, with instructions to fight the Knight's army led by Sebastian. He had decided to disobey his king, helping to ensure that the Knights took Heractus without spilling blood. The second time he had been in the company of Siavash's shadow, his soldiers serving in the Lord of Ishari's army. Once again, he had kept them out of the fighting on the battlefield.

'Your Majesty,' he said, inclining his head to Theron.

There was no trace of irony or sarcasm in the words, but nonetheless they hung rather awkwardly in the air, and Belwynn could see that Theron felt it too. Last time they had met was on the battlefield by the Pineos, after the fighting. Theron had stabbed Prince Straton to death and then turned on Diodorus, deciding to spare him at the last moment.

'I swore an oath to serve you,' Diodorus reminded Theron in his doleful voice, glancing across at Belwynn, as if reminding her that she had witnessed it. 'I have stripped my county of its people and we have brought as much with us as we could,' he said, waving a hand behind him.

When Belwynn looked now she could see that while the front ranks of the count's force was made up of soldiers, behind them were the ordinary men, women and children of Korenandi.

'A good thing that you did,' said Clarin, interjecting when it was not really his place to do so. 'We need all the warriors we can get.'

If Theron was irritated by Clarin he didn't show it. He rode up to Diodorus and they embraced one another. As Belwynn had suggested to him back at the Pineos, Diodorus was more useful as an ally than as a dead enemy. His soldiers, fresh and well-equipped, would make a significant improvement to their defences.

Diodorus signalled to his people to resume their journey, and they turned around to return to the fortress.

Clarin nudged his horse alongside the count's.

'Don't suppose you have arrows in those carts of yours?' he asked hopefully.

'We have arrows,' Diodorus confirmed unhappily, 'but Korenandi has never been able to supply large numbers of archers.'

'Ah,' said Clarin with a grin, 'don't worry about that.'

***

JESPER ALLOWED himself a little smile of relief as the river Drang revealed itself ahead of them. They had endured a hellish few days, fighting their way across Vismaria, a country where the Drobax ran amok. They had run virtually the whole way, desperately trying to keep pace with Oisin. When the Drobax threatened them, the King of the Giants would hurl himself at them, his spear striking the creatures down before they got close to landing a blow on him. After Stenk had been beaten to the ground by one attack, Oisin had simply pulled the injured Krykker along in the sled, ropes taut around his shoulders and waist, still able to travel as quickly as Jesper could run. He kept watch all night while they slept. It seemed that his rest of hundreds of years had given him an inexhaustible supply of energy.

Now, the Giant yelled out into the river at the top of his lungs, his voice just as powerful as the rest of him.

Jesper looked behind him, anxious that the noise would draw more Drobax.

He could see movement on an island in the middle of the river. There were Krykkers, and they began to lower a drawbridge that reached out into the river, before resting on a rocky outcrop. Two of them proceeded to make their way along the bridge onto the rock. Next, they lowered a second drawbridge towards the bank where Jesper and his friends waited.

Oisin reached out and grabbed the bridge as it descended, pushing it down into place. Stenk had got to his feet, but swayed alarmingly, and the Giant simply picked him up, before carrying him across the bridge.

'You next,' said Gunnhild, prodding Jesper forwards. He had learned not to argue with her and followed behind Oisin.

Soon all four of them had made it onto the island in the middle of the Drang. The Krykkers were quick to pull up the two lowered drawbridges, before any Drobax that might be watching were encouraged to try their luck.

The Krykkers stared at Oisin open-mouthed.

'You have our thanks, friends,' said the king, beaming at them. 'But we are in a terrible hurry. Our mission is to take this spear I carry, and Bolivar's Sword,' he added, gesturing at the weapon scabbarded at Stenk's belt, 'across the Lantinen to Dalriya.'

His words did little to wake the Krykkers from their open-mouthed stupor.

'We crossed with the army of chieftain Wracken,' said Gunnhild, doing her best to explain what was happening. 'We must speak with Lord Sevald of the Vismarians as soon as possible, about securing a ship.'

Finally, one of the Krykkers summoned the discipline to speak. 'Only a few soldiers returned from that expedition,' he said. 'Our chieftain Wracken, as well as Lord Sevald, never made it back.'

'Jodivig?' asked Stenk. 'Chieftain of my tribe, the Dramsens of Dalriya?'

The Krykker shook his head. 'Nor him. Those who returned say all three stood their ground so that a few could escape.'

Oisin put a hand to his head. 'So many sacrificed themselves so that I could be brought back here?' he cried. 'Then all the more reason for us to find a way to Dalriya. But I swear, if I am able, that I will return to Halvia and repay this debt I owe.'

***

RIMMON TRIED to ignore the rank smell that travelled on the wind. Instead, he focused on Peroz's expression as the servant of Diis walked towards their position. Normally so full of disdain, the Isharite couldn't help a look of pleasure escaping across his face. Rimmon looked over towards Herin. The Magnian saw it too—he wore a satisfied smile of his own.

'The whole city is taken?' Peroz asked.

'No-one lives,' said Herin.

The three of them turned to look at Heractus, the gates to the city torn apart, billows of smoke still wafting into the sky from inside the walls. Herin had it manned by Haskan soldiers now, but Kull's Drobax had taken it, destroying everything in their path, inflicting all manner of atrocities on the unfortunate Kalinthians who had taken shelter inside. It had been a terrible mistake on their part, to imagine the city walls would keep them safe.

When the Haskans were sent in, the Drobax had already begun to eat the corpses of the dead. It had taken an effort to force them back out of the city, some retaining their grisly spoils as they left. The Haskans had burned the corpses. Heractus was now a sanitised version of the city that had been taken yesterday.

'And it was our host only?'

'All by ourselves,' confirmed Herin. 'So we get all the credit.'

'This is very good,' said Peroz. His smile made Rimmon want to shudder. 'For Lord Siavash will soon be coming to join us here.'

'Siavash is coming to Kalinth?' Rimmon asked. 'Why?'

There was something odd about the whole thing. Four hosts sent to Kalinth was a disproportionate use of resources in the first place. Now Siavash would come here himself? What made this country, lightly populated, already on its knees, so important?

'Lord Siavash has a great personal interest in seeing Kalinth destroyed. He has ordered us to march to the fortress on Chalios immediately, where the remnants of their forces will be gathering. Not only that,' said Peroz, his smile becoming even more repulsive, 'he has ordered the dragon here. It has already destroyed the Krykkers and the Brasingians. Now we will see it in action for ourselves.'

Rimmon and Herin shared a brief look. Four hosts, a dragon and Lord Siavash himself? There was something going on they hadn't been told about. Perhaps Peroz, for all his superior attitude, didn't know either.

'And will we be given the honour of taking the fortress?' Herin asked, his look intense. 'We have given Lord Siavash King Mark, the Shield of Persala, and now Heractus. Surely we are the most deserving?'

'Surely,' agreed Peroz. 'I will be making our case to him. And I can be very persuasive.'

XVII

A WEAPONTAKE

I T TOOK SOREN A FULL DAY TO RECOVER from his expenditure of energy. He had drained all he could, from himself and from Onella's Staff, and now he paid the price for it. But as Tana had promised, the Asrai cared for him. They carried him out of the cavern, to a shaded spot under some trees. They laid him down in a strange bed, a length of cloth tied with rope between two trees, that swung about every time he moved. First they made him drink a frothy, fishy broth, that tasted of seaweed and fish guts. After a long sleep, they then brought him more palatable things to eat: fruit and vegetables that they must have foraged from the island, a fish they had smoked, the flesh succulent and tasty. He saw no more than six of the Asrai the whole time, all of them females. How many of the creatures there were altogether, where and how they lived, he still had no idea. The Asrai were not about to reveal such information to him. Their queen had been captured and enslaved by an outsider. Arioc had killed one of their number. Even if they understood Soren was an enemy of their enemy, that didn't mean they considered him a friend.

Soren chafed at the delay. Moreover, he found that his telepathy didn't work, meaning he had no way to tell Belwynn about his success, or to hear from her about how things went in Kalinth. He knew that he had left her in a perilous situation. He thought that the same magic that hid the islands from detection may also have prevented his thoughts from leaving. But intriguing as the mysterious islands were, he knew that he had no time to solve their riddles. He needed to leave as soon as possible. The Asrai would keep their secrets, and maybe that was for the best.

The next morning Soren was on his feet, ready to go. Tana appeared.

'The Asrai are ready to fight the Isharites once more,' she said. 'Where must we go?'

'Most of the other weapons are in Kalinth,' he explained. 'We need to return there as soon as possible. Do you know where Kalinth is?'

'Across the sea to the north. We must swim a long way to get there. Five Asrai will accompany us. But I am the only one who will step on land. The Cloak protects me, but nobody else.'

'Swim to Kalinth?' Soren responded. 'I can't. I don't have the power to go that far without stopping. If we return to North Magnia, we could catch a boat from there.'

Tana made a face. 'Asrai do not travel in boats,' she said. 'We will accompany you to Magnia. *You* can catch a boat.'

Soren was not surprised to find Morlin patiently waiting for him on the beach. The bodyguard had got used to watching him walk into the sea every morning, taken in his stride the fact that Soren created a bubble of air and roamed around the ocean in it. But he looked more than a little taken aback by the sight of the six green-haired Asrai, bobbing up and down with the waves, their dark eyes peering at him.

'What are they?' he asked, pointing.

'Asrai. Morlin, I need a boat. Could you get me to Wincandon? I am hopeful that the princesses might procure one for me.'

The soldier agreed to take him to Wincandon immediately. With one backward glance at the sea, he urged his horse up the path that led off the beach.

Irmgard and Elfled were more than keen to help, grateful to be able to do something useful. With some feminine persuasion, and a not inconsiderable sum of money, they persuaded a North Magnian captain to risk the voyage.

They came down to the harbour to see Soren off. Morlin accompanied them, a respectful distance away, but close enough to intervene should they need protecting from Asrai.

As Soren made ready to board, the two princesses looked more than a little disappointed. They gazed out to sea, but it seemed that the Asrai had moved further out from shore, nervous of so many humans.

Still, something made Soren wonder. Something in his senses told him there was a presence, perhaps a salty smell that was more than just the tang of the sea.

'Tana?' he called out, unsure of what he was doing.

A rustling sound made him turn around. Tana revealed herself. She was standing ankle deep in the waves, the Asrai Cloak a shimmering wetness about her body.

'Oh!' said Elfled, startled, though Soren could see that she was intrigued too.

Elfled approached the Queen of the Asrai. Soren went with her. Princess Irmgard, more hesitant, followed behind.

'Queen Tana of the Asrai,' Soren introduced her. 'Princesses Elfled and Irmgard.'

Elfled stopped where the waves soaked the sand. Tana moved forward then, until they were face to face.

'I'm so pleased to meet you,' said Elfled. She reached out a hand.

Tana looked at the hand held in mid-air, as if wondering why it was being offered. Then she took it in her own webbed hand. She turned it over, looking at the palm, then up to Elfled's face. Her other hand reached out for Elfled's belly.

Irmgard gasped and Morlin strode towards them, but Elfled shook her head at him, and he stayed where he was.

'You are with child,' Tana said, in her hushed, breathy tone.

'Yes.'

'It is a boy. He will become a great king.'

Elfled's eyes widened in surprise. 'Thank you,' she said. 'And thank you for visiting our lands. Please know that you are always welcome here.'

Tana withdrew her hand from Elfled's belly and released the princess's hand. It looked to Soren like she was considering Elfled's words. 'Then I offer you the same. Refuge on our islands should you ever need it.'

'I am most grateful. We will pray that you succeed in your quest to stop the Isharites.'

Tana gave a little shrug at that. 'Farewell.'

The Queen of the Asrai turned around and then disappeared. They all watched, transfixed, as her feet left impressions in the wet sand, and then splashed into the water. Then she was gone.

'She shouldn't have touched you like that,' Irmgard chided, nervous sounding.

'It is fine,' said Elfled, her voice distracted, as she looked out to sea. 'It would be very easy to convince yourself that such a meeting never happened. You must tell us where their islands are,' she said to Soren.

'When I return I will draw you a map,' he promised. 'But now I must leave.'

Elfled and Irmgard both embraced him. Morlin gave him a soldierly pat on the shoulder. Then it was time to board his ship.

Soren, still weak from the prolonged use of his magic, took the opportunity to sleep on the voyage north. He relied on the North Magnians to wake him if there was trouble and they did, more than once. The captain and his crew were edgy, hugging the coastline and pulling into the creeks along the way at the slightest sign of danger. The boy high up in the crow's nest would holler if he saw the Kharovians. One time a ship came close enough for Soren to make it out, sleek and silent in the moonlight; deadly looking.

The Asrai who swam into and out of view by the side of the ship didn't help the mood on deck. The sailors muttered prayers to various sea deities at the sight of green hair floating on the surface, or a splashing sound followed by the glimpse of webbed hands and feet.

But as they neared their destination without major incident, some of the sailors came to see the Asrai as benevolent protectors who had brought them luck. *Superstitious fellows*, Soren thought to himself, finding it all rather distasteful.

It was a relief to see the mountains of the Krykkers come into view. He had contacted Belwynn on the voyage, pleased to tell her of his success. But she had dire news. A huge army had invaded Kalinth, far larger than the force they had managed to see off a month ago. The Kalinthian forces had been defeated, and the survivors had retreated to the fortress at Chalios. His friends had escaped, and Toric's Dagger and the Jalakh Bow were safe. But he had to reach them as soon as possible.

A call came from the crow's nest. The boy pointed slightly to the port side. 'Ships!' he called out.

Soren followed the captain to the bow of the ship. They looked out, but it was hard to see much more than shapes on the horizon.

'Which way are they sailing?' Soren asked, concerned.

'Towards the land of the Krykkers. The same harbour we are heading for. We will have to pull in to the coast and wait until they are gone.'

Soren wasn't convinced. 'I would like to know who they are. They may not be Kharovians. Can your boy tell us?'

The captain made a face. 'Not without getting closer, and I'll not risk my men or my ship in doing that.'

'Please,' said Soren. 'I am a wizard, and we have the Asrai in the water. We will be safe enough if we get a little closer, just to see who is heading to the Krykker lands. It might be important.'

The captain sighed. 'A little closer, then. But at the first sign of trouble I'm turning her around.'

They continued on their course, the ship chopping through the water, the atmosphere on board tense.

'Three ships,' the boy shouted down when he was sure what he was seeing. 'First one is a Vismarian longship. The other two are Kharovians, closing in on her. She's not going to make it.'

'That's close enough,' began the captain, but Soren was already rushing over to the port side.

The Kharovians, with help from the dragon that the Isharites controlled, had destroyed their rivals in the Lantinen Sea. Siavash had said as much himself before the battle at the Pineos, and Maragin, chief of the Grendals, had confirmed it. Meanwhile, Rabigar had gone to Halvia to search for the Giants' Spear. Why else would a single Vismarian longship risk crossing the Lantinen, if it didn't have Rabigar on board, or at least some vital news to pass on? Soren knew that he couldn't risk that longship getting sunk.

'Tana!' he shouted at the sea, hoping that the Asrai would be able to hear him. 'Tana, I need your help!'

The captain blanched at the idea of calling out to the Asrai. 'I need to turn this ship around,' he muttered.

'Wait!' shouted Soren, pointing at him. Soren knew very well that people didn't like wizards pointing at them, and the captain stayed still and said no more.

Tana appeared in the sea by the side of the ship, and Soren could see the distinctive green hair of the other Asrai nearby.

'There is a Vismarian ship up ahead,' he shouted down to her, pointing in the general direction. 'It is being chased down by two Kharovian vessels. There is a chance that the sword of the Krykkers and the spear of the Giants may be on board. Is there anything you can do to help?'

Tana studied him for a moment, her black eyes giving nothing away, before pushing herself away in the direction of the Vismarian boat. The rest of the Asrai followed her.

Soren shared a look with the rest of the crew and the captain as the Asrai swam out of sight. 'Wouldn't you like to see what the Asrai do to the Kharovians?' he asked them. 'That would be a story to tell your grandchildren.'

The Magnian sailors looked at their captain, expectant. 'Alright, dammit,' he yelled. 'Follow on.'

Soren knew nothing about ships and sailing, but it seemed to take an age for their vessel to reach the confrontation. As they appeared, so one of the Kharovian vessels left, perhaps deciding that the arrival of the Magnians turned the odds fully against them.

The Vismarians had stopped. Armed men lined the deck of the longship, but it didn't look like they had done much fighting. Looming over the Vismarians was a creature literally twice their height. It held Soren's attention for a while, his mind not quite believing what it saw. Of course, a part of him knew what he was looking at. An Orias—a Giant. He could see that it grasped a massive spear in its hands.

Somehow. Somehow Rabigar had done it.

The feelings of disbelief and relief dominated him in such a way that it was a good while until he registered the sounds of screaming. Turning to the second Kharovian vessel, he saw that all was chaos. Kharovians were dying on their ship, as green-haired creatures ran amok. Some sailors tried to fight back. A Kharovian approached one of the Asrai, a curved sword held before him. Suddenly, he went flying, sent tumbling by some invisible force.

Of course, Soren knew full well that the force was Queen Tana, made invisible by her cloak. The Asrai, whom the Kharovian had looked ready to skewer only a moment ago, now launched itself at the sailor as he lay prone on the floor, its teeth sinking into his neck.

The resistance was all but over now. Some of the Kharovians had jumped into the sea to escape. Maybe they would be rescued by their sister vessel—unless the Asrai decided to return to the water, in which case they wouldn't stand a chance.

It suddenly occurred to Soren that the Vismarians may not react well to their arrival. An unknown ship, preceded by terrifying creatures that emerged from the sea, could justifiably put someone on edge.

'We are allies,' he shouted over to the longboat, trying to use Onella's Staff to help his voice carry across the water.

He could see the figures on the boat put their heads together in discussion. At least that suggested they had heard him. He then saw the giant raise its great head.

'Marvellous news!' it shouted in a deep male voice. It needed no magic to make its voice heard. 'We are in sore need of allies! I see that the Asrai are with you as well. Let us disembark in the land of the Krykkers and affirm our alliance!'

The captain of the ship turned to Soren with the glassy-eyed look of someone who had seen too much for their mind to process.

'Well now, captain, let's not tarry. Best to do what the giant suggests.'

Their arrival at the harbour of the Krykkers did not go completely unnoticed, even though it was night. Drobax could be seen descending the slope to the shore. They had little time for talk, and there were few of them to defend against the Drobax. For the Vismarians and Magnians who had brought them here were keen to get back home before more Kharovian ships arrived. As for the Asrai, as she had explained, only Queen Tana set foot on the land. Her five followers departed too, presumably back to the islands, though whether they intended to detour via the Kharovian sailors left bobbing in the water, Soren couldn't say—and didn't want to know.

This meant that Soren and Tana stood with only four others, none of whom he knew. There was a Krykker warrior, who looked like he had been on the wrong end of a battle somewhere. One arm was bandaged and there was bruising along one side of his head, with the black crust of dried blood. It was not Rabigar, he was much younger looking, but Soren spotted Bolivar's Sword on his belt. The Orias was there with what must be the Giants' Spear. Up close, Soren could see his skin was green. Never mind that. Up close he was huge. A woman stood with them. She looked small next to the giant, but she towered over the rest of them—fierce looking, with all the accoutrements of a warrior. Finally, a young man, with long, blonde hair and a bow on his back. Like the woman, he was dressed in the furs of a Vismarian.

'What happened to Rabigar?' Soren asked them, fearful of what they would tell him.

'He lives,' said the woman, 'but he took a bad injury from a white wyrm, out in the wastes of Halvia. He was not strong enough to travel back with us.' She nodded at the young man. 'Jesper's family is caring for him.'

'My father and sister are skilled healers. He is in good hands.'

'I'm pleased to hear that,' said Soren, his attention turning to the Drobax, the first of whom had nearly reached their position on the shoreline. There were about twenty or so headed towards them, but the danger was that they might attract hundreds. 'Look, I think the introductions will have to wait until we deal with this. Do you have any idea where we should go?' he asked the Krykker.

The Krykker pointed ahead, towards a rock face. It looked like there had been a rock slide, chunks of stone of all sizes lying at the bottom of it. 'That is a blocked tunnel,' said the Krykker. 'We won't be able to get in that way, but if we head in that direction, there's a better chance of being seen.'

It didn't amount to much of a plan, but Soren knew from his last visit that the only way of getting to meet Maragin was if her rock walkers found you— the routes in and out of the underground tunnel network were too well hidden for them to simply stumble on one by chance.

Without another word, they moved. The Giant's long strides took him ahead, spear aimed at the nearest Drobax. The creatures closest to them paused, realising that waiting for superior numbers was the best way to survive the encounter.

'I will put a shield around us,' Soren shouted as they moved to catch up with the Giant. 'If you stay within it's perimeter, you will be safe.'

'I will guide you while we walk,' said the Vismarian woman, as if she knew that Soren would need some help while he concentrated on his magic.

The Vismarian named Jesper took position on the other side of Soren. He strung his bow and put an arrow to the weapon. Meanwhile, Tana—Tana was nowhere to be seen.

Soren sighed. It was all very well having an Asrai and a Giant on their side, except that they didn't seem to want to fight as part of a unit. The huge, green figure was far beyond the perimeter of Soren's shield when he engaged with the Drobax. Despite the size of the spear he carried, he thrust it forwards lightning-quick. The blade plunged through the Drobax as if it were ripe fruit, only stopping when his hands reached the body. He then leaped forwards and sent the blade into a second Drobax. Both creatures were now spitted on his spear. He lifted them up, flicking the weapon so that they were flung away onto the ground.

Soren had never seen anything like it, and the Drobax stared wide-eyed with horror, before backing away. Jesper hit one of them full in the chest with an arrow. Another collapsed to the floor, seemingly for no reason, though Soren realised that Tana must have worked her way towards them, and would have her sharp teeth at its throat. That seemed to be the final straw. The Drobax turned and ran.

Taking the opportunity, they made for the rock wall as fast as they could. A figure appeared to one side of it, then two more. Krykkers—probably rock walkers, who had emerged through the rock that protected them from the Drobax who roamed above ground.

The figures waved for them to come, indicating they should hurry. Soren didn't need to be told twice. He stopped his shield spell, instead using Onella's Staff to help him scramble over the loose stones towards the waiting Krykkers.

Maragin was not far away, still able to keep an eye on events above ground, while her small force of Krykkers remained beneath it. They were based in a series of underground rooms, seemingly constructed for the very situation the Krykkers now found themselves in. There were rooms for storage and for sleeping. They were taken to a meeting room, where Maragin waited for them, their Krykker guides departing with a nod from their leader. There was a stone table and chairs; the Giant was given a rug on the floor to sit on. Pillars carved from the rock supported each corner of the room, and shelves full of fat, stubby candles lined the walls. It lent the moment some sense of grandeur, which was good, for there was no doubt in Soren's mind that it was deserved.

It was only now, in the relative safety of their underground hideout, that the introductions were made, followed by the sharing of stories. After Soren had introduced himself and Queen Tana, now visible again, he sat back and listened to the tale of those who had arrived from Halvia.

He learned that as well as Jesper, the Vismarian, there was his countrywoman, Gunnhild. The Krykker's name was Stenk and the Giant named himself Oisin. It was Gunnhild and Stenk who knew the full story, and of the two it was Gunnhild who did most of the talking. Stenk had the look of a man who, once sat down, had resolved never to get up again.

'A Vismarian crew agreed to take us across the Lantinen,' Oisin told them, as the story neared its end. 'They have few ships left now, and the Lantinen seems thick with Kharovian vessels. I judge we were lucky to make it. Of course, we may have been sunk, were it not for the arrival of the Asrai,' he said, nodding to Queen Tana. 'I knew your Queen from long ago,' he added. 'We fought together at the Battle of Alta. She wore the same cloak you now wear. And of course, Bolivar fought with us, too. We stopped the Isharites that day—but did not defeat them. We need to do better this time around.'

Soren spoke then, telling his story, ever since Toric's Dagger was found to be missing from its resting place in the temple in Ecgworth. He explained how the quest for the weapons of Madria had taken him across Dalriya, finally to the islands of the Asrai, who had agreed to play their part once more in the war against the Isharites.

'I have been honoured to play my small part in such a story,' said Stenk, surprising Soren by getting to his feet. He pulled Bolivar's Sword from its scabbard. 'Before we left him, Rabigar entrusted me with a message. He told me that my chieftain, Torinac, was the first to wield Bolivar's Sword. He was slain fighting the Isharites in Haskany. Rabigar took it then, believing it was his to wield. He told me that they had both been wrong. He said the sword should have been yours, Chieftain Maragin.'

Maragin gave the Krykker a piercing look, but said nothing.

'He bid me to take it from him,' Stenk continued, 'and if I made it back to Dalriya, to come here and deliver the weapon to you. I'm pleased that I was able to fulfil the mission he gave me. But the sword is yours now.'

He offered it to Maragin. She took it, hefting the weapon, feeling the weight of it. Maragin, chieftain of the Grendal clan, wasn't one for sentiment or ceremony. Soren knew that she and Rabigar had a unique relationship. He knew that she had just been given the greatest honour a Krykker could receive. But she made no mention of either.

'Very well,' she said. 'It looks like I am leaving my homeland with you. Stenk, I would ask you to remain here. You are too injured to trek across the mountains. But there is much you could do here to help us.'

'Of course,' the Krykker replied, collapsing back into his seat.

'We have the sword, spear, staff and cloak,' Maragin continued. 'Where are the other weapons?'

'The dagger and the bow are in Chalios,' Soren answered. 'The Shield of Persala is the one weapon we don't have, and I can't be sure of its whereabouts. But we know it is in the hands of the Isharites.'

'Dear friends, we must first travel to Chalios,' said Oisin, his deep voice resonating around the chamber. 'There, six of the weapons will be taken, coming together for the first time in centuries. From what you have told us, Madria has chosen your sister as her champion. She may be able to guide us to the whereabouts of the shield. Remember, we are merely the instruments of Madria. The war you have been fighting is coming to an end. Soon it will become a battle between gods, and that will decide what becomes of Dalriya.'

XVIII

ESSENBERG

THE NORTH GATE OF ESSENBERG was closed and barred, as the last of the stragglers made it into the city. The reinforcements from Burkhard Castle, exhausted looking, were found space inside the city walls: Rainer, the Emperor's chamberlain, efficient to the last.

The reactions of those inside Essenberg couldn't have been different. Edgar was overjoyed to find that Farred was amongst the survivors of the siege. Duke Coen was there too, his Thessian veterans with him. Coen was a good man to have in a situation like this, and Edgar took pleasure from the look on Salvinus's face when the mercenary leader realised that the man who had bested him at the Battle of Lindhafen was now in charge.

If there were reasons for Edgar to be pleased, the Empress Hannelore looked devastated. She kept asking where the Emperor was. She seemed to be under the impression that if she asked often enough, she would get an answer she could understand. But whoever she asked, the answer was the same. Baldwin had taken the Kellish and the Luderians east, away from Essenberg, leaving his family in the capital. Moreover, Hannelore's brother-in-law, Duke Walter, had taken the final third of the imperial army west. Adalheid, mother of Jeremias of Rotelegen, had been waiting to greet her son, only to find that he and his men had gone with Walter's Barissians. But she was a woman inured to hardship, and she didn't complain. She led the tearful Empress away to the castle, though Edgar doubted that Hannelore would get much in the way of sympathy.

Coen looked ready to drop, but he stood and explained the situation to Edgar and the other leaders who had come to meet him. The Isharite army that had taken Burkhard Castle was less than a day behind them. Baldwin and Walter had decided to lead the enemy away, in an attempt to save Essenberg. No-one present believed that Essenberg would now be spared—the capital of the Empire was too great a prize for Siavash's generals to ignore it. But they would undoubtedly divert some of their forces to chase Baldwin down, and that might give Essenberg a chance to hold out for a while longer.

They didn't have long to find out. The Isharite army arrived the next morning, marching along the Great Road. The great artery of the Brasingian Empire had made the Empire rich, but now it was proving to be a weakness, for it took the enemy straight to its heart. Whatever impact Baldwin's move had made, and Edgar knew it must have had some, it hadn't stopped thousands of Drobax from advancing on Essenberg. Edgar had been told all about the creatures, how the Isharites controlled hordes of them, totally unlike the armies of men. But now, watching them surge close to the walls of the city, he realised that he had not fully understood. If these monsters weren't stopped, the human kingdoms would be swept away.

Edgar stood on Baldwin's Bridge, the River Cousel flowing into the city underneath him, along with Prince Cerdda and Farred. Cerdda looked pale with shock, while Farred looked more resigned. He knew more than perhaps anyone else about the relentless nature of their enemy.

Duke Coen had merely confirmed the Magnians' deployment. From Baldwin's Bridge their soldiers stretched west along the walls of Essenberg. Wilchard commanded the men on the Valennes Gate, where the road led to the capital of Guivergne. The Middians, under Brock and Frayne, had been given the walls around the Coldeberg Gate. The southern troops were not, therefore, in the immediate line of fire, because the Drobax were still confined to the north side of the river. If they were to take Essenberg, of course, it would mean they had crossed the Cousel. Nowhere in Brasingia would be safe.

South of the Coldeberg Gate, the men of Gotbeck lined the walls all the way to the southern tip of the city, where the Cousel left Essenberg behind and continued its course to the Itainen Sea. The Gotbeckers, deprived of their leader, Archbishop Godfrey, had been given the safest section of the wall.

Coen had given his Thessians the toughest task. They defended the entire eastern half of the city, outside which the Drobax now gathered. Coen had taken this responsibility from Salvinus, instead leaving the mercenary captain with the defence of the strategic sites within Essenberg. Most important of these was the castle, inside which were Baldwin's wife and three children. Should their defences start to fail, Salvinus had to evacuate the royal family from the city. Edgar strongly disliked the idea of leaving their safety to Gervase and his mercenaries, but ultimately that was a matter for the Brasingians.

More and more of the Drobax gathered, surrounding the eastern half of the city, many rows deep. Edgar fancied they were close enough to be within bowshot, but the archers on the walls were waiting for them to attack, when they could make best use of their limited supply of arrows.

'What if we turn these catapults around?' Cerdda suggested.

The catapults on Baldwin's Bridge were currently aimed at the Cousel, designed to stop a naval attack from Guivergne. But the Isharites had no boats.

'It's a good idea,' Edgar agreed. He pointed to the nearest group of Drobax, who lined the east side of the riverbank and would be sent against the nearest section of wall, where Coen's Thessians met his own position on the bridge. 'We could target the Drobax there. I've no doubts the rocks will carry that far.'

The princes gave the order and the line of half a dozen catapults were shifted from their north-westerly position along the course of the Cousel, to due north.

The Drobax they were targeting peered up at them, watching. Any human unit would have retreated from the obvious danger, but the Drobax did nothing.

'Let's try them out,' Edgar suggested.

It required little calibration of the machines to strike the Drobax. They stood so deep and wide that they were hard to miss. A couple of rocks strayed to the left at first, splashing harmlessly into the river. Some hit the ground in front of the enemy, churning up the earth. But soon all the catapults were hitting their targets every time. Those Drobax who took a direct hit were defenceless, without any kind of armour to lessen the blow. Soon piles of grey bodies and rocks lay together, splattered with dark red gore.

It might have been coincidence, but the drums of the enemy sounded then. As far along as Edgar could see, the Drobax began to move, running for the walls of Essenberg. They carried no equipment, not even a ladder. But their numbers were terrifying, and he feared that the large North Gate, standing across the Great Road, would not hold for long.

Cries of alarm drew his attention closer to home.

'They're jumping into the river!' Farred warned him.

Hundreds upon hundreds of Drobax were hurling themselves into the Cousel. The river was thick with their bodies. They couldn't swim, but instead floated along with the current. Those who got into difficulty struggled in the water and drowned, pulling any unfortunate creature close enough with them in their desperation. But while many drowned before their eyes, more kept coming, getting closer to the bridge.

And they had moved the catapults.

The archers on the bridge and atop the Valennes Gate fired into the river, hitting the easy targets that floated there. But again, this was a numbers game, and they couldn't kill them all. The arches of the bridge were the next obstacle, funnelling the Drobax into narrow spaces where dangerous eddies swirled.

Edgar ran to the inner side of the bridge and looked over. It wasn't long before the Drobax reappeared. The first were hit by arrows and sank to the bottom of the river. But more came behind them. It had taken the Drobax a matter of minutes to breach the city walls by using the river. Those who had survived the perilous journey were floundering awkwardly. But nevertheless, they were making their way to both banks of the river. On the west bank some had found their way to the Market Quarter, where the Magnians and Middians were stationed. On the east bank, the Drobax left the river in the Castle Quarter. Not so far from where the Empress Hannelore and her three children were being kept. Still others, unable to get to either side, floated further downriver, towards Albert's Bridge.

When Edgar returned to the outer side of the bridge, he could see that the Drobax were still coming—hundreds more entering the Cousel, the quickest path into Essenberg.

He locked eyes with Cerdda and Farred. 'This is a disaster,' he said.

'We need to take some of our men down to the bank, stop them as they try to climb out of the river,' said Cerdda.

'Agreed. Farred,' Edgar said, turning to his friend. 'Get a message to Duke Coen, warning him that the Drobax have got into the city. He'll soon find his men surrounded, and the royal family needs to be moved.'

Farred nodded. 'Anything else?'

'Hold the bridge for as long as you reasonably can, but no meaningless sacrifices. Take everyone out via the Valennes Gate.'

'Understood.'

Edgar wasted no more time. He took a few men with him, Brictwin included, who was never far from his side. Cerdda did the same. They left the bridge and moved west along the city walls, heading for the Valennes Gate.

Wilchard, efficient as ever, saw their approach and came to meet them on the wall. He had already seen the danger.

'What do you want to do?'

'Give us a hundred men each,' said Edgar. 'We'll take them to the river. You stay here but get ready to open the gates. I don't know how long we can hold them back.'

Edgar and Cerdda took their men down from the walls into the city. The Valennes Road led from the gate into the market square. This was where the Brasingians made their money, goods from all over Dalriya finding their way here to be traded under the protection of the emperors. But it was empty now, the Isharite forces only a few hundred metres away. What exactly they would do with Essenberg, Edgar didn't know. But he knew that an era of freedom was at stake. Sometimes men don't realise that they're living in a golden age, until it ends.

They crossed the square, making their way to the river. Once he got within sight, Edgar could see that it was full of Drobax. About fifty of them had now climbed from the Cousel. They reached back into the river, grabbing onto the creatures that floated past, pulling them onto land. If Edgar allowed this to go on much longer, this part of the city would soon be overwhelmed.

Cerdda nodded at him, then led his North Magnians towards the Drobax who had gathered further downstream. That left Edgar and his men with those who were closer. The prince waited until his counterpart was in position, then called out a charge.

Both groups of Magnians drew weapons and streamed down towards the river. The Drobax turned to face them. They were thin, pallid, grey-skinned things, dripping wet from the river. Many had lost whatever weapons they had, and those that had been retained were primitive looking clubs and spears. For a moment Edgar almost felt sorry for them. What dark magic had driven them here? But there was no time for such thoughts now.

As he neared them, he focused on one, noticeably bigger than the rest. It held a large, spiked club. He startled when it opened its mouth and shouted 'Attack!' in a brutish voice. But Edgar was experienced enough now not to let that affect him for long. He feinted at it with his sword. The Drobax lost no time in making a vicious swing of its own. Edgar waited a split second to see its trajectory. The monster was swinging the club up towards his head. Edgar rolled underneath the swing, felt the whoosh of air above him, then came up and thrust his sword into the creature's chest.

The Drobax let out a cry of pain, but it wasn't done yet, bringing the club back down. Edgar tried to pull his blade free, but it didn't come easily. He was forced to let go, turning aside at the last moment as the club came down. He took the blow on his back and side, his armour protecting him from the full effects of the strike. It left him winded, but that was better than a broken arm.

He rolled away again, getting to his feet and drawing his dagger from his belt. But the Drobax had other problems now. Brictwin appeared—a series of fast sword slashes too much for the wounded creature, ending in a vicious crack to the head. The Drobax didn't get up from that blow, and Edgar was able to retrieve his sword.

They marched down to the riverbank, where the Drobax were now on the defensive, trying to maintain their improvised bridgehead. But Edgar's Magnians outnumbered them, and they succeeded in driving the last of them back into the river. That made their job easier. They could patrol the bank, deterring the Drobax from attempting to climb out, slashing down at those foolish enough to try.

It gave Edgar a chance to survey the situation. The Cousel was thick with Drobax bodies in both directions, and there were no signs of an easing off. Many had drowned, some of them washing up in the shallow water, but presumably many more had now sunk to the riverbed. Farther along, Prince Cerdda and the North Magnians had succeeded in driving the rest of the Drobax back into the river, so that the whole stretch of riverbank as far as Albert's Bridge was clear. Beyond the bridge was the Army Quarter, and he just had to hope that the Gotbeckers who manned the walls there were alive to the threat.

Edgar turned his attention to the opposite side of the river. Here, things were not going so well. No-one was preventing the Drobax from climbing out of the river into the Castle Quarter. Consequently, more and more of the creatures were making for this stretch of bank, where they were pulled out and sent on their way. The ground rose up beyond the river, so it was impossible for Edgar to see what was going on over there, though not so hard to imagine. The Drobax would be charging at the walls and the North Gate. Coen's Thessians would be hard-pressed. Edgar was sure that Farred would have passed on his warning by now. But that didn't mean Coen could do anything about it.

The siege continued in such a way for some time: the Magnians protecting the Market Quarter, while more and more Drobax found their way to the Castle Quarter. It was no surprise to Edgar when activity on Albert's Bridge grabbed his attention. He could see Cerdda waving at him.

'Come,' he said to Brictwin, before telling his men to keep to their positions on the riverbank. They walked briskly along the river. Edgar's back and side felt stiff and bruised, but the injury didn't seem serious.

They reached Cerdda, who pointed to a group of armed men coming off Albert's Bridge.

'Salvinus's men. They have the Empress with them.'

Edgar watched as the mercenaries, armed with spears and shields, moved quickly off the bridge, before forming up and making space. Next came Hannelore with her three children—Katrina, Liesel and Leopold. Their faces were full of fear, immediately making Edgar wonder what horrors they had witnessed on their journey from the castle to the bridge. Afterwards came the other key members of the court who were being evacuated with them: Rainer; Archbishop Decker; the Duchess Adalheid; and a young woman with blonde braids. Farred had told him that the apprentice of Archmage Gustav had come to the city with the army, and he supposed it was her.

Finally, Gervase Salvinus and the rest of his soldiers followed behind. Many held weapons that were red with blood—they had obviously fought their way across the city. Others carried heavy-looking bags, no doubt the valuables of Essenberg Castle, stripped bare before they left, not to mention the gold thalers that Salvinus had been promised for his services. A score of Cordentine crossbowmen were positioned at the end of the bridge, their hand-held machines pointing to the other side, in case the Drobax tried to give chase.

Edgar and Cerdda approached the group.

'Princes Edgar and Cerdda,' Decker acknowledged them. 'You have held the Market Quarter?'

Hannelore said nothing, her eyes wide. She looked ready to bolt at any moment. Her daughters had braver faces on than she did.

'We have,' Edgar replied. 'And the Castle Quarter?'

'Completely overrun,' said Salvinus brusquely. 'I have my orders to get the Empress and her children out of here, so excuse me if I don't tarry to share stories.'

'What of Coen?' Edgar persisted.

'He's alive,' Rainer answered. 'He's retreating the Thessians into the Cathedral Quarter and will then bring them across the First Bridge, before following us south to Lindhafen. We would appreciate it if you could hold Albert's Bridge for a while longer to give Coen time to affect his manoeuvre.'

'Of course,' Cerdda agreed, although Edgar wondered why Salvinus's mercenaries couldn't do it.

'We are all most grateful,' said Rainer. 'Then you must get your own men out of the city.'

'We hold the Valennes Gate and the Middians have the Coldeberg Gate,' Cerdda said, 'so our exits are secure.'

'Well,' said the chamberlain, with a nervous glance at his empress, who still stood silently, but was clearly impatient to get going, 'good luck to you both.'

With that, the royal family was led away. Gervase murmured instructions to his crossbowmen, before turning to them. 'They'll hold here for a few minutes until you can replace them. But then they're gone.' He smiled, his scar creasing. 'Remember, Prince Edgar, my men don't expect me to get them killed.'

With that he was gone, following his bags of gold, no doubt paid handsomely for retreating from Essenberg.

Edgar tried to let his bitterness go. He turned to Cerdda. 'Holding both Baldwin's Bridge and Albert's Bridge is stretching our forces as far as they can go. We need to make plans for a quick retreat, as soon as Coen is across. There's no value in staying in Essenberg now, and we don't want to be fighting off the Drobax every step of the way.'

Cerdda was never allowed to reply. All Edgar saw was Brictwin lurching towards him, before his bodyguard bundled him to the ground. They crashed down, Brictwin on top of him, but Edgar still heard the whistles of the crossbow bolts going past.

Brictwin was quick to get to his feet and pull Edgar up, even though Edgar could see that he had a bolt in his upper arm. Turning, Edgar could see the Cordentines running away. Hot anger took over, and he began to follow them. They wouldn't have time to reload before he was on them. He would kill every last one.

Brictwin grabbed him, pulling him back.

'No, Your Highness. I can't let you.'

'And I can't let them get away with it.'

'Edgar.' Brictwin rarely used his name. 'Prince Cerdda,' he said, pointing.

Cerdda was on his back. The first bolt had hit him in the chest, the second in his abdomen. The third was in his neck.

Edgar rushed over and grabbed his hand. Cerdda's eyes were wide with shock. Blood frothed from his mouth as he choked on it. Perhaps he was trying to speak, but no words came.

Edgar held his hand and spoke to him. He didn't know what words he used, but he spoke of Magnia, of Cerdda's wife Irmgard, of his mother Mette, and of his sister Elfled. By the time that Cerdda's soldiers had realised that something was wrong and had rushed over to their fallen prince, he was dead.

Edgar stood shakily. The North Magnians looked at him silently. Many emotions fought for control over him in those moments, one decision after another came and went in his head as he struggled to think clearly, to fight off the powerful urge for revenge. He must try to do what was right. He thought of Elfled, pregnant with his baby, and that was enough to give him a measure of self-control.

Finally, he took a deep breath. He was able to speak, even though his voice shook as he said the words.

'You must take your prince's body now,' he told them, 'to the Coldeberg Gate. Tell lords Brock and Frayne what happened here. They have horses outside the city. They should take the road to Coldeberg. From there you can cross the Midder Steppe and take Prince Cerdda's body home.'

Cerdda's men said little before they left, but did as he had asked. Edgar looked about him, his mind dangerously empty now, unsure what to do. All he could think about was killing Gervase Salvinus, but that would have to wait. From the bank of the Cousel his men shouted a warning.

'The Drobax are coming,' Brictwin said.

Edgar walked to the bridge. He looked to the other side. The bridge was so wide that the creatures could come six abreast and still have room to swing a weapon. He put a foot onto the bridge.

Brictwin grabbed his arm. 'We must go, Your Highness,' he warned.

'Yes, I know. I'm not about to throw my life away. Thank you, by the way. For saving it.'

Brictwin nodded, still wary looking, as if he feared that Edgar was about to charge at the Drobax who were making their way towards them.

Instead, Edgar stood on the bridge and looked downriver. 'Look,' he said to Brictwin, who stood next to him.

From the vantage point of Albert's Bridge, they could look down on Margaret Island, where the First Bridge crossed the Cousel. Many of the Drobax who had floated past them downriver had scrambled onto the island in the river. They were now being engaged by Coen's Thessians, who were trying to break their way through and access the bridge that would take them to the west bank of the river. On the east bank more Thessians were gathered in the Cathedral Quarter, holding off a swarm of Drobax until the First Bridge had been cleared and they could cross. Edgar knew that Coen would be in the thick of the fighting in one location or the other.

'It looks to me like they'll make it out,' Edgar said. 'There's no sense in us staying here.'

'Agreed,' said Brictwin, keeping an eye on the Drobax, who got ever closer.

Edgar moved quickly now, off the bridge and back to his men, giving them the order to retreat.

'I should have been more wary of Salvinus, when I saw him talking to his crossbowmen,' he said to Brictwin as they made their way back to the Valennes Gate. 'It just didn't cross my mind that he might give such an order in such a situation.'

'That's because you're a better man than him,' said Brictwin. 'These Brasingians are weak and treacherous,' Edgar's bodyguard ventured to add.

He stopped there, but Edgar knew well enough what Brictwin thought. That they shouldn't be here at all. That they never should have left Magnia.

Farred and Wilchard were waiting for him, and soon the Magnians were on their way north-west along the Valennes Road. Somewhere up the road Wilchard had stabled their horses, ready for just such a retreat.

Edgar only looked back once. Essenberg was taken, and with it Kelland joined Rotelegen as duchies lost to the enemy. The Brasingian resistance was now scattered. How much longer would the Empire last?

Edgar wouldn't mourn the end of the Brasingian Empire. That was where Brictwin misunderstood him. Edgar knew that this wasn't a war between the Isharites and Brasingians. The Drobax wouldn't stop at the borders of the Empire. Sooner or later they would be sent to Magnia. And Magnia had no great fortresses, or rivers, or cities to defend. The end of the Brasingian Empire meant the end of Magnia, and of everywhere else.

XIX

ALLIES

'EVER SINCE I TOOK THAT SPEAR to the calf in Samir Durg, all I've done is walk,' Jurgen grumbled to his cousin, the pain in his leg giving him a temper.

Wisely, Rudy ignored him.

At first, Jurgen had just been grateful that they had escaped from the Isharite army after the battle outside Heractus. After all, it had been after such a defeat that they had been captured and taken to Samir Durg in the first place. But once the immediate threat had subsided, his mind switched its attention to the agony of walking. There was also, at the back of his mind, a little guilt at having left Clarin behind.

They had been lucky, probably, that the battle had been fought at night, giving them the chance to use the darkness to move unnoticed. They had tried to follow the Kalinthians south, but with the enemy all about, it had seemed far safer to head east. They were moving through enemy occupied territory, but the Isharites would be focused on sending their forces after King Theron's army. Two men making their way in the opposite direction could easily be overlooked.

They knew they had made it into Persala by now, but otherwise, their ignorance of the geography of the area left them unable to say more than that. Neither had they developed any kind of plan, or destination. Everywhere about here was conquered territory. It seemed there were no safe havens any more. So they kept walking, and the futility of it was close to driving Jurgen to despair.

When the ambush came it was almost a relief.

They were walking in the countryside, but parallel to a road—with the vague, unspoken notion that if they followed a road, they would probably end up somewhere. The half-dozen men had taken their time over the ambush. Really, they had invested much more effort than was necessary. Three came from behind and the other three appeared from the direction they were walking in, timed to perfection.

Rudy and Jurgen drew their weapons anyway. They had agreed long ago that they weren't going to let themselves be captured again.

'Steady now,' said one of the men, friendly enough. He was tall and thin, hands holding a spear lightly enough to suggest he was used to holding one. He held up a hand to tell his associates not to go diving in quite yet. 'Unless you're better swordsmen than you look, fighting it out isn't your best option.'

'Dying here is as good as anywhere else,' Jurgen said, surprised that his voice came out as steady as it did.

'We'll kill if you want,' said the man. 'But it wasn't in our plans.'

'What was?' Rudy asked. 'Who do you fight for?'

'I'd like to think that outnumbered six to two, you'd have the decency to tell us your loyalties first. Then I might reveal ours. Your accents are Brasingian, if I'm not mistaken. If so, you've strayed a long way from home.'

Rudy shrugged. 'We're friends of Zared. He should be the rightful king in these parts.'

Mention of Zared clearly had an affect on their ambushers, though they hid it enough so that Jurgen couldn't tell if it had been wise to give the name or not. The leader kept any emotion from his face. 'Zared is an easy enough name to play with. It doesn't mean very much by itself.'

'How about Cyprian?' Jurgen said. 'Another friend of ours.'

The man's eyes narrowed. Cyprian's name had done the trick, though it remained to be seen whether it was for good or ill.

'Cyprian, eh? Well it just so happens that Cyprian is a very short walk from here. Maybe we could take you to see him and let him decide whether he counts you as friends or not.'

'How do we know you're telling the truth?' Rudy demanded.

The man gave an exasperated look. 'Not that I want to be accused of tyranny, but we're the ones with the numbers in this situation. Your job is to hope and pray that I speak the truth, not make demands. I am growing a little tired of this, truth be told.'

He gave his spear a spin to add a little emphasis to his words. Jurgen decided that there was something about the man he liked.

'We'll go with you,' he offered. 'But we keep our weapons. Yes, it's unusual in a situation like this, I fully concede. But when you've spent time in Samir Durg, you put a higher price on liberty than life.'

Their captor, if that was the right word for it, raised an eyebrow at that. He knew about Samir Durg, Jurgen could tell. These were Zared's men.

The man made a play of giving a sigh and contemplating his response. But Jurgen knew he would take them to Cyprian. He knew they had wandered aimlessly, without much thought or a plan, and yet still somehow stumbled upon an undeserved stroke of luck.

***

A STRANGE kind of peace descended on Baldwin as he led the men of Kelland east. Some of the Luderians had stayed with him. Others had taken his offer and left, to return to whichever part of their duchy they called home.

Baldwin considered what might happen to Luderia. He knew that its duke—his father-in-law, Arne—would stay holed up in Witmar until the enemy came to his walls. The north of Luderia was forest. The people might decide to escape there. They could conceivably give the enemy the run-around for some time.

Further east, the Atrabians were used to defending their hilly lands—Baldwin's father, Bernard, had learned that the hard way. They might even bring the Confederacy into the fight. To the south, his brother Walter would put his men behind the walls of Coldeberg. Coen would do his best to hold Essenberg, before falling back on Lindhafen. And should Lindhafen fall, there were other options. His allies in Magnia. Cordence, even.

Kelland would fall. That was the hard truth he had been forced to swallow. But somehow, despite that, he had hope. Farred's friends, with their talk of ancient weapons. They could still win through. And that was a burden they carried, not him.

The peace that fell on Baldwin came firstly from knowing that the Brasingian resistance would carry on without him. Secondly, that he had done the best he could. He had defended Burkhard Castle for as long as possible. He had got his soldiers out when it fell. They had sent thousands of Drobax to hell. If he could do it again, he might change one or two things, but none of them would have changed the outcome. Baldwin used to worry what the historians might write about his reign. That he would be remembered as a failure. But he couldn't control that. He found that when he judged himself, he was sympathetic.

They made it to the town of Könighausen. It had done well in recent years as the last stop on the road from Witmar to Essenberg, growing in size. Now Baldwin had to tell the townsfolk that the Isharite army was close behind. They must pack up what they could and leave.

They were frightened, but they hadn't lived through what Baldwin's soldiers had lived through in the last three weeks, and it was difficult to muster much sympathy. Baldwin could see that the townsfolk saw as much in the dead eyes of his soldiers, and they soon got to work preparing to leave, not wasting time or energy on useless complaints. They couldn't carry half as much as they owned, which was a welcome boon to Baldwin's men, whose supplies had run out yesterday. They settled themselves in and around the town's inns and taverns and got to work. When a barrel of beer or wine ran dry, they changed it for a fresh one. Any spare food was given to them and any animals left behind were soon slaughtered and roasted, either in the big pits in the taverns or outside on the many fires the Kellish soldiers shared. It mattered little to Baldwin that the fires continued through the night. *Let them see us*, he told himself. *We're supposed to be leading them away from Essenberg, and anyway, my men will fight better on a full stomach.*

The next day Baldwin led his men east. He had decided on his destination during the night. He had lain awake for much of it, unable to shake off the thought that it would be the last night of his life.

The ridge had already come into view when his men reported that the Isharites had been spotted behind them. It gave them ample time to reach it first, even though his scouts reported that the enemy were on horseback.

When they gained the ridge, Baldwin gave brief orders on the army's deployment. In truth, it was surely obvious to every man there. They would defend the ridge, forcing the enemy to come at them uphill. Behind them lay the beginnings of a small wood, a good place for any survivors to escape to. A marsh to the east would prevent the Isharites flanking them that way. To the west, it was possible for them to get around, but it would take a good two hours. If they tried it, Baldwin would spot them and order a retreat into the woods. No. The ridge wasn't so high that the enemy had to worry about such tactics. They would attack them here, he knew.

The ridge allowed a clear view of the enemy's approach. The cavalry came first, followed later by units of well drilled infantry. There were no Drobax to

196

be seen. The Isharites must have sent their monsters to Essenberg. A wave of fear passed over him; fear for his wife and children. But surely Coen and Rainer and whoever else led the defence there would get them out of the city long before there was any danger to them.

Baldwin was torn away from his musings when his name was called. Some commotion was occurring at the back of the ridge. He marched over, looking where his men pointed into the woods.

Not possible! His heartbeat raced. Had the Isharites somehow used magic to transport a force to the rear of his troops? But the sense of panic faded when he spotted the banners of the soldiers in the treeline. The Leaping Fish of Atrabia.

'Quiet!' he commanded angrily, raising a hand. He was angry that his men had given him such a scare, angry with himself for not properly scouting the woods. Such laxity could have led to disaster.

One man detached himself from the Atrabians in the woods. He came on foot, and Baldwin knew it was Prince Gavan, even though they had never met.

'Leave us,' he said sourly, and his men returned to their positions. Some cast dirty looks at Baldwin or at Gavan, but he had no interest in dealing with such minor insubordination. If they fought and died on this ridge, he could forgive it.

'Your Majesty,' said Gavan.

He was softly spoken, perhaps ten years younger than Baldwin and a couple of inches taller, his hair dark as was typical of his people. He wore full armour apart from his helmet, allowing Baldwin to look his subject in the eye. Gavan was a subject who had refused two orders from Baldwin to raise troops for the Empire. According to the law of the land he should have been stripped of his title and hung, drawn and quartered by now. But here he was, living and breathing, commanding the men of Atrabia.

'Prince Gavan,' Baldwin said. 'I saw you attack the Isharites on the Great Road. You're back for more?'

'If you want our help we will give it,' Gavan replied, a slightly quizzical expression on his face. 'I must admit, I haven't been able to fathom what your strategy is, Your Majesty.'

'Come,' said Baldwin, 'let's look upon the enemy together and decide what is best.'

They walked together to the front of the ridge and looked down at the army that approached.

'You can see for yourself,' said Baldwin. 'Instead of Drobax, human invaders have been sent to kill me. Men from Haskany and Persala. Even with your men, they still have us three to one.'

Gavan looked at him. 'While the Drobax have been sent on to Essenberg?'

'Exactly. So here I am tying up the Isharites' best soldiers. If I was in Essenberg instead, do you think I could have stopped the Drobax?'

Gavan shook his head. 'I start to see the strategy. The enemy is divided.'

'Good. And should those bastards strike me down here, and suffer some losses while doing so, where should they go next? Chase you into Atrabia? Try to take Luderia? Barissia? Thesse? Gotbeck?'

Baldwin could see Gavan think about it. 'The Isharites chop off one head and five new ones appear. I understand fully now. But must you die here, Baldwin? I can cover your retreat into the woods. We have horses with us.'

Baldwin considered it. If it made sense, he would do it. He didn't have a death wish. 'My men are at least well fed today. Tomorrow they won't be. And they will be marching on foot, while the Haskans chase us on horseback. You can delay them, but you can't stop them from catching us. Better to fight here, I would say.'

'Then we will fight with you,' Gavan said.

'An honourable suggestion,' Baldwin admitted. He gestured around them. 'But my men fill this ridge. You would be of more help in the woods, covering a retreat; or a flight. You might prevent a massacre if you could do that.'

'Of course. But won't you join me there? The Empire will do better with you alive than dead.'

Baldwin nodded. 'Maybe. But I escaped from Burkhard Castle while good men died to keep me alive. I'm not minded to do that again. I've made my peace with dying here.'

The mention of Burkhard brought a look of pain to Gavan's face, as Baldwin hoped it would.

'You know,' said Gavan, 'since your father conquered Atrabia, your family are devils to my people. My cousin permanently stirs up trouble for me, talking of a rebellion against the Empire. I am called coward and traitor for resisting such calls. If I had obeyed your orders and tried to take soldiers to Burkhard Castle, my people would have killed me, put my cousin on the throne and you would have faced a full-scale rebellion. You understand, I say this not to apologise. Just to explain.'

Baldwin shrugged. When put like that, Gavan's predicament sounded all too true. Walter had argued with him more than once about Atrabia. But Baldwin hadn't wanted to listen. When it came to their father, he wouldn't hear a bad word. Part of him had known that Walter was right. But when you're the older brother—when you're the emperor—you don't always have to do what's right. That seemed more than a little silly now.

He held out a hand. Gavan took it. At the last, they had found some kind of reconciliation. It might have felt irrelevant—too late. But for some reason, it didn't.

'You know,' said Baldwin, 'looking at those men coming for us, I wondered whether the Isharites plan to turn Brasingia into another satellite state. Will they try to appoint a new emperor, to recruit Brasingians into their armies, as they did with Arioc in Haskany?'

Gavan smiled grimly. 'They could try, but they would find it didn't work. Brasingians follow their dukes to war, not their emperor.'

'Yes. And that might turn out to be our greatest strength. Well, we have an understanding, Prince Gavan?'

'We do, my lord.'

Gavan returned to his people in the woods. They would be ready to counter-attack when the Kellish needed them.

Meanwhile, the Haskan cavalry were making their way up the slope to the ridge where the Kellish stood. They wore fine armour and they carried lances, that from horseback would give them a superior reach to Baldwin's men, despite the height advantage the ridge afforded. Behind them were thousands of infantrymen, with spears and shields. They had waited in reserve at the bottom of Burkhard Castle, while the Drobax and the dragon had taken the fortress. They were fresh, while the Kellish were battered and bruised from the horrors of the three-week siege, and had marched all the way here on foot.

It wasn't a battle Baldwin could win and he knew that he would die on this ridge. Nonetheless, a strange kind of peace had descended on the Emperor of Brasingia. It was strong enough to carry to his men, and when it came to it, they fought and died with him.

***

RIMMON WAS ON EDGE. Four hosts marched south to Chalios, making their night camp amongst the monotonous Kalinthian heathland. The foul smell from the Drobax was impossible to escape, whatever direction one took. But the army had been joined by other, even more disturbing visitors.

Firstly, Lord Siavash was here. With him had come the entire Order of Diis, black cloaked figures fanatically loyal to their leader. It was known that Siavash rarely left his Tower in Samir Durg, from where he had plotted his rise to the top. But now he was in Kalinth, his dark order with him, marching with his four hosts to a fortress held by the remnants of the army they had defeated outside Heractus.

It made little sense from a purely military point of view and Rimmon knew enough to piece things together. He had been there when Herin had won the Persaleian Shield from his brother. He had served under two members of the Council of Seven, Queen Shira and the red-eyed wizard, Pentas, during their ill-fated insurrection against the Isharites. He knew about the weapons of Madria, that they were the only things Siavash truly feared in Dalriya. He didn't know everything, for Siavash was careful to keep his plans to himself and his closest followers. But he understood that a victory at Chalios would, in some way, mark the end of the resistance from Madria and her followers.

It wasn't just Siavash who had come. With him—inside him—was the god of the Isharites. Diis. Whenever Rimmon got close to this presence he felt a wave of malevolent power roll towards him, like a giant clawed hand, making him shudder involuntarily every time. What he felt now was just a taste of the power that would be unleashed when Diis destroyed his rival Madria. The thought was so terrifying that he did everything he could to block it from his mind.

Finally, as if more evidence were required of the fate that was in store for Dalriya, a creature from nightmares had arrived yesterday evening. The story was that Siavash and Diis had summoned the dragon from another world, perhaps the one Diis had left to come here. Like many others, Rimmon had found himself moaning pitifully as the green lizard unfurled its long wings and landed on Kalinthian soil. Kull was one who at least made a play of being unconcerned. He had laughed when confiding to Rimmon that he had been ordered to serve the creature a supper of ten live Drobax. Despite the instinctive fear that almost everyone felt at the presence of the dragon, the fact that it would fight on their side against the enemy worked to blunt it. Few thought ahead like Rimmon did. When Chalios was destroyed, when the last opposition to Diis had gone, where would the dragon be unleashed next?

Rimmon was waiting for his tent to be made ready, when the half-human, half-Drobax abomination that was Kull found him. Everywhere he turned there were disturbing creatures. While Kull didn't have the kind of power or intelligence that made him a threat, Rimmon didn't trust him in the slightest.

'Herin wants to see you,' he said.

Rimmon thought about making a dig about Kull being an errand boy, but any kind of insult was water off a duck's back to the Drobax leader, and so he gestured for him to lead on. The sooner the meeting began, the sooner it would be done, and he could retreat to the refuge of his tent.

Herin's tent was already up. Well, he *was* the general of one of the hosts, commanding a mix of Drobax, Isharites and human soldiers. And his star was rising—his latest achievement was the sacking of Heractus, carried out by his forces. He had already got Siavash the Persaleian Shield, thereby preventing Madria's followers from securing the full set of Madria's weapons. All these triumphs were good for Herin, and reflected well on his lieutenants, too: Rimmon himself, and Peroz and Kull.

Given his current status, Rimmon had found it all the more surprising when Herin had acceded to Kaved's demands to lead the assault on Chalios. Herin's host would follow on, the second to reach the fortress. But with everything at stake here in Kalinth, Rimmon feared that Herin had given their rivals a golden opportunity for glory that might outshine their own. Still, Herin was a canny operator. Rimmon had learned to respect the Magnian's shrewdness during their time together.

When he pushed through the flap of the tent, Rimmon found Herin sitting at a table facing him. He was ready to start dinner, a large platter covered by a domed metal plate warmer in the centre of the table. It looked like Herin's food was substantially superior to the slop Rimmon was given.

As Rimmon stopped in front of the table Herin looked up at him. The mage sensed Kull slink into the tent after him, the hair on the back of his neck standing on end at the thought of the Drobax behind him.

'We'll arrive at the fortress tomorrow,' Herin said, 'with the assault coming the day after. Time is beginning to run out.'

Rimmon nodded. 'Have we been given orders? What of the dragon?'

'I'm not privy to what the dragon will do. If it is deployed, it will make breaking in much easier. If not, the Drobax will be sent over the walls anyway. Some crude ladders and such have been made, and we have only a few siege engines. Still. The defenders won't have the numbers to stop the Drobax getting in.'

He made it sound all so easy.

'And what of these weapons?' Rimmon asked him. 'Those who serve the goddess are inside. Maybe they will put up some sort of resistance.'

Herin smiled tightly. 'Madria's champion is in there. Siavash wants her killed, of course. But if they were able to stop us, they would have done so at the Battle of Heractus. They will have fewer who can fight now than they had a week ago.'

'So it should be easy.'

'Yes. Which is something of a shame.'

'A shame?'

'Indeed. What will happen when Kalinth is defeated? By all accounts Brasingia is already on its knees. They will push further south. It won't be long until they reach Magnia.'

What game is this, Rimmon thought to himself. *A poor one.* 'Of course, Lord Siavash will take the whole of Dalriya. This is hardly news.'

'Come now, Rimmon. I know you fought with Pentas. You tried to free your country from the Isharites. You understand my position completely.'

'Everyone knows my past,' Rimmon countered coldly. 'Lord Siavash forgave me and many others. I have served him faithfully since.'

Herin waved his hand in an irritated fashion.

'Please, Rimmon. This is not some piss poor attempt to make you incriminate yourself. Even if you think I'm not above that, at least admit I would do a better job of it. We both know that should Siavash succeed here, it is the end. For all of humankind, even such as us, who have served Ishari. I'm asking whether you will join me in turning against them at this crucial moment.'

Rimmon's heart was beating fast. Was Herin really serious? Inside, he agreed with everything the man was saying. But he had been pardoned once. He knew he wouldn't get a second. They would destroy him.

'What can we do to stop them?' he demanded.

Herin gave him a quizzical look. 'We command a host, Rimmon,' he said, as if talking to a stupid child. 'Come now. If it is fear, or lack of faith in me, then say so. But don't try to argue that we are not in a very good position right now to strike a serious blow.'

Turn their host against Siavash? Switch sides? It was a daring plan. Not enough to stop Siavash, but still, the thought of it was enticing. And what was the alternative? Continue to help Diis destroy Dalriya? Was that course any less stupid?

'Alright, Herin. I'm in. But how do we begin to get this host to do such a thing? The first inkling that Peroz gets about such a plan it will all be over.'

Herin smiled again. It was a proper smile this time, reaching his eyes. They lit up with mischief. He removed the metal dome from his platter. Revealed was the head of Peroz on the plate, sitting in its juices.

'I've already dealt with him,' Herin said unnecessarily, enjoying the reveal. 'It should buy us a bit of time to come up with a plan.'

'I'm glad you said yes,' said Kull behind him.

Rimmon turned to face the Drobax.

'I would have had to kill you otherwise.'

Rimmon glanced down at the knife the Drobax gripped. He had no doubt Kull would have slaughtered him on the spot if he had refused to join their insurrection. And yet it was strange.

'Why would a Drobax turn against the Isharites?' he asked him.

'Look at me,' Kull replied, a serious tone replacing the normal mocking one. 'Look at my people. Do you not think I have as much reason as anyone?'

XX

VIGIL

MONEVA SAT WITH GYRMUND atop the cliff at Chalios. They were taking advantage of a small sliver of time they could call their own. They had enjoyed little time to themselves since they had first met, both recruited to help retrieve a stolen Magnian relic. It had seemed a simple enough task back then, when Herin had offered it to her. So much had happened since. Perhaps the strangest of all was that she would find love with the ranger who had led them through the Wilderness. She wondered sometimes, if all this should end and they both lived, what it would be like. Would their relationship, born in turmoil, survive the banality of everyday life?

Soren is here, came a voice in her head.

She gave Gyrmund a wry smile.

'Did you hear that?' she asked him.

Yesterday Gyrmund had spent some time alone with Belwynn, as she established a telepathic connection with him, just the same as she had done with Moneva. Moneva was prepared to do almost anything to defeat the Isharites. Still, a petty and jealous part of her didn't like the fact that Belwynn could have such a private conversation with Gyrmund, when she couldn't.

'I did,' he replied. 'Could we pretend that we didn't?'

'I think she would track us down pretty quickly.'

He nodded, yielding to the inevitable, and got to his feet.

We're coming, Belwynn, Moneva said, as Gyrmund helped her up.

She looked out past the defences of Chalios, where the army of Ishari that had followed their retreat from Heractus now gathered, more and more of them arriving by the hour. An optimist might think Soren has arrived just in time, she thought to herself. But really, what difference is he going to make?

They descended the stone steps that led down into the vast open chamber of the fortress. It was crammed with people now, all having to live together with no privacy. It smelt of stale sweat and worse, and an uneasy atmosphere pervaded the area. They were holed up in here like a fox gone to ground, and beyond the walls, the enemy had found their lair. There was no escape plan now. Nowhere else to run to. No words of comfort to share.

Moneva picked her way quickly through the groups of people sitting together on the rough floor, until she reached the massive gates that led outside. Here she could breathe fresh air again, but the narrow space ahead was flanked by the walls and towers that defended the approach to the gates. Soldiers manned these defences, their numbers boosted since the arrival of Count Diodorus and his troops. They peered down at Moneva and Gyrmund as they walked towards the barbican, and the feeling of claustrophobia lingered.

They found their friends in a ground floor room of one of the barbican towers. They were the last to arrive and a conversation had already started, with at least four people speaking at once. Belwynn was with Theron and Clarin. Of the new arrivals, Moneva only recognised Soren. Otherwise, there were half a dozen strangers—strange being the operative word. The strangest of the lot had to be the Giant. Green skinned, he had to stoop to fit his body inside the room, leaning on the spear that was obviously the last of the weapons of Madria they had been tasked to find.

The conversation that swirled around the room was about Rabigar, and for a dreadful moment Moneva thought that their Krykker friend was dead. Instead, several people were trying to explain that he had suffered a bad leg wound and had been left, hundreds of miles away, on the far side of Halvia. A female Krykker now wore Bolivar's Sword at her belt, and while Moneva had never met her before, she had certainly been told of Maragin, the chieftain of Rabigar's clan.

Her gaze fell on Soren, who was staring at her. Why, she couldn't understand, but now he had her attention he made his way towards her.

'Please, excuse us for a moment,' he mumbled to the rest of the room, who were too occupied in conversation to pay much attention.

Save for Gyrmund. 'Am I excluded from this meeting?' he asked, jovially enough.

'Yes, I would say so,' Soren muttered. With a hand on her shoulder, he guided Moneva back out of the room.

Gyrmund watched them go, a look of concern on his face. Moneva tried to give him a reassuring smile.

She racked her brain thinking about what kind of message Soren could have for her. Outside the room, he looked around irritably. He obviously wanted to find somewhere private but didn't know the layout of the tower. Moneva led the wizard to a small storeroom, barely large enough for them both to fit inside.

'What is it?' she demanded.

'I wanted to tell you first, before it came up in conversation,' he said. 'Arioc was in the land of the Asrai.'

Mention of Arioc's name was like a punch to the gut. Moneva hadn't been expecting it.

'To cut a long story short, he was hiding there. When I arrived, there was a brief struggle. Tana, the Queen of the Asrai, killed him. Ripped out his throat, I think.'

Arioc was dead? She felt suddenly lightheaded. Her legs went weak, and she put a hand to the wall to support herself. A mix of emotions assailed her. Bile rose as she revisited what Arioc had done to her. There was relief that he was dead, anger that someone else had done it, that she wouldn't get the personal vengeance she craved. A kind of cold emptiness, too. Was she supposed to feel better now he no longer took breath? She wasn't sure that she did.

She looked at Soren, concern for her etched on his face. She had always seen him as rather cold: driven, ambitious, without much time for personal relationships. That he had thought of her feelings amidst all his other burdens surprised her.

'Thank you for telling me, Soren. I appreciate it. I'm glad he's dead. This Queen Tana, she is here? I didn't get a chance to find out who was who.'

'I will introduce you. Arioc took her captive—she had her reasons to want him dead, too. Tread carefully with her, Moneva. She is on our side. But she is dangerous.'

Moneva shrugged. 'So am I.'

After the introductions were made and the new arrivals given time to recover from their journey, the real meeting began. This was a meeting about magic, about the weapons of Madria, and only those with a direct involvement had been invited. Even Theron, ruler of this place, had decided to stay away. They returned to the tower room of the barbican, for it was the largest space they had that lent some privacy. The enemy army beyond Chalios was a reminder, if it were needed, that time was scarce.

'If we leave to one side, for the moment, the question of the Shield,' said Soren, 'let us agree what it is we are meant to do from here.'

Six of the weapons of Madria were present in the room: Moneva had Toric's Dagger at her waist; Gyrmund had the bow; Soren the staff; Oisin the spear; Maragin the sword; and Tana wore her cloak. Moneva was no sorcerer, but even she could sense the power in the room now that all six weapons had come together in one place. Clarin shifted uncomfortably in his chair at Soren's mention of the shield. Although no-one else blamed him at all, the fact that he had found the weapon and then had it taken from him still weighed heavily, she could tell.

'We must find Siavash and kill him,' said Belwynn. 'The real enemy is Diis. He must be destroyed, and He inhabits Siavash.'

'But that's what we did in Samir Durg,' said Gyrmund. He gestured at Moneva. 'Moneva killed Erkindrix at Samir Durg, and Diis simply left that body and joined with Siavash. What's to stop that happening again?'

'I need to do it. To be there,' Belwynn answered. 'Elana was Madria's champion then, and she wasn't in Samir Durg. Madria must use me to destroy Diis.'

'But that didn't work last time,' said Oisin, his voice a rumble of thunder.

Moneva had thought the strangest thing about the Giant was his appearance: full twice the size of anyone else, save for the Vismarian woman, Gunnhild. But it wasn't. She had learned that Rabigar had woken him from an impossibly long sleep. The King of the Giants had done all this before. He had been at the centre of the events hundreds of years ago that had led to the Cracking of the World; had fought with mythical figures like Bolivar the Bold. And he spoke about these events as if they had just happened yesterday.

'We closed in on Erkindrix that day, some of us had to fall to get to him, but that only made the rest of us the more determined. The Jalakh archer, Turgen, struck him full in the chest. Bolivar sliced into him with his blade, with just as much force as I did with my spear. He was impervious, you understand? Erkindrix couldn't be killed. Then Diis called forth terrible powers. The very earth erupted with fire. It was all we could do to save the weapons and escape. Our chance had gone.'

Oisin stared ahead, reliving his memories. His words silenced the room.

'But which one of you was Madria's champion?' Belwynn asked him quietly.

'The one whom Madria spoke to was the Avakabi. Masego.'

'Avakabi?' Moneva asked.

'A Lipper,' Soren replied.

'He carried the dagger,' Oisin continued, 'but he was killed when the seven swordsmen of Diis attacked us. Oh—'

Realisation dawned on the Giant and his face crumpled. 'We failed,' he cried, almost wailing. 'We failed to protect Madria's champion. So many lives have been lost because of us.'

'Bolivar didn't fail,' hissed Maragin, her face tight with anger.

Oisin ignored her, his head drooping as he looked at the floor, disconsolate. Gunnhild gave him a consoling pat on the knee.

'So,' said Soren in his calm manner. 'We know that Belwynn must be there and she must be kept alive at all costs. We must consider Toric's Dagger, too. Is it mere coincidence that the dagger was used to kill Erkindrix in Samir Durg, and again to destroy Siavash's shadow at the Pineos?'

'When other weapons, such as the bow, didn't hurt him,' Gyrmund added.

'Then the next question,' Soren continued, 'is where to find him? Samir Durg again? If so, how do we get there?'

Everyone looked at Belwynn. She turned her head to one side and made a face, as if she were listening, or thinking. The mannerism reminded Moneva vividly of Elana, and a lump suddenly came to her throat. She missed the priestess, who had seemed to carry the weight of her responsibility with ease. Belwynn was somehow more vulnerable than she had been.

'I think Siavash is coming here—Diis with him. Just as we are talking about killing him, so he must be set on killing me. Doing so would clear away the last obstacle to their victory. And with the Shield in his hands, he fears me less.'

'So it comes back to the Shield,' said Soren.

'Do we need it?' Moneva asked. 'If it is this dagger that kills Diis, then why worry about the Shield? Especially since we don't know where it is.'

'My sense is that we need it,' Belwynn answered her. 'Elana used to think so, too. But you could be right.'

'We don't know for sure where it is,' said Soren. 'What if Siavash has brought it with him? Maybe we could somehow get our hands on it? If it is in Samir Durg, then I am with Moneva. There is no possibility of travelling there and back in time. Chalios would fall long before any of us could return with it. We may have to risk going for Siavash without it. I am not sure.'

'Perhaps we need a little time to think?' Oisin asked.

'Perhaps so,' Soren agreed. 'But time is fast running out.'

Moneva looked across the room at Queen Tana of the Asrai. Their eyes met. It was like looking into a bottomless black pool, yet it felt to Moneva like she was looking into the eyes of a kindred spirit. She couldn't be sure that Tana was thinking the same thoughts as her. But she fancied she was.

'You killed Arioc,' Moneva said. 'I wanted to do that.'

Tana regarded her with inscrutable, dark eyes. But her mouth rose into what could be interpreted as a smile. Moneva could see rows of sharp teeth inside. The Asrai licked her lips.

'I'm sure there were many who wanted him dead. We are just two. I won't deny that the taste of his blood in my mouth was sweet. But who performed the act matters much less than the act itself.'

Moneva nodded. Soren had warned her that this creature was dangerous, and she sensed that now. There was a bestiality about her. She looked at the cloak, the weapon that Soren had searched for. It clung tightly to the Asrai and had a cloudy sort of transparency, revealing as much of her body as it concealed. Tana noticed her gaze and gave Moneva a wicked looking smile.

'I was thinking we could visit the enemy camp tonight,' Moneva said. 'I'm used to moving about under the cover of darkness, and if your cloak truly makes you invisible, you should have no problem either.'

Tana disappeared. Moneva knew she was still there and could feel her presence.

'You want to see if they have the shield,' came Tana's voice, a susurration on the air, before the Asrai reappeared.

'Yes. It's worth the risk. And if they don't, we can console ourselves by killing some of the enemy. Even the odds, ever so slightly.'

Tana's smile returned. 'When do we go?'

Moneva waited for as long as she could, but she and Tana were both eager to go, and they left the fortress not long after sunset. Maybe it was wrong, but she hadn't told Gyrmund she was leaving. He would have asked her not to go.

She told Soren instead. The sorcerer didn't object to them risking their lives, but he was worried about them losing their weapons to the enemy.

'I should go with you,' Soren said. 'You may need my help.'

'Soren, you're as agile as a one-legged crab. This really doesn't fit your skill set. Remember, I can communicate with Belwynn now. If we get into trouble, I'll warn her.'

Soren looked rather glum at this. Moneva supposed it must be hard for him, suddenly sharing a gift that he had thought was a unique attachment he had with his sister. Not that he would ever complain about something that might help them to defeat Diis. He was as obsessed with the idea as she was.

Moneva and Tana approached the enemy camp. Moneva stayed close to the Asrai woman. Her cloak meant Tana was an ideal accomplice for this task, but what about her eyesight, or her understanding of the threats they would face? It was safer to keep an eye on her.

Moneva touched Tana's arm to stop her, and they crouched down. 'They've set up a perimeter,' she whispered. 'Humans, probably Haskans. There's one there,' she said, pointing, 'and one over there, to the right. I think we'll find they'll have guards positioned at regular intervals right around the camp. Either we leave and find somewhere less well defended or try to get through here.'

'Here,' murmured Tana. 'We don't have time to waste.'

'Agreed. You take that one, I'll take the one to the right.'

Tana turned to look at her, frowning. 'I will take both. You might be seen.'

'I won't be seen,' hissed Moneva, offended by the idea.

'You *might* be,' Tana insisted. 'And I *won't* be.'

Moneva scowled. Stupid Asrai bitch was right. 'Alright,' she said through gritted teeth.

Tana turned invisible and left, leaving Moneva to watch and wait. The first soldier was moving about: stretching, practising his combat moves, perhaps to stay awake. After a set he would stop and look out. The sound of Tana's movement would be hidden while he was exercising, and that was the time Moneva would have chosen to strike.

Sure enough, mid-lunge, he suddenly sprawled to the ground, and didn't get up.

Moneva began to move towards that location, but slightly to the right. She went at a crouch, moving fast, looking around in all directions. A movement to her right caught her eye. The second soldier, perched on a rock, lurched backwards. Moneva changed course, making for the soldier's position. Tana reappeared, her victim's blood around her mouth.

'Come,' whispered Moneva. She didn't stop, moving ahead towards the camp now. If the perimeter had been set up properly, the guards should be able to check on each other now and then, to ensure that there wasn't a breach. It was possible that their intrusion might soon be noticed.

The Asrai turned invisible again, but Moneva could hear and sense her moving next to her. She wasn't as quiet as Moneva, but she had to admit, Tana moved well.

Soon they were approaching the tents of the soldiers. The Haskan defences had been poor. No doubt they weren't expecting an attack, and anyway, the Isharites had such a large force they didn't need to care if they lost a few soldiers from a night attack.

The priority was the shield, but the sleeping soldiers before them were too tempting for Moneva and Tana to ignore. They attacked together, Moneva with a short sword in each hand, Tana content to use her teeth. They killed quickly, before the soldiers knew what was happening, before they could make much of a sound. It wasn't until the fifth tent, when a soldier screamed in terror as Tana loomed over him, that they had to stop. She ripped into his neck, silencing him, but by then the camp had begun to stir. They departed quickly—Moneva's swords dripping with viscous blood; Tana's face and chest red.

Their bloodlust somewhat satiated, Moneva and Tana focused on searching for the shield. Moneva soon became disheartened. It had sounded simple enough back at the fortress, but in the midst of the enemy camp, she soon came to appreciate just how large and sprawling it was.

While the Haskan unit they had attacked was laid out to an organised, geometric design, the Drobax simply lay down where they had stopped, out in the open, sometimes for miles in any direction. What was more, they weren't asleep like the human soldiers had been. Moneva caught glimpses and sounds of the foul creatures copulating in the moonlight, turning her stomach. Once they came across a group of about ten Drobax sat around in a circle, making guzzling noises. Moneva saw that they were eating one of their own. Disgusted, she moved towards them, intent on killing them all, before Tana dragged her away. If the Asrai was appalled by what she saw, she didn't show it. She seemed intent on their search, and they kept to it, as the night hours began to pass.

They had to find where Siavash and the leaders of the army had made their camp, or where the carts full of supplies were located. But with no order to the area, they were reduced to simply hoping that they might stumble onto somewhere of interest. As their fruitless search continued, the middle of the night approached; the time when they should give up and return to the fortress.

'Hello,' came a voice from the darkness.

Moneva tensed, looking about for the speaker. Something at the back of her mind told her she recognised the voice, but she had no time to think when an attack could be imminent.

Beside her, Tana disappeared. Moneva heard her moving off in one direction and warily followed, trying to stay in touch with her ally, while peering into the darkness.

Two figures appeared at once. Ahead of Tana, a flame-haired man; he was tall, youthful looking. To Moneva's right, a second man, equally tall and powerfully built, dark hair swept over to one side. She knew this man. It was Herin.

Stunned, she didn't react as the red-haired man held out a hand in Tana's direction. She sensed that magic was being used, though there was nothing to see.

'I have her held,' said the sorcerer confidently.

Damn it. She should have brought Soren along after all.

Herin stepped forwards slowly, both hands raised in the air.

'Thank you, Rimmon. We're not actually here to fight,' he said to Moneva. 'I just want to make sure the pair of you don't slice me into pieces before I get my words out.'

Herin looked meaningfully at the swords Moneva held. She didn't feel like putting them away. Toric's Dagger weighed heavily at her belt. She wondered whether Herin knew she had it; whether he knew that Tana had the cloak.

'I had actually hoped that some of you might come here. It makes my life a lot easier. I thought if anyone did try it, it would be you.'

Tana reappeared. Moneva could see that she was held tight by whatever spell the man called Rimmon was using.

'What do you want?' she asked Herin.

'Don't worry, I'm not after the weapons. I've actually come to give you something.'

He clicked his fingers. Out of the shadows came a Drobax.

'This is Kull.'

It was taller, more human-like than the usual ones. She had seen such creatures at the Battle of Heractus; heard stories of them. It held something in its hands, covered in a dirty looking cloth. Moneva looked on apprehensively, as the creature pulled the cloth away.

'The Shield of Persala,' Herin announced, as if he were performing a circus trick.

The shield was made of a dull metal. There was nothing remarkable looking about it. Moneva eyed it suspiciously.

'Is this some kind of joke? How would you have the Shield?'

'Does Clarin live?' Herin asked suddenly.

'Yes.'

'He is well? Fully recovered?'

'Yes.'

Herin let out a sigh of relief that seemed genuine.

'The others? Belwynn and Soren?'

'Belwynn and Soren live. Gyrmund, too. We lost Elana and Dirk.'

Herin looked to the ground momentarily, a pained expression on his face.

'Clarin must have told you how I took the Shield from him. It had a leather cover, with a horned man painted on it. I took the cover off and put it on another shield, before handing that in to Siavash. I've never been so scared in all my life.'

'Truly, Herin? You're not lying about this?'

'Of course not. Diis was there too, you know, staring out from inside Siavash. Anyone would be scared.'

'You know what I mean, you fool!' she demanded, though she couldn't help her lips twitching in amusement.

'It's the Shield,' he confirmed, nodding at Kull. The Drobax stepped towards Moneva, offering it. With a little reluctance, she sheathed her swords, before grabbing the Shield. Kull stepped away.

'Do you think I can stop now?' Rimmon asked. His face was red and moist with sweat.

'Tana?' Moneva asked sharply. 'Will you stay still?'

'Yes.' The Asrai hissed with anger, but when Rimmon released her she didn't charge him, restricting herself to a bare of the teeth in his direction.

'I don't suppose Clarin will forgive me,' Herin said.

'You know Clarin,' Moneva said. 'He's not one to hold grudges like some people. So all this subterfuge on your part was for this moment?'

'This moment,' Herin agreed, 'and hopefully some more. When I was in Samir Durg, I got a sense of the power the Isharites had. And I was full of desire for revenge. I decided that escaping to fight and lose another day wasn't enough. If I could rise to a position of power within, I could do far more harm as a traitor than as an enemy. My luck was in choosing to serve Siavash. All of a sudden, he had won, defeating Arioc and his other rivals. He wanted generals who knew how to lead men and fight. He didn't worry too much about loyalty—he had his Order for that. When I took him the Shield, I was given my own host. So here I am, with one more trick up my sleeve, I hope. Tomorrow, we will attack. The first host will be led by Kaved.'

'Kaved?' Moneva asked. Gyrmund had told her he had seen the Krykker at the Battle of Heractus, but this was another surprise.

Herin smiled bitterly. 'He had his moment of glory when he killed Shira, Queen of Haskany.' He briefly glanced over at Rimmon before continuing. 'That won him a promotion early on. He will lead the attack on Chalios. My host will come second. I will order it to attack Kaved's force,' he said with a grim smile.

'Why would they do that?'

'Because I will order them to do it. You can see for yourself that my two lieutenants are in on the plan. Whether the rest follow my order or not, we will find out tomorrow. Either way, that is the opportunity for the Kalinthians to attack, to crush Kaved's attackers between our two forces. Ordinarily, the Kalinthians would never believe me. But I have given you the Shield of Persala as a sign of my good faith. And you all know that I seek vengeance on Kaved.'

Herin had recruited Kaved at the same time as Moneva, and the Krykker had betrayed them to Duke Emeric and Gervase Salvinus. Herin had felt personally responsible ever since, especially for what the jailers in Coldeberg had done to Rabigar. Moneva understood Herin, knew how much it meant to him.

'I will persuade them that you speak the truth,' she said simply. 'Is there a message for Clarin or anyone else?'

Could she see tears in his eyes? He shook his head.

'I don't know what else to say. Please just tell them what I have done, and why. That is enough. There is a chance I will see them again. If I don't, I'm ready for the consequences.'

Moneva nodded, dropping the Shield to the ground. She made up the distance to Herin then, and took him by surprise by giving him an embrace. He hugged her back, looking slightly embarrassed when they parted.

'There was a time,' she whispered, so that only he could hear, 'when I was ready to love you, you know?'

He nodded. 'Of all the foolish things I've done in my life, walking away then was perhaps the most foolish of all. But you and Gyrmund—?'

She nodded.

'Loathe as I am to say it, you are better off with him.'

'I am. Good luck tomorrow.'

'You too.'

Moneva retrieved the Shield of Persala. She and Tana turned to the east, keen to return to the fortress while the night still hid their passage.

'Farewell Herin,' she said over her shoulder, not looking back.

'Until next time,' he replied.

XXI

THE SIEGE OF CHALIOS

CLARIN WAS IN THE MAIN CHAMBER of the fortress of Chalios. In his hands he held the Shield of Persala. The first thing Moneva had done was to hand him the weapon, before recounting to those gathered her night-time meeting with Clarin's brother, Herin.

Clarin struggled with his emotions. He felt some pride had been restored. He had been embarrassed about losing the Shield to Herin, though there was nothing else he could have done in the circumstances. But most of all he had been embarrassed by his brother. The Herin he had always looked up to had become a craven supporter of the Isharites. Now it appeared that Herin had been playing the Isharites all along, looking to inflict the most damage on them as possible. Moneva told them of Herin's plans to turn his force against Kaved's today. He believed that Herin was telling the truth. He told the others as much, and none of them openly doubted him.

Despite all that, Clarin still hurt. What hurt, he realised, was that Herin had done it all without him. He had left Clarin at Samir Durg with no explanation—Clarin had been forced to leave, forced to assume Herin was dead. Then, when Herin intercepted Clarin's smaller force in Persala, he had maintained the pretence, not choosing to confide his secret to him. Choosing instead to fight him—to infect him with poison. No doubt Herin thought of himself as the great hero, delivering the Shield at the last moment. But Clarin couldn't forgive him. At first, when Moneva began to tell her story, he had felt jealous that she had been the one to find Herin, not him. But the more he thought about it, the more he was glad of it. He had no interest in speaking to his brother any more.

As everyone tried to digest Moneva's news, Clarin's friends couldn't help peering at the final weapon of Madria, their hands almost itching to touch it. He understood. Oisin's spear was impressive, but too large for anyone else to hold properly. Tana's Cloak, well—it wouldn't do to stare at that too long. This shield was altogether more accessible.

He let Gyrmund hold it first. His friend rapped it with his knuckles.

'Metal,' he said. He lifted it into a pose, slotting his forearm into the straps. 'Not as heavy as it looks. But still...'

'I don't mind it,' Clarin said. 'I'm used to using a shield.'

Gyrmund passed it on to Theron, who tried the weight out for himself, a serious expression on his face. 'I'll get a shoulder strap made for you right away,' he said. 'It will spread the weight around nicely. We'll need something to attach it to, though.'

'When I was given it, it had a leather cover,' replied Clarin. 'Quite pretty it was—colourful, with an image of a god on it.' He wracked his brain, trying to recall the conversation with the old Persaleian flamen, Ennius. 'Ludovis,' he remembered. 'A bearded chap with horns.' He glanced at Belwynn. Ennius had demanded a name from Clarin before handing over the shield. It was only her name that the priest had accepted. When he had woken up in Kalinth, he had discovered that Elana was dead, and Belwynn had become Madria's chosen. The ways of gods were strange, and Clarin didn't try to make sense of them.

'I may have something you can use,' said Diodorus. Compared to his usual demeanour, the count looked positively enthusiastic. 'It will have the winged horse of Kalinth on it, you understand?'

'I would be honoured. After all, I'm fighting for Kalinth, aren't I?'

Soren and Belwynn were following the conversation with rather bemused expressions. Clarin grinned. The twins weren't very interested in weaponry, which was ironic given the nature of the quest they had taken on.

Soren cleared his throat. 'I was wondering, given what Herin said, whether our plans for today should change?'

Once the topic of military strategy was mentioned, eyes naturally turned to Theron. It irritated Clarin, but he had come to accept it as something that wasn't going to change.

'Not much,' said the king. 'The walls must still be defended. But if there is an opportunity to counter-attack, we will be ready. The Knights will be held on standby. Everyone else, however, will be needed on the walls.'

Of course, thought Clarin. The Knights will get the glory, while everyone else gets to die on the walls. Still. With the Shield of Persala in one hand, and Cutter in the other, it might be fun.

***

GYRMUND STOOD with Soren and the Count of Korenandi. They were on the wall walk above the gates of the barbican. They faced due west, directly into the face of a cataclysm heading their way.

'That is only one of four hosts?' Diodorus asked them, his voice incredulous.

Uncountable numbers of Drobax came for them. So too did regiments of human soldiers from Haskany and Persala. He could hear the barking of Dog-men. In amongst all this would be the Isharites themselves, some of them magic users. This force would overwhelm them. Suddenly, Herin's claim that he would switch sides and lead his own units against this force looked like the only ray of hope they had.

'Prepare your men,' was Soren's reply to the count.

Diodorus nodded, taking a moment to compose himself. Gyrmund was more sympathetic than Soren. The count had taken his wife and children to Chalios. They, along with Lyssa and every other non-combatant, were in the huge stone fortress behind them, the great gates locked tight. It was a mighty stronghold, built to be impregnable, but no-one could design a fortress to withstand the numbers that came for them now. Gyrmund didn't like to think about what might happen to them.

Diodorus left without another word. The soldiers of Korenandi had the task of defending the barbican. At least they were fresh, Gyrmund mused, unlike the bruised and battered survivors of the Battle of Heractus that manned the walls behind them. He heard the count's raised voice, giving out final orders, reminding his soldiers of the tasks they had been given. His shock at the size of the enemy force was gone now. In front of his men, he was the confident commander.

Two great towers formed the centrepiece of the barbican, jutting out proudly from the walls. Slits in the towers allowed archers to fire from all angles, while great rocks could be dropped from the high battlements. Each tower had a catapult on its roof, ready to fire into the attackers. In between the two towers and beneath where Gyrmund and Soren stood, ran the metal-bound wooden gates that would be the obvious target of the attackers. A metal portcullis had been lowered in front of the gates to protect them. A few feet behind the gates, a second portcullis was down.

Gyrmund pulled on the string of the Jalakh Bow, stretching his muscles. Two buckets full of arrows leaned against the wall in front of him. The archers of Kalinth were positioned in the barbican and all along the walls and towers behind them. There were enough of them to disrupt the attackers. But the enemy had more Drobax than they had arrows.

The front ranks of the enemy were in range of his bow now. It was no surprise to see that the Drobax came first, arrow fodder in the eyes of their masters. Gyrmund wasn't minded to use his arrows yet—not on them, not when he might yet miss.

The Drobax came wildly. Many veered to either side of the barbican, sent past its formidable defences to the walls that connected it to the fortress proper. Moneva and his other friends commanded the defences there. He mustn't worry about them—just trust that they would hold off the enemy.

That still left thousands of Drobax who now came in a rush to the gates of the barbican. He could see now that many groups of slower moving Drobax carried rudimentary siege equipment. There were long ladders, thick tree trunks to be used as rams, large wooden panels to defend them from Kalinthian missiles.

The first Drobax had reached the barbican. The Kalinthians were firing arrows. Above the cacophony, Gyrmund heard the catapult to his right launch its first rock, then the one on the other tower followed. The rocks couldn't miss, landing on the Drobax that milled about in front of the barbican. Now was the time to use his arrows. Half a dozen Drobax were bringing a ram towards the portcullis, trying to push their way through the mass in front of them. Gyrmund took out the one at the front on the near side, then the one directly behind, the Jalakh Bow thrumming loudly with each release. With no-one taking the weight of the front corner, they pitched over, the ram crashing to the ground.

As soon as another Drobax moved in to help lift the ram up, Gyrmund shot them. While this was happening, the Drobax pulling at the great metal portcullis with their bare hands were crushed by rocks heaved over the sides of the battlements. A mound of dead bodies began to pile up in front of the barbican, while the catapults continued to launch more rocks into the air, which crashed into unarmoured Drobax wherever they landed.

Despite the losses they were taking, the Drobax came on. The large panels they carried were now linked together, forming a wooden wall that made its way forwards. They brought it down in front of the ram, defending it from Gyrmund's arrows. He stopped shooting, reluctant to waste a single arrow. Behind the panels, he could glimpse more rams, and ladders, getting readied for a massive assault.

Next to him, Soren acted. Holding forth Onella's Staff, he directed a blast of magic at the panels, pummelling many of them over. A roar went up from the Drobax behind and they came, dragging rams and ladders with them. Gyrmund made shot after shot, focusing on the rams, which he thought were the greater danger. Arrows and rocks flew at the Drobax, but not enough to stop them.

A loud crackling noise next to him drew Gyrmund's attention away. Soren was under attack, defending against a magical blast of energy. He was already red with the strain. This was why Gyrmund was here. Never mind the Drobax.

He slotted a new arrow to the Jalakh Bow and searched for Soren's attackers, tracing the source of the magical blast. There. No doubt at what they considered to be a safe distance away, were two black cloaked figures, next to a unit of mounted Haskans. Both had their hands held out in front of them, channelling their power at Soren after he had revealed himself. Gyrmund aimed carefully. The first shot had to hit, or he would be in trouble. He released the arrow and it struck one of the Isharite wizards in the chest. The man staggered backwards, his attack on Soren stopped.

The second wizard raked his magic blast away from Soren and towards Gyrmund. He quickly snatched up another arrow before running away along the wall.

'Gyrmund!' Soren called out.

Turning back, he could see that Soren was now holding off the magical attack, more comfortable now he had just one opponent. Gyrmund took aim, allowing himself time for a kill shot. He struck the second wizard in the face, and he crumpled to the ground. But Gyrmund wasn't finished yet. Returning to his post, he grabbed a third arrow, searching for the first wizard again. He knew he had only injured him with the first shot, and it wasn't safe to leave him alive.

He spotted him. He was clambering onto a horse, the rider helping him up to sit behind him. Gyrmund decided to wait. When the rider turned around to leave, Gyrmund drew, aimed and released. He hit the wizard in the back of the head, and he fell from the horse.

'Are you alright?' he asked Soren.

'Fine,' said Soren. He sounded tired, but that was all.

Gyrmund tuned in to a crashing sound. He risked looking over the wall in front of him and saw the portcullis getting pounded. The Drobax were using rams, but also the rocks that had been dropped down from the battlements. Ladders were propped up against the barbican towers, taking away the attention of the defenders. Just as he decided to act, he heard another noise. Then he saw. Diodorus was raising the portcullis.

'I'm going to help,' he called out to Soren, who waved him away.

Grabbing a handful of arrows, Gyrmund made his way over to the nearest tower and descended the stairs to the bottom, then out onto the open area behind the barbican. Two rows of walls and towers extended from the barbican all the way to the fortress, and he could hear the sounds of battle raging. Somewhere up on the south wall were Moneva and Belwynn; on the north wall, Clarin.

Ahead of him was the second portcullis, and looking through the gaps in the latticed grill he could see the gates of the barbican—could hear the crack as the Drobax smashed into it. The gates were made of thick wood, bound by iron, but they wouldn't stop a sustained assault by so many Drobax. He just hoped that the gamble Diodorus was taking would pay off.

One of the gates shuddered, and suddenly it was falling towards Gyrmund and the portcullis he stood behind. The Drobax were through the gates and charging towards him. They were desperate to smash their way through the portcullis, the last obstacle to them getting inside the outer defences of Chalios. The defenders were just as desperate to stop them.

Gyrmund targeted a group carrying a heavy looking ram. He fired, the first went down. He fired again, but this time the angle through the portcullis was too tight, and the arrow clattered into the metal and dropped harmlessly to the ground. The Drobax got to the portcullis, pulled back the ram, and swung it with an almighty crash. Gyrmund took his time now, getting close to them, safe as he was behind the portcullis. He fired at close range, downing one, then another, then a third. Now those who remained dropped the heavy ram to the ground, making an obstacle for the rest of the Drobax to come.

But come they did, surging through the gap where the gates had been, a swarm of Drobax bringing their rams and rocks, filling the space, barging their way towards the portcullis. Gyrmund only had a couple of arrows left now.

The portcullis at the front of the barbican began to lower.

Now, Diodorus gave his men the order to attack. Through the murder holes on each side of the tunnel came arrows. Through the murder holes above was poured a red-hot concoction of ash, sand, water, charcoal and whatever else they had been heating up. The Drobax screamed in agony, unable to retaliate. Steam rose all around them, and the smell of burning flesh. Weapons and siege equipment clattered to the floor as they covered their faces.

And still the first portcullis lowered.

For the vast majority, they realised too late. As the portcullis fell into position, the Drobax inside found themselves trapped, and the defenders were able to kill them at their leisure. Beyond the barbican thousands of Drobax remained, howling in frustration. Inside, between the two lowered portcullises, lay their siege equipment, out of reach.

***

BELWYNN STOOD with her sword drawn on the south wall. Along the wall, in the towers, were her Madrians. By her side was Moneva, nominally in charge of the archers, though once the Drobax had arrived it was impossible for her to shout orders out and be heard. That wasn't a problem for Belwynn, who could warn her Madrians about any threats with her telepathy. Somewhere in the general vicinity was Queen Tana of the Asrai. But since she was using her cloak to go about her business unseen, it was impossible to know where.

They were in trouble. Belwynn could warn her Madrians all she liked, but that didn't mean they were able to stop the enemy. The Drobax had succeeded in placing huge ladders at intervals all along the wall. Many of the ladders didn't end until they were way above Belwynn's head, and it was far from easy to stop the Drobax who climbed up them.

Neither were they having much luck pushing them away from the wall. They were positioned at such an angle that it generally wasn't possible. The Madrians had enjoyed a bit more success pushing them to the side. But down below, thousands of Drobax were holding the ladders in place. Large wooden panels had been erected around the foot of the wall to protect them from the rocks that the defenders had thrown at them.

More and more Drobax were making it up the ladders, from where they could jump onto the wall walk. At first they were despatched easily enough, but as time wore on it was becoming more difficult, and the numbers of injured and dead was rising.

Belwynn saw Oisin approaching a while before he reached her position. He was hard to miss. She stared in fascination, soon realising that ahead of him strode Gunnhild, the Vismarian woman that Rabigar had befriended. She cleared a path for him, guiding any Madrians in their path away, wielding a giant hammer when she came upon a Drobax. As Belwynn watched, the hammer connected into the chest of one of the creatures and sent it flying over the wall.

Oisin, meanwhile, was deploying the Giants' Spear. His height allowed him to lean over the edge of the fortress wall. From there, he struck the blunt end of the spear into the ladders, until the wood snapped. When he was done, the ladders were left well short of the top. If the Drobax wanted to reach the top now, they had to scramble up the stone wall for the last part of their journey.

Oisin turned to give Belwynn a little nod of greeting, and then he and Gunnhild continued on their way.

Belwynn and Moneva shared a look.

'I like them,' Belwynn said.

***

CLARIN LOOKED down from his tower roof on the north wall. A new threat had arrived, with the potential to be more of a danger than the Drobax had been. The creatures had made a good show of it at first, clambering up their ladders and onto the wall. It had given Clarin an opportunity to test the Shield of Persala and he had soon got used to its weight.

There was more, though. He had found that when he struck the Drobax with it, they had gone flying backwards, with more force than they should. Clarin had been around Soren enough to have an open mind about magic, and there was surely something supernatural about this weapon. His opportunity was relatively short-lived, however. Once the giant Oisin had arrived, snapping the ladders of the Drobax, the fighting had petered out, the creatures able to do very little to get past the solid defences of the fortress.

Now, though. A Haskan force had made its way to the north wall. Totally different to the Drobax, these units marched in rigid formation. And they came not with ladders, but with catapults. Four of them, pulled along on wheeled carts. This, Clarin realised, could be a problem. As far as he knew, they had nothing to stop a catapult.

Catapults here, he advised Belwynn. *Four of them. Any on your side?*

No, none here. That doesn't sound good, Clarin. I will tell Soren. Are they firing at you?

Not yet. They're setting them up at the moment.

The Haskans were training the catapults at different sections of the wall. Maragin's position further along the wall was targeted by one of the machines. One of them rather alarmingly pointed at the tower Clarin stood on.

Peering at the catapults with him was Jesper, the young Vismarian who had come from Halvia. Clarin had resolved to keep an eye on him. In fact, the lad had proven to be surprisingly strong given his slim build, pulling his bowstring back with steady hands many times, and accurate with it too.

'Do you think they're in range of bow fire?' Clarin asked him.

Jesper didn't look convinced. 'Just in range, perhaps. But they'd not land with much force or accuracy.'

Clarin nodded in agreement.

Then the catapult fired.

'Incoming!' Jesper shouted, diving for cover.

It was hard to explain, afterwards, why Clarin didn't do the same. He couldn't say more than it was a feeling he had. Instead of trying to avoid the huge rock that came hurtling towards the top of the tower, Clarin moved towards it and met it with the shield. Only a minimal amount of the force that the rock carried reached Clarin's arm and shoulder. Instead of crushing him, the rock rebounded from the Shield and dropped down onto the Drobax that remained at the bottom of the wall.

Slowly, incredulously, he turned the Shield over to look. The leather cover Diodorus had given him wasn't looking as appealing as it once had. But the Shield itself was undamaged—not even a dent.

Clarin laughed heartily and turned around to show Jesper.

White faced, the Vismarian looked a little more appalled than Clarin would have expected, but he did try to crack a smile.

XXII

TIPPING THE SCALES

*B*ELWYNN, SOREN SAID, HIS TONE SERIOUS. *We think the next army is coming. Herin's.*

She looked out from the south wall. A sea of Drobax, only a few human regiments. No siege engines. Nothing so dangerous she couldn't leave.

I'm coming, she replied.

Of course, Moneva went with her. Tana reappeared and accompanied them as well. Moneva pointed to the queen's face, and the Asrai lazily wiped away the blood.

As they walked towards the barbican, she saw Clarin down in the courtyard. He was gesturing towards his soldiers on the north walls.

Clarin? she asked. *Is everything alright?*

I'm evacuating the walls, he said. *Those catapults have made it too dangerous up there. But they're not going to blast through any time soon.*

We think Herin's army is approaching, she told him.

I'm coming, he replied, his tone giving nothing away.

They all met on the wall of the barbican. Belwynn gagged from the horrendous smell. Hundreds of dead bodies lay beneath them. Down below, the men of Korenandi were dragging Drobax corpses and wooden logs out of the barbican tunnel, ready for the Knights to make an exit. Doing her best to ignore the gruesome sight, she looked at the scene in front of Chalios.

While Kaved had sent most of his forces to attack the fortress, he had kept others in reserve. Beyond these lines a new force, approximately the same size Kaved's had been, was marching towards them. Like Kaved's, the bulk of it was made up of Drobax, but there were other units, too.

'The moment of truth,' muttered Soren, as the two forces got within range of each other.

It may be time to make ready, Belwynn warned Theron. Somewhere in the main hall of the fortress, behind the great doors, waited the Knights of Kalinth, and their mounts.

We will be ready on the signal, Theron assured her.

There was a silence amongst them, then, as they studied the movement of Isharite units on the plain before Chalios. All the while the Drobax pulled on the portcullis beneath them, and behind them rocks from the catapults occasionally thudded into the north side of the fortress.

'They're attacking,' said Clarin at last, apparently confident about what he saw. 'But only some.'

'That's what it looks like,' agreed Gyrmund.

'We shouldn't be surprised,' said Soren. 'If that order has gone out, not all will obey it.'

'Enough have obeyed to give us a chance, though,' added Clarin. 'It will be a confused mess down there.'

'So we are agreed?' Diodorus asked, a strain of anxiety in his voice. 'Theron wanted to be told immediately.'

Everyone concurred, and Diodorus moved to the east wall of the barbican and waved a flag depicting the Winged Horse of Kalinth. Moments later, the great gates to the fortress were opening. Tentatively, the armoured steeds of the knights left the fortress, stepping down from the rocky floor of the hall onto the smoother path that led to the barbican. Astride them were the Knights of Kalinth, helmets on, their armour polished, lances pointing to the sky. There were not so many as there had once been, but they remained an impressive sight.

'Raise the portcullis!' Diodorus shouted, and the cranking noise of the winch began as the knights moved towards them. Leontios and Theron led them, and Belwynn could see Evander and Philon too.

'What news?' Theron shouted up to them.

'It is as Herin told us,' Moneva shouted down, no doubt pleased that he hadn't misled her.

'Though as chaotic as you might expect,' Clarin warned him. 'There is a Haskan force with four catapults, close to a thousand feet from the north walls. That could be your first target.'

'Very well,' Theron raised an eyebrow towards Leontios, who nodded his agreement. They snapped their visors down and readied their lances.

The Drobax began to scramble under the portcullis, the first easily dealt with by the defenders in the barbican. As it rose higher, more of them surged through, and a few began to make it to the end of the tunnel, emerging onto the path where the Knights waited. Gyrmund took care of these, but it was time for the Knights to move.

Leontios let out a great shout, and those at the front levelled their lances. Then they began to move, picking up as much speed as they could, until they were entering the barbican tunnel themselves, the armoured horses buffeting aside any Drobax who tried to stop them. Gyrmund and the other archers now helped by trying to clear a path in front of the barbican, before the Knights emerged, barging aside any resistance, then streaming away to the right, in the direction Clarin had suggested to them.

The cavalry was out, and next an infantry force started to come together. Maragin, the Krykker chieftain, had taken on the role of Clarin's second-in-command, and she was down there already, shouting out orders, trying to get soldiers into formation. Clarin left to join her. Oisin appeared too, with Gunnhild and Jesper. Once ready, they began to march for the exit.

'The sword, the spear and the shield,' murmured Soren, as their friends looked up one last time before entering the tunnel. Where the Knights had simply aimed to barge their way out of Chalios onto the battlefield, Clarin's force was there to kill whatever was in front of them. Shouts and grunts and swearing filled Belwynn's ears. Clarin's force—slowly, methodically—began to push the Drobax backwards, cutting and hammering their way forwards. Such a counter-attack would have brought Kaved's reserves onto them only a few minutes ago. But now that Herin was engaging these forces, they were free to act.

Belwynn ordered the Madrians down from the south wall. It was time for them to go too, to take this chance to inflict a defeat on the Isharites. They turned to Diodorus, who was now tasked with holding the fortress with only the soldiers of his county.

'Good luck,' he said to them.

'Get those portcullises down as soon as we are gone,' Gyrmund reminded him.

'I will.'

Of course, no-one spoke the truth. If something went wrong on the battlefield and they didn't return, it wouldn't matter very much if the portcullises were up or down.

Belwynn and her brother and her friends left the barbican and took up position with the Madrians. She stood on the front row, but she was well protected. To her left were Moneva and Gyrmund, with dagger and bow. To her right, Soren and Tana, with staff and cloak. Inside her head, somehow, was Madria.

It was clear to Belwynn, as she led the Madrians out of the fortress, that they were taking a step towards ending this conflict. Somewhere out there were Siavash and Diis. They had come to kill her and to destroy Madria. Belwynn doubted that they would turn from their course. And she wasn't going to, either.

***

NONE OF THEM had known exactly what would happen once Herin gave the order to attack Kaved's host. Peroz was dead, of course, and they had succeeded in eliminating a few Isharites who would have opposed them. But that left thousands and thousands of individuals who now had to weigh up their response.

Did Herin's order, as he claimed, really come from Siavash, or had the Magnian turned traitor? Was it safer to wait, and stay away from the fighting, with the risk that they were accused of disobeying orders? It was not an easy situation to be put in.

Predictably, the response varied. Many a Haskan refused the order, though Rimmon persuaded others to act. What surprised him the most was the number of Drobax who followed the order, heading straight for the unsuspecting soldiers in Kaved's ranks. Once it had been Isharite mages who controlled the Drobax. Now it seemed it was Kull they looked to, and Rimmon honestly doubted that was any improvement.

'There,' Herin said, pointing to a location on the battlefield. The general appeared to have little interest in anything save for his vendetta. He nudged his horse forwards. Rimmon and Kull exchanged a look before following him, a dozen soldiers hand-picked by Herin coming too.

In the chaos of the battlefield, it wasn't hard to come at Kaved's position by surprise. Before his soldiers could react, Herin's were in amongst them, blunt weapons clubbing them to the ground, sharp weapons driven into bodies. Herin himself, implacable looking, had dismounted, and was making his way to the Krykker.

There was only one Isharite mage, and of course he was Rimmon's responsibility, whether or not Rimmon could match his power. His face buried in the cowl of a black cloak, he was all too obvious to spot. But Rimmon waited. He waited until Kaved told the mage to attack, waited until he sent a blast of magic at Herin, who dived out of the way just in time.

That was the moment for Rimmon to strike, when the mage was attacking, less able to defend. He summoned his magic and placed it around the other mage, suppressing him. The Isharite struggled, straining to remove Rimmon's hold on him. Herin, back on his feet, marched towards them.

'Get him!' Kaved bellowed.

The Isharite mage focused on Rimmon; focused on Herin's approach.

Behind him, Kull struck, a long spear punching through his back, under the ribs, and coming out of his stomach. There was a momentary look of surprise, and then he was thrown to the ground.

Herin held his hands out to Rimmon and Kull. 'Me now,' he said, drawing his sword. 'Don't intervene.'

'Well Herin,' rasped the Krykker, doing his best to retain an air of confidence, as Herin's men finished the last of his soldiers. 'You decided to roll the die. You caught me by surprise, I'll admit, but only by killing yourself along with me.'

Herin smiled. 'I told you I'd come for you.'

'You did. I suppose I should feel honoured that you've sacrificed everything just to put a blade in me. Though as much as I like to believe in my own self-importance, I think this is about more than you and me. This is Herin deciding to play the hero after all. In the end, you couldn't shake off that puerile side of you, however much you tried.'

'Come on, Kaved. We'd all like to see you go down fighting, not throwing insults. It's just you and me. My men won't intervene.'

Kaved shrugged. From his belt he drew a short sword and a hand-axe. Herin approached with his sword held in two hands. The talking had stopped now, and Herin's soldiers gathered around in silence to watch the combat. Everyone wanted to see this, Rimmon included. Kaved had killed his queen. Watching him die here would be pleasing.

Herin had the greater reach and he prodded his crystal blade in Kaved's direction, trying to entice him into coming forwards. Kaved didn't take the bait, though, moving to the side, just out of reach of the tip of Herin's sword.

Again, Herin jabbed, again Kaved moved, but the next time he went for it. Even though Herin must have been expecting it, it happened too fast. As Herin nudged his blade forwards, the Krykker pushed it aside with his sword, and then spun inside, his axe whirling. Herin tried to spin away, but the axe head connected with his hip, and he let out an instinctive yelp of pain. As he spun, his blade slashed down, scratching harmlessly along the Krykker's chest.

Kaved smiled wolfishly and attacked again. He was powerful, his arms swinging in a blur as he got closer to Herin, who was forced to back away. First the sword, then the axe, they came for Herin from a different direction every time, impossible to counter.

Stepping backwards, Herin went down on one knee and swung his sword around, chopping at the Krykker's legs. Kaved evaded the swing and kept coming for Herin, but this was perhaps what Herin had intended. As Kaved reached for Herin with his sword, Herin's blade was already sweeping upwards. Unable to withdraw in time, the razor-sharp crystal met the Krykker's wrist and sliced clean through it. For a brief moment, Rimmon thought Herin had won, but Kaved's axe had been moving too. It crunched into Herin's gauntleted hands. The axe wasn't sharp enough to repeat what Herin's sword had done, but it was strong enough to break Herin's grip, and his sword dropped to the ground.

Herin seemed to move on instinct, circling away to avoid the backswing of Kaved's axe. Despite holding up a bloody stump, the Krykker's face was a picture of manic exultation, as he followed Herin, his axe swirling. Weaponless, Herin tried to move away, but he tripped.

In an instant, Kaved was on him. Rimmon's eyes barely followed what happened next. From his belt, Herin had drawn a seax. He raked the thick blade along Kaved's forearm to the hand that held the axe, where it lopped off a couple of fingers. The axe spun away to the ground and now it was Kaved who stood weaponless, with only half a hand left.

They stared at one another for a moment, blood running down the Krykker's arm, dripping onto the floor.

'Do you know who made this blade?'

'Oh, fuck off, Herin.'

The seax went in and out, there was a spurt of blood, and Kaved's body sank to the ground.

***

BELWYNN MARCHED her Madrians ahead, positioning them in the centre of the battlefield. Off to the right, back in the direction of the fortress, the Knights of Kalinth were picking off the catapult crews who had threatened the north walls. To her left, Clarin had led his unit against a Haskan force. Some of the Haskans fought on horseback, giving them an edge, but Clarin's force had a giant with them. Oisin, King of the Orias, was the only figure Belwynn could make out at this distance. He towered over his enemies. As he whirled the Giants' Spear around, giving him a reach perhaps four times the length of anyone else, it mattered little whether the target was on foot or horseback.

'Their centre is broken,' Gyrmund commented. 'Little point in us trying to reach them, the Haskans won't hold much longer.'

'Then what do we do?' Belwynn asked.

She found the battlefield hard to read. In the distance, Herin's forces fought with Kaved's. In theory they should be helping, but when Drobax fought with Drobax, it was hard to tell which force was on their side. If they led the Madrians closer, it might even prompt the Isharite forces to stop killing each other and turn on them.

'There is no point risking lives that don't need risking,' said Soren. 'We are in a good position here to watch what unfolds and intervene if necessary. I don't see a reason to do more yet.'

Nobody disagreed. Belwynn looked at the Madrians who lined up behind them. Citizens of Heractus and the surrounding settlements for the most part, they had given their loyalty to Elana, and now to Belwynn. They had lost their homes, yet still fought for Madria, uncomplaining. Belwynn certainly didn't want to put them in any more danger than she had to.

So they waited awhile. It was a surprisingly hard thing to do in the midst of a battle, more nerve-racking somehow than marching or fighting. But wherever they looked, as best could be made out, their forces were on top, and Kaved's were in disarray.

Then, they saw Ishari's response.

Herin's treachery must only have been known to Siavash for a matter of minutes. Far too short a space of time to mobilise the units that remained at his disposal and send them into the battlefield. Instead, he had sent the dragon.

Gyrmund was the first to realise what was going on. He pointed into the sky. Others across the battlefield were doing the same. A palpable sense of dread spread among all creatures, whether they were loyal to Siavash, Theron or Herin.

Belwynn had been told about the dragon, how it had devastated the Krykker armies and forced that proud race to flee Dalriya. It had sunk the fleet of the Sea Caladri, said to have been the greatest in the world. And on his visit to Magnia, Soren had heard rumours that it had next been sent to the Empire, where the Brasingians were holding off the Isharite threat in Burkhard Castle. It was here now. Did that mean the Empire had fallen? Was this the last place in all of Dalriya that still resisted?

The dragon grew larger in the sky. Its long wings were beating hard, propelling its thin, snake-like body towards the battlefield. It was green, just like the dragon from the song of Stephen. She had sung that song at the High Tower, a song dear to the Knights of Kalinth.

'In Chalios there dwelt the beast,' she whispered the first line from the song, her throat tight with fear, barely aware of what she was saying.

The dragon dived, heading for the ground, and a wave of nausea hit Belwynn. It was some distance from their position, flying towards the thickest part of the fighting, where the armies of Herin and Kaved clashed. Once within range, it righted itself, opened its maw, and released an orange and yellow jet of flame. Screams of agony could be heard, as the monster engulfed the combatants in flame, indiscriminate in who it targeted. Men and Drobax, those who were loyal to Ishari and those who had dared to defy their masters, all burned. When the dragon was finished, few could have been left alive. It beat its wings again, climbing into the air, neck swivelling as it sought out its next target.

'We need to stop this creature now, before it destroys us all,' said Soren, taking a step forwards, leaning on Onella's Staff. Gyrmund moved with him. He took an arrow from his quiver and put it to the Jalakh Bow.

'You can't leave Belwynn,' Moneva warned them. 'If you fail and it comes for her here, all will be lost.'

Belwynn sighed. 'Then I will go with them.'

Moneva looked at her, torn, unsure what was best. She nodded. 'Alright.'

Stay here, Belwynn told the Madrians.

She took a step to join Soren and Gyrmund. Moneva and Tana did the same. The five of them began to walk towards the dragon.

They couldn't know what orders the dragon had been given, or indeed what orders it understood. Right now, it looked like it was intent on laying waste to the battlefield. But at any moment it might decide to change course and head for the fortress, and then they would be in trouble. The only resistance Chalios might offer was whatever archers Diodorus led who had kept some arrows, and a couple of catapults on the barbican towers. Meanwhile, Lyssa and the other children were in the central chamber of the fortress. Soren was right. They had to stop the dragon now.

It continued to scour the battlefield, as if looking for something. Meanwhile, all those fighters within range of the beast, whatever side they thought themselves on, had begun running away from it, in whatever direction they thought safest.

'Can you reach it with an arrow, Gyrmund?' she asked him.

He considered it. 'I can probably hit it. But I can't target specific points from here. I was thinking the eyes, or at least the face.'

'The wings, too,' Tana added, the Asrai's voice a murmur that made Belwynn's skin crawl.

'Strike it anywhere for now,' Belwynn said. 'Draw it within range.'

Soren gave Belwynn a look. Should the dragon come for them it was only his magic that might save them. But he didn't argue.

Gyrmund drew back the string of the Jalakh Bow, aimed, and released with a loud twang. Belwynn followed the flight of the arrow, allowing herself a grim smile as it struck home. The dragon hadn't seen it coming, but now turned its great head in their direction. It beat its wings and began to come for them. Gyrmund was ready, firing a second arrow in its path. This time, it was able to swerve out of the way, showing greater aerial agility than Belwynn had expected. It let out an angry sounding roar and kept coming.

'Over there,' said Moneva, pointing.

To their left they could see Oisin the Giant, running towards them, his long legs eating up the distance. Some way behind came Clarin and then Maragin.

'At least we will have all the weapons together against it,' Belwynn said.

Surely, that would be enough?

Before they knew it, before Oisin could reach them, the dragon was diving towards them. Gyrmund fired one last arrow, striking it in the neck. The dragon screamed with rage, but the injury didn't seem to weaken it. Opening its mouth, it sent its flame at them, intent on destruction.

Soren acted, placing a shield that covered the five of them. As the flames came, Belwynn instinctively turned away from them. She felt the heat of the fire, but Soren's magic had protected them.

Screaming in frustration, the dragon wheeled away. Tracking it, Gyrmund sent another arrow that tore through one of its wings. This time, the arrow had an effect. Belwynn could see the creature wobble clumsily in the air for a while, before drifting down to the ground. The dragon furled its wings, turned in their direction and came for them on its four legs.

'Well done, Gyrmund,' said Moneva.

'It can't fly?' Belwynn asked.

'Hard to tell,' said Soren. 'Maybe it's decided not to risk more injury to its wings. Look, I don't know how many more times I can hold back those flames. And the more magic I expend here, the less I will have later.'

'I'll try,' said Gyrmund, fitting yet another arrow to his bow.

The rest of them looked about helplessly. Toric's Dagger was no use, and what could Tana do, bite the creature? Wait, Belwynn said to herself, as an idea began to form. But it disappeared when she heard the sound of hoofbeats. Turning to look, her heart dropped. It was Theron. He had come alone. He was riding for the dragon, a lance tucked under his armpit.

'Oh no,' she said out loud. 'Gyrmund, try to distract it.'

Gyrmund's eyes had widened at the sight of the lone knight charging the dragon and did as Belwynn suggested, firing one arrow after another, favouring speed over accuracy. The dragon sent a flame in their direction and the arrows disintegrated.

'Oh Madria,' said Belwynn. If the Jalakh Bow wasn't going to work, what would? 'Moneva, give Tana the Dagger.'

Moneva frowned at first, then when comprehension dawned, she tossed the weapon to the Asrai, who caught it and immediately disappeared.

The dragon was dangerously close to them now. Belwynn could see its reptilian eyes studying them and she fought against the fear that the creature induced. It suddenly swung its head around. Oisin was running at it, his huge spear gripped in both hands. The dragon sent out a burst of flame and he was forced to throw his body to the side to evade it, dropping his spear. Gyrmund shot yet another arrow and now flame arced towards them, forcing Soren to defend against it yet again.

From the corner of her eye, Belwynn could see Theron approaching, his lance levelled at the dragon's back. Again, the words of the song came to her lips. 'No men to fight for him had he, But Stephen had his chivalry.'

Please Madria, she prayed, *don't let the dragon see him.*

But Madria was silent.

The dragon's tail whipped out. Belwynn followed its path as if in slow motion. It went straight for Theron, too late for him to change course, connecting with his mount with incredible force. Both horse and man sailed into the air and Soren used his magic again, cushioning their fall to the ground.

Belwynn's gaze was torn away from Theron as the tail whipped again. At first, it looked like it connected with thin air, but then she heard the cry of the Asrai queen, who suddenly appeared in view, flying through the air, and again Soren held out Onella's Staff to stop her crashing to the ground.

As he did so, the dragon turned to their position, and Belwynn thought they were done. Moneva stepped in front of Belwynn and Soren, swords drawn, a brave but hopeless gesture.

But the fire that was building in the dragon's throat never came. It swung its neck around and sent it at Oisin as he recovered his spear. Into the path of the flame came Clarin, the Shield held in front of him. Belwynn fully expected to see him turned to ash, but the Shield deflected the fire back at the dragon. It screamed its rage, tottering backwards on its hindlegs.

Then Oisin came, the Giants' Spear held steady in his hands. His height allowed him to drive the long weapon up, into the neck of the beast. The Spear pierced the scales, coming out the other side. The dragon opened its mouth to send its deadly fire at him, but he was still moving, still gripping the Spear, and then using his strength and momentum to give the Spear a mighty wrench. Still stuck in the creature's neck, the Spear dragged the creature off balance, and it fell to the ground with a mighty crash.

Belwynn could see the great beast's chest heaving. It tried to rise once, but with Oisin pinning its neck to the floor, it was useless. Moreover, the deep wound the Spear had caused had clearly done it severe damage. The dragon was dying. As Belwynn and the others tentatively began to walk towards it, Oisin put a boot to the neck, yanked the Spear free, and sent the blade into the dragon's head. The chest heaved one last time, and then was still.

Belwynn ran over to Theron, who was on his feet. 'I'm fine,' he said, though he didn't object to Belwynn helping him walk to the dragon.

Tana, too, was back on her feet, wordlessly handing Toric's Dagger back to Moneva. Belwynn let out a breath of relief. She had nearly got the Asrai woman killed.

As they all stood in a circle around the corpse, Maragin reached them, panting. 'I missed it,' she said, sounding disappointed, her face so stony that Belwynn couldn't tell if it was a joke or not.

'I thought I might be the hero and kill the dragon,' said Theron, ruefully. 'Like Stephen.'

Gyrmund nodded. 'I was sure I would fell it with an arrow in the eye.'

Oisin gave a chuckle. 'Come, come, dear friends. Don't you know that the Giants' Spear was made for killing dragons? Though I don't mind admitting, you all helped a little by distracting it for me.'

XXIII

FUGITIVES

TO JURGEN'S MIND, THE TOWN of Comagenta was an uninspiring choice for what the Persaleians had planned. It was laid to the same design as all the other urban centres in the country, but with no variation whatsoever, no attempt to add its own unique contribution. Still, Cyprian assured him that it was the right location, and that was crucial to the plan they had devised.

Zared was the man behind it all. King of Persala, king-in-exile, rebel and pretender to the throne—Jurgen had learned he had many titles here in Persala, depending on one's point of view. Jurgen still thought of him as balding Zared, the young man who had been his fellow prisoner in Samir Durg. Whatever one called him, Zared had been sending his supporters into Comagenta for weeks now, gradually infiltrating the town. Many towns like this were susceptible, their citizenry depleted, most of the men conscripted into the Isharite armies. Comagenta was Zared's town now, and he hadn't needed to kill anyone to do it. Any opposition had been cleared out, along with the children and the vulnerable. This wasn't a good place for them to be.

In the town hall, Jurgen and Rudy stood with Zared, Cyprian and the other leaders, as the plan was rehearsed one last time. Each of the principal actors had to tell Zared what they would do, and when. Jurgen didn't have to. Lame, not nearly as mobile as Cyprian, or his cousin Rudy, he hadn't been trusted with very much.

Everyone shook hands with Duilio, before the mighty warrior mounted his horse. It was a big beast—had to be, to bear that man's weight. Someone handed him his spear, and he turned his steed around. They watched him go in silence for a while, the clop of his horse's hooves the only sound.

'Well,' said Zared. 'That is it. Everyone to their positions now. Remember, the gods are with us. But it doesn't hurt to send them a prayer one last time.'

Jurgen and Rudy clasped hands. 'Good luck. Be careful.'

Rudy grinned, and then he was gone.

Jurgen left the hall. Outside, Zared's soldiers were finishing off the barricade that stretched across the main street of Comagenta. Jurgen made his way to the tall trader's house where he had been allocated a spot. He didn't rush. There was no hurry, and his legs still pained him when he walked. He made his way to the top room that faced onto the street. Waiting for him was the machine that Cyprian had given him. Jurgen had never spent enough time with a bow to get very good at it. These Persaleian crossbows didn't require nearly as much practice, though. He took a sitting position. Just as Cyprian had taught him, Jurgen placed his feet on either side of the stave, then pulled the string back until it locked into position on the trigger. The machine was now ready to fire, and he didn't need to hold it in place, like the big-shouldered archers had to. He placed the crossbow next to his set of quarrels by the window and sat down again. He had an excellent view all along the street from here. Now all he had to do was wait.

It was a comfy place to wait before a fight. Standing in the darkness outside Heractus had been harder. Creeping along the walls of Samir Durg much more terrifying. He would rather have avoided all the horror of the last year. But he had to admit, it made moments such as this easier.

He heard them only just before they came into view. The Shadow Caladri always came quietly, on foot—their clawed feet making next to no noise. No-one from the northern realms needed warning of the danger this deadly race posed. Their nights were often filled with stories of their dark deeds. In Rotelegen stories, they were the sinister force behind the rise of the Persaleian Empire. But one didn't have to go into history to learn of their impact. In the early spring of this year the shadow ones had crept through this land into Haskany, where at Simalek they had helped their Isharite ally, Siavash, defeat his rivals.

No doubt they were on their way to help him again. Zared didn't share everything, the whys and wherefores, but Jurgen and Rudy knew too much not to work it out. The Shadow Caladri must be on their way to Kalinth. That was why Cyprian was so sure that Comagenta was the right place for an ambush. And however they had come upon their information, they had been right, Zared and Cyprian: for here they were, marching down the main street of the town.

Duilio had led them here, and they had followed. Everyone knew the reputation of Dorjan, king of the Shadow Caladri. He ruled with an iron fist.
238

Perhaps the Caladri had assumed it would be the same in Persala, hadn't considered that there might be rebels leading them into a trap. They marched down the street, and it was only when the barricade was before them that those at the front stopped, sensed that something was wrong.

'Come on, Duilio,' Jurgen whispered to himself, feeling edgy. 'Get out of there.'

Even now, perhaps, the Caladri didn't understand. They seemed to be arguing with Duilio, gesturing angrily at the roadblock, and then up at him on his horse. Suddenly, the big man pulled back his spear, and then thrust the weapon into the chest of one of the Caladri leaders. Why? Perhaps it was their general, and the champion had thought their lives were a good swap. Whatever his reasoning, the Caladri were now quick to draw their weapons and they fell on him, cutting him down from his horse and finishing him as he lay bleeding on the street.

With Duilio gone, it was time to act. Jurgen picked up the crossbow with care. He was not completely confident with it and didn't want to knock the trigger with his clumsiness. He fitted one of his quarrels against the string, and then leaned out of the window, taking aim. Missiles were already raining down on the Caladri from both sides of the street, and from behind the barricades. Jurgen pulled the trigger and let his quarrel join them, losing sight of it amidst all the others.

No problem. It either hit or it didn't, and there was no point giving it any more thought. He turned the machine about and put his feet to the stave again, pulling the thick string into position. Placing his next quarrel onto the tiller, he looked out of the window.

In the shock of the attack, it was hard for the Shadow Caladri to decide whether to push their way through the ambush, stay and fight, or retreat. But they were responding now, and it looked like they had chosen to fight. Jurgen allowed himself a small smile. The Caladri fired back at their ambushers. Jurgen could see some of the barricades across the street moving, seemingly of their own accord. Somewhere, the Caladri magi were at work. He thought to find one and kill it with his crossbow, but he could see no obvious signs of magic being used. Magi were devious beings, after all. Squads of Caladri were barging into the buildings along the street, but Zared's warriors had another surprise for them. Jurgen could see flames in half a dozen buildings already, as well as at the barricade, and the fires would only spread. Cyprian and Rudy were both part of the fire crew. Moving quickly from one location to the next, they had been setting alight ready-prepared piles of tinder and wood as soon as the Shadow Caladri had arrived. Each minute that passed meant the flames grew higher and made it more difficult for their enemies to escape.

Jurgen fired, and then leaned back into the room to cock his weapon a third time. Taking more care this time, he peered out of the window. He was met with an eerie sight. A strange, mist-like substance swirled along the street, and when it met the fires it suppressed them. The magi of the Shadow Caladri were gaining them the upper hand. At the near end, Caladri soldiers were starting to break through the barrier that had been erected. The defenders there had been dispersed by Caladri arrows and it would not hold much longer. Aiming carefully, Jurgen was rewarded when his bolt hit one of the Caladri in the back, sending it to the ground. He ducked quickly back into the room before he was spotted.

It was obvious that they could not contain the Caladri much longer. Jurgen cocked his crossbow once more, his hands shaking somewhat now. He sat there for a while, not ready to move. Where before he had a simple task, options now crossed his mind. Should he stay here or head back down to the street? When was it time to retreat? If he left it too long, he would find himself trapped in this room while the Caladri began entering buildings, hunting for their enemies.

A new sound from outside persuaded him to come to the window again. He held his crossbow up first, just in case a Caladri was waiting for him to reappear. No missiles came his way, and he dared to put his face in harm's way again. The sound he heard was the whistling of arrows being fired. It came from the east, from the direction the Shadow Caladri had arrived from. Jurgen fired his own weapon and then peered down to the far end of the street. He breathed a sigh of relief. The trap was being closed.

The Blood Caladri had come. The Shadow Caladri at the far end of the street were now retreating from the fizz of arrows that were being sent into their exposed rear ranks. But they had failed to fully clear the barricade and there was little option for them but to make for the buildings on either side of the road and hope to fight their way through. Jurgen didn't give them much of a chance. Zared's soldiers would be ready.

Jurgen stared at the crossbow. It wasn't a very fair weapon, in his mind, and it hadn't been a very fair fight. He didn't feel like using it again. But the

Shadow Caladri had been stopped, and they would have gone to Kalinth to help Siavash. For some reason an image of Clarin came to him then. His big friend wouldn't have thought much of his complaints about fair fighting. The Kalinthians had been horribly outnumbered by the Isharite forces. That invasion was hardly fair. Samir Durg wasn't fair. He set his jaw. He took a deep breath and pulled back the string of the crossbow one last time, before slotting another quarrel onto it. It was time to go.

The door to the room burst open. A Shadow Caladri warrior stood there, a desperate look in his face. Probably looking for somewhere to hide. He ran at Jurgen, sword in hand. Jurgen just had time to aim and shoot. The quarrel hit the Caladri square in the forehead and it collapsed, dead.

'Well, well,' he said, and gave his weapon a gentle pat of thanks.

No-one stayed in Comagenta for long. The buildings were broken and burned, and the main street ran with blood. Not to mention the danger of an Isharite army coming to investigate, or of Shadow Caladri reinforcements being sent.

Jurgen followed the crowd, as fast as he could, to a field outside the town. It was only when he got there that he found his cousin Rudy was alive and unharmed; Cyprian, too. The army of the Blood Caladri stood apart, but Zared was talking with two of them, perhaps their leaders.

'I must admit,' Jurgen said. 'I had my doubts that the Blood Caladri would show up.'

'Me too,' said Cyprian. 'But that's why we have kings. If it had been left to a vote, we'd never have trusted them, and where would that have got us?'

Jurgen supposed that made some kind of sense.

'I hope it's important,' said Rudy. 'This victory, I mean,' he added, when they looked at him quizzically. 'I hope it means something.'

They turned to look over at Zared, and found that he and the two Caladri he spoke with were looking at them. 'Rudy! Jurgen!' Zared called out.

With a surprised look at one another, the cousins made their way over.

'These are my friends from Rotelegen,' Zared said. 'This is King Lorant of the Blood Caladri, and Queen Hajna.'

'Your Majesties.'

Jurgen bowed, and then offered them both his hand. They each took it, then Rudy's.

'King Zared tells me you were in Kalinth not too long ago,' said the Caladri king. 'With your friend, Clarin. We know Clarin and his brother Herin. Elana, Soren and Belwynn. We would dearly like to know how they all fare.'

Zared nodded encouragingly and Rudy and Jurgen shared what they knew. Jurgen found that when they told the story to the two monarchs, it all seemed so much worse than even they had thought. Both Lorant and Hajna looked particularly devastated when they were told that Clarin's friend Elana had been killed. Jurgen supposed that was sad, but not having ever met her, it hadn't seemed so important to him. Then, their story ended with the invasion of Kalinth, of the Isharite hordes defeating King Theron's army outside Heractus. In one way it was nice to see that these Caladri cared so much about what happened to their friends; but their ashen faces made him feel uncomfortable.

Hajna did her best to thank them and gave them each a little smile. 'King Zared tells us that you have been away from your homes in Rotelegen for some time. Unfortunately, the duchy has been overrun by the Isharites and isn't safe. But we have sheltered some of your people in our realm. We are returning there now, and we would be happy to offer you both sanctuary with us. I still have faith that the Lady Onella will save Dalriya, and that one day it will be safe for you to return home.'

He had only just met her, but Queen Hajna seemed like a very wise person to Jurgen. If she still had faith, after all he had just told her, then so should he.

'Well?' Rudy asked him.

Rudy was probably happy to stay here in Persala and play the outlaw. But Jurgen ached. He was tired and he needed to rest.

'Yes please, Your Majesty.'

***

THE MAGNIANS, of both north and south, left Essenberg by the road to Valennes. This stretch of the road ran parallel to the Cousel, the river on their right, protecting them from the Isharite forces that had taken the territory on the other side.

Little more than a month ago, Farred had come the other way, down the river. He had come with a warning for the Empire, of a dragon that had devastated the lands of the Krykkers. How quickly that dragon had ruined the defences of mighty Burkhard. Where was it now, he wondered. For the

Isharites hadn't even sent the creature to Essenberg. They hadn't needed to. His thoughts turned briefly to his friend, Gyrmund. The last time they had met was in Coldeberg, when Gyrmund had plans to travel north, to the lands of the Jalakh tribes. He hoped he had met with success; hoped he still lived. Hoped it wasn't his turn to face the dragon now.

They marched quickly, unsure how swiftly the Drobax that had taken Essenberg might follow their retreat. Once they reached the wooded grove where Wilchard had stabled their horses they could relax somewhat. Mounted, they were able to put some distance between themselves and the enemy who had taken the capital. The mood remained sombre, however—no-one much interested in conversation. It wasn't because they had lost the great city to the enemy. It was because Prince Cerdda had died there, and not at the hands of the Drobax. He had been killed on the orders of Gervase Salvinus, and the Magnians' hatred for the mercenary was so strong now it hung in the air with them, almost a physical substance that could be touched. Prince Edgar's face was full of a cold rage and no-one, not even Farred or Wilchard, chose to interrupt his brooding.

Instead Farred rode ahead, leading a group of men he trusted to scout the area. The Valennes Road was taking them to the western part of Kelland, a land he had travelled through once before, when he and Prince Ashere had taken their soldiers to Burkhard. It was a strange land, full of giant karst rocks—not easy for humans to live in.

It wasn't long into the afternoon when they encountered a scouting party from a different army. There was no drama. Farred recognised the scouts, knew many by name. They were Duke Walter's men. After sending a message back to let Edgar know, Farred rode on to speak with the duke.

Walter was surprised to have encountered Farred, shocked when he learned that Essenberg had already fallen.

'Baldwin and I had strengthened Essenberg's defences no end,' he said. Someone less calm than Farred might have taken offence at the implication that the defenders of Essenberg had let the brothers down. The truth was, no-one had foreseen that the river was such a weak point in the defences when dealing with the Drobax: not Baldwin or Walter, not any of the defenders, until it was happening. Until it was too late to stop.

'Salvinus got the Empress and the children out, via the Great Road,' Farred told him, to Walter's evident relief. 'Edgar believes Duke Coen will have managed to follow them out. But we have bad news and it is important I let you know before you meet with Edgar.'

Farred told Walter about the murder of Prince Cerdda, killed in a foreign city he had come to save. Walter looked to the heavens and for a moment it looked like he might crack; the predicament he was in was perhaps too much for him. But he fought to regain control.

'I will speak with Edgar and the North Magnians,' he said at last. 'If I have any say in it, Salvinus will pay for his crimes. We crossed the Cousel upstream at Vordorf, destroyed the bridge there to stop the Isharites from following. I had thought to track back to Essenberg, see if we could help. But your news changes that. There seems to be nothing else but to make for Coldeberg.' He sighed. 'Between you and me, I never much liked the place. But it seems that as well as becoming its duke, I am destined to die there.'

They cut south, staying the night outside a small Kellish village. Walter warned the elders of what had happened and what was coming, telling them to escape to the south and west; to Coldeberg if they had nowhere else to go. The Brasingians were in full retreat, but soon they would run out of places to run to.

The next day, they hit the road to Coldeberg, allowing for a faster pace. But the vast majority of Walter's men, the Barissians and men of Rotelegen who had survived Burkhard Castle, walked on foot, and were close to exhaustion.

Edgar, mollified a little after hearing Walter's apology yesterday, gave the order for his men to dismount and give their horses to their allies. Hard stares followed this, especially from the warriors of North Magnia who had lost their prince. But most did as he asked, and got a grateful response from those they helped, their feet blistered and bleeding from the walking they had done.

There was one more night spent out in the open by the Coldeberg Road, but the next day they reached the capital of Barissia.

Coldeberg was still powerful looking, built on a hill with high walls, its castle dominating the skyline.

'It must be one of the most formidable places of defence in Dalriya,' Wilchard commented as they approached the town gates.

'True enough,' Farred replied, too tired to see the positives. 'But there is no river here to act as an obstacle. Once the Isharites surround Coldeberg, there is no escape. We need to persuade Edgar not to stay here.'

244

Chastened somewhat, Wilchard nodded his silent agreement.

Safely inside Coldeberg, Walter soon had everyone in good accommodation and well fed. Farred shared a room in the castle. Nothing was expected of anyone except sleep, in a bed, without the discomfort and fears of the last few weeks.

Farred slept the rest of the day and through the night. He woke feeling tired and groggy, but the feeling of utter exhaustion, of having pushed yourself beyond your physical and emotional boundaries, had dissipated somewhat. He found he was able to think a bit more clearly, able to find a degree of optimism amid the hardship and disaster of the last month.

He left his room and found his prince. Edgar and Wilchard had found a quiet spot in an antechamber just outside Walter's private chamber. Edgar motioned for Farred to sit.

'We have some news,' Edgar began. 'The Middians passed through the city a couple of days ago. Didn't tarry for long, apparently,' he added, his expression showing his distaste.

Farred could tell that Edgar had become dissatisfied with the efforts of Brock and Frayne in the campaign, especially considering they had taken large payments for their services, and the Magnians had received nothing. But Farred clearly remembered Brock's contribution at Burkhard Castle last summer, and couldn't begrudge him and his people a reward now. Would it have given Edgar more satisfaction if they had returned to the Steppe with men dead and their wives widowed?

'The North Magnians carrying Cerdda's body went with them. It shouldn't be long until he arrives home now. According to Walter, the Duke of Morbaine led an army through the Steppe to Guivergne, to go to the aid of his brother, the king. If Guivergne falls, we may have Drobax coming from the north as well as the east.'

'I think it's time you return home as well.'

Edgar furrowed his brow. 'I think not, Farred. Once Coldeberg falls, the Isharites will be heading west, to Magnia. We must prevent that from happening for as long as possible.'

'Then keep a force here, if you wish to,' Farred countered. 'But Magnia needs a leader, for when they do come. With Cerdda and Ashere dead, it must be you.'

'I can't ask my warriors to fight here, most probably die here, while I slink off home to my family.'

'Of course you can. You're the Prince! You give the orders.'

'Careful, Farred. You know how much I respect you. But I don't appreciate the facetious remarks.'

Farred nodded, looking down to the floor. But he raised his eyes to stare across at Wilchard.

'The trouble is,' Wilchard began, 'Coldeberg doesn't give us choices. When the Isharites send their Drobax here, the city will be surrounded on all sides. There are no secret caves, there is no river to complicate things. No escape route, in other words. When Coldeberg falls, everyone inside its walls will die. So I urge you, Edgar, as your friend and your steward, heed Farred's advice. If Cerdda lived, it would be different. But as things stand, you are needed back home.'

Edgar sighed, visibly wrestling with the dilemma he was in. Farred admired him all the more for it—a ruler who struggled to do the right thing. 'I will think about it,' he grudgingly conceded.

In the end, they persuaded Edgar to leave. Cerdda's death had eroded the Prince's commitment to the Empire, in a way that the arguments of his advisers alone never could. Farred volunteered to stay behind, and the Magnian warriors were given the choice to stay with him. There were precious few who did, but some men, those who had served with Farred at Burkhard Castle and lived to tell the tale, those with a mad streak to their nature, waved off Prince Edgar and the Magnian army from the walls of Coldeberg.

If Edgar had left it much longer, the decision would have been taken from him. Farred stood on the castle walls with Walter and Jeremias, the young duke of Rotelegen, watching as the Drobax arrived. All three knew what to expect. It took them a good while, but as Farred had predicted, the numbers of the creatures allowed them to encircle the walls of the city. When the evening came and the sun went down, and the light from the Drobax fires sparkled in the blackness, the three of them were still there, looking out.

Walter turned to Farred. 'So. You've seen their army. And you've seen this castle.'

'We'll kill many,' said Farred.

The two men chuckled. Jeremias looked at them as if they had gone mad. Because there was nothing remotely funny about it.

XXIV

THE SEVEN

*I*T IS TIME TO FACE DIIS, Madria told her.

Although Belwynn felt terrified at the prospect, there was also a sense of relief. It would soon be over, one way or another.

She went to Soren first, and they found Theron and Herin. The two men were talking by candlelight. Like most people, they had not yet tried to sleep, the tensions of the battle still in their minds. What was left of Herin's forces remained outside the fortress, not trusted to pass inside. But despite the attrition to his once great army, it was still greater in number than Theron's. They had to come to an agreement on the strategy for the next day, for it was inevitable that Siavash would send the rest of his forces against them.

'We are leaving,' she told them simply. She didn't need to explain why.

Theron nodded, trying to control his emotions as she tried to control hers. She had her duty and he had his and they had to part now, with many things between them left unsaid, and little hope that they would both live through the next day.

I love you, he told her.

I love you too.

Herin stood, looking awkward. 'That was a brief reunion,' he said.

Belwynn felt like it would take years to peel back the layers around Herin and find the real man. She didn't have the time, couldn't really understand what he had done, and why. But she knew that his actions today had saved them all from destruction.

'Thank you for what you did,' she said, and he seemed to welcome the words.

'I could ask Clarin to see you,' offered Soren.

Herin smiled. 'No need. He has made it clear that he doesn't want to speak to me. I'd ask you to look after my brother, but I think his job is to look after you. Good luck.'

She nodded. Belwynn looked at Theron one last time. They shared a long moment, as if trying to hold back time, stop it from driving them apart. Then

Belwynn left. She thought Theron might use their telepathic link to say something else. But all she could hear behind her was Herin's voice, talking of formations and manoeuvres.

'Belwynn,' Soren said, as they made their way out of the barbican. He had an anxious look on his face, and he tapped at his head. 'This may be the last chance we get to talk, as alone as we can be.'

As alone as we can be? Tapping his head? He was talking about Madria. She knew he still had his concerns. It was as if he feared that the goddess was listening in somehow.

'I understand.'

'You remember,' he continued, 'when I was a prisoner in Samir Durg? Siavash got into my mind, took everything in it from me, except for our link.'

He paused, searching for the right words. 'We will not all return from this. I hope some of us will, though. I want you to understand that having someone in your head—like I did. It's wrong. Someone reading your every thought; someone controlling you. It could get to the point where you can no longer tell your own thoughts from theirs.'

Belwynn understood Soren's fears for her, she truly did. But she was worried about facing Siavash, about Madria confronting Diis. If she survived that, then she might worry about other things. Still, she could tell Soren needed to be reassured. She put an arm about his shoulders and leaned in. 'Trust me,' she whispered.

She found Moneva and Gyrmund on the cliff top. She knew they came here to find a small measure of privacy and felt guilty that she was taking it from them.

'It is time to go,' she told them.

They were quick to rise to their feet, these friends of hers, and she was grateful for them. Gyrmund picked up the Jalakh Bow, slinging it over his shoulder. Moneva already had Toric's Dagger at her belt.

'I think,' Belwynn said, 'that I should take the dagger. Remember what Oisin said? I must be the one to use it. And I don't want to risk your life if I don't need to.'

'I think not,' said Moneva firmly. 'I am coming, and I will make sure you do what you have to.'

Belwynn looked at Gyrmund, but she found no support there. He knew better than to tell Moneva to stay behind while the rest of them faced danger.

'Very well,' she agreed, defeated.

They descended from the cliff top and entered the great chamber of the fortress. Belwynn found Evander. He was sitting with his back to the wall, his arms around his knees. Next to him lay Lyssa, fast asleep. She crouched down next to the girl, put two fingers to her own lips, and put them to the girl's head. She turned to Evander. She nearly asked him to look after her but stopped herself. She knew she didn't need to ask. So instead she just smiled, and he smiled back; a boyish smile, even though he was a man now.

Belwynn, Moneva and Gyrmund left the Great Chamber and walked to the barbican. Both portcullises were already raised for them. Looking out on them from above was Count Diodorus. He raised one hand as they passed underneath. When they were through, he called out the order, and the portcullises were lowered.

Waiting for them outside the fortress were the holders of the remaining weapons. Soren had gathered Clarin, Oisin, Tana and Maragin. They all turned to look at her. It was wrong that these champions had to look to her. It should have been Elana standing here. But it was her, and she had to be strong enough to meet the challenge.

'We need to find Siavash,' she told them. 'I don't know his exact location. But I trust that Madria will guide me.'

'Come,' said Tana. 'Moneva and I have been to their camp. We will lead for now.'

They followed the Asrai's lead. A dark feeling grabbed at Belwynn as they set off. Many of these people were precious to her and she was leading them to their deaths.

Madria, I must speak with you, she demanded. *What if I say no? What if I refuse?*

Then Diis will win, Madria replied.

The people I care about will die anyway, Belwynn said. *You must give me more than that.*

Once Diis is destroyed my strength will return. I will have the power to give you one of them back.

What do you mean?

One who is dead. I will have the power to bring one of them back. If such a reward is what you ask of me, I will give it.

250

***

'I NEED that fortress and everyone in it destroyed,' Siavash told his generals.

Both men nodded, Linus with too much enthusiasm, Etan with too little. He only had these two left now—only two hosts remained of the four he had taken to Kalinth. They still outnumbered the enemy by a huge margin. He shouldn't even be questioning the inevitability of victory. But yesterday had left him feeling uneasy. Yes, some of Kaved and Herin's soldiers had limped back to the camp unscathed, but Herin's treachery had effectively destroyed half of his army.

He dismissed his generals from his tent. The battle for Chalios was in their hands now. There were even greater contests to be won. Siavash must prepare for these, but his doubts refused to disappear.

His thoughts turned to the dragon. There was something inescapably symbolic about its death. Diis was unhappy: Siavash could sense his god's anger. His Lord blamed him. Siavash had believed that his reforms to the Isharite military would prevent the kind of treachery Pentas had inflicted on them, but he had been wrong. He feared that if Diis had now lost faith in him, he would be replaced.

And if all that wasn't enough, of course the shield Herin had brought to him had been a fake; a cheap trick. That meant that Madria's champion might have all seven weapons. The victory of Diis—that had seemed all but assured—could, conceivably, end in His destruction. Of all the threats he now faced, even to his own life, that was the one Siavash must prevent.

'Come,' he said, and the black-robed followers of Diis went with him. They left the camp, left the Drobax and human slaves and Dog-men and all those base instruments behind. It was the Isharites who would yet win this, and of the Isharites, it was the Order of Diis that remained his most powerful institution. The servants of Diis were utterly loyal, steeped in magical power; they were the ones who could be relied upon to complete His task.

They met outside in the open air, a hundred black cloaks gathering, darker than the night.

'We have a decision to make,' Siavash began. 'Despite our superiority, Madria may have succeeded in acquiring all seven of her weapons. If so, my proximity to her champion may not be wise. We must determine the best location to hold, until our armies complete their work.'

The first priest moved towards him and bent the knee. 'I am returned from Samir Durg with grave news, Lord. A Jalakh horde, numbering in the tens of thousands, has descended upon our fortress from the Steppe. It is said they are led by a new khan, by the name of Gansukh. Stripped of our fighting men, the fortress may not hold out. If it falls, all of Ishari will be open to the Jalakhs.'

Stunned, Siavash grimaced. But he didn't have the time for emotion. He had to focus on what could be controlled. 'We had thought the Jalakhs would remain a sleeping giant, but it seems they have been stirred. We cannot doubt our enemies are behind this. But it is a crime that must be punished later. If a return home is out of the question, then where?'

A second priest approached to give his news. 'I am returned from Persala, where I investigated the failure of the Shadow Caladri to answer your summons. I found a great slaughter of them in that country, many killed by the arrows of the Blood Caladri. An attempt to head east may also put you in peril, my lord.'

The meeting went silent. Siavash put a hand to his mouth and thought through his options. The hard truth was that he had few. Turning and running like dogs in the night, with nowhere to go, simply wasn't acceptable. Their enemy might track them down anyway.

'We still have the largest army in Dalriya by far, right here in Kalinth,' he decided. 'So it makes little sense to go elsewhere. I have decided to retire to the capital of this wretched country. Heractus. You will all accompany me. There we will wait for our armies to complete their work, and when we receive news of their victory, we will lead them north and remind Dalriya of our power.'

His priests nodded their assent. It was indeed the best decision.

'Harith?' he asked.

'The Seven are here,' said the servant, gesturing at the figures he had brought with him.

At least Harith had some welcome news. The seven figures stepped forward a pace and then took their turn to kneel. The greatest warriors in Ishari, they were chosen to act as the champions—the guardians— of Diis. It was the highest honour, each of them receiving an original diatine crystal sword, the weapons that had defended their Lord at the Battle of Alta. They hung at their belts now, amongst the holiest of relics.

'Welcome,' Siavash said to them. 'The Seven have only ever had to draw their swords in anger once before, and I call you here only as a precaution. But it doesn't do to leave things to chance. I trust your weapons will be coated with the deadliest of poisons. Just in case.'

***

TANA AND Moneva led them away from the fortress, towards the Isharite army, under cover of darkness. Belwynn doubted their path, however. The rest of them couldn't creep about like those two, and night would never be enough to hide a Giant from view.

Madria spoke to her then. She stopped still and the others stopped with her, giving her anxious looks.

'They are travelling to Heractus,' she told them.

'Madria said so?' asked Clarin.

She nodded, looking at Soren's face. She could see him racking his brain for a plan that might get them there. She could see the others turning to him expectantly.

'Madria will help me to take us there,' Belwynn said. 'She can use the power that the weapons have when they are together.'

There were some surprised faces, but no-one questioned what she said. Belwynn could read her brother's feelings. He had worked so hard for his magic, and here was his sister, about to do something he couldn't.

Please don't be jealous of me, Soren, she said to herself. I never asked for this, and I don't want it.

They formed a circle of eight, holding hands.

Warily, Belwynn worked to open the connection between herself and Madria. She was fearful of it, unused to it. She knew it was strong, had tasted the power that day in Heractus, when Elana had lain dying in her temple and asked Belwynn to take her hands. It had blown through her like a raging fire.

Now, she needed to control it. She needed to link with her seven companions, and she needed to think of a location near Heractus that she could safely transport them to. When she asked for the power she needed, it came.

She began to feel that lurching sensation she had first experienced in the lands of the Grand Caladri. Her stomach roiled in protest and most of her senses abandoned her.

They were moving.

***

JESPER LOOKED out from the cliff top of Chalios as the sun began to rise. The walls down below remained in the shadow of the huge cliff, but beyond them the battlefield of the day before was revealed. Bodies lay strewn, mostly where they had fallen. Some had been moved, and even now Herin's Drobax, their strange new allies, were out there, stripping bodies of armour, upgrading their rudimentary weapons with hard steel.

So many had been killed that his mind reeled. And yet he found that his mind couldn't rest, needed to process what he had experienced. Back home, Jesper had only ever met two hundred people in his entire life. He had known them all by name, an extended family that supported one another. He must be able to see something in the region of fifty times that number of bodies out there. Fifty times more people, if one called the Drobax people, than he would have ever met in his lifetime if he had stayed at home. All dead. And today they would do it all again.

'Not a pretty sight,' said a voice behind him.

It was Herin. One might call him the architect of the slaughter, since he had sent one huge Isharite host into battle against another. Jesper wondered what it was like to carry that much death on your shoulders. But he didn't wonder enough to ask the man. There was something about him that cautioned you to choose your words very carefully.

'You met Rabigar,' said Herin, part statement and part question.

'Yes. Really, I am here for Master Rabigar. When he decided he was too ill to travel, I offered to come in his stead.'

'*Master* Rabigar, is it?' said Herin with a twist of a smile. 'Well, you have big shoes to fill, Jesper. And how was he when you left him? How ill, exactly?'

'He took a bite to the leg from a white wyrm. By the time he reached us it was heavily infected. My father had to cut it off above the knee or he would have died.'

Herin grimaced at the details.

'Father was confident he would recover, given time. But the journey across Halvia was too difficult for him to make in that condition.'

The comment made him recall those intense, exhausting days of canoeing up the Nasvarl, and then trekking through the Drobax-infested lands of Vismaria. Oisin had virtually carried them to the lands of the Krykkers, his physical strength seemingly limitless.

When Jesper looked up he saw that Herin was studying him. Herin turned his head to look out across the fortress to the battlefield.

'Rabigar and I were betrayed by a friend of mine. Kaved. That was how Rabigar lost his eye. I killed Kaved yesterday.'

Jesper was unsure what to say. There was something grand, something formidable about these people. Rabigar, wielder of Bolivar's Sword, had crossed Halvia to wake King Oisin. Yesterday he had seen Herin's brother, Clarin, deflect a catapulted rock away with his shield. Herin himself had fooled the Lord of Ishari and stood here to tell the tale. Jesper couldn't help but feel out of his depth, yet somehow fortunate to be amongst them.

'Come,' said Herin. 'The enemy will be moving out now the day has dawned. Time for one last war council.'

'Oh,' said Jesper, feeling a little awkward. 'I wasn't invited to a war council.'

'You just were.'

Jesper felt honoured. There were only ten of them at the council. It felt like there should be more, and he was sure he wasn't the only one to feel that way. Of course, King Oisin left a gap when he was gone. But seven others had left with him—seven of their best, taking the weapons of Madria with them—and those that remained now had a heavy burden to carry.

Jesper stood with Gunnhild, Herin, and Herin's two lieutenants—the red-haired wizard, Rimmon, and the Drobax, Kull. Across from them were the Kalinthians—King Theron, along with Grand Master Leontios and a few others.

'I know the enemy, as much as that helps us,' said Herin. 'Linus will come first, eager to destroy us and win all the glory. Etan will let him, keen to hang on to what he has. It means we will only face half of them at first. Of course, half of them are still more than enough to finish us off. We just need to decide how to play it.'

'My mind hasn't changed,' said Theron. 'Our walls held yesterday thanks to Oisin, Soren, Gyrmund and the others. Without them, the enemy will get in. Much as it seems counterintuitive with a fortress such as this, I'm minded to fight it out with you and your army.'

Herin nodded. He seemed pleased with the decision. 'Well one thing's for sure, Linus won't be expecting it. I assume you will leave part of your force behind the walls?'

'The Madrians were able to fight well when Belwynn was with them, but are a much diminished force without her. They will man the barbican and the walls. Otherwise, the rest of the Kalinthian infantry will make up the right wing, as we discussed. Count Diodorus will lead them,' he added.

Diodorus nodded glumly at being given the honour. He didn't seem pleased, but Jesper had never seen the man crack a smile, so it was hard to tell.

'I will lead the left,' said Herin. 'Rimmon will be with me. Gunnhild and Jesper are invited too if they wish to join us?'

Gunnhild smacked the head of her war hammer into the palm of her hand. 'Just put me somewhere I can use this,' she replied.

That left a wide centre division, made up purely of Drobax. There were enough of them, but Jesper wondered if they would hold against the onslaught; wondered even if they could be trusted.

'Will Linus notice our disposition?' Theron asked Herin, sounding unsure.

'Kull?' said Herin, inviting him to speak.

'The Drobax front ranks are all fitted with human armour and weapons. No-one is going to tell them apart from the other two divisions unless they are specifically looking for it, and that's not likely.'

'You will lead your people?' Leontios asked the creature. 'Do you care that they will take the brunt of the attack?'

Kull leered at the Grand Master. 'I will lead them, along with the other half-breeds. But don't make the mistake of thinking we care for them. Our mothers were raped by the Drobax to make our kind. I would gladly see them all dead, and after today's battle—whatever happens—we will have taken a step closer to that objective.'

There was little anyone could say to that, and soon afterwards Theron and the Knights left them to it. Jesper and Gunnhild joined Herin's division. He positioned it quite a distance behind Kull's, and farther to the left than the walls of Chalios. Jesper could see that Diodorus had done the same, on the other side of the battlefield.

Herin's force was made up primarily of Haskans and Persaleians, men who had decided to throw their lot in with their general. There were even some Dog-men, terrifying looking things that fought only with tooth and claw. Jesper would never have imagined he would be fighting on the same side as such creatures. But if it kept the enemy away from the women and children inside the fortress, then the strangeness of it would be worth it.

Just after Herin had declared himself satisfied with their position, they heard the beat of drums from the west.

'Stay close,' Gunnhild said to him. 'They're coming.'

XXV

A CLASH OF GODS

BELWYNN TRANSPORTED THEM TO A PLACE she knew. Not far out of Heractus was a quiet piece of countryside, where a stream idly gurgled along, and wild flowers grew. She had taken Lyssa there once during their time in Heractus. Just the one time, even though the girl had loved it. She wished she could have had more time with Lyssa. Feelings of guilt, of self-pity, tried to surface. She pushed them aside. There was no time for that.

When they stopped, they had to take time to recover until the nausea wore off. She glanced at her brother, worrying about his stamina. But Soren seemed alright, though he clutched Onella's Staff so hard his knuckles turned white.

Most of them knew the way to Heractus, but Gyrmund led, taking on his habitual role without comment. It was only a short walk before he stopped them, gesturing ahead to where the walls of the city were now visible.

Belwynn had not taken to the dull grey of Heractus at first, but she had developed an affection for the place. She wondered at Siavash's decision to come here of all places. This was where the Temple of Madria was, where Elana had spread the faith. But then she was reminded of darker experiences. Siavash had come here once before, or at least his shadow had. He had killed Sebastian and Prince Dorian in this city. He had killed Elana. And now, his armies had taken it, no doubt slaughtering all of those who had stayed. For Siavash and for Diis, it was a place of victory.

'I can't see anyone on the walls,' Gyrmund said.

'Siavash has not brought an army with him,' said Soren. 'But his followers will be here. We need to get in unnoticed.'

'I know a place,' said Moneva, a wistful expression on her face. 'Where the walls are not quite so high. It was used to get things in and out of the city from time to time.'

Belwynn gave her an enquiring look.

'If, for example, certain innkeepers didn't want to pay the city tolls on spirits.' Moneva grinned. 'When I found out about it, those innkeepers agreed that they should pass on some of their savings to their customers. Or to me, anyway.'

'Well, I'm glad your days as a soak turned out to have some use,' said Belwynn archly. 'But how do we approach this spot without being seen?'

'I have been thinking about that,' Soren said. 'Now is the time to try it.'

He closed his eyes in concentration, drawing on the power of the staff he clutched in one hand, the other held open before him, as if he were reaching out to touch some hidden object. Belwynn sensed the magic he was using but it was a gentle, whispering kind of magic. Motes of light emerged around each of them, *from* each of them, floating in the air with no apparent form or purpose. Then, they began to coalesce into shapes, growing larger and more defined, and Belwynn could see what her brother was doing. The lights were taking on the form of each of them. They became stunningly accurate recreations, from Oisin's height and skin tone, to Maragin's tough torso and muscled arms, to Tana's shimmering cloak and webbed fingers. Belwynn gasped, wanting to reach out to touch Soren's creations, but fearful she might break the spell if she did.

'They're beautiful,' she gasped.

But Soren wasn't done yet. Each image began to move, again faithfully capturing the idiosyncrasies of each one of them: Moneva's lithe steps were just as accurate as Clarin's brawny stomp. Belwynn watched a version of herself walk with them, and saw everyone else watching too, astonished looks on their faces.

'That is the greatest magic you have ever made,' she told him.

Soren opened his eyes and looked at his creations, a ghost of a smile on his lips. 'They will walk up to the East Gate. I think it will cause enough of a distraction for us to get to the walls unseen.'

'Surely it must!' Oisin enthused.

'Even for one of your proportions,' Maragin added.

Oisin gave a hearty laugh, before he remembered they were supposed to be quiet.

Belwynn linked arms with her brother, knowing that he would need help with his movement while he concentrated on such a complicated piece of magic.

Moneva took them to the place she remembered. It was an anonymous looking spot outside the city walls, but the ground did rise here, making the walls that bit more accessible. They debated the best option to get into the city. In the end, Queen Tana grabbed onto the butt of the Giants' Spear and used her Cloak to turn invisible. Oisin proceeded to lift his weapon up above his head, reaching high enough for her to clamber over the wall.

Then, they simply had to wait. Tana was taking a long time. Belwynn feared that they had been seen; feared that Siavash had his wizards waiting for them; that Tana had been captured. But all she could do was wait and hope.

Eventually, a rope was dropped from the wall above them. Oisin clambered up first—it wasn't such a great distance for a Giant. When he was on the wall, he was able to pull everyone else up, one by one, until they were all inside the city. Moneva took them to one of the nearby inns she had mentioned. They gathered amidst broken furniture, discarded objects and dried pools of blood, all a testament to what had happened here.

'I had a look around,' said the Asrai. She spoke in a natural whisper all the time, though something about her voice put Belwynn even more on edge. 'There are black-cloaked Isharites in the city, but they only occupy two locations. One group is at the castle by the east gates, watching the approach of our—' she paused, searching for adequate words, 'other selves. The rest are in a building near the centre. I'm not sure what this building is—'

'The Church,' Belwynn said. 'He's in the Church of Madria.'

That building belonged to them. To her and to Madria. To Elana.

'You're sure he's at the Church, not the Castle?' Clarin asked her. 'If necessary, we could split up, check both locations.'

Belwynn shook her head. 'He's there. I can feel it.'

'Good,' Soren said. 'That means we can ignore everywhere else and just focus on that one location. We need to keep hidden for as long as we can, but we must be prepared to be discovered. When that happens, remember this is about getting Belwynn to the Temple. If it comes to it, the rest of us can be sacrificed.'

Everyone nodded. A cold feeling of dread gripped Belwynn's stomach and spread to her chest. *I will have the power to give you one of them back*, Madria had told her. Belwynn shook her head, doing her best to rid the thoughts from her mind.

They left, moving quickly and quietly down the side streets of Heractus, weapons in hand. Belwynn took one of Soren's arms and Clarin held the other and they followed as fast as they could. Suddenly, without warning, Soren stumbled, and he would have crashed to the ground had Clarin not got a firm grip on him.

'They've broken it,' he rasped, breathless. 'The ruse is gone. They will be looking for us now. We must hurry.'

Soren recovered his feet and they began to run. *Only half a mile now*, she said to him. *We've nearly done it.*

But it wasn't to be. Ahead of them, Gyrmund was firing the Jalakh Bow at the top of the street. A figure in a black cloak was felled by his arrow, but more came.

'Down here!' Moneva shouted, indicating an alleyway that led to the back entrance to the church.

A flash of light flew down from one of the roofs, straight for Belwynn. Soren put up his staff and knocked the blast aside. The blast briefly lit up the whole area. The place was crawling with black-cloaked Isharites. Not only at the top of the street, where they now charged towards Gyrmund, but on the rooftops as well. At least one was a wizard; most likely more.

Clarin grabbed her and pulled her towards Moneva's alleyway. She turned to see Soren following close behind. Oisin and Maragin had already gone ahead, the spear and the sword in their hands, ready for any ambush. As Belwynn watched, a blast of magic came for them. Reacting quickly, Maragin met it with Bolivar's Sword, and somehow the weapon stopped the blast, the Krykker still standing, unharmed. Oisin launched the Giants' Spear up at the assailant. Pierced through by the huge spearhead, the black-cloaked Isharite toppled forwards and fell into the alley, his body meeting the stone paving with a wet thud.

Oisin and Maragin waved Belwynn into the alley. She looked up the street at the lone figure of Gyrmund, now down on one knee, firing his bow as fast as he could. The sound of the bow cracked loudly, surely drawing more of the enemy towards him. She saw him fire up, catching one of the Isharites on the roof above him in the throat. Then Clarin pulled her on, and Tana was with them, and Soren too, gripping Onella's Staff in both hands, ready to defend against another attack. They tentatively followed Oisin and Maragin, but the rest of the alley seemed clear. Belwynn turned around to look at Moneva. Her friend looked away from Gyrmund and back to her.

Jamie Edmundson

'I'm sorry,' Moneva said. She drew her short swords, holding Belwynn's gaze for a while longer, before turning away and disappearing up the street to help Gyrmund.

Moneva! Belwynn shouted into her mind, using their telepathic link. *The Dagger!*

Trust me, Moneva replied.

'Come,' said Soren. 'We need to go.'

'Toric's Dagger—' said Belwynn, loathe to leave.

'I'll go after her,' said Tana suddenly, running in Moneva's direction.

Belwynn, said Soren sternly. *We have to go.*

Belwynn watched the Asrai go, until Tana disappeared before she even turned into the street. No, it's all gone wrong already, she told herself. But she allowed Soren and Clarin to lead her away.

***

MONEVA RAN for Gyrmund, as fast as she had ever run for anything in her life. Black forms lay prone in the street around him, but more Isharites had come and they were on him now. With no time to fit another arrow, he defended himself from a sword thrust with the bow, backing away. The crystal swords sparkled as their wielders thrust towards him. He let out a scream as one connected, slicing through armour and gouging deep into his thigh, and then a second struck him under the shoulder.

Moneva threw her first short sword, taking one of the Isharites in the side. It was enough to give them pause, make them turn to look at her rather than at Gyrmund, who dragged himself backwards, until he slumped against the wall of a house.

The Isharites came for her and she ran at them. Their swords flashed, their reach much longer than hers. Moneva swerved and spun away, only just avoiding the razor-sharp blades. Half a dozen of them surrounded her now. She pulled Toric's Dagger from her belt, but it wouldn't do her much good against these killers.

'I'm sorry, Belwynn,' she muttered.

Then, she watched in shock as one of the Isharites' necks seemed to explode open in a gush of blood.

Tana.

Suddenly, a faint hope.

Then, a song of blades. The Isharites sent their crystal swords into the Queen of the Asrai. Invisible though she was, she had revealed herself to them and these dark lords of Ishari were ready to face Madria's champions. Moneva, too, stabbed with her sword and with her dagger, her arms moving the fastest of all with her short blades. Tana found another neck, then a face, before she was impaled so many times she could no longer move. A sharp pain at her forearm caused Moneva to drop her sword, then a messy slash on her opposite hand took away fingers, and she lost Toric's Dagger, too.

When it was done only one of the Isharites remained, his sword levelled at her. That was how close they had come. He smiled, a surprisingly generous sort of smile, as if sharing with her the satisfaction of a hard-fought combat. Then an arrow appeared, lodged in the side of his head, and he collapsed.

Tana's body was revealed with her death. She lay amongst the Isharites in a pool of blood that continued to expand. One of Moneva's hands was a ruin, and she couldn't feel the opposite arm, but somehow, she managed to bend down and pick up Toric's Dagger. Then she moved over to Gyrmund. His bow fell to the ground with a clatter and he pointed behind her.

Moneva turned. Two more black-cloaked figures, near the entrance to the alley. They had seen her, but she held no interest for them now. They took the alley. They were going for Belwynn.

Moneva tried to feel regret.

But Gyrmund lived, so she couldn't.

***

THE ALLEY opened onto the church courtyard. There were only five of them now, their numbers cut so quickly. Oisin and Maragin were the first to enter, looking for trouble, but the space seemed empty. Belwynn, with Soren and Clarin either side of her, followed them in.

The rear entrance to the church was only yards away now, but Soren wasn't happy.

'Something isn't right,' he warned them.

Then, suddenly, Soren was shooting backwards, landing back in the alley, Onella's Staff skittering away from his grasp. A fog—a magic induced haze that had somehow hidden the courtyard from sight, disintegrated before

Belwynn's eyes. It revealed seven Isharite warriors, muscled and deadly-looking, each holding a crystal sword of a different colour. With them were two black-cloaked wizards.

'The Seven,' murmured Oisin, readying his spear.

'We are to take you to Lord Siavash,' one of the wizards said, speaking to Belwynn. 'Tell your champions to lay down their weapons, or we will kill you all.'

'Go fuck yourselves,' said Clarin.

Then it began. One of the wizards targeted Oisin, but Maragin launched herself in front of the Giant, Bolivar's Sword suppressing the magic blast. The second launched the same kind of blast at Belwynn. This time, Clarin pushed his shield towards the attack, and the blast was returned from where it had come, the crackling energy crashing into the wizard who had sent it, knocking him to the ground.

Belwynn turned and ran for Onella's Staff. She grabbed the weapon and placed it in her brother's outstretched hand.

He rose and turned, just in time. He placed a shield around them both. One of the crystal swords, pale yellow in colour, connected with the edge of Soren's shield and recoiled backwards.

The Isharite warrior bared his teeth in frustration. Behind them, the fight was desperate. The Isharite warriors were incredibly fast and agile. Holding their light swords in two hands, they made Belwynn's friends look slow and cumbersome by comparison.

To one side of the courtyard, Oisin held off three of them, his great spear twirling in his hands, the butt striking out in one direction, the blade in another. But despite his size and skill, the enemy had opened up vicious-looking wounds in his arms and legs. At the back, Clarin and Maragin had somehow fought their way towards the remaining wizard. Clarin used the Shield to hold off the Isharite warriors, counter-attacking with his own crystal sword. But like Oisin, he hadn't been able to stop them entirely, and he bled from several wounds. Maragin, meanwhile, had worked her way to the wizard. Eyes bulging in panic, he threw whatever power he had left at her, but Bolivar's Sword negated it all, and the Krykker thrust the sword into his neck. Leaving him to die, she turned and fought her way next to Clarin.

Come, Soren said to Belwynn, and they moved to join them, until Soren was able to cover Clarin and Maragin with his shield.

'You need to protect Belwynn,' Clarin said to Soren breathlessly. 'Their weapons are poisoned. And it won't be sleeping poison, like Herin's,' he added with a grim smile.

Belwynn looked at the wounds up and down Clarin's body. Maragin looked a little better: the crystal swords had scratched, but not penetrated her tough hide. But neither would last very long; nor would Oisin. They were the ones who needed her brother's protection. And she knew that he wouldn't be able to hold his spell forever.

'We need to get Oisin,' she said, as four of the Isharites circled around Soren's shield.

'On my call,' Soren shouted. 'Now!'

For a split-second, Belwynn watched them. The four Isharites were shoved backwards into the other three. Somehow, Soren was able to send a blast of magic at one of them, sending him crashing to the floor, whilst still moving with his shield. Then Clarin and Maragin were swinging their swords, forcing their way through to the Giant.

They were going to make it. Belwynn turned and ran. She ran for the door to the church. Her fear told her to look behind her, but she didn't stop. She got to the door and then she was in, slamming it shut behind her.

She knew where to find Siavash.

***

ONE OF the Isharite warriors lay unmoving on the floor of the courtyard, but that still left six of them. They stood about them, but wary now of getting too close. They weren't able to break through Soren's shield, but Oisin's long spear could still reach them.

Soren held his shield steady, letting them catch their breath in its protection. Onella's Staff helped supply him with the stamina to keep it going for a while yet. Hopefully long enough to see off the remaining warriors.

'Where's Belwynn?' Clarin asked, and a cold feeling crawled into Soren's gut. Concentrating on his magic, he hadn't noticed her go. They looked around the courtyard, but Soren understood what she had done.

'She's gone into the church.'

'Alone?' demanded Oisin, his voice still strong despite his wounds.

'You need to go after her, Soren,' Clarin said quietly.

'No. Not yet. If I leave you here, you die.'

'You said it yourself,' said Maragin. 'The rest of us can be sacrificed. We can't afford for your sister to lose.'

Soren knew they were right, but that didn't mean he could just leave them here, without protection.

'Then let's kill these bastards now.'

'Glad to,' said Clarin. 'But whatever happens, you get into that church. There's no point in you getting stuck with one of those swords when we're full of poison already.'

Soren turned towards the Church of Madria. He took down the shield, freeing his magic. The Isharites came for them. He pulled his magic inside him, his desperation to save Belwynn making it all the stronger. He released it at the Isharite in front of him. The warrior tried to defend himself with his crystal sword, but it couldn't stop Soren's magic from getting to him, a fiery blast leaving a blackened corpse behind.

He had magic left, and turned it on the next Isharite. But this one leapt to the side, not about to make the same mistake as his dead comrade. Soren tried to follow his movement, but he was too fast. He rolled towards Soren.

Damn, Soren thought, as he saw the tip of a rose-coloured sword come for him. He just didn't have the reactions of these killers.

Inches from his body, the sword was met with a shield, Clarin launching himself at the enemy. The Shield of Persala slammed the Isharite's blade to one side, and then Clarin's own sword followed, striking point first into the guts of the Isharite.

Soren turned to Clarin, who gave him a beaming smile. Behind Clarin, an Isharite thrust his sword into the big man's back. Seconds behind was Maragin. Bolivar's Sword swung and cracked into the side of the Isharite's head, felling him.

Clarin kept his eyes on Soren as he crumpled to the floor. The crystal blade had struck something important inside Clarin and he lay there, not moving or speaking. Soren knelt on the ground next to him and held his friend's hand for the seconds of life he had left. For some reason, that smile never left his face.

Soren got to his feet, surveying the courtyard. The Seven were dead, while Oisin and Maragin remained on their feet.

'I'm sorry,' said the Krykker. 'But we should go now.'

Soren nodded.

Oisin gave a little whistle. 'We've got company.'

Two black-cloaked figures emerged from the alley into the courtyard. Would this ever end?

'Go,' said Maragin. 'There might be more.'

Soren nodded. He had to find Belwynn. Wordlessly, he walked to the door of the church, Onella's Staff taking his weight.

'Give us victory,' the King of the Giants bellowed at him when he reached the door. Soren turned around to take a last look. Oisin was twirling the Giants' Spear. Maragin had picked up the Shield of Persala.

He pulled open the door.

Belwynn? Where are you?

***

BELWYNN TOOK the corridor to Elana's private room. It was where Siavash had killed the priestess. She knew, as much as Madria knew, that was where they would find them.

Siavash was waiting for her, only one black-cloaked attendant with him.

'Belwynn,' he said, as she entered the room, 'you made it. A fitting place to end it all, don't you agree?' he asked, waving a hand at the room.

Belwynn hadn't been to the room since Elana's death. It had been left untouched.

'Your champions didn't make it?' he asked.

'They may be on the way,' she said.

Siavash smiled at that, but she could tell that he was nervous. No-one really knew what would happen here.

'Check her, Harith,' he said.

His attendant approached her, putting out his hands to search her. She knew what they were looking for.

'Get off me,' she said, slapping his hands away.

'Oh really, Belwynn,' Siavash chided.

He shot an arm out and Belwynn found that she was held immobile.

Harith patted her down. 'Nothing,' he said.

She could see Siavash visibly relax.

'Good. You know, if you had tried to use the dagger, I would only have taken it from you.'

'Release me,' she said.

'I think not. This is one of the strange things about Madria's choices, isn't it? Her champions. Why you, Belwynn? Your brother would have surely made more sense. He might have been able to give me a challenge. But you offer nothing, do you? My Lord, Diis, is stronger than Madria. I am stronger than you. It really is a foregone conclusion, isn't it?'

Belwynn called on Madria and the goddess came to her. She felt that power course into her, the heat of it, the pain of her body trying to hold divine forces inside a mortal shell. It was time for the gods to have their contest. This man's prattle was irrelevant.

'Of course, you weren't really her choice, were you? I gutted Madria's *real* champion in this room, didn't I? You just happened to be here when it happened. It was you or nothing, I believe.'

Belwynn and Madria released their power as one. Siavash's hold on her was flicked aside like it was nothing, and they turned on Siavash, pouring their power at him. He sank to his knees, his face red with the strain. Then a pair of eyes behind his kindled into life. They were like black coals and they regarded Belwynn at the same time as they looked past her, at Madria.

'At last,' Diis spoke, and his voice was the essence of terror, and Belwynn flinched at the presence of a being she should never have met. 'It is time to take Dalriya.'

Siavash and Diis struck back with a dark power, a power that came from another realm. Diis had come to conquer, and to do that he would kill Madria. For a moment the two gods wrestled for control and Belwynn could feel the ground shake and the air crackle. But Diis was the stronger. As he pushed back, Siavash got to his feet, and as he began to win, it was Belwynn who was forced to her knees.

She screamed out loud as a clawed hand entered her mind. It was searching for Madria, and when it found her it would be the end.

Belwynn? Where are you?

There were voices in her head. Through her pain, she couldn't tell who was speaking, or how many voices there were. Could it be a trick? A way for Diis to locate Madria? She had to hope not. She had to risk a reply.

I'm in Elana's room. Come quickly.

'Who do you speak to?' The words came from Siavash's mouth, but they sounded more like Diis.

Angry, the god scoured her mind for what it wanted. The pain was intolerable, and Belwynn had to fight to stay conscious. She feared that if she gave up—if she withdrew her defences and left the battle, her mind would be open for Diis to find whatever he wished to. Not just Madria, but all the people she had a connection with. Soren. Theron. Clarin. Moneva and Gyrmund. Lyssa. No. She wouldn't let that happen.

Then suddenly, there was blissful release. The pain had gone. Belwynn had a moment to herself, alone in her own world, to appreciate the absence of pain, before fear kicked in. Did that mean Diss had won? She forced herself to wake. Her eyes snapped open.

Soren had found her. Siavash's attendant was slumped, broken-looking, on the floor. Her brother was standing over Siavash, both hands on Onella's Staff, using the weapon to drive a burst of magic at his enemy. The man who had tormented him in Samir Durg was pummelled by Soren's attack, arms in front of him, desperately trying to hold off the magic.

Belwynn got to her feet, struggling to stand. In a daze, she tried to think what she should do. Try to escape? That didn't seem to be an option.

Madria, she asked, trying to locate the goddess. *We need to help him, with whatever strength you have.*

From somewhere, she felt Madria answer the call. She felt her gather her strength for one last attempt.

But Diis had returned. Belwynn felt the power of the god as He forced aside Soren's attack. Then Diis was on the offensive. Soren put up a shield, but it was breached in moments. Diis pulled Soren towards him. Siavash's hands grabbed her brother and an unstoppable shock of divine power was turned against him. Soren was thrown onto the floor like a rag doll, his staff skittering aside, his body finally broken for good.

Belwynn stared at her brother's body. They were here because of him. Their mother's death had driven him to search out as much power as he could, determined to change the world for the better. That ambition had left him here. Belwynn had lost her mother, then her father, and now her brother.

Diis came for her then. She tried to find her emotions. Tried to feel anger, vengeance, anything that would make her fight. But Soren's death had left her feeling nothing but emptiness.

Siavash grabbed her and the claw of his spirit returned to her mind, ready for his final victory. The agonising pain returned and Belwynn had nothing left to fight it with, swooning dangerously close to oblivion.

Then she felt something. It wasn't something in her mind. It was something physical. A weight in her hand, a familiar feel to it. A dagger.

Realisation dawned. She forced her eyes open. She stared, past the cruel face of Siavash, into the remorseless black eyes of Diis.

'Die!' she screamed.

Toric's Dagger came down, the blade penetrating Siavash's skull.

And then Madria was alive. Belwynn all but disappeared, as she became a vessel for a god. She could taste Madria's rapture. The goddess had waited a long time for this moment, carefully moving her pieces, suffering setbacks and beginning again with a divine patience. Now, she knew she had finally won. Her power blazed through her weapon and into Diis. Siavash was killed, his body slumping to the floor. The spirit of Diis was free. It searched frantically for a new host, heading for the only other living being in the room, ready to force himself upon her.

But Madria was upon him. Bodiless; defenceless; vulnerable. Belwynn had never been sure whether a god could be killed. But then she felt it happen. A great, malevolent presence was gone, a great vacuum where He had been. Into the vacuum Madria poured herself, more powerful than she had ever been. The only god left in Dalriya. She was supreme.

Madria allowed Belwynn to return. She felt her lungs gasping for breath, her frail mortal body restarting to keep her alive. She saw her brother's body and turned away, looking for someone else.

Next to her, Moneva appeared, the Cloak of the Asrai about her. One hand was raised, blood pouring from a wound where her fingers had once been. Her other arm hung at an awkward angle. But she had done it. She had brought Belwynn the dagger.

'You did it?' Moneva asked, looking at the body of Siavash, much less aware than Belwynn of what had just happened.

Belwynn returned her gaze to her brother.

'We did it,' she said.

XXVI

SHADOWPLAY

I T WASN'T CLEAR WHO WAS SUPPORTING WHOM. Leaning against one another, Belwynn and Moneva exited the Temple of Madria, out into the courtyard. It was a scene of bloody devastation. The bodies of the Seven, as well as several black-cloaked priests of Diis, were strewn about, the putrid smell of death hanging heavy in the enclosed space. Oisin and Maragin sat beside each other, leaning against the courtyard wall. Too exhausted, too injured to move, they turned their heads at the approach of Belwynn and Moneva. Laid out before them was Clarin. They had placed the Shield of Persala by his side.

'No,' Belwynn said, crouching next to him.

'I'm sorry,' Oisin rumbled, a dry croak all he could muster. 'He died bravely, saving your brother.'

She turned to look at them. 'Diis is destroyed. Soren and Clarin gave their lives for that. They would be satisfied.'

Madria's words repeated in her head. *I will have the power to give you one of them back.*

Moneva was examining Maragin's wounds. 'Poison,' she said. 'It will kill them.'

'Gyrmund?' Belwynn asked her, ashamed it had taken her so long. 'Tana?'

'Tana is dead. Gyrmund was alive when I left him.'

'We'll bring them here. Then I will ask Madria to restore her champions.'

***

JESPER HELD still, as he had been ordered, while a swarm of Drobax hit the front ranks of their army. It was Drobax fighting Drobax, a brutal massacre. Hundreds fell, while the leaders of each side held their main forces in reserve.

'Linus will wait for us to be softened up before he sends in his better soldiers,' Herin assured him, perhaps sensing Jesper's uneasiness. His bow was on his back and the enemy were in range, but Jesper did as he was told, even though his hands itched for his weapon. On his other side, Gunnhild tapped the blunt end of her war hammer into the palm of her hand. She also seemed impatient to join the fight. They were fighting in Herin's unit now though, and this was his plan—his, and Theron's. They had to see it out.

Herin's Drobax had the better of the fighting at first. Kull had ensured that the front ranks had the pick of the armour and weaponry that had been collected from the battlefield, and that gave them a considerable advantage against the poorly armed Drobax that Linus had sent against them.

But Linus had the numbers. When his dead fell, they were soon replaced, whereas gaps appeared in their own lines that weren't filled, weak points that began to be exploited. Their Drobax began to retreat. Jesper could hear the shouts from Kull's kind, giving the order to move backwards. It was orderly enough, surprisingly so from the usually mindless Drobax. But the enemy began to gain in confidence, whooping in excitement.

As Kull's Drobax were pushed backwards, the front line of their own division became exposed, and some of the Drobax came at them. They came in disorganised groups, screaming a challenge.

'We need your sword and shield for this,' Herin told him. 'We fight as one.'

The Drobax ran at them. Only at the last second did Herin's front line take a step forward to strike out or put a shield in the way of a Drobax spear. Then they returned to their positions, not leaving their place in the line. Jesper was quick to learn, and quick to realise he could best serve as a shield man. On one side, a Vismarian swung a hammer that broke bones and stove in skulls. On the other, a Magnian flicked out a deadly crystal blade, slicing and puncturing wherever it was sent. Jesper supported them, using his shield to cover their attacks, and receiving grunts of approval in return.

Only when Kull's Drobax had retreated further towards the fortress behind them, did Herin finally give the order to move. As the enemy Drobax pushed forwards, focused on defeating the retreating force in front of them, they revealed their flank. Herin swung his left wing around to face them.

'Now would be a good time to use that bow of yours,' he advised Jesper.

Jesper strung his bow. They advanced slowly, and he was able to pick his targets with ease.

***

GYRMUND LIVED, and although badly injured, his wounds didn't have the smell of poison on them. Between them they carried Tana's body back to the courtyard, laying her down next to Clarin. She was naked without her Cloak and so they covered her with a blanket, though Belwynn doubted that the queen would have cared very much about such things.

You said you would bring one back, Belwynn said to Madria. *I ask you now to return all three of your fallen champions.*

That cannot be done, Belwynn.

It can! Belwynn argued. *I felt the power that came to you when Diis was destroyed. What else would you use it for?*

If I could, I would, Belwynn. But once a life has departed it cannot return. There are still things beyond a god's power. Many things.

But you promised me, Belwynn pleaded. *You said you would have the power to give one back.*

You know how that is done, said Madria. *Diis did the same thing. I can take your shadow and you can place it into one of them. If that is what you want, I can do it.*

Something broke inside Belwynn at these words. The goddess she had devoted herself to had lied to her; used a cheap trick to get what she wanted. She had been a fool not to see it. Madria had used Elana, used her—would go on using her to get what she wanted. The goddess inside her didn't love Belwynn at all. And what was more, she had never claimed to. Belwynn had imagined something that simply wasn't there.

And Soren had tried to warn her about Madria's control over her. *It could get to the point where you can no longer tell your own thoughts from theirs,* he had told her. She had felt it when Madria had destroyed Diis, how little left of herself there had been. So what now? She saw Madria's plans, they had been there all along if she hadn't been so blind: marriage to Theron; Queen of Kalinth; spreading her influence across the realm and then beyond it. A life purely governed by the whims of Madria.

That was no life.

Very well, she told Madria. *Then that is what I will do. One of my choice.*

The thought of reanimating Soren's body, shuffling it around with her shadow inside? Or Clarin, the man who had loved her, who had dreamed of buying a farm and growing old with her? His mind and soul gone but his body restored as her personal puppet? It was monstrous and revealed Madria's lack of humanity. But if the goddess wanted to play cheap tricks, then Belwynn could play too.

But what of the four who survived? she asked. *Two of them are dying. Surely, you can heal them now? They are still useful to us. They could be sent back to save Chalios.*

Very well, Madria agreed. *Though it will cost me much in power to do both. These must be the last things you ask of me.*

I promise.

Belwynn saw to Oisin and Maragin first, for they were most in need. The pain in their faces eased, and the bad smell disappeared. But their wounds were far from completely healed and would need time. Such had always been the case with Elana's healing powers. Perhaps it was true what Madria said. There were things beyond a god's power. Next, Belwynn treated Gyrmund and Moneva. When she was done, they looked much better, though Moneva had lost two fingers and they would not be returning to her.

'Madria can send you back to Chalios, to help Theron. I need to stay here for a while longer. There is something more that needs to be done.'

Moneva looked at her suspiciously. Belwynn forced herself to ignore her friend and turned to Maragin.

'I would ask you to stay with me,' she said to the Krykker. 'I have a favour to ask of you and I think you are the only one who could do it.'

'Of course,' said Maragin.

'You may need your sword,' Belwynn added. 'But not the shield.'

Maragin gave the Shield of Persala to Moneva and took her place by Belwynn's side.

Moneva looked hurt, but Belwynn had to be strong enough to ignore it.

'After all that has happened, I think I should stay with you,' Moneva said.

'I must do this alone. I will need Toric's Dagger one last time, then you can have it back for good. Trust me,' said Belwynn, and she found that she could bring a light smile to her face.

Moneva knew she couldn't argue.

Madria's power surged into Belwynn. Moneva, Gyrmund and Oisin were sent away from Heractus.

***

HERIN'S WING crashed into the exposed flank of the enemy Drobax, cutting a bloody path into them, with little resistance. Jesper pushed ahead with his shield, using his sword when he had to. Either side of him, Gunnhild and Herin kept him right. They could have gone faster, but Herin wanted discipline, and so his front line moved forward at the same pace.

On the other side of the battlefield, Diodorus's wing would be doing the same thing. The Drobax had been slow to react, intent on chasing Kull's Drobax all the way to the fortress. But the walls of Chalios would keep them hemmed in. And now, Jesper could hear the rumbling sound of the Kalinthian cavalry. Hidden from view until the time was right, they would circle around the Drobax and come at them from the rear. The trap they had set would be closed.

For a while, they continued to make progress in their own little part of the battle, the Drobax unable to respond to their predicament. But then Herin's wizard, Rimmon, came to him with news.

'The Knights are not able to join us. Linus has sent his Haskan cavalry against them. They have had to face them instead.'

'Shit,' said Herin. 'It was always going to be a bit much to expect Linus just to sit back and watch us destroy his army. If we leave the Knights alone, they'll be outnumbered and overwhelmed. We'll have to support them. Halt!' he shouted.

'Halt!' shouted Rimmon, and then Jesper joined in.

'Halt!' boomed Gunnhild, and that did the trick.

They disengaged from the Drobax, leaving behind a confusing mess of bodies. They retreated across the gore and the maimed remains of Drobax that they had made, before Herin swung his wing back round to face in the direction they had begun the battle. Only now was Jesper able to see the situation that Rimmon had described. The Knights of Kalinth had joined together in a thin line in front of them. Towards them came the massed ranks of the Haskan cavalry, perhaps four times as many as the knights had. Soon Theron would have to order his men into the charge. Everyone knew that the Knights of Kalinth were the better horsemen. But the numbers of the enemy more than evened the contest.

'March!' yelled Herin, urgency in his voice now and they moved forwards swiftly. Herin was keen to intervene and swing the odds back in their favour.

But when Jesper looked into the distance, he saw that the enemy had infantry units of their own still held in reserve.

Herin looked at him. 'Yes, I know,' he said, just loud enough for Jesper to hear him. 'Hard to see us winning from here. But we can still fight well.'

Jesper nodded, an uneasy feeling gnawing at him. Would he be brave enough to go down fighting like Herin and Gunnhild? He hoped so.

He caught sight of something between the two cavalry forces. A shimmering, a glimpse of movement, perhaps. Then three figures appeared where there had been none. Two looked like soldiers, but the third was huge. It was a Giant, and it towered above everyone and everything else. Oisin Dragon-Killer.

'Hold here,' said Rimmon, before sprinting forwards.

'Halt!' called out Herin, holding up a hand, and his unit stopped. They watched, and they waited.

The Haskan cavalry came on, and Jesper heard the crack of the Jalakh Bow echo across the battlefield.

'Gyrmund,' said Herin, and Jesper couldn't tell if the Magnian was pleased to see his countryman or not.

Gyrmund targeted the less well armoured horses of the Haskans. Cruel, perhaps, but effective. Many went down, and the disciplined cavalry line became ragged.

Oisin shouted out across the battlefield. Jesper heard his voice, but amidst the cacophony of horses charging, and Drobax slaughtering one another, he couldn't decipher the words.

The Haskans kept coming. Gyrmund kept firing. Rimmon kept running. Oisin kept shouting.

Then, Rimmon held out his hands, and the Giant's great voice was suddenly amplified. It roared and echoed across the battlefield. The Haskan cavalry pulled up. Pockets of fighting continued, but much of it stopped.

'Hear these words! Siavash is killed! Diis is dead! The war is over! Know my words to be the truth, for I am Oisin Dragon-Killer, King of the Giants, Last of my Kind, and I would not stand here making false claims. Go back to your homes now, for you are free!'

A chill ran down Jesper's spine, to be hearing such words. Some people cheered, but mostly, there was a heavy, exhausted, sense of disbelief. Not that anyone there thought Oisin was lying. It was more that the world had suddenly changed, and the mind wasn't able to absorb such news quickly.

'There are only three of them,' said Jesper. 'Oisin, Gyrmund and Moneva. Where are the others?'

'They are not here,' said Herin grimly. 'And I think that tells us all we need to know.'

***

I AM surprised by your choice, Madria told Belwynn. *But pleased.*

You won't be so pleased soon, bitch, Belwynn thought to herself, trying not to let the thought leak out.

It was time. Belwynn experienced a horrible, rending pain, as her shadow was stripped—cut—from her body. A sick feeling of horror swamped Belwynn, but she did what she had decided she would, forcing her shadow into a corpse.

Maragin stood by her, keeping Belwynn's trembling body on two feet.

'I know your beliefs,' Belwynn whispered into the Krykker's ear. 'I know them from Rabigar. You reject magic and gods.'

Maragin nodded, her face pale, a bleak grimace all it could show.

Belwynn could feel the inanimate shell of a body regain life. Organs, bones, blood, flesh and skin were remade by Madria's magic, and by Belwynn's shadow. There are some things gods can't do, Belwynn considered, and yet this is a powerful and a terrible magic.

The body laid out before them began to flap and jerk, as Belwynn tried to control its movement. Finally, it stood.

I have given you one back, Madria declared.

Belwynn nodded. She took Toric's Dagger and gave it to her shadow. Her shadow clutched the hilt in its fingers awkwardly, until it mastered the grip. She made her shadow raise Toric's Dagger high, and then she brought it down onto her own head.

Through her shadow's eyes, Belwynn watched her body fall to the floor, dead. Most of Belwynn was gone now, yet her shadow remained.

A scream of fury emanated from Belwynn's body as Madria was forced from her host. A transparent, ghost of a thing floated before them now.

What did you do? Madria demanded.

'I decided,' Belwynn's shadow said, working hard to make the lips of her new body form words. 'Dalriya doesn't need *any* gods.'

The ghost flew at Belwynn's shadow, but there was no life there to join with. So it turned instead to Maragin, seeking to bond with another.

'Krykkers don't deal with spirits,' Maragin said decisively. She raised Bolivar's Sword, and the blade repelled Madria's ghost.

Lost, Madria turned about, searching for another creature. But Maragin didn't give her another chance. Bolivar's Sword came down, it cut through the goddess like splitting mist, and the mist evaporated before their eyes.

Madria was gone.

'Rabigar would be proud,' said Belwynn's shadow. 'So would Soren.'

***

THE TOWN walls of Coldeberg still held. Farred had been a little surprised by the ferocity of the Barissians. Down to meagre rations, on little sleep, and less hope, they had fought off every attack. Of course, everyone knew the consequences if the Drobax got in. Having only one option can sometimes make a person even braver than they believed themselves to be.

Of all the hardships in Coldeberg, it was perhaps the isolation that got to Farred the most. They had no way of knowing what else happened in the Empire. Was Lindhafen besieged also? Had it already fallen? How were things in Magnia? What of Gyrmund and his friends, and the weapons they had put their faith in?

Even though it was not his rota, loud shouts lured him up to the castle walls. He found the two dukes, Walter and Jeremias, looking out. Walter grabbed his arm and pulled him to the wall so he could see for himself.

The Drobax were leaving. They marched to the east, in the direction of the Great Road.

'What can it mean?' Jeremias asked.

Farred considered the question. But every way he looked at it, it seemed like there was only one answer that made sense.

'It's over,' he said.

Epilogue

Two months later

ASERVANT LED THEM TO THE GARDENS of the Imperial Palace. Jurgen offered his arm, and the Duchess Adalheid took it without comment. She was a stern woman, and yet for some reason they seemed to have struck up a warm relationship over the last few weeks. *Perhaps,* Jurgen considered, *because we walk at the same pace. And speak only when necessary.*

The gardens were pretty, that was for sure. It was pleasurable to take their time, inhaling the scented air, only the sound of buzzing insects and the crunch of the crushed stone path under foot. The murmur of voices guided them, and they came to an open spot, with wooden benches and a table set up with drinks.

The King of Persala came to greet them. He bowed to Adalheid and laid a kiss on her hand. He gripped Jurgen's hand firmly and flashed him a smile. It was a special relationship they shared, ex-prisoners of Samir Durg. A relationship that Jurgen doubted would ever be broken.

'It's a lovely spot,' said Jurgen.

'Isn't it?' said Zared. 'Slightly better than a hole in the ground, eh?'

'The negotiations go well?' Adalheid inquired.

'They do, Duchess. King Koren has his own objectives and has proven to be flexible in order to get them. Haskany will be returning our eastern lands to us, which was always our main goal.'

'As they should,' said Adalheid. 'Congratulations. It is a relief to see that diplomacy is being given a chance over war.'

'Yes, I think we are all thoroughly sick of war. Cyprian will be pleased,' he said to Jurgen. 'His home city will be returned to Persala soon.'

Jurgen grinned. 'He is here?'

'No, this isn't Cyprian's sort of thing. But I will make sure he is told. I am sure he can be persuaded to do something useful for me. Mayor of Lumberco, perhaps?'

Jurgen smiled. 'Mayor Cyprian? Well, we have all gone up in the world, haven't we?'

'Come,' said Zared. 'Meet my other guests.'

Adalheid put her arm through Jurgen's again. This time, he knew, it was for moral support. For King Koren, uncle of Shira of Haskany, had not only had a hand in the conquest of Persala, but the invasion of Rotelegen as well. He had been a leader of the army that had defeated Adalheid's husband, Duke Ellard, in battle, making her a widow and taking away all but one of her sons. Jurgen and Rudy had fought in that battle too, and had ended up in Samir Durg as captured prisoners.

Zared made the introductions.

'I am grateful that you are here,' Koren said.

'Of course. My son sends his apologies, he is at the coronation in the Empire. But he was keen that Rotelegen should be represented, for we have suffered just as much as the northern realms, and have a stake in what happens next.'

'Indeed. Peace between our realms is my highest priority now. Though I have been seeking to persuade King Zared that more than peace is necessary. The Jalakhs are loose, their numbers as large as the days when they terrified the north. Ishari is all but gone now, swallowed whole by Khan Gansukh. I have heard that not a single Isharite has been allowed to live. Only a northern alliance will dissuade him from casting his ambitions south next year.'

Jurgen had escaped from Samir Durg—he knew the geography. Haskany would be trembling in fear of a Jalakh Empire. No wonder Koren had come here to negotiate.

Adalheid and Koren were able to conclude their conversation and keep it civil. Finally, time to speak with the third king of the north. Theron of Kalinth looked older than Jurgen remembered him, his bones protruding somewhat, as if there wasn't an ounce of fat left on him.

He greeted Adalheid politely.

'We met once, in Guslar,' Theron reminded her.

'I remember,' said Adalheid. 'I asked you to fight the enemy. You did that and more. Dalriya is grateful.'

Theron murmured his thanks, but seemed unmoved by the words. He remembered Jurgen, too, even though their paths had only crossed for a short while. Jurgen had fought for Clarin, and Clarin had fought for Theron, that was the truth of it. There hadn't been much love between the two men. But they had both loved Belwynn.

It was impossible for Jurgen to look at Theron and not think of the woman who had saved them all from Siavash. From Diis. It was said that by the time Theron arrived in Heractus to find her, Belwynn and Clarin were already in their graves, buried next to one another in the cemetery of the Church of Madria. Soren on his sister's other side. He wondered what the king thought of that.

They excused themselves after a while, having said not very much. Jurgen knew that of all the people who had gathered in Baserno, King Theron was the one who would go down in legend, the rebel knight who took on the Isharites and won. Yet he was the one who seemed the most sombre of them all.

When he and Zared took a chance to have a quiet conversation alone, he said as much.

'He must have a lot on his mind,' Zared said. 'Kalinth was badly ravaged by the end. Not as bad as Rotelegen, of course, but worse than here. Then, of course, what happened with Belwynn. No-one really knows the truth of how she died. It's said that she survived the initial encounter with Siavash. Still, I think he will be alright, given time. He told me there was a girl he and Belwynn cared for.'

Jurgen nodded. 'Lyssa, I think her name was.'

'Yes. He has officially made her his daughter. So, he has family. That is important.'

'It's about time you were thinking of a family yourself, King Zared?' Jurgen suggested.

Zared smiled. 'No time for such thoughts, I am afraid. How is Rudy?'

'Spending all his time on the farm. No interest whatsoever in politics.'

'Good for him. You know, I think of Samir Durg very often still. I think of Clarin a lot especially. I think, really, he was a forgotten hero in all of this.'

'Yes,' said Jurgen. There had been something noble about Clarin. He hadn't been surprised to learn that he had died defending the twins. 'What news of Herin and Gyrmund?'

'Gyrmund has completely disappeared. Herin, well, part of me wishes he would disappear, too. I am sure he is up to no good somewhere, but I don't think he'd dare come back to these parts.'

'And yet, what he did helped to defeat the Isharites, you could say,' Jurgen said, looking surreptitiously about them, since such sentiments were not universally shared.

Zared shrugged. 'You can say if you like. The man killed my father, remember. If I ever get my hands on him, he'll pay for it. But one thing's for sure. If our little group of escapees hadn't made it out, things might have ended very differently.'

'Indeed. We can agree on that, Your Majesty.'

***

AFTER THE ceremony in church, Coen's coronation as Emperor of Brasingia had turned into a lively affair. His guests had been warmly welcomed into his hall. Food and drink were liberally provided, and music played. It was hard to imagine that Lindhafen had been besieged by an army of Drobax a mere two months ago. Edgar was pleased he had brought Elfled with him. She was enjoying herself, and anyway, she was much better than he was at being charming.

Still, none of that meant that Edgar had forgotten he was here on business. He had sought out virtually every political leader for a private conversation. In the aftermath of the wars, Magnia still needed as many allies as she could get.

King Glanna had made a rare expedition away from Cordence. One of the few nations not affected by the wars, the Cordentines were keen to make a profit from the peace. Then there was the host himself, of course, Duke Coen of Thesse and Emperor of Brasingia. A man Edgar knew well and had a good relationship with. After all, Edgar had helped Coen to save his duchy from Emeric only last year. The first ever emperor from Thesse, elected unanimously. In truth, there had only really been one other alternative for the throne, and Walter had been quick to back Coen for the job. Edgar believed Coen would make a good emperor. Brasingia needed the southern duchies to aid the ravaged north of the Empire, and Coen was best placed to make that happen.

All the other dukes were here. Edgar had spoken with Jeremias of Rotelegen, and Arne of Luderia. There was much fevered whispering at the presence of Gavan, Prince of Atrabia. But Edgar had found the man easy to talk to, and surely his willingness to come here was a good thing for the

Empire. Edgar had even been introduced to the new Duke of Kelland, young Leopold. One had to feel sorry for the lad, no doubt still grieving for his father. He had no idea who Edgar was, and must have felt overwhelmed by the whole process. Edgar knew well enough what that was like. Still, one of the dukes of Brasingia was his uncle, and another his grandfather. He didn't lack for support. Surely, he would grow into the role in time.

The only one missing from the room was the Archbishop of Gotbeck. Godfrey's death had left a vacancy in the duchy, and Edgar supposed that filling it would be one of Coen's first tasks.

That left only one duke, and Edgar now made a beeline for Walter.

'Your wife is looking well,' said the Duke of Barissia as they grasped each other in a friendly hug.

'Thank you. It all seems to be going to plan, though I understand she will get considerably larger soon.'

Walter shrugged. 'I'm afraid I'm the last person to know of such matters. How are things in Magnia? You know, I thought there might have been a coronation there by now.'

Cerdda's death had left the throne of North Magnia empty. A delicate situation, but one that could unite Edgar's country if handled well.

'No plans on that front until our baby comes,' said Edgar.

Walter nodded. 'I suppose a boy would help you out.'

'It is a boy.'

'You're that sure?'

Edgar smiled. 'Well. Elfled has been told, on good authority.'

Walter looked at him quizzically, and Edgar shared the story of Elfled's meeting with the Queen of the Asrai.

'We have lived through strange times,' Walter said on hearing the story. 'Please accept my condolences for your cousins, Your Highness.'

'Thank you, Walter,' Edgar said. 'And take mine for your brother. I'm consoled a little by the high regard they are held in, from whoever I speak with.'

The hurt from Belwynn and Soren's deaths had remained raw for Edgar. Apart from his mother, who was frail and remote anyway, they were the last of his family. With Elfled losing both her brothers, too, it had not been an easy time at home. Mette had not taken it well, and Irmgard, Cerdda's widow, was heartbroken. Edgar was just glad that he and Elfled had each other.

'Mention of this brings me to certain requests I have to make of you,' Edgar said then, and Walter sighed, a little melodramatically.

'Magnia is still seeking justice for the death of Prince Cerdda.'

'I would like to see Salvinus in chains, too,' said Walter fiercely. 'And I don't care if he is punished in the Empire or in Magnia.'

'And you promise to remind Coen of the importance of this issue?'

'Of course. I know Coen wants the same as you and I. But you had best speak to Glanna about this, too. That is the most likely place the bastard has hidden himself.'

'I've spoken with Glanna. I've told him there will be no new trade deals with Magnia until Salvinus faces justice. I would appreciate it if the Empire held the same line.'

'Yes, yes, I'm sure Coen can be convinced of that.'

Edgar still wasn't convinced. For all his crimes, Salvinus had taken Hannelore and her children from Essenberg to the safety of Lindhafen. Edgar doubted how much appetite there really was in the Empire to see him captured. But he had pressed as hard as he could.

'One last thing,' Edgar said, glancing about the room. 'Farred has requested that I release him from his obligations to me. He wants to serve you in Barissia. I am willing to do so if you are willing to be his lord.'

'Of course,' said Walter, keeping his voice neutral. It was well done. 'He will be a good man to have with me. But you will lose a useful ally.'

Neither Farred nor Walter were willing to tell Edgar about their relationship. And that was alright. He just wanted them to have some years of happiness together. By Toric, if the last two years had taught him anything, it was you must take your chances when they come.

He smiled. 'I have Wilchard. He's running things for me as we speak. I shouldn't be greedy. Well, those are my requests, Your Grace.'

'Your Highness.'

They shook hands. That was Edgar's business in the Empire done. There were enough good men in this room for Brasingia to flourish. He was now free to return home with his wife. It was their chance for some happiness.

***

RABIGAR STOOD by the shore of the Lantinen Sea, in his homeland. The rock of the Krykkers was underfoot. There had been times when he had feared he would never make it back here. But when a mighty, green-skinned Giant had appeared at Nemyr's house, he had started to believe it was possible. Oisin had dragged his old body across Halvia and over the sea so he could be here. It was more than he deserved. But he was grateful beyond words.

He had returned to a Dalriya free of the Isharite menace. The price its people had paid had been high, the Krykkers no less than any others. But he stood here with a fully healed Stenk, and the woman he admired and loved—Maragin, chieftain of the Grendals. His people had suffered, but they had a future.

The three Krykkers waved at the ship that now pulled anchor and left for the west. Two figures on deck stood out, taller by far than anyone else.

'Goodbye, dearest friends!' called out a booming voice. 'Don't be sad! We will meet again!'

Oisin and Gunnhild were bound for Halvia. They would march into Vismaria and reclaim it. Rabigar wondered how they had the stomach for more war. The task they had set themselves would not be easy or swift. But if anyone could do it, of course, it was them.

A fourth figure stood nearby. Rabigar had thought young Jesper might be returning with them to Halvia, but the lad had decided on a different course.

Once the ship was out of sight, Rabigar hobbled over, still awkward on the false leg that Nemyr had constructed for him.

'Where did Herin tell you to meet him?'

'Guivergne, he said.'

'Guivergne? Why Guivergne?'

'I honestly don't know, Rabigar.'

'Probably because Guivergne is about the only place no-one has heard of Herin. You know I got this following Herin on some foolish adventure?' Rabigar said, gesturing to his eyepatch.

'Yes, you have said,' Jesper replied. 'But a man needs some excitement when he's young, wouldn't you say?'

'I can't remember what men need when they're young, lad. All I know is, I'm done with excitement.'

It was clear that the lad wasn't going to listen to his advice, and he left Jesper to say his farewells to Stenk. Even if he couldn't tell Jesper what to do, he had made it quite clear to Stenk that the young Krykker was staying put.

Maragin took him by the arm and they looked out to sea for a while.

'That is the end of the weapontake,' she said. 'The weapons are dispersed again—the Spear returns to Halvia. Already, the whereabouts of others are unknown.'

Gyrmund and Moneva had apparently told no-one where they were going, except that Gyrmund had said it was a place they could never be found. Rabigar supposed that if anyone knew of such a place, it would be Gyrmund. He felt it would have been nice to see them one last time, before they left. But he didn't begrudge them their isolation, their chance to be alone together at last. They both carried their scars, but Rabigar was inclined to think they would heal in time. They would have a good life together.

'Of all the friends I have lost,' he found himself saying to Maragin, 'it is Belwynn I struggle to come to terms with. I loved her, like she was my daughter, you understand? I know you and the other champions did your best to protect her. But it does seem so unfair.'

Maragin faced the sea. He watched her from the corners of his eyes. Her lips parted, as if she was about to speak, but then closed. He knew full well that Maragin wasn't telling him something. She had confided in him to an extent, telling him that Belwynn had decided to kill Madria, and thereby herself. But he knew there was more to it than that.

Well, he had time. Maybe after a while she would be ready to tell her secrets.

He sighed. Knowing Maragin, she would take them to her grave.

***

TORSTEIN SAT ON the pebbles of the beach, deep in his thoughts. The sun shone and the wind buffeted. His boat was put away and his catch was ready to take home. He never used to do this. When Elana was here, he would rush home. Now, he was in the habit of sitting here, wasting some time before he returned. He wasn't being fair, he knew. His two daughters needed him all the more now that their mother was gone. And yet, for some reason, he did it all the same.

It had been a year since she had left. Longer, since Elana had become infected with her strange religion—started hearing a voice in her head. Sometimes he thought it would make life easier if she had died. It was hard, knowing that she could still be out there somewhere. Hard, answering the confused questions of his daughters. Their perfect mother had suddenly become a different person and, as far as they could understand it, rejected them.

He sighed. He should get going. As he stood, he heard the crunch of someone walking on the pebbles. It was unusual to find someone else on this empty stretch. He looked across. A woman, long hair blown by the wind, was approaching him.

His breath caught in his throat. It looked like Elana. Not possible. Surely, not possible that one day she would just wander back into Kirtsea, back into his life, as if nothing had happened. She walked up to him and stopped. She looked uncertain, afraid even.

A silence and a distance hung between them.

'Elana?' he said finally.

'I have come home,' she said.

He hadn't been willing to believe it until he heard her voice—his wife's voice.

He closed the distance between them and pulled her into him. He held her close and kissed the top of her head.

'You're back?' he asked, still not quite daring to believe it, fearing it was a cruel dream. He had suffered plenty of those in the last year.

'I'm back,' she said, into his chest. 'Back for good.'

I hope you have enjoyed reading The Weapon Takers Saga. It is a story that has been buzzing around in my head for a long time. I'd like to think that the world of Dalriya is big enough to support another book or two. But for now, other worlds await me.

Many thanks to everyone who has supported me. A special thank you to my wife, Julie, for all the support she has given me—with this project and with everything else.

Final thanks go to my beta readers: Lisa Maughan, Phyllis Simpson, Marcus Nilsson & Ian Edmundson.

CONNECT WITH THE AUTHOR

Website:

jamieedmundson.com

Twitter:

@jamie_edmundson

Newsletter:

Download the free prequel story *Striking Out* by subscribing to:

https://subscribe.jamieedmundson.com

'The best way to thank an author is to write a review.'

Please consider writing a review for this book.

The Giants' Spear

Jamie Edmundson

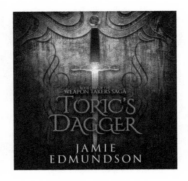

TORIC'S DAGGER

The quest doesn't have to be over! Now you can listen to The Weapon Takers Saga on audiobook, beginning with Toric's Dagger. Available on Amazon & Audible.

CPSIA information can be obtained
at www.ICGtesting.com
Printed in the USA
LVHW020803111119
636959LV00002B/282